PRAISE FOR THE 13TH [

"*The 13th Continuum* manages to be smart, surprising, ⌐ a good time, all at once. That's hard magic to pull off, but Jennifer Brody makes it seem easy. Swift and surprising, this novel is such a confident debut. Here's to many more."

o o o Victor LaValle, author of *New York Times* Notable Book of the Year, *The Devil in Silver*

"The books I loved as a YA reader profoundly informed my life. So I'm excited for all who are about to discover *The 13th Continuum*. Jennifer Brody has brought muscular, propulsive writing and big ideas to bear on an ambitious, dystopian landscape that dares to look past the near horizon. And dares to hope."

o o o Mark Ordesky, Executive Producer of *The Lord of the Rings*

"With meticulous world-building and an epic scope, Jennifer Brody has created a fascinating sci-fi story. Readers will flip the pages, anxious to answer a question that will determine the future of humanity: Will they reach the surface?"

o o o Pintip Dunn, author of *Forget Tomorrow*

"We've all had those novels that make us sad when they end, not because we didn't like the story or characters . . . but because we liked them too much and there will never be another 'first time' to experience it. *The 13th Continuum* is one of those kinds of books. In cases such as these, re-reading is good, but telling your friends to go pick it up so that you can vicariously live the story through their first time is about as close as you can get to that feeling you had during your first read. So that's what I'm doing now. Go read this book. It's fun, it's sad, it's completely unique, and it's an absolute breath of fresh air. In a post-apocalyptic genre you thought had no new stories to tell comes this surprisingly conceived book. Don't wait for the movie that's no doubt to follow and let yourself be spoiled—read the book and pass it on."

o o o Kirby Howell, author of *Autumn in the City of Angels*

RETURN OF THE CONTINUUMS

JENNIFER BRODY

RETURN OF THE CONTINUUMS

The Continuum Trilogy
BOOK 2

TURNER
PUBLISHING COMPANY

Turner Publishing Company
Nashville, Tennessee
New York, New York

www.turnerpublishing.com

Return of the Continuums

Cover design: Maddie Cothren
Book design: Glen M. Edelstein

Library of Congress Cataloging-in-Publication Data

Names: Brody, Jennifer, author.
Title: Return of the Continuums / by Jennifer Brody.
Description: Nashville, Tennessee : Turner Publishing Company, [2016] |
  Series: The Continuum trilogy ; book 2 | Summary: Myra and her friends
  form an unlikely alliance in hopes of surviving long enough to reach the
  First Continuum, to learn the secret behind humanity's destruction and the
  hope for its survival.
Identifiers: LCCN 2016000708 | ISBN 9781681622583 (pbk.)
Subjects: | CYAC: Science fiction. | Adventure and adventurers--Fiction.
Classification: LCC PZ7.1.B758 Ret 2016 | DDC [Fic]--dc23
LC record available at https://lccn.loc.gov/2016000708

9781681622583

Printed in the United States of America
16 17 18 19 20 10 9 8 7 6 5 4 3 2 1

To all those who have the fire in their hearts to keep fighting
even against the greatest obstacles.

CONTENTS

There is no escape—we pay for the violence of
our ancestors.
—Frank Herbert, *Dune*

There is a place that still remains
It eats the fear it eats the pain
The sweetest price he'll have to pay
The day the whole world went away
—Nine Inch Nails, *The Day the World Went Away*

Chapter 0
THE FINAL CHOOSING

Before the Doom

Professor Divinus hurried across the Harvard Yard. His crimson robes rustled around his ankles, concealing the wool-lined slippers that sheathed his feet. The Memorial Church bell was chiming. Class had just let out.

"Who knew biophysics could be so riveting?" one student said to him after he finished lecturing in Sever Hall. That was why he still taught freshmen when he could have reserved his talents for graduate students. They weren't jaded by the rigors of scholarly life; they remained refreshingly open-minded and malleable, if perhaps a bit naïve. *We could all use a little more of that*, he thought.

His slippered feet found the paved pathways and avoided trampling the well-manicured lawn, lest he incur the wrath of the strict groundskeepers. Some familiar students called out to him as he passed. "Good morning, Professor," they said before they dashed off to their next classes with their bags slung across their shoulders.

Divinus nodded back in response and murmured a few terse platitudes, but his face remained serious. His pace suggested the urgency of his errand. In a fit of nervousness, he groped for the package tucked inside his robes to make sure that it was secure. It was far too precious to risk dropping. His fingers probed the hard outline of the leather case. *Still there*, he thought with a small sense of relief.

It quickly evaporated.

Usually he kept his mind busy by thinking about the complexities of his plan and the endless preparations it required, but in moments like these, when he found himself alone and his mind unoccupied, his thoughts drifted to terrible places. He stared into the crowd of students rushing across the Yard and imagined their faces melting off in a white-hot blast of radiation, the flesh dripping from their skulls like candle wax.

Now isn't the time, he thought and pinched his wrist. That snapped him out of it. He reached Widener Library and rushed up the many steps as fast as his achy joints would allow. He flew through the double doors and down the once grand halls. Shelves spanned the entire length of the building and stretched up to the ceiling. They were empty, aside from the thick layer of dust that had collected on them.

Once this library had been filled with all the collected knowledge of humanity—some of it prophetic, some erroneous, some plain silly and forgettable—but all of it had existed because men and women saw fit to put pen to paper, or later fingers to keyboard, in an attempt to illuminate the greatest mysteries of the universe. The emptiness on the shelves and in the hallways saddened him.

It reminded him of the legendary Library of Alexandria. Built in the third century BC, it was one of the largest and most significant archives of the ancient world. Famously, it burned down, resulting in the destruction of its many books and delicate papyrus scrolls, thus becoming symbolic for the loss of cultural knowledge. He prayed that same fate would not befall the First Continuum.

He approached a golden door marked with the Ouroboros seal—a snake swallowing its own tail, entwined around two words. He spoke them aloud: "Aeternus eternus."

The computer registered his voice. The door dilated to reveal an elevator. He boarded it, and it began to descend with gathering speed. The rapid acceleration made his head spin and his ears pop. He clung to the railing, feeling the infirmity in his body with its brittle bones and rickety joints. Old age had caught him by surprise, coming on suddenly and absolutely. He still pictured himself as a freshman, complete with a bad case of acne and unruly, carrot-orange hair, though he hadn't had either in many decades.

About twenty minutes later, the elevator halted and the door dilated. Ceiling panels flashed on one after the other and illuminated the underground chamber.

"Good morning, Professor Divinus," said a voice that seemed to emanate from everywhere and nowhere all at once. "The others are waiting for you in the control room."

Divinus knew that he shouldn't dawdle, but something drew his attention. His eyes grazed over the rows of cryocapsules that covered the entire length of the chamber. More than half of them still remained empty, but soon they would be filled with the clumpy, embryonic buddings of life. He felt a sense of comfort at the simple knowledge of their existence—these last vestiges of hope tucked away in frozen slumber. But it was fleeting. His mind ticked and hummed with worries.

"Professor, may I suggest increasing your pace?" the voice came again. Still unfailingly polite, it sounded less confident this time.

A smile tugged at Divinus's lips, as he lingered in front of the capsule housing the impressive species *Canis Lupus*. "Noah, how long have we known each other?" he asked.

"Is this a trick question?" Noah said, belying some puzzlement this time. "Professor, you programmed me. Thus, we have been acquainted for the entirety of my existence, which amounts to exactly thirteen years, thirty-four days, seven hours, twenty-one minutes, and fifty-two seconds—"

"In that case, you can come right out and say it," Divinus cut him off before the calculation could dissolve into nanoseconds

"Very well. Professor, you're late."

"Much better, Noah. Your interactions are improving."

"I've been practicing," Noah said, sounding flattered.

"Have you been perusing my book suggestions?"

"I scanned a few of the old movies you recommended. I especially enjoyed *2001: A Space Odyssey*, though I found it a bit farfetched that a computer would turn on his creators and try to murder them. But mostly I've been monitoring the network feeds. Humans have a boundless appetite for social interaction, don't they?"

Divinus cocked his head at that revelation. He spent as little time as possible on such mind-numbing, time-sucking pursuits, but he was in the minority.

"Indeed, they do," he replied.

"If I may be honest, I find it curious," Noah went on. His voice turned ponderous, another trick of the programming. "I'm content to exist in complete isolation."

"We designed you that way for a reason," Divinus said with a smile; it quickly faded. "I'm afraid there may be a lot of isolation in your near future."

At that unhappy reminder, Divinus dragged his gaze away from the cryocapsule and its embryos—tiny, nascent beings that were rigid with cold and lit up from below with emerald light. In his younger days, he never would have gotten distracted this way, but as he'd aged past the point of no return—as he often thought of it—his mind had become a far less dependable and sometimes wholly unpredictable organism.

Green arrows lit up on the floor beneath his feet, but he didn't need their help. He knew the route by heart. He hurried through the interconnected chambers and, finding the door to the control room already unlocked, he whisked through it and took his place at the head of the long table. Twelve men and women turned to look at him. They all wore the same matching crimson robes, their lapels marked with the Ouroboros seal.

"Theo, thanks for deciding to join us," Professor Linus said with a thick, cockney accent that made him famously difficult to understand when he lectured. They had been randomly paired together as freshmen roommates in a closet-sized, drafty room in Wigglesworth Hall. "Weren't you the one who called this bloody meeting?"

"Indeed, Wendell," Divinus replied. "And I apologize for my tardiness. Time is short, and we haven't a moment to lose. As you know, the Final Choosing is upon us." When he said that, his face appeared to age by ten years, but the illusion quickly vanished, replaced by a look of sheer determination. "If there are no objections, let's get started," he said and manipulated the screen, pulling up the first case file.

Above them, a holographic image materialized of a man with caramel skin and close-cropped, salt-and-pepper hair. His military uniform cleaved to his lanky, muscular frame. The projection rotated slowly so that everyone could get a good view; it appeared so lifelike that it almost seemed like he was standing in the room with them.

"Professor Singh, you nominated this candidate?" Divinus said, flipping through the file.

"Guilty as charged," Singh said, raising his hands in mock surrender. With his boyish countenance, he was the youngest person in the room by a good two decades, but that didn't mean he was any less worthy of inclusion in this formidable group.

"Care to do the honors?" Divinus said.

"Gladly," Singh replied in a lightly accented voice that he projected with confidence. "My sworn brothers and sisters, meet General Milton Wright." He gestured to the holograph with a sweep of his hands. "His credentials are impeccable. Four-star general in the United States Army, Commander of the US Army Forces, and Chairman of the Joint Chiefs of Staff during the Arctic Seas Resources Conflict—"

"Clearly, he's qualified," Divinus interrupted, painfully aware of their limited time. His eyes swept over his colleagues' faces. "All in favor say *aye*."

"Aye," rang out twelve times.

"It's decided then—he's officially Chosen," Divinus said, making a note on the file. "Now where should we place him?

One of the space colonies . . . or maybe underground? The construction plans are ahead of schedule on the Sixth and Seventh, though we've hit delays with the Ninth."

The professors voiced their opinions, talking over each other at times, then another vote ensued. Divinus nodded his approval and manipulated the screen, placing the General on the list for the Second Continuum, one of the space colonies. This would trigger the top-secret notification process, so that even while they were huddled together working through the rest of the case files, their sworn brothers and sisters at other universities around the country would spring into action and contact the candidate.

Without delay, they moved to the next case file—a projection materialized of an older woman with a swish of long, white hair and piercing blue eyes. Cassandra Beth Knowles was a Nobel laureate in economics whose books topped the bestseller lists. Despite a contentious debate and a close vote, she failed to make the cut.

"Nay" rang out a few too many times.

Divinus leaned back in his chair and rubbed his tired eyes—the Choosing was a wearying process. For every individual that they could save, he always considered the billions that would perish should the Doom come to pass. And that didn't include the plant and animal life, most of which was sure to be obliterated in a rain of fire and brimstone that would make the mass extinction of the dinosaurs look like a picnic.

Many hours later, when they were all bleary with exhaustion, they reached the final case file. It was larger than the rest, and some might have felt more important, though Divinus refused to think of human lives that way. His fingers manipulated the screen and opened the file. A holographic image of a family—a father, mother, and their two impeccably dressed daughters—materialized posed inside a familiar room. The walls were white and circular, and the navy rug under their feet featured a prominent seal.

"Saving the best for last, Theo?" Professor Linus said,

raising his scraggly eyebrows. "Or have you got something else up your sleeve?"

"Why do you always think I'm up to no good?" Divinus asked.

"Because you usually are," Linus shot back. Chuckles erupted around the table.

But then Divinus turned more serious again. "My sworn brothers and sisters, I trust that you're already familiar with President Elijah Wade and his family?"

"Only the most famous family in America," Professor Bishop interjected, pushing her straight, blond hair off her shoulders. She heralded from the History Department with a specialty in Digital History, an area of study that used communication technologies to collect historical data. She was also one of the most popular professors on campus, regularly invited to dine at the Houses with her students.

"In my opinion, President Elijah Wade will go down in history as one of our most consequential presidents," she continued. "His domestic agenda alone has reshaped our nation in the midst of a severe financial crisis, not to mention his immigration reforms that opened up our borders and his numerous foreign policy accomplishments."

Divinus nodded. "Thank you, Professor." He turned his attention to the others. "On the Choosing, what say you?

"Aye," rang out twelve unanimous voices.

"The Wade family is officially Chosen," Divinus said, manipulating the screen and marking their file. "Now the harder part. Where should we place them?"

"Right, we need to consider the secure evacuation routes," said Professor Quaid, pulling up a map and zooming in on the portals near Washington, DC. He was a professor of Engineering and Applied Sciences and responsible for logistics. "The President is a high-profile candidate, so we can't rely on the normal procedures."

"Excellent point," Divinus agreed. "Anyone else care to chime in?"

"President Wade served in the Navy prior to entering

politics," said Professor Ronan, a middle-aged woman with a severe bob who chaired the Psychology Department. "He commanded a nuclear submarine. He has training and exposure to the extreme pressures of the deep. Based on my analysis, he would likely feel most at home in a deep-sea environment."

"I concur, Professor," said Linus. He was a professor of Political Science and in charge of vetting candidates who held elected office or worked for the government. "His Naval record is immaculate."

"Interesting . . . one second . . . let's see," Quaid said as he manipulated the map. "There's a portal at the United States Naval Academy in Annapolis, Maryland. That would provide an expeditious and secure evacuation route from the White House."

"But which deep-sea colony?" Singh asked.

"Well, we've got five to choose from," said Quaid. He pulled up images of the trenches—jagged gashes marring the bottommost depths of the ocean. They were the byproducts of extreme tectonic violence when one plate was pushed down beneath another plate, creating a rift in the Earth's crust. They had been selected for their remote locales, shielded by miles of saltwater and rock. Each trench now housed a colony. Divinus found himself thinking about the colorful name for the deepest parts of the ocean—the Hadal Zone—so named for Hades, the Greek god of the underworld.

The professors debated the pros and cons of each colony. Quaid marked up complex risk assessments, Ronan spoke about the different demographics, and Bishop talked about the historical significance of their choice, but Divinus was barely listening. Instead, his attention was focused on the projection of the President and his family. He knew that he was breaking protocol by not calling for a vote, but he did it anyway. He placed the Wade family on the list for the colony where he knew they belonged.

Silence engulfed the table when the others saw what he'd done. Quaid looked up from his calculations and frowned. "The Thirteenth Continuum?" he said, pushing his tablet away. "But why that one? The Twelfth has a larger occupancy capacity, and the Eleventh in the Mariana trench might prove a safer choice due to its greater depth."

Divinus thought for a moment. "My sworn brothers and sisters, science is the foundation of our work, but the Choosing goes way beyond any of our science."

"An educated guess?" Bishop suggested.

"More of a hunch," Divinus admitted.

"A hunch?" Linus chuckled. "You're going soft on us, Theo."

Divinus smiled. "All in favor say *aye*."

"Aye," reverberated through the room.

They'd finished with the last case file. But before they could adjourn, Divinus stopped them with a fluttering of his wrist. "We have one last order of business to consider today." Without ceremony, he removed the hard leather box from his robes and slid it onto the table. The top was marked with the Ouroboros seal.

"Is that the last one?" Singh said. "They've finally finished it?"

Divinus cracked open the box to reveal a golden armlet nestled on rippling folds of soft, black velvet. The surface looked almost liquid, as if its solid state were merely an illusion. He removed it and held it up for the others to see. As he handled the device, the "13" stamped on the interior became visible in a vivid flash of emerald light.

"The Bioscience Engineers outdid themselves this time," he said, admiring the complex device that felt feather-light in his palm. "It's their finest work yet."

"And we're sure it's safe?" Singh said.

"For the proper Carrier," Divinus replied. He didn't bring up the numerous failures along the way—the lives lost perfecting the complicated bonding process.

Professor Ronan leaned forward, the golden light from the Beacon catching her sharp cheekbones. "Who should we nominate to be the Carrier?" she asked.

Divinus fiddled with the armlet.

"Theo, don't play bloody games with us," Linus said. "You've already got someone in mind, don't you? Well, out with it already. No need to keep us in suspense."

Divinus didn't deny it. Instead, he shifted his gaze from the Beacon to the projection still hovering over the table. He focused in on Elianna Wade, her bright eyes filled with the innocence of youth and unsuspecting of any impending burden.

"The President's daughter?" Singh guessed.

"Elianna Wade," Divinus confirmed. "Fifteen years old. Born in Tulsa, Oklahoma, but relocated to Washington with her family following last year's election. Currently enrolled as a sophomore at Sidwell Friends."

"Her test scores are only average," Linus said, tapping his tablet and flipping through her transcripts. "Surely, there must be a more qualified candidate? What about her sister . . . Sari Wade? She's younger, but her scores are more impressive."

"Wendell, test scores aren't everything," Divinus said. "Not by a long shot. Look at her empathy rating—it's off the charts. The highest score I've ever come across."

Approving murmurs rumbled around the table.

"I officially nominate Elianna Wade to be the Carrier for the Thirteenth Continuum," Divinus went on, sensing that the time was now. "All in favor say *aye*."

Twelve voices reverberated through the room. It was settled—there were no dissenters. At that moment, the Beacon blazed to life with emerald fire as if it knew that its fate, and possibly the fate of humankind, had just been decided with one swift vote. Divinus replaced the device inside the box and tucked it back into his robes.

"Noah, book a flight to DC and inform the White House," Divinus said, rising from the table and swishing toward the door. "We haven't a moment to lose."

"Yes, Professor," Noah said right away.

And with that, in a swirl of crimson, Divinus swept out of the room.

PART I:
THE GREAT AWAKENING

A kind of light spread out from her. And everything changed color. And the world opened out. And a day was good to awaken to. And there were no limits to anything. And the people of the world were good and handsome. And I was not afraid any more.

—John Steinbeck, *East of Eden*

Excerpt from
"THE COVENANT TO RETURN TO THE FIRST CONTINUUM"

BETWEEN

PROFESSOR THEODORE DIVINUS and his
SWORN BROTHERS AND SISTERS, REPRESENTATIVES
of THE CONTINUUM PROJECT

AND

THE undersigned individuals, identified on the appendix
and hereafter referred to as the "CHOSEN," of
THE SECOND, THIRD, FOURTH, FIFTH, SIXTH,
SEVENTH, EIGHTH, NINTH, TENTH, ELEVENTH,
TWELFTH and THIRTEENTH CONTINUUMS

*Entered into on this day, in accordance with International
and Maritime laws.*

WHEREAS, the Earth faces the threat of the Doom;

WHEREAS, should the Doom come to pass, the surface
of the Earth will be destroyed and remain uninhabitable for
a thousand years;

WHEREAS, representatives of the Continuum Project have
made preparations to preserve the accumulated knowledge of
humanity and to ensure the continuing survival of the species
after the Doom has passed and humans can return to the surface;

WHEREAS, the undersigned CHOSEN have all agreed to
be bound by the terms hereof in order to fulfill their assigned
roles in the event of the Doom;

NOW, THEREFORE, the parties hereto covenant and agree as follows:

ARTICLE 1: THE CHOOSING

1. By accepting their selection and assignment to one of the aforementioned continuum colonies, the CHOSEN agree to abide by this COVENANT.

2. Failure to abide by the terms of this COVENANT will result in the expulsion of the CHOSEN from the Continuum Project, if such a violation occurs before the Doom, or lifetime banishment from their colony, if such a violation occurs after the Doom.

3. The adjudication of and punishment for any violation of this COVENANT shall be conducted and implemented by the representatives of the Continuum Project (including Professor Divinus and his Sworn Brothers and Sisters, hereafter referred to as the "PROFESSORS") if it occurs before the Doom, or by the citizens of their assigned colony in the manner set forth by that colony's customs and laws if it occurs after the Doom.

ARTICLE 2: THE EXODUS

1. In the event of the Doom, the CHOSEN shall be notified immediately. The CHOSEN agree to abide by the secure evacuation protocols laid out by the PROFESSORS, to report in due haste to their assigned port of exodus and to follow all instructions in an orderly and safe fashion.

2. Failure of the CHOSEN to report to their assigned port of exodus in a timely and expeditious fashion will result in the subsequent and immediate forfeiture of their place in the assigned colony and an alternate person being named to take their place in their assigned colony. Due to the exigent and

perilous circumstances elicited by the Doom, this forfeiture will not be subject to any formal objection or appeals process, but instead will be considered binding and irreversible.

ARTICLE 3: THE PERIOD OF EXILE

1. The CHOSEN agree to remain in their colonies for the entire period of exile (1,000 years) ("THE PERIOD OF EXILE") in order to allow for decontamination of the surface that will allow humans to safely and successfully inhabit it again.

2. Any attempt to return prematurely jeopardizes the welfare and safety of the colony, as well as the overall success of THE CONTINUUM PROJECT, and will therefore be punishable by a death sentence.

3. Each colony will be provided with one [1] CARRIER, preselected by the PROFESSORS, and one [1] BEACON. Before the exodus, the CARRIER will bond with the Beacon, as instructed by the PROFESSORS, and carry the device for the entire span of his or her life. Attempting to remove the device prematurely is strictly forbidden and will result in the instantaneous death of the CARRIER.

4. Each CARRIER will select an appropriate replacement to bond with the Beacon and become the next CARRIER in the event of his or her death. In this way, the BEACONS shall be passed down from one CARRIER to the next until such time as THE PERIOD OF EXILE has elapsed and the time to return to the surface has arrived.

5. Failure to properly pass the BEACONS down through the generations will result in the irreparable loss of vital information critical to the survival of the CHOSEN, and thus will jeopardize the entire mission of THE CONTINUUM PROJECT.

ARTICLE 4: RETURN OF THE CONTINUUMS

    1. After THE PERIOD OF EXILE has elapsed, the BEACON will alert the CARRIERS that the time to return has come.

    2. At such time, the CARRIERS shall lead the CHOSEN from their colonies back to the surface of the Earth, following the directions communicated by the BEACONS, which will function as homing devices and lead the CHOSEN to the proper coordinates for THE FIRST CONTINUUM. The BEACONS will then serve as the key to unlock and obtain entry into THE FIRST CONTINUUM.

    3. The CHOSEN agree to return to the surface of the Earth after THE PERIOD OF EXILE with peaceable and constructive intentions—or not to return at all, and thus to remain in exile for the remainder of their days.

    —THE NATIONAL OPERATION TO ARCHIVE HUMANITY

Chapter 1
THE DARK THING

Closer.

Closer.

Closer.

He could get closer to the girl now.

He pushed out his consciousness and probed the dreamscape, even the blurry edges that had not yet taken solid form, but the boy wasn't here to protect her. He flowed toward the girl like a malevolent fog, stretching out his ghostly tendrils. The closer he got to her, the more he could influence her thoughts and inject them with his darkness.

Blinded, she screamed

Trapped, she flailed.

Defeated, she folded.

He hovered over the girl for a moment, feeding on her helplessness. She convulsed and cried out in fear, and that was when he descended on her with his claws extended and his black jaws cracked wide open. Suddenly, a burst of emerald light exploded from her wrist. The light was like a living, breathing creature; it stabbed through him like a hundred thousand blades and drove him back into the shadows.

Pain blazed through him, followed by disbelief. Nobody had ever resisted him before. He seethed as the sunlight spilled into the dreamscape and stole the girl away. The fabric of this world began to fade, dissolving into nothing like a flimsy spider web spun in the dead of night that could not withstand the onslaught of morning.

He was still too far away from the girl. Even his great power, enhanced by the instruments, could not overcome this amount of space and time. But soon—very soon now—that would change. He was growing stronger as they closed the distance. The secret of the Doom, long hidden from him, would be revealed and unleashed again.

Soon he would claim the girl and what was left of this ruined world.

Or they would both be destroyed.

Chapter 2
WAKING AT DAWN

Myra Jackson

The sun crept over the horizon and hit Myra full in the face, rousing her from what had been a tumultuous slumber. *Another nightmare*, she thought groggily. Her muscles ached from tussling with some imaginary monster, and her throat felt raw. She was curled up next to the heater, but it had long since gone cold. Its solar panels needed to recharge.

With a shiver, she pulled the bedroll around her shoulders to ward off the night's remaining chill. It gave way easily, and that triggered alarm bells in her head: *Tinker!*

She bolted upright. Her little brother's weight usually kept it anchored in place. They slept together for extra warmth, but also because it provided a small sense of comfort lacking in this desolate world of the Surface. Back home in the Thirteenth Continuum, a remote colony nestled at the bottom of one of the deepest ocean trenches, where she shared a tiny bedroom with her brother, she often longed for her own space and a little bit of privacy, but now that the whole world with its vast skies pierced by a billion stars was her bedroom, she found that she only wanted to keep Tinker closer.

She blinked in the early morning light. The sun cast a razor-thin streak of pink across the horizon. The landscape was volcanic and blackened, scarred by the Doom. No organic life survived on the Surface, at least not that they'd encountered since they washed up here a week ago. To the west, a crisp mountain range rose up and poked at the sky, and to the east, the ocean churned and sloshed, rasping up against the shore.

She spotted two more bedrolls splayed around their campsite, which was perched on a rocky ridge overlooking the sea. They were lumpy with the bodies of her other companions—Paige and Kaleb. Both were still sound asleep. They were her best friends and they'd all escaped from the Thirteenth Continuum together. But the spot right next to her where Tinker always slept was empty and cold to the touch.

That made the alarm bells in her head blare louder.

"Tinker!" she called out and burst to her feet, kicking off the bedroll that twisted around her ankles and threatened to trip her. The golden armlet fasted to her right wrist pulsed faster and brighter, struggling to keep pace with the racing of her heart.

She felt another presence stir deep inside her. It was Elianna Wade—or rather, it was the amalgamation of her memories, thoughts, emotional cadence, basically everything that the Beacon had downloaded and preserved from its first Carrier. This presence manifested itself in the form of a womanly voice that only Myra could hear.

Stay calm and look for him, Elianna communicated. *You'll find him.*

How do you know? Myra thought, feeling panic ripping and roaring in her ears. They didn't have to talk out loud to communicate—Elianna could read her thoughts.

He couldn't have gone far, Elianna replied.

But he doesn't have to go far to get hurt, Myra thought back. *You know Tinker, he's absent-minded and prone to accidents—and that's on a good day.*

She scanned the vicinity, looking for his diminutive form. Though he was eight years old—almost nine—he was about half the size of other kids his age. He also sported a thick pair of glasses that perched aslant on his nose; they were held together by screws and duct tape and the Oracle knew what else. Unlike Myra, who had curly brown hair and resembled their mother, Tinker had fine, blond hair like their father. But she didn't see him anywhere.

In two seconds, she ascertained that his pack was missing and a set of footprints led down to the beach. She didn't wait for Paige and Kaleb to wake up; she struggled into her boots, limping forward as she tugged them on, and took off after the tracks.

"Tinker!" she yelled as she ran.

Adrenaline pumped through her veins, pushing her faster. She spotted a small figure huddled on a rocky outcropping that jutted over the sea. In his dark coat with the hood cinched up, he blended into the volcanic terrain. His bony legs dangled over the water as the rough waves churned and spit around him. Why didn't he answer her? Were her cries drowned out by the ocean? Or was he injured?

She didn't know, and that terrified her.

Myra sprinted down to the beach and scrambled up the narrow outcropping, picking her way over the twisted rocks. They felt pockmarked and prickly under her palms. She reached the edge and grabbed Tinker's shoulder. He had a glazed look in his eyes. It took a moment for it to fade.

"Good morning!" he announced as if nothing were amiss. Ever since they'd discovered true morning—the kind where the sun rose and drenched the world in brilliant light— it had become his favorite greeting. He said it all throughout the day.

"No, it's not a good morning," Myra said. She tried to keep the anxiety out of her voice, but it found a way in anyway. "Pretty far from it. You scared me to death."

"No, I didn't," he said in his raspy voice. She had to strain to hear him over the roaring of the waves. "You're alive."

"Half to death then. You can't just wander off like that! What if you hurt yourself? Or what if you got lost and couldn't find your way back to camp?"

"But I didn't," he pointed out logically. "I'm perfectly fine."

She scowled. "But what if you did?"

"You're right, I should have told you."

"Now you're just saying that," she said with a frustrated sigh. She settled down next to him. The icy wind bit into her cheeks, turning them pink. She zipped up her jacket and tightened the hood. "What're you doing out here anyway? It's freezing."

"I couldn't sleep . . ." He fidgeted with the portable computer clutched in his lap; it lay open, but the screen was dark. "You were having another nightmare. Kicking and moaning in your sleep. It woke me up."

The nightmares were something new. Before she found out that their colony was running out of oxygen, Myra was a sound sleeper. Too sound, really. Waking up at the crack of dawn to the automatic lights had been one of her greatest challenges.

"Did I say anything in my sleep this time?" she asked as an especially large wave slapped the rocks and misted them. She licked her lips and tasted the briny water.

"Nothing that made any sense . . . something about *darkening* . . . or maybe *dark thing* . . . and I think you called out another name . . . you kept repeating it over and over . . . and your Beacon was flashing really fast . . ."

Her cheeks reddened. "Aero?"

He nodded. "He's one of the other Carriers, isn't he?"

"I think so," she said, fingering the golden cuff shackled to her right wrist. It throbbed with steady greenish light. The truth was that Aero had only ever visited her in dreams. The Beacons connected them together, but she wasn't good at controlling it yet. She felt like Aero was real, but the scientist in her wanted to scream out in protest:

But you don't have any proof! Just feelings and visions and dreams!

Worse yet, he hadn't contacted her in over a week, not since their first night on the Surface. His absence left her doubting his existence, even as her heart beat emphatically and told her that he was out there somewhere.

Tinker tapped on his computer, but the screen remained dark. It was his most prized possession and the only one of its kind in their world. He'd built it himself from scavenged parts, but it had gotten drenched when the kraken attacked their sub, along with a lot of their provisions and supplies.

"Any luck with the repairs?" she asked.

He shook his head. "Nope, it's ruined. Saltwater is corrosive." That was something Myra understood well. Back home, where she worked as an Engineering apprentice, a lot of her job involved combating saltwater and its destructive powers.

"I'm so sorry, Tink," she said and squeezed his shoulder. "But don't worry. When we get to the First Continuum, you can build a whole new computer. I bet they have tons of spare parts there, even more than back home in Sector 10."

Tinker absorbed her words in his silent way. The only sound for a long time was the crashing of the waves on the rocks. Finally, he broke the silence.

"Do you think they're still alive down there?" he asked, his eyes fixed on the choppy water. The question caught Myra off-guard. It took her a moment to find her voice. Not a day went by that she didn't worry about the fate of their colony. They had to escape from Padre Flavius and the tyrannical Synod, fleeing in a submersible that her father built and making for the Surface in the hope of finding it livable again.

"Of course they are," she said, trying to make her voice sound upbeat and confident—the way a parent should talk to a child—but it frayed and cracked under the strain. She wasn't up to the task. It made her miss her father like a knife to the heart. The last time she saw him he was locked up in the Pen for conspiring against the Synod.

"That's why we're doing this," she added, feeling the determination swell in her chest. "We're going to find a way to save them. They haven't run out of oxygen yet."

"But they will soon," Tinker said. "If we don't hurry."

His statement hung in the air like a poisonous cloud.

Myra couldn't dispute it; he was just stating the facts. Her father's words echoed through her head. *Eight months at the most, before the levels drop too low.* He was the one who had discovered that the Animus Machine was failing and their colony was running out of oxygen. Even though he was the Head Engineer, he couldn't fix it. Everything depended on them.

"The First Continuum will help us," she said and mussed his hair. *They have to help us. They're our last hope.*

Tinker glanced down at his computer. "You know how back home we put people out to sea after they die? I want to give my computer back to the Holy Sea."

"Tink, are you sure?" Myra said, taken aback. She couldn't imagine him without his computer—it was like his fifth limb. But when she glimpsed the look in his eyes, she knew that he had already made up his mind and nothing she said would dissuade him. He was as stubborn as they came, just like their father.

"It can't be fixed," he said with a shrug. "Besides, it's heavy to carry around and takes up a lot of room in my pack. No point in keeping it around if it's broken."

"Alright, but only if you're sure," she said and watched as he shut the computer, folding it in half like creasing a piece of paper. She could see the rust that had already crept into the joints and corroded them. He was right—the computer, like so many other things they'd lost, was beyond saving. The Holy Sea may have provided them with safe harbor from the Doom, but it also had the power to destroy anything that it touched.

"Do you want to say a prayer?" she asked.

Tinker's eyes darkened. "Nope, I don't believe in them."

He cast his computer into the sea. It sailed out, spinning end over end, and plummeted into the waves. It sank quickly, subsumed by the deep.

o   o   o

They returned to camp to find a worried Kaleb and Paige waiting for them.

"Myra, you can't just run off without telling anybody," Kaleb said, rushing over to her. His face was tense, but it softened as he thrust his arms around her.

Her body stiffened at his touch. She had to force herself to return his hug. She felt his warm breath kissing her neck and resisted the urge to squirm away. What was wrong with her? Why couldn't she just love him back the way that he loved her? She stayed entangled in his arms for as long as she could stand it and then pulled away.

"That's what my sister told me," Tinker rasped. He shrugged off his pack. It slumped on the ground, emptier without the sturdy weight of his computer to prop it up.

"Well, it applies to both of you," Paige cut in with a stern voice. Her long, blond hair was bunched into raggedy tangles, and her delicate features were smudged with dirt. Myra hadn't seen her own reflection since they left home, and though she'd never been as effortlessly beautiful as Paige, she wondered if her appearance had also disintegrated. She reached up and felt the sharp ridges of her cheekbones and the significant tangles in her curly brown hair and pulled her hand away. It was smudged with black residue.

"Sorry, I wasn't thinking," Myra said. She dug her boot in the ground, feeling guilty for upsetting them. "I woke up and Tinker was gone . . . so I guess I panicked and went after him. I promise it won't happen again."

"Swear it on the Oracle?" Kaleb said.

"On the Oracle and the Holy Sea," Myra replied and swirled her hand over her heart. They shared a smile, but then her Beacon throbbed and she heard Elianna.

The day is wasting—it's time to get moving.

The Beacon's pull was impossible to ignore. Myra couldn't imagine trying. The device was both a blessing and a curse. Kaleb noticed the look in her eyes.

"Let me guess—Elianna says it's time to go?" he said with a melodramatic sigh. "She's worse than the teachers at the Academy."

"At least she's got a plan," Paige interjected. "I quite like plans. Wait . . . she does have one, doesn't she?" she added, casting a worried glance at Myra.

Myra laughed, but then her Beacon flashed. Her eyes glazed over as images of their circuitous route to the First Continuum shot through her head, courtesy of Elianna.

It was far—really far.

A matter of months on foot, not weeks.

"Right, we washed up near a place called the Outer Banks," Myra said after she absorbed Elianna's message. "We'll have to travel the rest of the way on foot. Elianna wants us to keep heading north, following the coastline so that we stay close to a water source. It's also a good landmark to keep us from getting lost."

"Translation—walking, walking, and more bloody walking," Kaleb grumbled as he tugged his socks over his blisters, wincing from the pain. "I think my feet might fall off before we get there."

Paige shot Kaleb a devilish look. "I doubt they'll fall off, but if your blisters burst, your skin might slough off."

Kaleb looked appalled. "Slough off? That sounds horrific."

"It's not pleasant, but it shouldn't kill you."

"Fantastic, I feel so relieved."

"Enough complaining," Myra said, hopping to her feet and packing up her bedroll. "The sooner we get moving, the sooner we get there. That means you, Sebold."

"Fine, Jackson," he groused back with a good-natured grin.

As the sun rose higher and higher, arcing toward the crown of the sky, they packed up their camp and set off on foot toward the north to seize the remaining light of the day.

Chapter 3
MAGIC HOUR

Aero Wright

Aero watched the burned-out husk of his escape pod as the sun sunk below it. A blistering circle, then a shimmering crescent, then a flickering sliver, until it was finally obliterated by the sleek curves of the ship. Still the world would be bathed in golden light for at least a few more minutes—magic hour. Isn't that what it was called?

He remembered reading that somewhere, or maybe he'd learned about it at the Agoge, or maybe it came from the Beacon. Ever since he became the Carrier for the Second Continuum, his home colony located aboard a large spaceship that was originally designed to search for extraterrestrial life, his thoughts seemed like a jumble of fragments, loose ends, snippets of history and conversations and memories. He couldn't untangle them anymore, or summon up their origin. They were as much a part of him now as his arms or legs, or the sickle-shaped scar that marked his forehead.

As dusk began to fall, he made his way over the scorched earth. The temperature, which had risen perilously during the day, was now dropping rapidly. Sand gusted across the desert landscape; he tasted grit on his tongue. It was black, not reddish, but otherwise he could have been standing on the dead seabeds of Mars. He ascended to a high plateau and looked back at their camp, where they'd been stranded for the last seven days.

He picked out Wren's slender figure, hunched by the escape pod. He could tell from her movements that she was organizing their supplies and counting their rations, something she did several times a day, almost as a nervous tick. He shifted his gaze to the Forger in his crimson robes. He bent over the portable stove, brewing medicinal tea. It was so acrid and strong that Aero couldn't stomach the stuff, but it wasn't for him.

His eyes darted back to Wren. If he looked closely, he could detect a limp as she moved around and the outline of the brace encasing her ankle.

"Captain, just leave me!" she had grunted through gritted teeth right after they'd crash-landed their escape pod on Earth following their escape and banishment from the Second Continuum. "Damn it, I'm too injured . . . I'll only slow you down—"

"Not a chance," Aero cut her off as he carried her out of the wreckage.

"I'll catch up . . . when I'm better . . ." she protested, her face red and twisted with pain. Her ankle had already swelled up to twice its normal size and was possibly broken. She couldn't put any weight on it and yelped with pain when she tried anyway.

Still he refused to leave her, despite the myriad and linguistically colorful protests she hurled at him. Wren hadn't abandoned him when the Majors interrupted his duel with Vinick and ambushed him in the simulation chamber, and he wasn't about to abandon her now.

The Forger examined her ankle and determined that it was only a bad sprain; thankfully, it wasn't broken. Industrious as always, he fashioned a makeshift brace to stabilize it, but she was too injured to walk even short distances, let alone the thousands of miles to the First Continuum. "Two weeks rest, at least," the Forger told her as he secured the brace to her ankle. "If you try to walk on it too soon, you'll reinjure it."

"It's worth the risk," Wren said, even though Aero shot her a disapproving look.

The Forger tightened the brace, making her wince. "Lieutenant, this isn't something to take lightly. You could cause permanent damage to the ligaments."

"But staying here puts us all at risk! We're totally exposed out here in this desert. Vinick is searching for us. It won't take him long to piece together our trajectory. Our best bet is to keep moving—"

"We're not leaving you behind," Aero interrupted, even though he knew she was right about Vinick. "That's final, Lieutenant. Do you dare defy a direct order?"

"No sir," she said though she still looked defiant.

Suddenly, his Beacon flared, snapping Aero out of his memory. He looked down at the device fastened to his right wrist. The Ouroboros seal—a snake swallowing its own tail entwined around the words *Aeternus Eternus*—still glowed faintly, casting off greenish light. The golden metal also felt warm to the touch.

Vaguely, as if from very far away, he heard somebody calling his name. The voice sounded distant and ghostly.

Aero! Aero! Aero!

He immediately thought of Myra. Was she reaching for him? Was she calling to him? Or worse—was she in trouble? Or was it something else altogether?

But the signal faded before he could lock onto it. He felt frustration sweep through him, chased by a bitter dose of uncertainty. Unlike his Falchion, he wasn't skilled at controlling the Beacon yet. It was so different from anything that he'd ever encountered before. For all their complex science, the Falchions were weapons with a straightforward purpose, but the Beacon was something else altogether—part science, part alchemy, part magic.

Aero unsheathed his Falchion and cycled through some drills, partially to keep his abilities sharp but also because it helped to still his mind when he felt overcome by confusing emotions. He glanced at his blade and caught sight of his reflection in a flash of golden light—his short brown hair was beginning to grow out into longer curls, but his eyes were still dark brown, almost black, and the scar still marked his forehead.

He thought—*broadsword*—and the Falchion morphed from its default form of a curved sword and into the heavier, longer weapon. It cut and weaved through the air, leaving a trail of golden sparks in its wake. Soon perspiration dotted his brow and trickled down his face; it felt good to be moving his body.

Katana, he thought. The blade morphed into a Japanese Samurai sword. His Falchion was shifting a little sluggishly, he noticed, though nobody watching would have been able to tell. It needed a fresh charge. He'd have to talk to the Forger about it later.

He finished the last drill, crouching low and spinning when suddenly another blade collided with his *katana*. It was curved with a knuckle guard.

Talwer—that was its name.

He'd know the person who wielded it anywhere. "On guard, Captain!" Wren said with a puckish smile lighting up her face with its cobalt eyes and spiky blond hair.

Aero deflected her blow and took a step back to reset his feet. "I lost my official ranking when Vinick banished me, remember?" he said as he circled her with his Falchion at the ready, probing for openings. "I'm not a Captain without my army."

"You'll always be my Captain," she said and swung again.

"An army of two?"

She grinned. "I like our odds."

"Me too, Lieutenant."

They sparred for the next few minutes, their Falchions

blazing white-hot in the rapidly cooling air of the desert. Yesterday, the Forger had cleared Wren to start some rehabilitative exercises, though Aero doubted he'd approve of combat drills. But he didn't have the heart to deny her the thrill. They both lived for the heat of battle. It just meant that he'd have to end this quickly for her sake—or so he told himself.

He studied her movements for any weaknesses. Despite wearing an ankle brace and moving stiffly, she was still twice as good as any other soldier. He couldn't help but admire her abilities, but that didn't mean he was going to let her win.

He danced out of reach of her shorter, lighter sword, and swung when he spotted an opening. Sparks exploded around them, lighting up the plateau like fireworks.

In a flash, his sword stabbed at her left shoulder.

"Damn it," Wren cursed and shifted her Falchion into a shield just in time to block his blow, but the impact made her stagger on her injured leg.

"Have mercy, I'm injured!" she feigned, but then she twirled around lightning-fast and shifted her Falchion back into a talwer, catching him unawares and almost disarming him. He had to dig deep and use every skill that he'd mastered at the Agoge to battle her into submission.

"Mercy, mercy, I surrender," she said as she dropped her weapon and thrust her hands toward the sky, the tip of his Falchion pointing straight at her heart.

Aero lowered his blade; they were both panting and drenched in sweat.

"Sure you want to give up, Lieutenant?"

"*A good soldier knows when they've lost the battle*," she quoted their teachings from the Agoge. "Besides it's getting cold in this blasted desert." Goose bumps were already prickling their sweat-slickened skin.

Aero shifted his Falchion back into its default form and sheathed it in the scabbard belted to his waist. He gave her a respectful nod. "If it's any consolation, that's the best workout anybody's given me in a sparring match in a long time."

The robust sound of her laughter rang out, echoing through the desert, making Aero realize yet again how glad he was that she had accompanied him to Earth.

In the last of the dying light, they made their way back their camp, where the escape pod still rested against the rock formation that had torn a jagged hole in its hull. The metal gaped open like a nasty wound that hadn't been stitched up. The deflated parachutes trailed away from its nose. A deep trough in the sand led to the spot where they'd first touched down and somersaulted a few times before smashing into the rocks and bursting into flames.

In the long shadow of the ship, the Forger was tinkering with his special pack, the one made by the Order of the Foundry to function as a portable charger for their Falchions.

"What's Xander . . . I mean, the Forger doing?" he asked. Old habits were hard to break. Xander had been in their class at the Agoge before the Forgers chose him, but once he joined their Order, he left both the school and that name behind.

Wren followed his gaze. "He's trying to erect a shield to protect our camp from Vinick's sensors. Just pray that it works. If Vinick finds us . . ." she trailed off.

Aero frowned. "You can say it . . . we're dead."

Wren stumbled as they made their way down the steep embankment. Aero caught her arm and steadied her by pulling her close. They were only centimeters apart. He could feel her breath tickling his face and see the beads of sweat drying on her cheeks.

"How's the ankle?" he asked in a low voice.

"Almost good as new," she said with a forced smile and started down the hill ahead of him. He followed after her, studying her gait. "Seriously, I don't know what happened," she went on. "Must have stepped on a rock or something—"

"Liar," he cut her off. "And not a very good one."

She looked defiant for a moment, but then she dropped the act and stopped overcompensating. The hiccup in her walk worsened, allowing Aero to glimpse the full extent of her injury. It wasn't pretty.

"I told you, go on without me! I'll catch up once I'm healed."

Aero shook his head. "Not an option, I thought I made that clear."

"But sir—"

"If I'm still your Captain, then that's an order."

He winced as he remembered the soldiers from his unit that they'd left behind—Xing, Etoile, and Hoshiko. They'd fought bravely to help him escape from the Majors and probably died for their loyalty. Though they volunteered for it, he still felt guilty.

Wren picked up on the shift in his mood, and they both lapsed into silence, but it wasn't uncomfortable. Neither of them felt pressure to make mindless small talk. They'd served together for almost their whole lives so they were used to it. Eventually, as they neared the campsite, Wren broke the silence.

"So if you're not leaving me behind, then what's our plan? Sit here doing nothing until Vinick breaks the shield? Or finds some other way to track us?"

The mere mention of Vinick made Aero reach for the hilt of his Falchion. "As I see it, we've got two options," he said, coaxing his fingers to relax and release their grip on his weapon. "And I've got a feeling that you're not going to like either of them."

"What makes you so sure?" she said with a defiant look.

Spirited as always, he thought and had to suppress a grin. "Option number one is that we set off on foot once you're better. But according to my calculations, we're approximately two thousand clicks away from the First Continuum. That's based on what I could figure out from the Beacon and the old maps stored in the escape pod's onboard computer."

"Two thousand clicks," Wren repeated, letting out a low whistle. He could tell that she was doing the calculations in her head. "That's one hell of a hike."

"My thoughts exactly. Even if we manage to locate fresh water, our provisions will give out long before then, and the chances of finding anything edible are next to nothing. The

Doom destroyed all the organic life." He paused and scowled. "If Vinick hadn't shot us down, then I could have landed us closer to the First Continuum."

"You're right, I hate it," she agreed. "What's option number two?"

He shifted his gaze to the escape pod. She looked over, and then her eyes snapped back to him. Her face contorted with alarm. "The escape pod? You can't be serious? It's not designed to fly over terrestrial surfaces."

"Remember Emergency Combat Engineering at the Agoge?"

"You know I don't—I never studied."

He cocked his eyebrow. "Saved by the tip of your Falchion?"

"That's one way to put it," she said with a grin. Even though she did poorly in her academic classes, she was one of the top students in simulated combat. That's why she graduated with a decent ranking and passed her Krypteia. It was also the main reason why Aero chose her as his second-in-command. That, and her fierce loyalty.

"Well, good thing I was paying attention then. You're right—the escape pods weren't designed to fly over terrestrial surfaces. They're meant to provide emergency transport away from the mothership. But the engineers integrated a special workaround. It's a little glitchy, but it's possible to rig them up so they can fly short distances."

"How glitchy are we talking about?"

"I'm not sure," he admitted. "I've never actually tried it."

"And you said short distances. Look at the condition of that escape pod. The hull's shredded to hell, not to mention the fire. We put it out fast, but it did significant damage to the electrical systems. We're lucky there's anything left."

Aero winced. "I said you wouldn't like it."

"Please, tell me you've got another idea."

He shook his head. "What about you?"

She let out an exaggerated sigh. "Fine then, option number two—we repair the escape pod and rig it up to fly us to the

First Continuum. But we should work on it at night. That will make it harder for Vinick to track us. Not to mention the heat. It's much cooler at night, so we'll conserve more water that way."

"It's a deal," Aero replied with a grin. He loved how she always thought about logistics, no matter what the situation.

They reached the edge of the camp and approached the escape pod. The light had vanished, and the world was cloaked in darkness. An endless array of stars prickled the heavens, but no moon. The only other light came from the flickering of the lantern that the Forger had erected in the center of the camp. Aero looked up at the purple-black sky and pictured the Second Continuum's mothership orbiting Earth, blending into the stars. He wondered if Vinick had already deployed unmanned probes to search for them.

He felt the weight of the Beacon bonded to his wrist and thought about how simple his life had been before he bonded with it. Like clockwork, he rose with his soldiers and led them through their duties, until he closed his eyes at night like two leaden weights and fell into a dreamless sleep. But now everything was different—he'd lost his father, his army, and his home. It was as if his life had been divided into two distinct parts—*Before the Beacon* and *After the Beacon*.

The Forger stood up from his evening prayers and drew the hood of his robes over his shaved head. His eyes came to rest on Aero, and understanding flashed in them.

"Captain, you've come to a decision."

It wasn't a question.

"Yes, my Brother," Aero replied. "And we need your help."

The Forger bowed deeply. "At your service, Captain."

Wren pulled out the toolbox and started laying out various tools. Aero took a few strides toward the escape pod and laid his hand on the charred exterior. Blackened bits of paint and insulation flecked off on his hands. The ship was in bad shape. He had no idea if his crazy plan would work. He wished that he believed in prayers like the Forger.

Maybe then he wouldn't feel so lost.

"Let's get to work," he said anyway and reached for a wrench.

Chapter 4
THE BRIGHTSIDE

Seeker

The rustling of tiny feet reverberated through the Darkness of the Below and reached Seeker's ears. She was on the trail of a creature. She scented the air and settled on what it was—a ratter. And hopefully, a fat one. She hadn't eaten anything in many days. Her stomach was sunken and had even given up on grumbling at her to feed it.

Scratch, scratch, scratch.

The ratter scampered ahead of her, leaving a pungent trail of scent in its wake that made her mouth water. She ran faster, using her arms and legs to propel her through the black tunnels. Her muscles started to cramp and tremble, but she ignored the pain and tried to run even faster. She couldn't lose the trail or she would miss making her offerings. Like all Weaklings, she had to give the Strong Ones half of everything that she hunted and killed—slimy, dirty, furry things that skulked in the Darkness. It didn't matter what it was, if it wriggled and had a heartbeat, then she would hunt it down and devour it, crunching its tiny bones with her sharp teeth and slurping down the thick blood.

But lately, she'd gotten distracted. She'd missed her last two deliveries of offerings. If she didn't turn up at the altar with something edible soon, then Crusher would come after her. The Strong Ones might already be looking for her. That last thought made her heard thud,, sending more adrenaline cascading through her bloodstream.

Scratch, scratch, scratch.

The tunnel forked ahead. Seeker paused to scent the air. Her eyes, though large and very sensitive, could see nothing in the pitch darkness of the tunnels. The smell his her nostrils. That was how she knew—the ratter went to the right.

She careened after it and around a sharp curve, avoiding the sheer drop-off. Though the Darkness of the Below was impenetrable, she knew exactly where to place her feet, exactly when to turn—and exactly how to survive. Her prey was just ahead now. She coiled her body to spring when something large and hairy slammed into her and pinned her flat on the ground.

Pain shot down her spine and forced the breath from her lungs. One panicked thought shot through her head:

The Strong Ones found me!

The hair on her back bristled as she struggled to free herself, but it was futile. Though there were only two of them, she was no match for their size and strength. They were three times larger than her with thick frames corseted by rippling, veiny muscles.

"Smells like . . . Seeker," the first one said, sniffing at her face. Seeker could smell his putrid breath fogging her nostrils and recognized his scent—it was Biter.

That made her squirm even harder.

"Hey, get out of my way," the second one growled, shoving Biter away. This one was female. "Stop hogging the Weakling. I'm starving, just let me have a lil' nibble."

"Pincher, no nibbling!" roared Biter, knocking her away. "Not until we find Crusher! He wants his meals intact. He likes to sink his teeth into them while their blood is hot and they're still squirming." He seized Seeker and dragged her down the tunnel. "That's what happens to filthy Weaklings who don't make their offerings."

"Fine, no nibbling," Pincher agreed in a sulky voice. "But Crusher better reward us. This Weakling was hard to find. We've been searching the tunnels for days."

"He will," Biter said. "If you don't go getting greedy."

The mention of Crusher made Seeker flail around in a blind panic. He was the Strongest of the Strong Ones, and all the Weaklings feared him. A soft whimper escaped her lips, and more adrenaline shot through her system. She tasted metal in her mouth. One desperate thought cut through her panic:

The Door in the Wall.

The memory of it popped into her head. The rumbling and shaking as it dilated. The lurching from under her feet that made her stomach twist and her ears pop. The burning, stinking Light that made her eyes burn and her skin heat up. That was the reason why she'd missed making her offerings. It was also the reason why they hadn't been able to find her.

Biter held her in his ironclad grip—she couldn't fight her way out of this. Her only chance lay elsewhere. She twisted around so that her mouth was free.

"But I found it," Seeker gasped. "The Door in the Wall!"

Biter didn't let go, but his grip did slacken. "You're lying, Weakling! Nobody knows where the Door in the Wall is . . . it probably doesn't even exist."

"She is a bit squirmy," Pincher agreed. She stalked over to Seeker and pressed her nail deep into her neck. "Are you lying, Weakling? I'll slit your throat if you are—"

"No, I'm not! I swear it!" Seeker squealed, trying to twist away from her claw. "I found the Door in the Wall . . . it leads to the Moving Room . . . and the Brightside!"

Biter snorted. "What do we want with Doors in Walls and Moving Rooms?" "Yeah, what do we want with those?" said Pincher, pressing her claw deeper. "We want to eat you, that's what we want! Maybe we should start right now—"

"But do you ever get enough meat?" Seeker cried, feeling her throat constrict.

Pincher hesitated, and Seeker sensed an opening. She wriggled away from Biter's grip and scrambled to her feet.

"Crusher takes most of the offerings for himself, doesn't he? Leaves nothing but tubers for you? When was the last time your belly was full?"

"It will be," Biter growled,"once we feast on you."

Seeker tugged at her loose skin, pinching it between her fingers. "But you can feel my ribs sticking out—I'm not much of a meal. There's no meat on my bones."

"The Weakling has a point," said Pincher. "She's puny. If we give her to Crusher, then there won't be any meat leftover for us. He does take the best kill for himself."

"I can tell," Seeker said. "Now that I think about it, you do seem skinny—"

"Who you calling skinny, Weakling!" snapped Biter.

He struck Seeker with his fist, knocking her down. White light exploded in her vision, but it was worth it. She could sense their uncertainty growing like a tuber through bedrock. The only law in their world was survival of the strongest, and Strong Ones could always become Weaklings if they weren't careful.

Pincher paced around the tunnel in frustration.

"The Weakling is right! Crusher does take the best offerings for himself! Leaving nothing but gristle and scraps for us! He doesn't want us growing big and strong like him. Then we might take over, and he wouldn't like that, would he?"

"No, he wouldn't," said Biter. "Wouldn't like it one bit."

Seeker struggled back to her feet. "A lot more creatures live in the Light than in the Darkness of the Below! I can go to the Brightside and hunt for fresh meat. I'm very good at finding things. Then your bellies will swell and stretch and bulge until you grow strong like Crusher."

"More meat?" Biter said, licking his lips.

"I still don't trust this Weakling," Pincher growled, tramping around and sniffing at Seeker's face. "I say we feast on her now while we still can."

Silence rushed back into the tunnel as the Strong Ones considered their options. Seeker didn't know if what she'd said was true. She didn't know what lived on the Brightside. She had only been able to stay in the Light for a short amount of time before she fled back into the sanctuary of the Moving Room. But she was prepared to risk going back to the Brightside over certain death at Crusher's hands.

Please, thought Seeker. *Please let me live!*

"We'll let Crusher decide," Biter said at last.

o   o   o

Biter threw Seeker down in front of the altar.

She landed hard on her side as a greenish glow washed over her. Wincing at her bruised ribs, she cracked her eyes open. They landed on the source of the illumination— the Gold Circle. Their most sacred object lay in a stone alcove. Its surface cast off golden light that pulsed in a steady rhythm and lit up the cavernous room. At one end stood an arched doorway, and at the other a massive, obsidian throne. Tiny skeletons littered the floor, the remnants of recent feasting that had yet to be swept up by the Weaklings.

Biter and Pincher bowed down in front of the Gold Circle. "We worship the Light in the Darkness! May the Light never go out, so long as we shall live . . ."

Suddenly, a shadow stretched across the floor. Seeker jerked her head back and cowered away in fear.

"I see you've brought my meat," Crusher growled as he strode into the room, stooping over to pass under the doorframe. He was at least twice as big as the other Strong Ones with massive jaws and jet-black hair that covered his entire body. He stalked over to Seeker, towering over her. His eyes snapped to Biter and Pincher and narrowed.

"What took so long?" he growled, his lips pulling back from his teeth. "I was about to send Slayer to find you! Maybe I should feast on more than Weakling?"

Biter and Pincher exchanged a worried look.

"Oh, Crusher, Strongest of the Strong Ones," Biter said, bowing to make himself seem smaller. "This Weakling told us something we thought you'd want to hear—"

"Better not be a filthy trick!" Crusher snapped. "This Weakling is named Seeker, but she should be named Sneaker. She can't be trusted."

That made Seeker whimper with fear. Biter and Pincher also looked afraid. "But she says she found the Door in the Wall," Biter ventured in a shaky voice.

"Impossible!" Crusher roared. The muscles in his neck bulged out like thick ropes. He paced around the room, casting his hulking shadow across the walls. "It's been lost for ages! Nobody knows where it is! It must be a filthy trick—"

"But I found it!" Seeker said. "Oh, mighty Crusher, I can prove it! It leads to the Brightside! I will go up there and hunt and bring back fresh meat. More creatures live in the Light than in the Darkness of the Below."

Crusher licked his lips while he thought. Biter and Pincher followed the exchange with their sharp eyes, waiting to see what he decided. Seeker's heart beat against her ribcage like a drum, making her feel lightheaded and nauseous. Her empty stomach certainly didn't help matters. Finally, Crusher broke the silence.

"Weakling, you'd better be telling the truth!"

Seeker leapt to her feet and hopped around in an anxious dance.

"Yes . . . I will show you the Door in the Wall! And if I'm wrong . . . well, you can still feast on me! Oh, Strongest of the Strong Ones, you're bigger and faster than a Weakling like me. I can't possibly escape from you."

"The Door in the Wall?" Crusher repeated. "You know where it is?"

"Yes . . . yes . . . I will lead you to it!"

Crusher and the other Strong Ones exchanged a pointed glance. Though they didn't say anything, Seeker felt relief flooding through her like a drink of cool water after a meal. She'd won them over, and she was safe.

For now.

Chapter 5
ALL OF THE BIRDS

Myra Jackson

They spent the next few days walking, taking only short breaks for meals or thirsty sips of water, and sleeping when the daylight faded and night was about to descend. The early morning chill wore off, and Myra started sweating profusely. The sun beat down on her back like it was making up for all the years she spent away from its warmth.

She shed her jacket and tied it around her waist and glanced back at Kaleb, Paige, and Tinker. They were all sweating, the perspiration speckling their brows and staining their clothes darker. They continued hugging the coastline and traveling steadily northward, following Elianna's instructions and the siren call of the Beacon.

Occasionally, as they trudged along with their heavy packs weighing them down, they passed the scorched remains of manmade structures jutting out of the ground like gruesome memorials to the world that existed Before Doom. Most of them were so charred and damaged that they were unidentifiable even to Elianna, but occasionally her ethereal voice echoed through Myra's head with their foreign-sounding names:

Wharf.

Hangar.

Tractor.

Sometimes a vision accompanied her words of what the twisted hunk of metal might have looked like when it churned the fertile soil so that farmers could plant their crops and grow food, but as Myra trudged over the barren landscape, she found it difficult to imagine that this earth had ever been capable of growing anything.

As midday approached, Myra gazed up at the cornflower blue sky while Elianna told her about the birds that used to fill them—soaring, diving into the ocean in search of a meal, squabbling, mating, returning to their nests to regurgitate morsels of food for their hungry chicks. *Birds* . . . Myra thought as images of the winged creatures fluttered through her head. They seemed so magical and unfathomable like something out of one of her mother's fairytales.

When Tinker started to lag behind, Myra relieved him of his pack and coaxed him forward by telling him about the birds. Soon he was peppering her—and really Elianna—with questions about the whimsical animals, a noticeable bounce having returned to his step. But then he skidded to a halt by a steep bluff overlooking the ocean.

"They died, didn't they?" he rasped. "All of the birds?"

Myra probed Elianna for some answer. Her face fell when she heard the response. "Yes . . . they did . . . all of them. I'm sorry, Tink. I shouldn't have told you about them."

"No, I'm glad you did," he said as his gaze lingered on the empty skies. "It's too bad. I would have liked to see them fly, so I'd know what they really looked like."

"Well, maybe you will one day," Myra said and handed him back his pack.

Tinker shot her a quizzical look but didn't ask any further questions, and she didn't mention the last image that Elianna shared with her. It wasn't a memory, Elianna explained, only her projection of what must have happened to them in the Doom. In a flash, Myra saw the birds burst into flames and rain down from the sky like fireballs until their charred bodies shattered on the ground, breaking into a million tiny pieces.

At midday, they stopped for a quick lunch by a small outcropping of rocks. Beneath them, the ocean stretched endlessly into the horizon. No birds hovered above it or dove into the frothy waves in search of a meal.

These skies are dead, Myra thought.

Kaleb spotted the frown on her face. "Hey, cheer up, Jackson," he said, taking a sizable bite of his kelp bar and finishing it in two swallows. "It can't be that bad."

She felt the fatigue and worry rushing through her. Her hand impulsively shot out to her pack, where she kept their provisions. She hadn't told the others yet, but they'd lost a lot of their supplies when the kraken destroyed their sub and were fast running out of food. She didn't want to worry them, not when there was nothing that they could do about it. So she pushed it from her mind and put on a brave face.

"You're right. We're still alive, aren't we?"

"Speak for yourself—I'm starving, and I can't feel my feet."

Myra pinched his ankle.

"Holy Sea!" he cursed. "That hurt!"

A mischievous smile lit up her face.

"I'm no doctor, but I think you can feel them just fine."

"That was my *ankle*, genius. My feet are numb with huge blisters. I'm pretty sure necrosis is setting in. It's only a matter of time before they fall off—"

Myra silenced him with a kiss. She wasn't sure what came over her exactly, only that seeking refuge wherever she could get it seemed like a good plan at the moment.

She fixed him with a shy grin. "I'd still love you even if you were a footless cripple. I'd hoist you onto my back and carry you to the First Continuum."

"Since when are you so cheerful?" he asked, a bit dazed from her attentions.

"Since I got to eat lunch, I guess."

He draped his arm over her shoulders and pulled her close. She snuggled into him and allowed him to comfort her, wishing that it actually worked, but she felt just as stressed as ever. They lingered in the shade of the rocks and gulped water from their flasks, but soon Elianna urged them onward again. They walked for the rest of the day, traversing rocky cliffs and rockier paths, curving inland when the shoreline proved impassable, but always following its trajectory, wending their way toward the north.

As the sun began to set, vanishing behind a growing mass of pink clouds to the west, they finally broke for camp. Kaleb and Paige hiked down to the beach to refill the flasks while Tinker took over the cooking duties. Myra measured out some dried beans and rice and passed them over and then quickly replaced the satchels in her pack. He didn't seem to notice that their supplies were running low.

"Need any help with that?" she asked as she unfurled her bedroll next to the stove. It was her father's invention and ran on some sort of battery power. She rubbed her hands together and held them up to the burner. The evening was fast turning colder.

"No thanks," Tinker said with his lopsided smile. "I've got it."

A few minutes later, Kaleb and Paige returned with the filtered water and settled down around the stove, spreading out their bedrolls. Paige squinted at the sky.

"See that over there? I don't like the look of those clouds."

Myra followed her gaze. They had grown considerably larger since that morning. Their lumpy, dark shadows now obliterated the setting sun completely. The wind had also picked up, whipping down from the mountains, and it was cold and smelled . . . *wet.*

"Me neither," Myra said, yanking her bedroll up.

"Think they're coming this way?" Kaleb asked as he watched Tinker stir the pot to prevent clumping. "I've kept my eye on them all day. I think they're getting closer."

"I'm not sure . . . but . . ." Myra trailed off.

Paige cocked her head. "But . . . what? By the Oracle, you have to tell us."

Myra set her lips. "Elianna says weather moves from west to east."

They all took this in solemnly. When the rice and beans were tender, Tinker seasoned them with a pinch of sea salt and some dried herbs and passed around bowls. They ate in the fading warmth of the stove while night fell firmly around them, and then they retreated to their bedrolls. Myra watched as the others, exhausted from the long day, fell asleep around her one by one. Tinker was soon snoring softly next to her.

But still she lay awake in the gathering dark despite her bone-deep weariness. She thought of the mental exercises that Elianna had taught her. They were supposed to help her control her mind—and the Beacon.

Inhale . . . Elianna communicated. *Exhale . . . Inhale . . . Exhale . . .*

Myra shut her eyes and worked hard to steady her breathing. Somewhere in the middle distance she heard the faint whooshing of the waves as they beat up against the shore. She tried to match her breathing to the ancient rhythms of the sea. When she felt her mind on the cusp of drifting off, she probed for Aero and called out his name, like he did every night.

Her ghostly voice roiled through the dreamscape.

Aero . . . are you there? Can you hear me?

But he didn't respond.

She wasn't sure why he'd been absent from her dreams these last few nights. Of course, she wasn't very good at controlling the Beacon yet. Neither was he. Maybe that was it. But doubt lingered in her mind anyway. She missed him more than she cared to admit. She tried calling for him again, even though Kaleb was sleeping only a few feet away, which made her feel terribly guilty. She probed for Aero using the Beacon.

Aero . . . I'm calling you!

Her disembodied voice rippled through the dreamscape, but still he didn't respond, nor did he materialize before her like he always had in the past.

Only the Dark Thing hovered in the shadows.

Watching. Waiting.

Then coming *closer*.

And the dream quickly became a nightmare.

Chapter 6
WHEN THE LIGHTS COME ON

Jonah Jackson

T he darkness is alive," Jonah said and chuckled to himself. The fit made his broken ribs ache. He winced from the sharp pain. He was losing his mind, wasn't he? The endless night of the Penitentiary was like a living, breathing organism. The darkness pulsed and breathed and consumed anything that moved. Taking up the entirety of Sector 3, the vast prison had been constructed after the initial occupation of the colony when the Synod seized control. Rows upon rows of steel cages stretched up and down the sector, their bars ascending to the low ceiling.

Beep!

The sector door unlocked—someone was coming.

Jonah's heart heaved. He could see nothing in the pitch darkness, but he could hear things—the rustling and scratching of rats, the stirring of other prisoners, their curses against the Oracle. He could smell things too—putrid things, rotting things.

Slurp!

The door dilated, and a flashlight beam careened around Sector 3. A Patroller stepped through the door; the key ring fastened to his waist chinked with each step. Jonah recognized him right away—it was Baron Donovan. He'd been in his daughter Myra's class at the Academy and was famous for dispensing brutal beatings. Another figure trailed behind him—it was a Red Cloak. The priest's crimson robes brushed against the floor.

"Piss on the Oracle, Red Cloak!" screamed a deranged prisoner through a mouth full of broken teeth. He rammed his head against the bars of his cell.

"Shut up, heathen!" yelled Baron. He unsheathed the heavy, lead pipe belted to his waist and swung at the bars. The noise it made was jarring. The prisoner scampered back with a strained whimper.

Baron lowered his pipe and aimed his flashlight forward again, and they continued through the sector. *Don't come to my cell*, Jonah thought in desperation, *keep moving!* Already his skin was burning in anticipation of another beating.

They marched down the row, coming to a stop right in front of his cell. Baron inserted a key into the lock and twisted it; the door swung open with a reluctant whine. His flashlight hit Jonah full in the face, blinding him.

"Well, hello there, heathen," Baron said. "Looks like you've got a visitor today. Are you going to behave like a good little prisoner? Or do I have to teach you a lesson? I know I shouldn't expect much from the likes of you. Your wife was a heathen. Your daughter was a heathen. Your son was a heathen. A whole family of heathens—"

"Don't talk about my family!" Jonah cut him off.

Anger shot through him like a fiery knife. He strained at the chains shackled to his wrists and felt them bite into his skin, but then he sagged helplessly.

Disappointed, Baron lowered his pipe. "Padre Teronius, he's all yours."

"Thank you, Patroller Donovan. You do the Oracle's good work."

Teronius stepped inside the cell, grimacing at the stench. Jonah's eyes snapped to his face. It was framed by a long, dark beard that was riddled with white hair. Teronius was one of the oldest and most respected priests. This caught Jonah's attention right away. Aside from Padre Flavius, none of the Red Cloaks visited the Pen.

Teronius glanced back at Baron.

"Patroller, you may leave us alone now."

Baron fidgeted with his pipe and glanced around nervously. "Padre Teronius, my orders are to stay with you! This heathen is unpredictable and dangerous—"

"What part of *now* didn't you understand?" Teronius said, his voice flushing with barely contained fury. He leveled his irate gaze on the young Patroller.

Baron bobbed his head quickly. "Sorry, Padre! Of course, I'll leave you alone. Just knock twice on the sector door when you're finished with him."

Teronius waited for him to exit the sector, and then knelt down before Jonah. His eyes roved over the prisoner, taking in his shattered, bruised body, the chains that bound his wrists, his dry, cracked lips, and the empty water cup beside him.

Jonah gathered what was left of his courage; it wasn't much. "Padre, why are you here?" he asked in a feeble voice.

A smile animated the priest's face. "Because I wanted to see the notorious heathen for myself. Padre Flavius wasn't wrong about you!" He held up his hands. "I can feel the evil wafting off your body. *The Book of the Oracle of the Sea* teaches us that 'to understand good we must face great evil . . .' Vinius Chapter 2, Verse 12."

"Padre, please have mercy," Jonah said.

Teronius drew his hand back and slapped Jonah clear across the face. "There's no mercy for heathens! Only the blessed waters of the Holy Sea can save you now."

"Do it then," Jonah said. "Put me out to sea already!"

"You'd like that, wouldn't you? Not until you've suffered and repented your sins! Your treasonous actions have had grave consequences. The uprising has begun, and it's all your fault. Your daughter inspired it by defying the Oracle's teachings—"

"Wait . . . what do you mean?" Jonah stammered. "My daughter . . . what uprising?"

Of course, he knew that there had been more unrest lately. The Patrollers kept dumping more prisoners in the Pen, but none of them talked for fear of beatings. This was the first news he'd gotten in weeks of what was happening outside Sector 3.

"Don't lie to me, heathen," Teronius snarled. "You expect me to believe that you didn't know about the uprising? This was your plan all along, wasn't it? For the Hockers to rise up against the Synod? And then for some sympathetic Factum to join them?"

"Factum, too?" Jonah said in shock. "The trades are working with the Hockers?"

"Don't play dumb with me!" Teronius said.

He leaned closer to Jonah, so they were only inches apart. The scent of sandalwood oil wafted off him. "Tell me about Engineering. How long has your old trade been plotting against the Synod? We know Royston, the Head Engineer, is involved."

"Royston?" Jonah said. "How is he involved in this?"

"He's a fool and a heathen!" the priest said and swirled his hand over his chest. "Thanks to his help, the rebels have barricaded themselves inside the Engineering Room. They call themselves Surfacers. And Royston isn't alone. He's working with a Hocker, who they call Chief. Despite her inferior status, she's proven difficult to contain."

"A Hocker? But . . . that's impossible," Jonah stammered. "Royston doesn't associate with any Hockers! He keeps to himself mostly, goes to work, then goes straight home. He never even married, has no kids. His whole life is Engineering."

Teronius pursed his lips in distaste.

"Tell me about . . . Maude Studebaker."

"What about her?" Jonah said in confusion. It wasn't just his arms that had atrophied; his brain also seemed sluggish from lack of use.

Teronius slapped him again. "Should I summon the Patroller back to jog your memory? I hear their pipes are very good at making people talk—"

Jonah held up his shackled hands to protect his face. "No . . . no . . . please! Maude was just my elderly neighbor! A harmless widow who watched my kids when I had to work late. Sometimes I helped her out with repairs to her compartment. Maintenance was always slow to respond to Hockers' requests—"

"You're a liar!" Teronius cut him off. "She's the leader of the Surfacers, and she's getting supplies into the Engineering Room somehow, even though we've cut off their Victus and shut down the Souk."

"Padre, I don't know anything about their supplies!" Jonah stammered but then pulled himself together. "But if I did know, I wouldn't bloody tell you!"

Teronius looked beyond furious. He leaned closer so that his lips were only millimeters from Jonah. "Listen carefully—and whimper like I'm torturing you."

The priest looked him straight in the eyes, so there was no mistaking what he said next:

"I've got a message for you from Maude."

Jonah flinched. Was this some kind of trick? Teronius saw the suspicion clouding his face and quickly whispered, "Jonah, please don't be afraid! I'm sorry I had to hit you, but it was an act for the other prisoners. We can't have them thinking that I'm a traitor, now can we? I have to protect my cover, or I won't be much use to the Surfacers."

Jonah frowned and spoke in a low voice:

"But why should I trust you? You're one of them."

"Right, it's natural for you to have doubts. Frankly, I'd be concerned if you didn't. Perhaps this will persuade you . . . ." He lowered his voice even more. "Before I pledged to the Church and took the name Padre Teronius, I went by another name."

"What name?"

"Walter Studebaker."

Jonah stared at the priest in shock. Of course, he knew that Maude once had a brother named Walter. But she never spoke of him, so Jonah always assumed that he had died in the same Pox outbreak that killed her husband and children.

"But I thought you were dead," Jonah said. "Maude never talked about you."

"Far from it! Though symbolically, when we pledge to the Church, we leave our old lives and our names behind. So it's a little like dying, I suppose."

"That means your parents were Plenus?"

Teronius nodded. "Our mother sat on the Synod. After my sister became a Hocker, the whole family shunned her. It was bad enough that she could have pledged to the Synod or the Church, but she chose a Factum trade—Records, of all things. We were humiliated when she failed her Apprentice Exam and got kicked out of her trade."

"Of course, your parents must have been horrified. I'm not surprised they shunned her. Even most Factum won't associate with Hockers, let alone the Plenus."

Teronius looked down with shame contorting his face.

"I'm not proud of it. Quite the opposite, in fact. But I was young and ambitious. I didn't want anyone to know I was related to a Hocker. I worried that it would tarnish my reputation. When the time came, I pledged to the Church, and I never spoke to my sister again. Occasionally, I'd see her peddling candy at the Souk—and feel revulsion."

Jonah absorbed this. "So then . . . what changed?"

"Since Padre Flavius took over the Church, I've witnessed many things that I wish I hadn't . . . dreadful things . . . unforgettable things . . . unforgivable things . . ."

Jonah felt his heart lurch. "My . . . wife?"

The priest nodded. "Your wife Tessa isn't the only one that Padre Flavius has killed over the years. He loathes anybody who poses a threat to his power, and he's willing to use any means necessary to silence them."

"The sacrifices?" Jonah guessed.

"Yes . . . once you make his black list, he'll look for any excuse to put you out to sea. He bribes greedy Factum to make up lies and testify against you, and he uses the Church to shield him, and the Patrollers to do his bidding. For many years, I've been praying to the Oracle of the Sea for guidance. And your daughter, bless her! She's what we've been waiting for! She's 'the Second Ascension' that Vinius wrote about."

"What do you mean? The Second Ascension?"

"Don't you see?" Teronius said, his eyes widening with excitement. "Myra was called by the Holy Sea to deliver us from this evil like it's written in *The Book of the Oracle of the Sea*. It's time for the class system to fall, time for the sacrifices to stop, and most of all—time for the reign of Padre Flavius and the Synod to come to an end."

The priest glanced around nervously. Though the sector remained dark and quiet, Baron could return at any moment, not to mention the other prisoners couldn't be trusted either. Their eyes and ears had grown sharp in the darkness.

"Look, I don't have much time. For all I know, Padre Flavius has already made the connection between me and Maude and ordered the Patrollers to keep a closer eye on me. You're not supposed to have any visitors, but I talked that young Patroller into letting me in. But he could realize his mistake at any second. So . . . listen closely . . ."

Jonah leaned forward as far as his chains would permit. The priest's lips brushed his ear. "When the lights come on, look to the heavens for salvation."

Jonah furrowed his brow. "That's the message from Maude?"

The priest nodded. "That's the whole thing."

"But what does it mean?"

"I'm sorry, that's all I know. Maude thinks it's safer that way, in case the Patrollers decide to arrest me." Teronius stood up and drew his hand back. "I'm sorry, but I have to do this. Grab my robes now and act like you're begging for mercy."

Jonah did as instructed and then steeled himself to receive the blow. The backhand caught him across the jaw, splitting his lip. "Curse the Oracle!" he cried out—more for show than from actual pain. The briny tang of blood flooded his mouth.

The priest rose to his full height and gathered his robes around him like he'd just suffered a great affront. "Serves you right, heathen!" he spat. "How dare you soil my robes with your impurity? May the Holy Sea have mercy on your black soul."

With that, Teronius spun on his heels and swished across the Pen. When he reached the sector door, he rapped his knuckles on it three times. A second later, it dilated with a slurp, and he vanished from sight. The door contracted as darkness flooded back into the Pen.

Jonah thought about everything that he'd just learned. Could the rebels actually overthrow the Synod? And what did Maude's cryptic message mean?

He didn't have a clue, but despite the depth of his confusion, he felt hope pulsing through his veins like a powerful stimulant. Maybe his children weren't dead. Maybe they had survived the journey to the Surface. Maybe they'd find the First Continuum—and a way to save their colony. One last thought ricocheted through his brain:

Maybe we still have a chance.

He waited in the darkness of his cell, but now his waiting had a purpose. *When the lights come on . . .* he thought over and over. *When the lights come on . . .*

He would be ready for what was coming.

He only hoped it came soon.

Chapter 7
NOT ON THE OLD MAPS

Myra Jackson

The nightmares were growing worse.

Myra no longer doubted that's what they were. Every morning, she woke shaking and drenched in sweat. She couldn't remember what they were about exactly. Only a vague residue of terror lingered once she opened her eyes, but somehow she knew that Aero wasn't in them. In the dawn light, she gazed out over the dead landscape and felt a shudder run through her. They were the only things alive out here. This world was primordial and volcanic. Was it even considered a world without life on it?

Despite their collective weariness, they shouldered their packs and set out following Elianna's directions. As they walked, the weather turned colder. Thick clouds skirted the mountain range. A damp, icy wind gusted out toward the sea.

Winter will be here soon, Elianna communicated. Myra didn't need to see the accompanying images of blizzards and storms to know that wasn't good news. But she kept it to herself for the same reason that she didn't mention their dwindling supply of rations. She didn't want to worry them, not when they couldn't do anything about it.

About an hour after they stopped for lunch on a cluster of rocks, they crested a steep ridge and were forced to halt. Before them, spreading out in every direction, was an enormous crater. Seawater swelled into the basin, smashing up against the blackened, twisted rocks. The drop-off was perilously steep. Myra signaled for the others to hold back and peered into it. Elianna's voice echoed through her head:

This shouldn't be here.

Myra could sense the confusion in her voice.

What do you mean? she thought back.

This crater isn't on the old maps, Elianna responded.

What were you expecting to find here?

A city . . . I thought maybe something would be left.

Elianna's words were freighted with sadness. An image from her memories flashed through Myra's head, superimposing itself over the crater. She saw *skyscrapers* and *streets* and *stoplights* and *cars* and *traffic* and *pedestrians* and *sidewalks*, and rising above the city, a single spire—magnificent and snowy white and pointing steadfastly toward the heavens.

Myra wished the others could witness these visions, but only she carried the Beacon. As she watched the memories, a realization dawned on her.

Elianna, did you live here? This city was your home, wasn't it?

Once upon a time, I lived here with my family, she confirmed. *We moved here after my father won the election. Millions of people lived here. This was the capital of our nation. We called it Washington, DC. But it's gone. All of it. There's nothing left.*

The image of the ancient city held fast for a moment before dissolving into thin air, leaving only a massive crater where this grand metropolis once stood. Myra wondered what could have caused such a vast wound in the earth.

Elianna heard her thought and answered:

Only one thing.

Her voice did not waver.

Elianna . . . please tell me . . . I want to know what happened here.

I can't tell you—but I can show you. This city must have been a target. This isn't a memory for I wasn't here to witness it, but it's what I believe happened.

The vision pierced through Myra's brain as if it were stabbing her. The city appeared again superimposed over the crater, but this time it was burning . . . no, it wasn't just burning . . . it was melting. The heat was so intense that Myra flinched back and screamed. The pedestrians were melting. The cars were melting. The buildings were melting. And that magnificent spire that rose above the city? It was melting, too.

Even the earth itself was melting.

Until there was only a smoldering hole left.

When the image faded, Myra was panting and her cheeks felt hot. She wanted to sink to her knees and cry out in pain. Elianna's voice rang through her head. *There's nothing more to see here. The daylight is wasting. We must continue onward. Let it go.*

o   o   o

Elianna directed them around the crater, and they curved inland. Now the shoreline was behind them, and the mountain range was straight ahead. As Myra walked, her Beacon began to pulse faster and grew warmer to the touch. A few hours later, when the sun was already well into its descent, they reached the westernmost edge of the crater.

Myra stopped and probed the Beacon for guidance; she expected Elianna to keep leading them around the crater, eventually turning them back toward the coast and then northward again. But Elianna's voice sounded uncertain. *Myra . . . do you feel that?*

You mean the Beacon? Myra said, glancing down at her wrist and the pulsing green light. *It's been doing that all afternoon. Wait . . . it's growing stronger, isn't it?*

Stronger and stronger. It's picking up a signal of some kind.

Aero, Myra thought right away. His name shot through her head. Elianna heard it. Their conversations—held only in Myra's head—were growing more fluid and natural.

The signal could be from another Carrier, but it's weak, so I can't be sure. As far as I can tell, it's coming from some-where in that mountain range. That could be why it's so hard to trace. The mountains could be blocking it.

Myra's gaze locked onto the mountains. She had never seen something so immense or forbidding in her life. Not to mention the dark clouds encircling the peaks and the cold wind emanating from them. She chewed at her lower lip while she considered their options. *Should we follow the signal?* she thought to Elianna.

Elianna's response echoed through her head:

You're the Carrier now—it's your decision.

Myra was so lost in the exchange that she almost forgot she wasn't alone. The others had stopped and were staring at her with worried expressions.

"Myra, what's going on?" Kaleb said, tapping her on the shoulder. "Are we camping here for the night?"

"Great idea. I'm beat," Paige said and slung off her pack. She plopped down on the bag and wiped the sweat from her brow with her sleeve.

But Tinker cocked his head at Myra.

"It's the Beacon, isn't it?" he said in his raspy voice. His eyes were fixed on the device peeking out of Myra's sleeve. "It looks like it's glowing brighter."

Indeed, it *was* glowing brighter. Myra felt that protective instinct rear up inside her. Before she knew what she was doing, she yanked her sleeve down to hide it from view. But then she relaxed and shrugged off her pack.

"Come over here," she said. "I've got something to tell you."

They gathered around in a circle by the edge of the crater with their heavy packs slumped around them. She told them about the mysterious signal from the mountains and how it could be from another Carrier. She finished by confessing about the strange dreams but omitted the parts about bonding with Aero. It just felt . . . well . . . too intimate.

"Other survivors?" Paige said after Myra had finished. "By the Oracle...you're positive?"

"Well, not positive," Myra admitted. "So far he's only visited me in my dreams. But I think he's a Carrier from one of the other Continuums. His name is Aero. From what I could tell, he also had to flee from his home and crashed on the Surface."

"Why didn't you tell us?" Kaleb asked, unable to hide the hurt in his voice.

"They were just dreams," Myra said, feeling her cheeks turning hot; she couldn't meet his eyes. "And I wasn't sure what they meant, or if they were even real. Plus, the signal is weak. Elianna doesn't know if it's coming from Aero. It could be nothing, only a glitch in the device. Or it could be coming from something else."

"Don't you see?" Kaleb said. "That doesn't matter. If there's even a chance there are other survivors out there, then we have to find them. You said the signal's weak, right? What if something happened to them, and they need our help?"

Paige frowned. "But what about our colony? They're still running out of oxygen, remember? Our families, our friends, everyone we love—they're all depending on us reaching the First Continuum. We can't waste time on wild detours."

"Paige has a point," Myra agreed, dragging her finger through the dirt. "Also, those mountains look steep. Climbing them could prove tricky, to say the least."

"Yeah, and look at the sky," Paige said. "It looks . . . angry."

They turned to look at the peaks shrouded by their halo of dark clouds.

Myra nodded. "I'm worried about that, too."

"Also, there's something else we haven't talked about yet," Paige said. "If something bad happened to the survivors . . . well . . . then it could happen to us, too."

They lapsed into silence while they all considered the enormity of their decision. *Myra, you have to tell them the rest of it,* Elianna communicated. *Now is the time.*

Myra knew that she was right; she'd waited too long as it was. She looked down and fiddled with the strap of her pack, feeling guilt sweep through her. "There's something else I haven't told you guys. I guess I didn't want to worry you."

Paige snapped her head up. "Myra, what is it? Just spit it out already."

"Well, you know how I've been rationing our supplies?" Myra said.

"How could I forget?" Kaleb said and patted his rapidly thinning midsection. "My stomach hasn't stopped growling at me this whole bloody trip."

Myra stifled a smile. Kaleb could always lighten the mood. But then she turned more serious again and forced herself to continue. "As you know, we lost a lot of supplies when the kraken attacked our sub. Our provisions are running pretty low—"

"How much is pretty?" Paige cut in.

Myra bit her lower lip. "Based on how I've been rationing them, we've got enough to last for about another two weeks. According to Elianna, we won't make it to the First Continuum before we run out."

She pulled open her pack and spilled out the meager contents for them to see. The satchels of beans and rice had shrunk markedly. Sugar seemed a distant memory. Only a tiny pinch of green tea remained; she was hoarding it. They had some kelp bars left—one of their staple foods that the Hockers relied on to stave off malnutrition and starvation—but even those would be gone soon.

Kaleb paled. "I knew it was bad, but two *weeks*?"

"How are we supposed . . . to get more food?" Paige stammered. "We haven't seen anything remotely edible since we got here. Just rocks, rocks, and more rocks!"

Tinker took it all in soundlessly. Maybe he had known about the provisions running low, or maybe he realized that nothing he could say would change their situation.

Myra turned to gaze at the mountains. Her Beacon

throbbed stronger than ever. It took every bit of her willpower not to run straight after the signal. "Right, I admit it's a long shot, but if the signal is coming from the other survivors, they probably have provisions. We're a whole lot closer to those mountains than the First Continuum."

"But you're not even sure that the signal is coming from he other Carrier," Paige pointed out. "Not to mention you've only ever met him in your dreams. How do you know he's real? And even if he is, how do you know we can trust him?"

Myra looked down in frustration. "I don't know . . . you're right. It's not logical, I get that. But I can feel that Aero is out there—just look at the Beacon!"

She held up her wrist. The device was pulsing faster and brighter, that much was undeniable.

"So let me get this straight," Kaleb said. "The way I see it we've got two choices—possible chance of starvation versus definite chance of starvation."

Paige didn't find that funny. "Those are some really great choices. I love how this adventure is shaping up so far." She aimed a pointed look at Myra. "Anything else you haven't told us?"

Silence descended over the group. Life on the road was wearing on Paige more than the others, Myra noticed. Her best friend's eyes had lost their sparkle, and her face looked hollowed out as though somebody had scooped the flesh from her cheeks. While the journey had also taken a toll on Kaleb, it had chiseled away his soft edges and added lean muscle to his tall frame, making him look even more handsome somehow. Tinker had also fared well. He seemed to have sprouted a whole inch since they'd gotten here.

In the end, they took a vote. The results spoke clearly— three to one in favor of following the signal. Paige was in the minority, and though she agreed to abide by the group's decision, she wouldn't take her eyes off the mountains. The clouds hovering over them seemed to have grown thicker and darker. Paige was right—they did look angry.

Paige chucked a rock toward them, but it landed only a few feet away with a dull thud.

"I've got a bad feeling about those mountains," she said before they started off again—this time to the west. "By the Oracle, I just hope I'm wrong."

Chapter 8
STEPPING INTO THE LIGHT

Seeker

The Door in the Wall opened and the Light came in.

The nasty, burning, evil, stinking Light.

But this time, Seeker didn't cringe or shy away. She didn't try to claw her eyeballs out either. She'd learned to keep them shut. To give them time to adjust first. Fear gripped her heart and squeezed it tight. She wanted to scurry back into the Darkness of the Below, but she couldn't return empty-handed or the Strong Ones would kill her.

Crusher had watched her enter the Moving Room. He had watched the Door in the Wall contract behind her. He had promised right before it finished closing that if she returned without fresh meat, he would devour her himself, feasting on her while her heart was still beating and her blood ran hot, just the way he liked it.

Seeker was glad when the Door in the Wall shut with a terrific rumble, and the Moving Room began to accelerate upward. She was ready for it this time. The lurching of the floor and the popping in her ears didn't bother her nearly as much, though she did feel nauseous, like when she'd eaten something that had been dead for too long.

The rumbling and shaking stopped as the Door in the Wall finished dilating. She peeled her eyes open in the Light. They were shielded by a device of her own making—a jagged slice of metal poked with holes and bent to fit over her ears. As her vision cleared, she beheld the Brightside for the first time. The harsh angles of the rocks and their protruding shadows frightened her. This place looked too pointy—too exposed—too much of everything. She preferred to slink in the safety of the Darkness.

But she couldn't go back now.

Not without fresh meat.

She raised her foot and inched it through the doorway. The Light fell on her toes, but it didn't burn like she expected. She wiggled them and watched them dance in the Light. She risked a tentative step forward and then froze with her eyes shut and her body retracted into a crouch. But still nothing unpleasant happened to her though she did startle when she caught sight of her own shadow following her every movement.

And then she took another step.

And a few more steps.

And then she was running on all fours.

Searching. Scenting. Stalking. *Seeking.*

This was a hunting trip.

Seeker promised herself that she wouldn't return without fresh meat. She wouldn't let the Strong Ones kill her. And maybe if she was successful—maybe if she found enough meat—then she could become a Strong One, too.

This thought both thrilled and terrified her. She had never allowed herself to dream of anything beyond her next meal. Could Seeker the Weakling become Seeker the Strong One? Was such a thing even possible? It had never happened before.

But hope stirred in her chest. It dug its roots deep into her heart, as her claws bit into the ground and propelled her forward. Her eyes grew sharper in the Light that warmed her hair and kissed her flesh. The world of the Brightside opened up in front of her and laid itself out at her feet. Over the miles and miles of blackened terrain, visible through the holes in her visor, she searched tirelessly for her prey.

Seeker would find meat, or she would die trying.

This she swore as she ran toward the Light.

PART II
THE SIGNAL FROM THE MOUNTAINS

I looked at the stars, and considered how awful it would be for a man to turn his face up to them as he froze to death, and see no help or pity in all the glittering multitude.

—Charles Dickens, *Great Expectations*

Chapter 9
A FLEET OF PROBES

The Majors

Y ou may enter, Major Rothman."
     Danika strode onto the bridge and saluted Supreme
General Vinick. He stood at the bow of the ship, his face
tilted toward the spherical windows, his hand resting lightly
on the hilt of his Falchion. Beyond the windows lay the
blackness of outer space speckled by a million stars. Though
not visible from this angle, Earth floated somewhere below
them. The Majors were scattered about the control room,
performing various duties.

She locked eyes with the other woman on the bridge.

Major Lydia Wright.

They were both soldiers from combat units recently
selected to join the Majors, but they had one other big
thing in common—the deserter Aero Wright. He was
her betrothed; Major Wright was his mother. *Thank the
stars our Connubial Ceremony never happened*, Danika
thought for the hundredth time in the last few days. The
shame of almost being wed to a traitor haunted her. It
drove her to serve the rightful Supreme General. She

wouldn't rest until the deserter was apprehended—or better yet—dead.

"At ease, Major," Vinick said.

She dropped her stiff posture. "Sir, you summoned me?"

He tore his attention away from the windows. His lips puckered with impatience. "Major, you've prepared the report on the *deserters?*" he said, emphasizing the last word like it was an expletive. "For your sake, I hope you have something good to tell me."

Danika felt her stomach churn with anxiety. Ever since her promotion, it had become a familiar sensation. "Sir, we reviewed the security footage. Unfortunately, our security array doesn't have a clear angle of the Docking Bay's corridor, where we discovered the bodies of Majors Oranick and Mauro. It's a flaw in our system that we believe the deserters exploited on purpose. The results of the autopsy came back from the Euthanasia Clinic. The deserters shot them with a blaster before they stole an escape pod and fled to Earth."

"Cowards use blasters," Vinick said. "Did you recover the weapon?"

"No, sir," she said, scanning the report on her portable tablet. "We swept the scene but it was clear. We're guessing it was tossed down the incinerator."

Vinick frowned. "Anything else?"

Danika nodded. "We picked up something interesting from the security array. One additional deserter escaped with them, sir."

Major Doyle looked up from his console.

"Another deserter?" he said, exchanging a glance with the Supreme General. Officially the Majors were of equal rank, but Doyle acted like Vinick's second-in-command. "It's not a soldier from their combat unit. They've all been accounted for. Most are dead, but the rest are being detained in the Disciplinary Barracks."

Vinick's eyes flared with rage. "Enlighten us, Major. Who's this traitor?"

Danika flipped through her report. "A Forger, formerly known as Xander Xavier. We pulled his records, and it turns out he was in the same class at the Agoge as the deserters before the Forgers chose him for their Order. We spoke to the Forgers. They claim they had no prior knowledge of his involvement with the deserters. They also said that Xander stole a portable charging station before he disappeared from the Foundry."

"So the deserters will be able to recharge their Falchions on the surface," Doyle said. "Very clever. Could the rest of the Order be involved?"

"Sir, we don't have any proof," Danika said, but then she frowned. "But they did seem resistant to the idea of talking to me. They could be hiding something."

"I don't trust them," Doyle said. His tapped at his monitor idly. "Their loyalty does not lie with the Supreme General and the Majors. They care too much about their damned science and their secret teachings."

Vinick nodded. "Let's investigate the connection further." He turned to face the monitors, where Earth was projected in three-dimensional form. "Major Rothman, where are we with tracking the escape pod?"

"As you know, we lost their ship in the upper atmosphere," Danika said. "But we ran a few flight simulations. Their escape pod sustained a direct hit from our ship's defense systems, so they couldn't have gotten far." She hit a few buttons on her tablet, and maps and flight trajectories popped up on the monitors. She pointed to a large landmass surrounded by water. "We've zeroed in on the area where we believe they crashed down—the North American continent."

"Can they repair the ship?" Doyle asked.

Danika was stumped. She hadn't anticipated this question.

But Major Wright stepped in and saved her. "Supreme General Vinick, I've studied the deserters' files. Engineering was not the boy's strong suit. His victories in Falchion-to-Falchion combat are what propelled him to the top of his class. The same goes for the girl. And the Forgers don't work on the ships—just the Falchions."

Vinick's face darkened. "Your son was good, wasn't he?"

"His file says undefeated," Wright said. "I've seen that only one other time in the school's records and they date back to the founding of the Second Continuum."

Danika knew that she should keep her mouth shut and only speak when spoken to, but she couldn't help it. Curiosity got the better of her. "Major . . . who was it?"

"Arthur Brillstein," Wright answered. Though she was talking about her late husband, she kept her voice devoid of emotion, like she'd been trained.

"The Supreme General?" Danika said without thinking.

"*Former,*" Vinick spat and unsheathed his Falchion, morphing it into a dagger. "He was also the deserter's father, but that didn't save him."

"Of course not . . . sir," Danika said and looked away. "You are the strongest soldier and our rightful Supreme General," she added, her heart pounding.

Vinick stared her down for a second longer, but then he retracted his weapon. He morphed it back into its default form and sheathed it at his waist. He flicked his eyes to the maps. "Deploy the probes," he ordered. "If they're down there, we'll find them."

"Sir, the whole fleet?" Doyle asked.

"The whole fleet," Vinick confirmed. His eyes snapped to Danika. "And Major Rothman, if we apprehend the deserters alive, what is your recommendation?"

"Execute them and retrieve the Beacon," she said without hesitation. Though emotions were frowned upon, anger flooded into her voice. "*No mercy in the face of weakness,*" she quoted from their teachings. "The Beacon belongs to the Second Continuum and the Supreme General—we can't have a deserter carrying it."

Vinick stroked the hilt of his Falchion.

"Do it," he said. "And don't disappoint me."

Chapter 10
BLACK RIDGE

Myra Jackson

As they walked to the west, the wind picked up and tore at their clothes. Soon dark clouds obscured the sun, casting the world into shadow long before night had begun to fall. Myra made sure that Tinker zipped up his coat and helped him with his pack when he lagged behind. Kaleb and Paige trailed after them in a single-file line.

That night they camped out in the open underneath the canopy of stars, but Myra slept fitfully. It wasn't because of the cold wind or the rocks underneath her bedroll. The nightmares came when she closed her eyes and didn't abate until sunrise. She woke with a scream on her breath and the metallic taste of adrenaline coating her tongue. Though the nightmare quickly dissipated from her conscious mind, she knew one thing for sure:

Aero wasn't in it.

They set off again the next morning, and soon the flatlands gave way to rocky foothills. They picked their way over them. If they strayed, Elianna corrected their trajectory or suggested an easier route. The foothills grew steeper and more treacherous. They summited the next ridge, and Kaleb slowed and cupped his hand to his brow.

"It that a mountain?" he said.

Myra followed his gaze to the steep peak ahead. "That's the beginning of the mountains. On the old maps, they're called the Blue Ridge Mountains."

Kaleb studied them. "More like Black Ridge, don't you think?"

He was right—the mountains looked black in the dim sunlight snuffed out by the gathering clouds.

"The Black Ridge Mountains," Myra said. "Let's change it then. I'll let Elianna know that it's an executive decision by the Carrier and her steadfast companion."

Kaleb grinned and adjusted the straps on his pack.

"What's so funny?" she said.

"I guess I never thought I'd be an explorer, let alone ever set foot on the Surface. I always figured I'd live a comfortable life as Plenus. Maybe follow in my father's footsteps and join the Synod one day, get married and start a family and then get a bigger compartment assignment. You know, the usual fairytale stuff."

This made Myra smile, but she also felt a pang of guilt tug at her heart. Would he be living that life if she hadn't come along and taken a sledgehammer to his world? But then she remembered the Animus Machine. Maybe he would be living that comfortable life—a fairytale life—but not for much longer. Likely only a few months, at most.

"Things never turn out how you plan," she said softly.

"Speak for yourself," he replied. "One of my plans is going to work out."

The way he looked at her right then made it crystal clear what that plan was. Her heart thumped faster as his eyes bored into her. He leaned over to kiss her, but she dodged it and picked up her pace.

"Hurry up, Sebold," she called back. "A whole world awaits us." She was talking to Kaleb—but she was thinking about Aero.

o   o   o

It began to drizzle shortly after lunch, and then to pour out-right near dusk. Their coats offered some protection, but as the deluge intensified, the rain found a way through cracks in their boots and seams and zippers in their clothes. Soon they were all soaked and shivering. The wind hurtled down the foothills and whipped eastward.

"Hurry, we need to find shelter," Myra said. She had to yell to be heard over the storm. The sun was setting fast, and it was getting harder to see, especially in the storm. With nightfall came colder temperatures and a greater chance of slipping on the rocks.

"Preferably someplace dry," Paige added.

They peeled off from the path and split up in search of a suitable campsite. Myra spotted a boulder across the way and peered under it to see if it was dry. Suddenly, a scream broke through the storm—a high-pitched, strangled shriek that signaled danger.

It was Paige.

Myra whipped around. Paige had been standing on the path right behind her, but now she was gone. Only the sound of the rain slapping the rocks remained.

"Paige!" Myra yelled. "Tinker . . . Kaleb . . . help me!"

She sprinted over to the spot where Paige was standing. With numb, slippery fingers, she pried the flashlight out of her pack. She shined the light around—and almost stumbled into the sinkhole. It hadn't been there before, she was sure of it; she'd walked across that exact spot only seconds ago, and it was solid ground, or so it seemed.

"Paige!" she called into the hole. "Can you hear me?"

Nothing.

With her heart racing, Myra aimed the flashlight into the hole but only saw unending blackness. Even the beam vanished after a few feet as if eaten alive by the darkness.

"Paige, are you down there?" she called again, her voice echoing out.

Still nothing.

Myra leapt into action. She swung her feet over the sinkhole when she heard footsteps behind her and then Kaleb's voice.

"Myra . . . wait! We don't know if it's safe!"

He grabbed for her arm, but she wrenched it away. "I'm going after her, now get out of my way."

Myra started lowering herself into the hole. The rain poured down even harder and gushed into the hole, making it slippery and perilous.

"Slow down!" Kaleb yelled. "At least, let me get a rope!"

Myra shook her head, making wet strands of hair stick in her eyes. Mud caked her fingers as she felt around for a solid handhold. "There's no time for that! Paige could be seriously hurt."

She didn't wait any longer. She clenched the flashlight between her teeth and felt around with her feet, searching for some foothold, anything to keep her from plummeting into the sinkhole. Finally, her right foot caught on something solid. She leaned her weight onto it—mercifully it held.

Myra began to climb down, moving as quickly as she could. The walls were slick from the rain and caked with mud. As she descended, she kept her ears sharp, listening for any sign that Paige was alive down there. But nothing reached them.

Myra glanced up—Kaleb and Tinker had their flashlights out and were watching with tense expressions. "Anything?" Kaleb yelled down at her.

"Not yet," Myra said. "And we're going to lose visual contact soon."

She didn't wait to hear his curses and objections; she scrambled down another few feet to where the tunnel curved sharply to the right. Kaleb vanished from her view. She was on her own now. She paused to free her right hand, plucking the flashlight from her mouth and aiming it down. Below her, spanned a great ocean of blackness.

"Paige!" she yelled into it. "Paige, please answer me!"

Still nothing. Just endless darkness.

Myra kept climbing down through the tunnel. A few minutes later it bottomed out into a large, underground cavern. Jagged rocks dripped down from the ceiling like knives. In the dim glow of her flashlight, she spotted a body lying face down.

It wasn't moving.

Adrenaline kicked in and took over. Myra leapt down the remaining few feet, landing in a crouch on all fours. She scrambled over to Paige and rolled her onto her back. Blood seeped from a nasty gash in her forehead, where she must have struck it on the way down. Luckily, she had landed on a pile of soft sand that cushioned her fall.

"Wake up," Myra said. "Please . . . wake up."

For a terrifying second, Paige remained limp. But then her eyes popped open. She coughed and sputtered. "Where . . . am I?" she gasped. She touched her forehead and pulled her hand away—blood coated her fingertips. "What . . . what happened?"

"We were looking for shelter from the storm," Myra said, relief flooding her voice. "And you fell through a sinkhole. By the Oracle . . . are you ok?"

"Yeah, I think so," Paige said, wincing as she struggled to sit up. "I remember looking around outside . . . it was raining pretty hard . . . but then . . . nothing."

"Right, I think you hit your head on the way down."

"That would explain the blood," Paige said, slipping into her medical persona. "A minor concussion, most likely. That can cause temporary amnesia in some cases."

Myra felt a rush of fear. "Amnesia? Is that serious?"

Paige shook her head. "No, it should be only temporary. My neck is a little stiff, and I'll probably have a killer headache tomorrow, but I should recover."

Once Myra ascertained that Paige was safe, she called for Kaleb and Tinker to join them in the cavern. Kaleb secured a rope around a boulder and lowered it through the sinkhole, and they climbed down it. Tinker went first, and Kaleb followed after him, carrying their packs. The bluish beams of their flashlights bounced around the cave—it was about ten feet square with sloping walls and loose sand covering the ground.

"Think it's safe to camp down here?" Kaleb asked, shining his flashlight around. "At least it's out of the storm and should give us a chance to dry off."

"I'm not sure," Myra said, her eyes roving over the cave. They were almost certainly the only people who had set foot down here in over a thousand years . . . if ever. Other tunnels branched off the main cavern, twisting their way through the rock to the Oracle knew where. She inspected one of them, peering into the pitch darkness. Something about the cave bothered her, though she couldn't say what exactly.

But Paige had no such qualms. She unrolled her bedroll and started stripping off her wet clothes. "I say we sleep here for the night, where it's nice and dry."

Myra hesitated, but Paige had been through a lot. Making her climb up the slippery rope and spend the night out in the storm seemed like too much to ask.

"Fine, we'll camp here tonight," she agreed.

o   o   o

They peeled off their wet clothes and boots and laid them out to dry, and then huddled together in their bedrolls by the portable heater. Soon Myra's shivering subsided, and she began to feel pleasantly drowsy. Tinker waved his hands in front of the heater, watching as their shadows danced through the reddish glow. He contorted his fingers into a fish and made it swim through the sea, and then shaped them into a bird that flapped its wings.

Myra watched his performance and smiled.

"That looks like an eagle."

"Nope . . . it's a bird," Tinker said. "It flies through the sky."

"No silly, it can be both. An eagle is a type of bird."

His eyes widened. "Are there more types? What are their names?"

And so Myra shut her eyes and summoned Elianna to the forefront of her mind. *Bird names*, she thought. And Elianna answered, sending the strange words swooping through her head: *Gull . . . sparrow . . . crow . . . hawk . . . blue jay . . . egret . . . flamingo . . . dove . . .*

Myra repeated them to Tinker. He flapped his hands, casting more bird shadows against the walls. A lopsided smile graced his lips. "I like it down here," he rasped. "It's kind of like the Secret Room back home, isn't it?"

Myra looked around. "Well, almost."

"Something's missing, isn't it?"

"A big thing, actually."

Tinker lowered his hands. "Do you think Rickard's still alive?"

His words hung in the air.

"Unlikely, isn't it?" Paige mumbled from her bedroll. A bandage graced her forehead. "Sorry . . . but you saw it. The 'Trollers were bludgeoning him to death. And even if he survived their pipes, he's probably swimming in the Holy Sea by now. How long have we been gone? More than enough time for Flavius to sacrifice him."

Silence descended over the group; Tinker stopped making animal shadows. As much as Myra usually tried to avoid thinking about it, the memory flashed through her head of Rickard being overtaken by the Patrollers as they fell on him and battered him with their pipes. He'd made it possible for them to escape in the submersible—he'd held the Patrollers back long enough for his father to get the portal door to close.

"Tink, there's always a chance," Myra said and ruffled his hair. "You have to believe that." She was talking about Rickard but also their father, who was locked up in the Pen.

Tinker slipped his hand into his sister's palm and squeezed it tight. "I believe," he rasped. "I do."

Once their clothes were dry, they put them back on for extra warmth and climbed back into their bedrolls. Gradually, they drifted off to sleep. Even Elianna seemed to have nodded out. But Myra stayed awake, gazing into the red glow of the heater. Rickard was still on her mind, and so was her father. Memories of them cycled through her head in a loop. She wondered what was happening in their faraway home tucked beneath the sea.

Paige is probably right, she thought glumly.

Despite what she'd told Tinker, her faith was wavering. The enormity of her task settled on her shoulders. She felt them sagging under the impossible weight. She wasn't just worried about her father—but everyone else in their colony, too.

Maude . . . the Bishop twins . . . Royston . . . Mr. Richardson . . . Baron . . . The names scrolled through her head in an endless list of everyone who she'd ever gone to school with, or passed in the corridors, or hated their guts, or loved without reservation. If she didn't make it to the First Continuum, then they would all suffocate to death.

And soon.

Myra let out a weary sigh and slumped on her bedroll. The noise from the wind and rain was muted; only a faint whistle blew into the cave. She inhaled and smelled the dampness coming from above. It hadn't let up yet. How long would the storm last? It was slowing their progress, and all the while, their supplies were dwindling. She slipped her hands into her pack and felt the satchels, counting out their provisions.

"One day . . . two days . . . three days . . . four . . ."

She stopped on *four*.

She'd told the others that they had two weeks left, but that was wishful thinking. Feeling dejected, she twisted over and stared at the ceiling. Restless thoughts thrummed and hummed in her brain. She knew from experience that sleep wouldn't come for a long time, not with the adrenaline surging through her veins. Indeed, sleep was far off tonight.

The rippling red light cast by the heater played tricks with the shadows.

And then . . .

Something darted across the ceiling.

Myra sat up, her eyes straining to see in the dim light.

She was about to reach for her flashlight when she exhaled slowly. *The heater is just playing tricks with my eyes*, she thought. Not to mention, she was exhausted. When was the last time that she'd gotten a decent night of sleep? "Bloody nightmares . . ." she cursed, flopping onto her bedroll.

She was about to drift off when it darted across the ceiling again. This time, she saw that it had hairy legs, and she heard scratching noises. Now she knew she wasn't imagining things. She snatched up her flashlight and slipped out of her bedroll, careful not to disturb Tinker who was curled up next to her, snoring softly. The scratching noises sounded like they were coming from one of the tunnels branching off the cave.

She clicked the flashlight on and followed the sounds. She heard the faint dripping of water, coming from the storm above. She ran her hand along the wall, causing bits of rock to flake off. She breathed in some dust and coughed hard.

"Hello?" she choked out. "Anybody . . . here?"

Her voice echoed down the tunnel and died out.

As she made her way down the narrow passage, the scratching grew louder. The Beacon pulsed faster and brighter. She rounded the corner—and felt something sticky and strong wrap itself around her body. She flailed her arms to free herself, dropping the flashlight. It hit the ground with a clang and rolled away. It came to a rest a few feet away. The beam illuminated the end of the tunnel.

Her eyes widened in terror. She tried to scream, but the sticky tendrils sealed her lips shut. She thrashed around harder, but the mesh held her tight. She could only stare at the pulsating nest as the creatures broke through the membrane with their razor-sharp pinchers. They had bulbous heads with roving eyes and rippling legs that scratched at the ground, propelling them forward with surprising speed. Their pinchers snapped hungrily at the air. And there were hundreds of them.

No . . . thousands.

Myra panicked, but no matter how hard she struggled against the webbing, it held her tight. Her mouth was still sealed shut, so she couldn't even scream for help. The monstrous creatures kept gushing out of the nest and streaming toward her. All she could do was watch as they got closer. She knew one thing for sure:

They meant to devour her.

Chapter 11
THE BREACH

Aero Wright

The alarm blared through the desert.

"Incoming probe!" the Forger yelled. "It's breaching the shield."

Aero looked up from where he was working with Wren to repair the escape pod's engine around the bow of the ship. Their camp in the desert had been calm and seemingly safe only moments before. It was still night, technically speaking, but the easternmost skyline had started to bleed from black to dark navy. He scanned the sky, but the probe was silent and invisible to the naked eye. He pictured the sleek, black-plated vessel, armed with powerful sensor arrays and deadly weapons that could torpedo them to dust before they realized that it was approaching. The alarm continued to blare.

Aero threw down his wrench and sprinted over to the Forger. "Turn that alarm off—it's not helping!"

The Forger disabled the alarm by pressing several buttons on his pack. It resembled an ordinary backpack until the protective cloth was pulled away to reveal a golden machine with levers, dials, and buttons marked with strange symbols that Aero didn't understand—but they meant something important to the Forger.

"It's Vinick, isn't it?" Wren said breathlessly when she reached them. "He deployed the probes."

The Forger toggled a lever and looked up grimly. "It's an unmanned probe scanning for life-forms . . . and it bears the markings of the Second Continuum."

"He must have tracked our trajectory," Wren said. She had a pair of ocular scopes slung over her shoulder. She hoisted them up and scanned the sky. "Come on . . . where is it? Damn it . . . where is it?" she thrust them down. "Has it locked onto our location?"

The Forger manipulated more levers. "Not yet . . . it only partially breached our shield on the first pass, but it's doubling back for a closer look. Its sensor arrays must have detected the anomaly."

Aero felt a jolt of adrenaline. That probe would be back any second and it was sure to detect them this time. "Can't you boost the shield's power?"

"Captain, I'm trying," the Forger said as he hit a series of buttons. A force field shot out of his pack and settled over the campsite in the shape of a large, translucent dome. But the shield was weak and flickering with emerald light.

"Damn it, the shield is leaking!" Aero said.

The Forger threw back his hood. "Captain, my pack can't generate enough power. It's maxed out! I'm doing everything I can, but it won't hold off that probe."

"Then we're dead," Wren said. Her fingers twitched at the hilt of her Falchion, but she didn't unsheathe it; she knew it was pointless. "Those probes are weaponized. Once Vinick sees the scans, he'll fire on us remotely and blow us to bits."

Aero looked around, but there was nowhere to hide in the naked desert. Everything was exposed in the morning sunlight. Plus, even if they could hide until the probe passed, it was sure to detect the crash site and the remnants of their escape pod. A biological scan would reveal a billion tiny traces of their DNA littering the landscape. That would prompt Vinick to send down a combat unit to investigate.

"How long until visual contact?" Aero asked.

"Sixty seconds," Wren reported as she peered through the scopes. "Fifty-nine, fifty-eight, fifty-seven, fifty-six . . ." she counted down the probe's approach.

Emotions threatened to overtake Aero and rob him of his capacity for reason, but he fought hard to stay calm. He glanced over at the Forger in his red cloak.

"Brother, there must be something we can do!"

The Forger knitted his brows together. "Maybe . . . but it's a long shot."

"We've got forty-five seconds before that probe nails us," Wren said with the scopes fixed to her eyes. "So whatever the hell it is, you'd better do it fast."

"Captain, give me your wrist," the Forger said.

"My wrist?" Aero said, taken aback. "But . . . why?"

The Forger yanked some wires out of his pack.

"The Beacon is a biological interface, right? We need more power to stabilize the shield, and your life-force has power, more than any battery or reactor. If you can channel it through the Beacon and direct it into the pack, then it might boost the shield."

"Right, how do I do that?" Aero said.

The Forger frowned. "No clue . . . but you've got to try or we're dead."

"Captain, forty seconds," Wren reported.

Aero thrust out his wrist to the Forger. Moving quickly, the Forger attached the wires to the Beacon, but Aero felt . . . nothing. He glanced at his wrist helplessly.

"It's not working," he said. "I can't feel anything."

Wren's eyes flicked to the sky. She had lowered the scopes. The probe was now visible to the naked eye. "Thirty seconds . . ." she reported in a hoarse voice.

The Forger shot her a warning look that said—*you're not helping.*

"Captain, look at me," he said. "You have to calm your mind using the exercises that we've been practicing. When you achieve stillness, you should be able to direct your energy into strengthening the shield."

The Forger continued talking, but Aero was no longer listening. He shut his eyes and tried to calm his mind. He heard the wind gusting across the desert and felt sand pinging his cheeks, but only in a vague and distant way, like it was happening to somebody else. He withdrew deeper into himself—sank into the recesses of his subconscious mind, where his worst fears and memories resided. He fell through them as if down a long, dark well with no bottom.

He saw his mother abandoning him in front of the Agoge . . . Major Vinick stabbing his father in the back while he watched helplessly . . . waking up in the simulation chamber after the duel and seeing the Majors with their Falchions drawn . . . he saw them slaughtering his brave soldiers . . . heaping their lifeless bodies into the incinerator . . .

And still he fell through himself for what felt like an eternity. The well seemed endless and filled to the brim with the polluted runoff of a thousand painful memories—

But then he stopped falling.

He was floating as if he'd suddenly become weightless, like in zero gravity. Light poured in from some unknown source, chasing out the darkness. He saw the outline of a figure haloed by the light—he wore a crisp uniform and had a Falchion belted to his waist. His gray-speckled hair was tightly shorn, and his eyes were steely gray.

"Father . . ." Aero whispered.

More figures fanned out behind his father, standing in tight military formation. It was a whole unit of Supreme Generals. Each one had once been a Carrier. *Supreme General Wright,* his father said. *We serve at your pleasure. What are your orders?*

Aero couldn't believe his ears. *But I am only a captain.*

Now the generals spoke in unison, their voices echoing out. *You are the Carrier of the Beacon and the rightful Supreme General.*

Aero felt their power surging through him. He issued

his orders, and then his eyes snapped open to the brilliant morning sunlight. He was back in the desert again with Wren and the Forger.

"Twenty seconds . . ." she said. "Until contact."

Aero turned his attention back to the shield. He felt as if he were moving in slow motion—he could sense the wind blowing as if it were a visible force and understood its trajectory. The stillness of his mind was absolute. No voices. No chatter. No emotions. He felt the power of the Supreme Generals—united in their purpose—surging through him.

He focused his mind and directed the power through the Beacon and into the Forger's pack. For a terrifying second, nothing happened. But then greenish fire blazed down his arm and into the pack; it spread out and encased their campsite in an impenetrable dome.

"He's actually doing it," the Forger whispered. "It's working."

Wren laid her hand on the dome, causing emerald light to ripple underneath her palm. "It's so much stronger now—like pressing against a solid pane of glass."

Aero opened his eyes. Wren and the Forger both seemed to be holding their breath. The probe passed silently overhead. It looked like nothing more than a black speck gliding through the predawn sky. But Aero could *feel* its sensor arrays probing for them, just like he could *feel* the wind kissing his skin. It swooped closer as the probing turned into prodding, like something physical trying to penetrate his body.

Aero gently pushed back against the sensors.

There's nothing here. Move on. You just see sand and an empty desert. Report that you found no life forms and no sign of the escape pod. Then go away.

The drone passed overhead at the apex of the sky.

And then it flew on.

Wren glanced at Aero and then back at the sky. "Captain, don't stop whatever it is you're doing," she whispered. "We've got to make sure it doesn't come back."

Aero held the shield in place; it took everything in him to

keep it together. After a few more seconds—when the probe didn't double back as was protocol if it had detected anything amiss—he let go of the shield. His legs buckled, but Wren caught him.

Their eyes met. "Starry hell, that was close," she muttered.

"Too close," he agreed. He sat down hard in the sand while the Forger worked to detach the wires from his wrist. Wren hoisted the scopes up and scanned the sky.

"Vinick must be orbiting," she said. "Why didn't he leave on Stern's Quest already? I'll bet he wants revenge for the duel. He hates losing, and he hates you."

Aero thought for a moment.

"Maybe . . . he's probably still furious about the duel. But I can't help thinking that it's more than that. He's too calculating to act on emotional impulse alone."

"He fears you then?" she suggested.

The Forger removed the last of the wires from his wrist. Aero massaged it gingerly. It was sore—in fact, now that he thought about it, his whole body was sore.

"It's possible, but I still think there's more to it."

"Well, what else could he possibly want?" she said, gesturing around. "We've been banished from the only place that we've ever called home. We lost our combat unit, and we're stranded in this godforsaken desert with a broken escape pod and no damned clue how we're going to get to the First Continuum. We've got nothing of value."

"We have one thing," Aero said.

His eyes darted to his wrist.

Wren followed his gaze. "The Beacon? But why would Vinick want it? He can't bond with it—he's too old. Even trying that would kill him. Besides, he wants to destroy it, remember? He thinks Earth is a dead planet. He wants to find a new home."

"That's true," Aero said, letting out a frustrated sigh. "I don't know. Maybe you're right—he wants revenge. He does hold grudges, just ask my father."

"You don't sound convinced," she said with a wry smile.

"Look, does it really matter what Vinick wants? We know he's looking for us, and we know he's dangerous. That probe sensed something. It might come back, and I want to be long gone before that. We've got to fix our ship—and fast."

He struggled to his feet, swaying unsteadily. He was worse off than he thought. He started toward the escape pod. Wren exchanged a worried look with the Forger.

"In your condition? No way. We can pick it up again tomorrow."

"I'm fine," Aero protested. "Just a little tired, that's all."

To prove his point, he limped over to the ship, but each step was agony. Every muscle in his body ached like he'd just fought in a grueling Falchion-to-Falchion drill. Even so, he forced himself to pick up the wrench and get back to work on the engine.

Wren shot him a disapproving glance, but she shrugged in defeat and went back to repairing the rudder while the Forger stayed with his pack. He unfurled a solar panel to capture the burgeoning daylight and recharge it. Midday peaked and the afternoon wore on. Aero tried to focus on the singed circuit board in front of him, but his eyes kept drooping. Eventually, the daylight waned and dusk began to fall, bringing with it a chill that cooled the sweat on their backs and summoned goose bumps to their skin.

At some point, as the sun was dipping below the horizon and transforming the sky into a vivid pink light show, the wrench slid from his hand and landed in the sand with a soft crunch. He didn't reach for it. Instead, he slumped against the side of the ship.

And then he slept deeply.

When Wren found him, she summoned the Forger, and they moved him to his bedroll. He was dead weight in their arms as they dragged him across the campsite. The heels of his boots dug twin rivulets in the sand. He didn't stir. Didn't even crack an eyelid. Didn't mumble in his sleep. He was dead to this world. Because he was already in another one, carried away by the soft but irresistible throbbing of his Beacon.

Chapter 12
BUGGERS

Seeker

The burning orb in the sky dipped at last.

Seeker could come out of her hiding place. She slunk from the cave and watched through her visor as the orb slipped below the horizon and dusk washed over the world. *The nasty Light is leaving,* she thought. She tipped the metal contraption up to her brow. Her muscles ached with a deep weariness. She'd been hunting for many nights.

"Filthy buggers," she muttered under her breath. And then she added for nobody's benefit except her own: "But no meat for Crusher."

Last night, she'd sniffed out a fresh bugger nest hidden deep in a crevice. She knew how to trap the nasty creatures and avoid their prickly pinchers, and how to break through their tough shells with her teeth to get to their juicy guts. Buggers kept the hunger from killing you . . . but they weren't very tasty. And they wouldn't satisfy Crusher.

That thought made her stomach clench. Her fight-or-flight response kicked in with a vengeance. She took off running, driving herself with her arms and legs. She vaulted down the ridge, careful not to slip on the loose rocks. When it bottomed out, she came upon a rushing torrent of water.

Fast water, she thought after she sniffed it. She slurped thirstily from the river and then sprinted away, ascending the next ridge and pausing at the top. She tipped her head back, drawing the air into her nostrils.

Clean and wet . . . not stale and dead.

Suddenly, her ears pricked up. She heard scratching noises. They were faint, only a small disturbance in the still night, but she heard them. She stalked after the noise, and then another scent hit her nostrils. She sniffed the air again and locked onto the position. Her stomach rumbled hungrily. From the scent, she knew that it wasn't another bugger nest—she hoped it was something meatier and tastier.

Something she could track.

Something she could find more of.

Something she could bring back to Crusher.

Chapter 13
THE NEST

Myra Jackson

The creatures swarmed out of their nest toward Myra. She struggled against the webbing, but it was no use. The sticky threads held her in place. Even her mouth was sealed shut, so she couldn't scream. She heard Elianna's voice in her head, but it sounded faint. *The Professor feared this might happen . . . mutated insects . . . carnivorous . . . radiation from the Doom . . . .* Then her voice fell silent, overwhelmed by the panic now seizing hold of Myra's mind.

Scratch! Scratch! Scratch!

Myra twisted harder as the first wave of insects scurried up the web. They were about the size of one of Kaleb's boots and twice as long. One slithered up the leg of her pants. She felt the clawing of its sharp feet and then stabbing pain as its pinchers tore into her flesh. Tears exploded in her eyes from the pain. One bit into her arm, another tore into her stomach. And then a deeper horror dawned on her. They weren't just trying to eat her—they wanted to burrow into her skin and devour her from the inside out.

In seconds, the insects were all over her body and still

coming. With one mighty pull, Myra wrenched her neck hard to the right—and the sticky threads ripped away from her lips. The pain was searing, but she didn't care.

She opened her mouth and screamed:

"Help! Somebody, help me!"

She kept screaming as one of the mutated insects scuttled up her chest and encircled her neck. It went straight for her ear and clamped its pinchers down. She felt a scorching sting when suddenly the creature let out a high-pitched shriek.

A hand ripped it off her neck.

"Myra, don't move!"

Kaleb's voice—it was Kaleb.

He had a flashlight and clutched a knife. "Hold still, I don't want to hurt you!"

He used the knife to knock the creatures from her legs and stomach. Myra glanced over at the slimy, pulsating nest—more and more were still swarming out of it.

"Kaleb, hurry!" she cried. Her heart thudded so hard that it almost choked off her voice. "More are coming—"

"I'm trying!" he said, as he started sawing at the web to cut her free—first one arm, then the next, then her right leg, then her left leg. Finally, he cut her loose.

"Run!" she yelled, and they took off down the tunnel.

The scratching noises followed them.

A few seconds later, they burst into the cave. Myra grabbed Tinker and wrenched him from his bedroll. She hustled him into his boots and dragged him over to the rope, which still dangled into the sinkhole. She hoisted him up as high as she could.

"Climb, Tink! We've got to get out of here!"

The sleepy confusion in his eyes was replaced by horror when he saw the mutated insects stream into the cavern. They gushed out of the tunnel in one pulsating, slimy mass of writhing pinchers and wriggling legs and roving eyes. Tinker didn't say a word; he just started climbing as fast as his little arms would carry him.

Kaleb jerked Paige from her bedroll and hurried her

over to the rope. He was carrying two packs slung over his shoulder. Paige turned white when she saw the creatures.

"What in the Holy Sea are . . . those?"

"No idea," Kaleb said. "But they want to eat us."

Paige didn't need to be told twice. She started scrambling up the rope, and then Kaleb followed with the two packs. Myra looked back. The insects swarmed over their campsite, tearing through their bedrolls and shredding the tough fabric with their pinchers like it was flimsy paper. *That would have been us if we were still asleep*, she thought.

"Myra, come on!" Kaleb called down. "What're you waiting for?"

She hesitated. "Our other packs and the heater, we need them—"

"Are you crazy? Just leave them! It's too late."

She wanted to salvage more of their stuff, but one glance at their campsite told her that Kaleb was right—it was too late. Everything was already destroyed.

"Myra, climb the rope now!"

That snapped her out of it. She started climbing the rope, right as the insects swarmed under her feet. She felt something clawing up her leg. She kicked violently to dislodge it, but it held on tight. She bashed her leg against the side of the hole, and finally, the creature shrieked and plummeted down, landing with a loud crunch. She scrambled the rest of the way up. Kaleb grabbed her wrists and lifted her out of the sinkhole. She flipped onto her back, panting hard. Kaleb retracted the rope, reeling it in one arm length at a time. His face twisted when he saw the end.

The tip had been . . . eaten.

Myra felt a wave of revulsion roil up in her.

"I think I'm going to be sick—"

She doubled over and retched, then sat down hard and wiped the sides of her mouth with her sleeve. Rain still poured down, and the wind was even stronger now. Lightning pulsed in the middle distance, chased by a deep rumble of thunder.

Myra checked the two packs. They had their clothes and

boots thankfully, but they'd left behind their bedrolls, the heater, and two of their packs—including hers.

"By the Oracle . . ." she cursed as tears welled in her eyes.

"Myra, it's going to be alright," Kaleb said and squeezed her shoulder. "They can't get us up here. I pulled up the rope, and I don't think they can climb out of the sinkhole." He slipped his arms around her shoulders, but she shrugged him off.

"No, it's not!" she cried. "We left my pack behind."

Paige flinched and looked over. "Your pack . . . with all the food."

"Exactly," Myra said, her voice thick with tears. "I never should have gone down that tunnel. I heard some noises . . . and I thought maybe it was the other survivors."

"Oh, they're survivors alright," Kaleb said, holding up the chewed-up rope. "Just not the kind you were expecting. Actually, it's lucky you went down there when you did. I'll bet they would have found us anyway—most likely while we were sleeping."

Myra shook her head as the tears kept falling, mixing with the cold rain that was quickly soaking her, too. "But don't you see? It doesn't matter! Without my pack, we're as good as dead anyway."

Even Kaleb didn't have a positive retort to that. And he kept his distance; he didn't try to comfort her again. Tinker came up beside her. His eyes were clear. He laid his hand on the Beacon.

"We can't give up now," he rasped. "Not after we've come this far. You have to believe. There's still a chance. We can find the signal from the mountains."

Myra looked at him through her tear-blurred vision. His glasses rested askew on the bridge of his nose, but he hadn't lost them in the escape. And behind the thick glass and wire rims held together with screws and tape, he had a determined look in his eyes. Suddenly, she felt ashamed for giving up when her brother refused to do the same.

She wiped her tears away and swept him up in her arms. "Tinker's right. Let's find somewhere to spend the rest of the night. Then we'll keep going in the morning."

"Fine, but no more caves," Paige muttered. "Out in the open this time."

Despite their circumstances, Myra choked out a laugh—a snotty, sickly kind of laugh. But it felt good to know that at least she still had a sense of humor.

"Agreed, no caves," she managed between fits of laughter.

o   o   o

With a few hours of night remaining, they settled under a narrow ledge that kept out some of the wind and rain, but not all of it. Without their heater or their bedrolls, the cold seeped into their wet clothes. They huddled together against the cliff-side and shivered. Beyond their flimsy haven, the sky rumbled and flashed, providing brief glimpses of the bleak, rain-soaked landscape that stretched out seemingly into infinity.

Myra pulled Tinker closer, trying to warm him up, and stroked his hair, feeling the fine strands sliding between her fingertips. In the middle of the night, a cascade of hail rattled down into their shelter accompanied by lightning and thunder. The chunks of ice—some as large as clenched fists—blanketed the ground and turned it eerily white.

Despite the raging of the storm, Myra was so exhausted that she finally fell into a deep slumber. Not even the clattering of hail could rouse her. The pulsing of her Beacon slowed in rhythm to her breathing. And then, suddenly—

She was somewhere else altogether.

Chapter 14
THE EYE OF THE STORM

The Dark Thing

The Dark Thing saw the girl materialize into the dreamscape. Every night he lay in wait for her to appear.

Her form flickered once, twice, and then stabilized. He flowed out of the shadows, unfurling his black tendrils toward her frail body. He was about to drive them into her like knives when suddenly another figure materialized into the dreamscape.

It was the boy.

Demon, be gone! he shouted as his weapon cut through the air, spitting and hissing out a rain of golden sparks. *Leave her alone!*

The Dark Thing fled from the girl, seeping back into the shadows. *Patience,* he told himself as he blended into the places where the light from their Beacons could not penetrate. He could cloak his form, making it invisible. Instead, he waited and watched them. The boy felt the threat had passed, so he sheathed his weapon and went to the girl. She was shivering and depleted. The sky above stirred with a rising storm. The clouds swirled darkly, unleashing a blast of lightning and a crackle of thunder.

There's a thunderstorm, the boy thought as he cradled her head in his arms. His Beacon flared, and it strengthened the girl. Her Beacon blazed back in response.

Not here, the girl thought. *It's dry as a bone.*

She cupped her hand to her brow. A million tiny stars glittered overhead. No clouds obscured the sky. No lightning pulsed in the distance. A dry wind stirred; it swept down from a wide plateau, carrying sand and grit and a velvety warmth.

You must be seeing the desert where we crashed down, the boy thought. *We've been stranded out here for weeks, trying to repair our damaged escape pod.*

Her heart sank with this knowledge. *Then it's not you.*

Sadness cloaked her voice. The boy frowned.

What do you mean?

We've been following a signal from the mountains. My Beacon picked it up. I hoped it was coming from you. But you're still too far away.

I'm sorry—you're right, it's not us.

She kicked the sand in frustration. *Then I've failed. I lost all our provisions. We have no food left, and we're growing weaker by the day. My brother won't last much longer, not without proper nourishment.*

You're not the only one who failed, the boy thought, toying with the hilt of his weapon. *I've been trying to fix our ship, but I'm not up to the task. I'm trained to fight, that's it. I know some basic mechanical stuff, but nothing like what this requires.*

This caught her attention. Her eyes snapped to the escape pod resting in the sand a few feet away. She took his hand, cupped it to her chest, and led him over to it. She inspected the engine, running her palms over the parts, and then smiled.

I wish I were actually here, she thought. *I could fix your ship. Back in my world, I was an Engineer. I've always liked fixing things.*

He laid his hand on her cheek, and their Beacons caught fire with emerald light. She wanted to ask him a million questions. She wanted to find out why he'd been absent from her dreams. But she didn't have to ask, not once they bonded. She just knew. She saw him working at night out of the desert's heat, away from the Second Continuum's probes. She saw Wren and the one they called the Forger helping him. She felt his frustration each time the ship failed to start, and then once it started, each time it failed to fly.

And he felt her fear and worry as she and her companions turned inland toward the mountains, driven off course by their dwindling supplies. As their food diminished each day, along with their morale and strength. As they sought shelter from the tempest in the cave. As the mutant insects tried to burrow into her skin and devour her—

Kaleb, he saved you, he thought as he absorbed the memory.

He's brave, she agreed. *Braver than I realized.*

He watched the memory play out. *We have a saying at the Agoge. "A soldier reveals his truest self when he's facing death." This must be true of your Kaleb.*

The girl shook her head. *He's no soldier.*

We're all soldiers now, the boy answered.

The girl stayed in his arms for as long as she could, and then as day was threatening to break, she led him back to the wrecked ship. Their bodies shone pale in the starlight. Her bare feet sank into the sand. Below the surface, it was still warm from the day's punishing heat. She traced the smooth line of the hull, placed her hands on the parts, felt where the circuits had been singed and severed, and explained how to fix the connections, where to solder the ends back together, her fingers finding the way.

But I can't, the boy thought. *This is beyond me. I'm only a soldier.*

She shook her head. *Now you're an engineer.*

She rifled through the toolbox and selected a large wrench. She handed it to him. *One step at a time like my father taught me. Use this to write the steps in the sand and then you'll remember.* She talked him through the instructions one more time, explaining everything slowly as if she were the Head Engineer and he was a first-year pledge.

When she reached the last step, something strange started to happen. First the air started to smell different—colder, wetter, electrically charged. And it felt different like the pressure had dropped suddenly. The girl snapped her head to the sky.

What's happening?

The boy's face darkened. He dropped the wrench and unsheathed his weapon. *The storm . . . it's growing stronger. I think it's seeping into your dream somehow.*

The girl saw the black clouds amassing overhead. They were bleeding into the dreamscape. Without warning, a dazzling flash of light ripped through the air, followed by an earsplitting rumble. Hailstones volleyed down, even in the desert landscape.

The storm! the girl thought. *It's here—*

Suddenly, a blaze of light lashed down from the sky and struck her full force. The boy was blown back several feet by the force of it. His Beacon exploded with green sparks and then fell dark. The Dark Thing howled in pain, as he felt the lightning ripple through him, too. The fierce blow of thunder that followed shattered the dreamscape, making it splinter like a mirror cracking into a million little pieces.

The world around them began to collapse, folding in on itself. The sky, the ground, the rocks, the sand—

Noooooo! the boy screamed and scrambled to his feet.

The Beacon on his wrist was smoking. He lunged for the girl, but his hands passed through her body as if she were made of smoke. She flickered once. Twice.

And then she vanished from the dreamscape.

Chapter 15
THE SKY LIT UP

Aero Wright

Aero woke soaked in sweat.

"Nooooooo!" he screamed. "Myra, watch out!"

The Beacon on his wrist was pulsing erratically and felt burning hot to the touch. He glanced around feverishly, feeling completely disoriented. Wren heard his anguished cries and sprinted over, followed by the Forger. But Aero shoved them both back and unsheathed his Falchion. He whirled around wildly.

"Hurry up!" he yelled. "We have to help Myra! She's hurt!"

"Myra?" Wren said, agilely dodging his Falchion. "What're you talking about? Starry hell, get a grip! And put your sword away before you hurt someone!"

Aero felt dizzy. The disorientation was overwhelming, making him sway on his feet. He searched his memory. "There was a thunderstorm and hail . . ." he managed with some difficulty. "I think Myra got struck by lightning . . . and then she vanished . . ."

"Thunderstorm? Hail? Lightning?" Wren repeated and exchanged a worried look with the Forger. "Captain, it was only a bad dream." She gestured up to the sky. "Look around for yourself—there's no storm here. The skies are clear as crystal."

Aero looked up at the sky and blinked a few times in the dawn light. There wasn't a cloud in sight, to say nothing of thunder, hail, and lightning. The sky was clear—as crystal. Wren was right. Myra and the storm had all been a dream. Even so, a terrible sense of loss flooded through him. *Maybe it was only a dream*, he thought. *But that lightning was real.* He knew that something terrible had happened to her.

Suddenly, burning pain shot up his arm.

He glanced down—his Beacon was scorched black and smoking. He dropped his Falchion and crumpled to his knees, letting out a howl of pain. The Forger saw the smoke. He rushed over to Aero's side to examine the Beacon. When he touched the golden metal, he jerked his hand back.

"Damn it, what's wrong?" Wren asked, her face etched with worry.

"The Beacon . . . it's burning hot to the touch. I've never seen anything like it." The Forger laid his hand on Aero's forehead. "Lieutenant, help me! He's burning up with fever—"

That was the last thing Aero heard before he passed out.

o   o   o

Aero slept, and the fever dreams became his reality.

Over and over again, he saw the lightning strike Myra and then watched in horror as she vanished from the dreamscape. She'd always faded away in the past—never flickered out altogether. The memories gave way to fearful imaginings. He saw her splayed out in the mud while her brave companions wept by her side. Her lips were blue, her skin charred. Her eyes gaped wide open—but she wasn't breathing.

Still the fever kept its hold on him and refused to relent. He sweated and hallucinated and cried out. Sometimes, distant voices reached him in his fugue state:

High fever . . . chills . . . why is he so sick? It was just a dream!

The Forger's voice: *Dreams aren't always just dreams—they can be conduits. You saw the writing in the sand, didn't you? How else do you explain that? Something damaged the Beacon, and now it's trying to repair itself. Just pray he's strong enough.*

Wren's voice: *And what if he isn't?*

Silence and then the Forger's voice again: *We're doing all we can. The rest is up to him.*

o o o

Many days passed before Aero woke up, and even then he still burned with fever.

Wren tended to him and made him drink water, cleaned up when he retched, and took him to relieve himself. It wasn't until the seventh day that the fever finally broke, and the Beacon cooled down and its pulsing became less erratic. The Supreme Generals returned with their incessant chatter like somebody slowly turning up the volume.

But Aero couldn't sense Myra at all.

She's really and truly gone, he thought and his heart sank.

Some time later, though he wasn't sure exactly how long, Wren roused him from his bedroll to take him to relieve himself. "Come on, you must be bursting," she prodded when he tried to shrug her off and sleep more. "It's been hours."

"It's fine, I can go on my own! You don't have to baby me."

He was well enough now to feel ashamed at his helplessness. He staggered up and tried to take a step, but he stumbled and would have fallen if she didn't catch him.

"Please, I don't think this counts as babying." Worry lit up her eyes, making her look older than her sixteen years. "Captain, whatever happened in that dream . . . you almost died. Besides, I saw much worse during my rotation in the Medical Clinic."

He didn't have it in him to protest further. He gave in, and she escorted him away from the campsite. She only had a slight hitch in her gait as she helped him limp along. Her ankle was healing well then. *At least one of us is mobile now*, he thought.

He took another halting step. "So, I've been out of commission for eight days?"

"Affirmative, Captain," she replied. "Eight long days."

"Starry hell," he cursed. He hated feeling . . . well . . . helpless.

"Got you out of working on the escape pod, didn't it?"

That teasing lilt was back in her voice, but he could tell that she was still really worried about him. They made it a few more halting steps. He had to pause frequently to catch his breath. Since when did walking a few meters make him this tired?

"Well, go ahead," Aero said. "I'm sure you're dying to ask about her."

"Her . . . sir?" Wren said, keeping her face composed.

His cheeks started to feel hot again, and it wasn't from the fever or the blazing sunlight. "Come on, you know—that girl I was ranting about before I passed out."

Now it was her turn to look embarrassed. "Uh, right, you can spare me the gory details. I'm pretty sure I get the gist of it. The Forger thinks that she's a Carrier from one of the other colonies. Apparently back in the day, the space colonies could communicate with each other through their Carriers. The Beacons connected them together."

"Yeah, that's what the old Forger told me before the duel with Major Vinick. But that hasn't happened in a long time, not since the Mars colony sprung an air leak, and the Fourth Continuum vanished on the dark side of Uranus—"

Wren threw her hands up. "You don't have to tell me again! I suffered through The History of the Continuums at the Agoge, too. Let me summarize it—they all died and we've been alone for the last seven hundred years."

"Until Myra."

"Exactly, until your *secret dream lover* showed up—"

He elbowed her, but he was still weak so it wasn't very hard.

"Hey, watch it," she yelped in a complete overreaction. Her hand darted to her weapon. "I could best you in Falchion-to-Falchion combat now."

"Only because I'm sick."

"Winning is winning," she replied with a smirk. "You said so yourself."

Then they both laughed.

After Aero did his business and Wren helped him limp back to the camp, he made her show him the writing in the sand. He'd heard the Forger talking about it. She helped him over to the far side of the escape pod. A large area on the ground was covered with plastic sheeting, weighted down with tools. Carefully, he peeled it back, revealing complex instructions and strange words that he could never have written by himself. He ran his finger over them, deepening the rivulets in the sand. He glanced up at Wren.

"Still think it was only a dream?" he asked.

"You've got me there, Captain," she replied as she gazed down at the strange writing. Her forehead scrunched up. "Though it all looks like gibberish to me."

"This gibberish is how we repair the escape pod. Myra showed me how to fix it. Back in her world, she was an engineer. A really good one. Her father, too."

He scanned the steps and miraculously remembered everything that Myra had shown him. But then he got to the last step and frowned. "She didn't finish telling me how to fix it . . . before the lightning struck her." He pointed to the empty space in the sand and felt a stab of sadness. The grisly scene replayed in his head again like clockwork.

"The last step is missing?" Wren said, kneeling down next to him and inspecting the writing. "Can't you try to contact her with the Beacon? Ask her what to do?"

He glanced at the golden armlet affixed to his wrist. It throbbed weakly with greenish light; it was still healing. Whatever happened in that dream damaged it badly and almost killed him—and he hadn't suffered a direct hit.

"I can't . . ." he said. "The connection is broken." He

coughed to disguise the emotion choking his voice, but Wren picked up on it anyway.

"You think she's dead, don't you?" she said in that direct way of hers.

He closed his eyes and searched inside himself. He probed at the Beacon—gingerly and gently, so as not to damage it further—and felt pain cascading up his arm, and worse, a deep sense of nothingness. He felt completely alone in the universe now.

Am I the only Carrier left?

He opened his eyes and met Wren's steady gaze.

"I hope not," he said. "But I fear it is so."

o   o   o

When he was strong enough, Aero worked day and night to repair the escape pod. He didn't care about waiting for darkness to fall, or if that probe came back. Fixing the ship was the one thing that he could do, even if at the end of his next journey, he found only Myra's grave. He'd sworn an oath to find her—and he wasn't about to break it now.

A few sleepless days later, he reached the final step, but the escape pod still would not fly, no matter what he tried. Despite Wren's and the Forger's protests, Aero kept working on the ship and kept not sleeping. Eventually, delirious with exhaustion and overcome by frustration and a crushing sense of defeat, he threw down his tools and kicked the sand, sending up a spray of grit that erased half the steps.

He stared at the empty space in the sand, and then he closed his eyes and probed with the Beacon, projecting his consciousness out through space and time.

Myra, he thought, *please come back. I need you.*

His Beacon flared and seemed to have healed, but he still couldn't sense her at all. Even his father remained silent on what to do now. Like Aero, he was a trained fighter, not an engineer. He couldn't help him fix his ship.

Aero was on his own now.

And that was when, in the middle of the day, he slumped

down in the shadow of the escape pod and didn't get up. He watched the sun arc across the sky and sink below the horizon, bathing the world in purplish light, but still he didn't move. He barely even blinked, though his eyes and lips were dry and he felt terribly thirsty. Wren came over and tried to make him drink more water, but he waved her away weakly.

He'd experienced moments of intense hopelessness before, first when his mother abandoned him on the steps of the Agoge, and then when Vinick killed his father and later banished him from the only place he'd ever called home. But he had never experienced true depression before. It pressed down on his chest like a crushing weight. Each breath was a struggle against the heaviness. He felt the most exhausted that he ever had in his entire life put together, and it wasn't from sickness or lack of sleep either.

Myra . . . she's gone.

That night, Aero slept restlessly and didn't want to wake up the next day, not even as the sun rose. He pulled the bedroll over his head and sank down into it despite the suffocating heat. But consciousness eventually found him, as it always did, no matter how much he loathed it. It yanked at his eyelids, tugged them open, wrenched him from sleep. He cracked his eyes open to a world stained by Myra's absence and his failure to fix the escape pod, and he only wished to shut them again.

He would have slept much longer, maybe even for the whole day, had Wren not shaken him awake and demanded that he drink and eat something. "Captain, with all due respect, I'm not letting you die on my watch. Now get up, damn it, and drink this."

He obeyed reluctantly and gulped the lukewarm water and choked down his rations, but they sat like a rock in his gut. His stomach gurgled and sloshed. He didn't care what Wren thought; he crawled back into his bedroll and pulled it over his head. The sun seemed too bright as it beat down on their campsite. The darkness was a welcome respite. He lay there for hours and tried not to think—not to feel.

It didn't work. It never worked.

Not really.

More days passed, and Aero did little except eat and drink whenever Wren demanded it. She and the Forger exchanged worried looks when they saw him moping about the campsite, or sleeping far more than was normal, but they didn't talk to him about it directly. He even neglected his Falchion. It needed a fresh charge, but he didn't hand it over to the Forger. He'd never mistreated his weapon before. He swore an oath at the Agoge to take care of it at all times. But he found that he just didn't care anymore.

Not about his Falchion. Not about fixing the escape pod. Not about reaching the First Continuum. And certainly not about himself. Nothing mattered anymore.

Not without Myra.

Chapter 16
SCENTS IN THE NIGHT

Seeker

Seeker was moving toward the sunrise.

And she was moving fast.

The world of the Brightside was changing; something was happening to the air and the burning orb in the sky. She didn't understand it, and that alarmed her. She'd first noticed the shift yesterday when the orb was dipping below the horizon and she was emerging from her hiding spot to hunt. The change was trivial—maybe she wouldn't have even noticed it at all—except for her sharp sense of smell and sensitive ears.

The air smelled wet.

Her ears ached from the change in pressure.

She shrugged it off and tried to focus on hunting ratters, but then the next morning, the shift intensified. Dark clouds rushed from behind the mountains and blocked out the burning orb in the sky, casting the landscape into shadow. Despite the breaking of dawn, she didn't need her visor to protect her eyes. The light was pale and dreary. As the day advanced, it only got darker. Her claws tore into the earth, churning the rocks and pushing her up to the highest ridge. She paused at the top to scent the air.

The valley splayed out below her. She felt something cold and moist on her skin. Droplets of water started falling from the sky, making her shirk back in fear. Burning light pulsed in the lead sky, and then a deep rumble tore through the air and rattled the ground. This light was different from the burning orb in the sky.

It felt more menacing.

Seeker muttered to herself. "Nasty light and nasty rumbling—"

Another rumbling wave stole her voice.

She leapt back in fear. Slowly and cautiously, she backed into a crevice carved into the cliff to wait out the disturbance. This cave felt safe and familiar. It reminded her of home, where no light or rumbling or water pierced the skies, for there were no skies, only rock ceilings. She missed the Darkness of the Below like a claw to the throat.

More light and rumbling tore through the Brightside. Warily, she peered out from the cave into the heart of the storm. The skies swirled thick and gray with clouds. Water poured down even harder, rushing down the ridges and growing into frothy black waterfalls. A vile wind whipped down the mountain passes and tore at her lair.

The light in the sky and the rumbling are moving away, she decided after watching the storm for a long spell. And so, she slunk out of the cave and continued moving toward the sunrise, skirting up the slippery paths, pausing at the top to scent the air. She'd been hunting for many weeks now and still hadn't picked up anything worth pursuing, except for the rotten odor of buggers and ratters seeping out of the ground. And this water was only making it harder to smell; it was washing away any traces.

By nightfall, the storm grew stronger again, forcing Seeker to find shelter in another cave. Her prize was a bugger nest. She spent the night feasting in the Darkness, and she almost felt like she was back home. Once her belly was stuffed, she crouched down and settled in for the night. Her coarse hair dried quickly and kept her warm. Usually she traveled at night, but this night was too dangerous. The water pouring from the sky was one thing, but the flashes of light and the rumbling were another.

They made her feel afraid.

It was safer in the Darkness of the Below.

The next day broke bright and clear. Seeker waited for the sun to arc across the sky and dip again, napping and hunting away the day, and then emerged from her lair as dusk was falling. She scaled the highest ridge and tipped her head toward the sky. Her nostrils flared as they pulled in air . . . it smelled wet and muddy . . .

But was there something else on the edge of the breeze?

She inhaled again and waited for her brain to register the scent. *Yes . . . something else . . . not a bugger or a ratter . . . something bigger and juicier . . .*

A thrill shot through her body.

She took one last sniff, surveyed the valley below with her sharp eyes, and then bolted away on all fours, careening down the cliffside at breakneck speed. She stopped only to slurp water from the rivulets that trickled down the rocks. The water tasted cold and clean. She drank thirstily. Every few minutes, she slowed her pace and sniffed at the air, and then adjusted her trajectory. The scent was growing purer and stronger. She was getting closer.

At long last, she had found something worth hunting.

Chapter 17
DISCONNECTED

Myra Jackson

Lightning erupted in the sky, and a loud crackle shook the earth.

"Myra!" Tinker shrieked. "Help, she's hurt!"

Kaleb burst awake and rocketed to his feet. Shards of rock whizzed past his head. One sliced his cheek. His ears rang, and he was blinded. Hail and rain pelted him. The wind lashed around the bluff sheltering them and ripped at their flimsy campsite. Paige appeared at his elbow, equally blinded and disoriented.

"What happened—" she started.

But then another bolt of lightning exploded in the sky, chased by earsplitting thunder. A fresh wave of hail clattered down. Kaleb spotted Tinker a few feet away. He stumbled over and found Myra lying facedown in the mud.

"Myra!" he yelled, but his voice came out sounding far away. His ears were still ringing. He knelt down and flipped her over. Her eyes were shut tight against the world. He cradled her limp body in his arms and shouted her name again, but she didn't stir.

Paige came up behind them with a flashlight. The bluish beam swept across their campsite—it wasn't more than a shallow scoop in the cliffside. The ground was peppered with lumpy balls of ice. For a split second, as the flashlight grazed over it, Kaleb saw where the lightning had blasted a chunk out of the cliff. The sunken area was scorched and still smoking.

Paige aimed the flashlight at Myra and inspected her closer. The sleeve of her jacket had been blown to bits, and a spider web of fresh burn marks snaked up her arm. Her Beacon was singed black. It didn't pulse with light, not even faintly.

Paige reached out to touch it but jerked back. "It's burning hot," she yelped.

"What . . . what happened to her?" Kaleb asked, still cradling her in his arms.

"I think she got hit by lightning," Tinker rasped, his voice quivering with fear. "I was sleeping next to her . . . and the explosion knocked me back."

"You can actually get hit?" Paige said, flinching back from the sky.

Tinker nodded. "Elianna told my sister about it. Lightning is made out of electricity. I think it's kind of like getting electrocuted, only worse."

Paige looked shocked, but then something inside her clicked. "Right, electrocution. I've seen that before in the Infirmary. Kaleb, fetch the packs!"

He ran to retrieve the two remaining backpacks, shaking off the crust of ice that had formed on top of them during the night, while Paige snapped into triage mode. She worked to stabilize Myra's neck and checked for spinal cord injuries. She talked as she worked, partially out of habit and partially to calm Tinker.

"No broken bones or neck injuries . . . she's breathing . . . that's a really good sign . . . her lungs sound clear."

When Kaleb returned with the packs, Paige rummaged through them and extracted a first aid kit. She yanked it open and pulled out a stethoscope. In a practiced motion, she bent over and listened to Myra's heart, moving the stethoscope around.

"Her pulse is strong. I don't detect a heart arrhythmia—"

"What's that?" Kaleb said. "It sounds bad."

"Irregular heartbeat. And it is bad. Electrocution can cause heart damage, even cardiac arrest in some cases. But everything sounds normal, thank the Oracle."

"Then why isn't she moving?" Tinker asked.

Paige hooked the stethoscope around her neck and reached for a pair of scissors and some ointment. "Well, electrocution can also cause keraunoparalysis."

"No idea what that is either," Kaleb said. "But again, it sounds bad."

Paige cut away what was left of Myra's shirt and started swabbing the stinky ointment onto her burns. "It means temporary paralysis. She should wake up soon. She's got a nasty burn on her arm, but the rest of her body looks unharmed. No burns . . . no bruising . . . not even any signs of trauma . . . at least that I can detect."

Paige stopped what she was doing and turned her puzzled gaze on Kaleb. "It's crazy, really. Based on the severity of these burns, she should be more injured. I can't explain it . . . it's almost like the Beacon absorbed the worst of the damage."

"The Beacon?" Kaleb said, jerking his gaze to the device fastened to her wrist. Its golden surface was now scorched black. Tinker inspected it, careful not to touch it.

"I think Paige is right," he said softly. "When the lightning hit her, it was almost like it got sucked in by the Beacon. I'll bet it did protect her. Otherwise, she'd be dead. Actually . . . we might both be dead."

Kaleb laid his hand on her forehead. It felt sweaty and hot to the touch. "Myra, please wake up," he whispered. "Come back to us . . . please come back."

But she didn't—she remained unconscious.

Paige worked to treat her injuries, but they were minor and not the cause of her unconsciousness. They waited by her body for two hours, hoping and praying, until despair started to set in. Kaleb stroked her forehead and wiped the sweat away, smoothing back her hair while Paige listened to her heart again. She straightened up and shook her head. "I don't understand it . . . she should have woken up by now."

None of them did.

Least of all Kaleb.

o   o   o

The storm finally relented as the sun rose and bathed the world in brilliant light.

Under assault from the sun, the hail strewn across the ground began to melt, dissolving into the sodden earth. The clouds dissipated and blew out toward the sea, erasing all traces of the storm. But still Myra remained unresponsive. Kaleb laid out a tarp and carried her limp body onto it. They gathered around her, stripping off their damp coats and laying them in the sun to dry.

"No point in being wet and hungry," Paige said.

"Just hungry, right?" Kaleb said, as his stomach grumbled. Despite their worries, overcome by exhaustion and hunger, they soon found themselves dozing in the warmth of the sun. At some point, a few hours later, Kaleb woke to Myra mumbling in her sleep.

"Desert . . . broken ship . . . the Dark Thing . . ."

She cracked her eyes open, then quickly shut them again and whipped her head from side to side. Kaleb bolted to her side and shook the others from sleep.

"Paige . . . Tinker . . . she's waking up!"

Paige tended to Myra, but she still wasn't coming around fully. She tossed and turned in a feverish sleep, her forehead burning hot to the touch. She kept having violent nightmares and mumbling nonsensical things in her hallucinatory state. She'd bolt upright for a second—her arms flailing around, her eyes unseeing—and then pass out.

Paige slung off her stethoscope and let out a frustrated sigh. "I need to monitor her heart for a few more days as a precaution, but her pulse is strong. She's breathing on her

own. I don't understand it! Her wounds are superficial, and
I've disinfected them. Why is she burning up like she has an
infection? It doesn't make any sense."

Myra thrashed around and moaned agitatedly. "Can't
feel him . . . can't feel her . . . can't feel anyone . . . even the
Dark Thing . . . they're all gone . . ."

"Hurry!" Paige yelled. "Help me stabilize her before she
hurts herself!"

Kaleb held her arms, while Paige cradled her neck. "Myra,
nobody's *gone*," Paige said. "We're all right here. Just open
your eyes and you'll see."

Myra writhed and mumbled. "No . . . gone . . . gone . . .
gone . . ."

Kaleb leaned over and whispered in her ear. "Myra, it's
Kaleb. Can you hear me? I'm holding your hand. You're not
alone. Nobody's going anywhere."

Myra wrenched her head back and forth.

"No . . . Aero . . . Elianna . . . gone!"

Then she lapsed back into unconsciousness, and the
fit subsided. Kaleb released her arms, but he was sweating
from the effort of holding her still. He ran one hand through
his hair. Without a trim, it had grown out into wavy, black
tendrils that dipped over his forehead and got into his eyes.

"By the Oracle, what's wrong with her?"

Tinker had a curious expression on his face, the kind
that he got when he was putting an especially difficult puzzle
together. "It's the Beacon," he said at last.

"Tink, what do you mean?" Paige said, looking up sharply.

He pointed to the device.

"See this charring on the exterior? And did you notice
how it's not flashing with light anymore? I think it got
damaged by the lightning, and it's making her sick. She can't
feel Aero or Elianna because the Beacon isn't connecting
them anymore."

Paige frowned. "But how can it make her sick?"

"Right, it's some kind of biological interface," Tinker
replied. "Really advanced technology. It's bonded to her body

and her mind. If we tried to remove it, that would kill her, right? And if it's badly damaged, I'm guessing that could have the same effect."

"Wait . . . you mean she could die from this?" Kaleb said.

"Only if the Beacon stops working," Tinker said quickly. He bent over and studied the device closer. Gently, he wiped away some of the black residue, revealing a shimmer of gold. Abruptly, it emitted a weak flash of greenish light.

Myra groaned and tried to wrench her arm away as if it was hurting her. But then the Beacon fell dark again.

"Look, it feels hot to the touch, almost like it has a fever," Tinker said. He sat back and thought for a minute. "I'm guessing it's trying to repair itself somehow."

"You mean . . . like it's alive?" Kaleb said.

Tinker nodded. "Exactly, it's part machine, part biological entity. It's probably working hard to regenerate itself, like how your skin heals after it gets hurt."

Paige absorbed that and felt Myra's forehead again.

"Well, how long will that take? Her fever is still really high. I gave her some medicine to bring it down, but if it doesn't drop soon, she could be in trouble."

"I don't know," Tinker said. His eyes were still glued to the Beacon. "It could take weeks, maybe even months. But that's only a guess. It was badly damaged . . . and that's if it can be healed at all."

A dark look passed over Paige's face. "But we don't have weeks or months."

"Days at the most," Kaleb agreed. "We finished the last kelp bars this morning, and without the Beacon to guide us, we're completely lost. Not to mention the weather. It's getting colder, and clouds are starting to build over the mountains again—"

"Storm . . . lightning . . . Aero . . ." Myra moaned and writhed, but she didn't open her eyes. She flailed around violently and then lapsed back into a fitful sleep.

Kaleb and Paige exchanged a worried look, while Tinker crawled over to his sister and laid his head on her heaving chest. His glasses were crooked, and his tiny face was crumpled with worry. "Her life is tied to the Beacon now," he said.

As if in response, the armlet flickered weakly. Was it trying to heal itself, or were those merely its dying gasps?

Chapter 18
SALVATION

Jonah Jackson

The automatic lights blazed on in the Pen.

"Myra!" Jonah screamed and burst awake. He was coated in sweat and panting. He tried to wipe his brow, but his arm only rose halfway before the chains snapped it down. He'd been having another nightmare, hadn't he? He tried to dredge up the details, but they were fading fast. Only a vague residue of dread remained in their place.

He blinked at the stark light that had shattered his dream. The automatic lights had turned on in the Pen. They burned with the fierceness of little-used filaments. The other prisoners—a mixture of Factum and Hockers, known as the Disappeared—shuffled around in their cells and stared up at the blazing lights with a mixture of wonder and confusion. Some swirled their hands over their chest in a superstitious gesture.

A few brave souls whispered among themselves. "Holy Sea, what does this mean? The lights never come on. The Pen's been dark for hundreds of years."

"Bet it's some new torture cooked up by the 'Trollers."

"And the Red Cloaks and their bloody Oracle."

Jonah had a similar cascade of questions tumbling through his mind and felt the same burst of confusion. The Pen was always dark, except when the Patrollers came through with their flashlights to deliver watery gruel or dispense beatings . . . or both.

But suddenly—

Beep!

The sector door dilated, and a group of rebels stormed through it.

Surfacers, Jonah thought. That's what Padre Teronius called them. He counted about twenty in all. Burlap masks shrouded their heads, obscuring their faces, and they wore navy coveralls with a golden symbol stitched onto the shoulder—a fist with the index finger extended up. They carried tools as weapons that he recognized from the Engineering Room—wrenches, hammers, crowbars, screwdrivers, blowtorches.

He strained against his chains to see what was happening through the bars of his cell. One of the rebels—most likely the leader—had a thick key ring. He started working his way down the cells, unlocking them as he went and releasing the prisoners. In the depth of his confusion, Jonah felt something click. He remembered Maude's message:

When the lights come on . . .

It was happening—and it was happening now.

"Drown the Synod and the Red Cloaks!" one prisoner howled as he burst from his cell. "The Oracle be damned!" He looked demented and half-starved with wild eyes and a scraggly beard that extended almost to his knees, but when one of the Surfacers handed him a hammer, he wielded it with a strength that defied his physical condition. The rebels started dispensing tools to the able-bodied prisoners so that they could join the fight.

"Put Padre Flavius out to sea!" called another prisoner. He looked terribly young, barely older than Tinker. The boy wanted to join up and fight. He reached for a wrench almost as big as his arm, but the rebel leader waved him off.

"Young brother, you can fight when you're older," he said

with a kindly lilt to his voice. "Hurry, make haste to Sector 4 where you'll be safe. The Engineering Room is stocked with Victus, medicine, and blankets."

The boy didn't need to be told twice. He bolted for the sector door and vanished into the corridor. The next prisoner released was an elderly woman. The rebel leader cranked the key and jerked her cell door open, the hinges emitting a loud whine.

"To the Surface!" she said as she hobbled out of her cell with a pronounced limp. She raised her fist up, extending her index finger to the ceiling. "For Myra Jackson!"

The chanting of his daughter's name took over the Pen. "For . . . Myra Jackson! For . . . Myra Jackson! For . . . Myra Jackson!" It became a battle cry.

Jonah couldn't believe his ears. His daughter a rebel hero?

Before he could fully process that, a black tide of Patrollers rushed into the Pen with their pipes unsheathed. They fell on the Surfacers with savagery.

"For the Oracle!" screamed Baron as he charged forward. "No mercy for sinners!"

He bashed a rebel's head, and it caved in from the blow. He grinned in satisfaction as blood sprayed his black uniform. He kicked off her mask, revealing that the rebel was a woman—a Hocker who sold spicy fish rolls at the Souk before the uprising. Jonah had often found himself stopping by Cynthia's booth on his way to work, and always found her coquettish smile and bawdy laughter charming.

"Nice work, mate!" cheered another young Patroller named Horace, and they clanged their pipes together in triumph. Jonah recognized him from Myra's class.

Mere children are fighting the Synod's war, he thought with a shudder of disgust.

"Surfacers together!" called the rebel leader with the key ring, and they pulled back into a tight circle. The Patrollers outnumbered them two-to-one, and they were trained at fighting. But the rebels didn't flee.

Instead, at their leader's command, they fell on the Patrollers, their tools clanging against Patrollers' lead pipes. The melee spilled over into the adjacent cells, as the rebels and the Patrollers battled for control of the Pen. The tinny sound of metal bashing against metal reverberated through the sector. Those prisoners still locked up grabbed their water cups and banged them against the bars, adding to the unholy racket.

Though the Patrollers were better trained, to Jonah's surprise, the Surfacers seemed to have acquired some fight training, too. Fighting in tight formation, they managed to drive the Patrollers back several feet. Jonah struggled against his chains, feeling them bite deep into his wrists, but he was trapped and helpless. Suddenly, Jasper locked eyes with him. They narrowed to slits, and he pointed his pipe at Jonah.

"Seize that heathen," the Patroller snarled to Baron and Horace. "Or Padre Flavius will put us all out to sea."

Jonah struggled harder, but it was no use. All he could do was watch while the Patrollers fought their way toward his cell at the back of the sector, cutting a bloody swath through the rebels. They wielded their pipes with a combination of precision and blunt force that proved lethal. The Surfacers fought back bravely, rallying behind their leader, but it didn't look like they could hold the Patrollers off much longer.

Jasper lunged forward, taking out a rebel with his pipe. He trampled over the body with his boots. He had almost reached Jonah's cell. Another minute and Jonah would feel the sting of his pipe. He braced himself for the beating, when suddenly—

The rebel with the keys tore off his mask.

It was Royston.

He was Jonah's second-in-command in Engineering, and more importantly, his best friend. Jonah felt a sudden rush of conflicting emotions sweep through him—surprise, joy, hope, terror. Their eyes met for a split second. Blood trickled down Royston's temples, and his cheeks were ruddy from exertion, but he looked feisty as ever.

"Jonah!" Royston called. "Here . . . catch!"

He tossed the key ring through the bars of Jonah's cell. They landed with a brittle clang and skidded a few feet, stopping several inches away from Jonah. He strained against the shackles, stretching his arm out—his middle finger just brushed the edge of the ring, but he almost pushed it out of reach. Frustrated, he jerked his head up.

Royston was battling both Jasper and Baron at the same time. His sledgehammer clattered against their pipes, and he drove them back a little. But he was winded and losing strength. "Royston, behind you!" Jonah screamed right as Horace swung his pipe at the back of his head. Royston whipped around in time to block the blow.

Jonah wanted to help his friend, but he had to free himself first. He took his eyes off Royston and strained against the shackles. He felt his shoulder almost wrench out of its socket, but it gave him an extra centimeter of reach—and that was all he needed. He hooked his pinky around the metal ring and dragged it toward him. Then, he worked to unlock the shackles, shedding the golden chains of his own making. He broke the key off in the lock so that the shackles couldn't be used again and then limped to the door. His knees felt like putty, threatening to buckle under his weight.

He flipped through the keys, searching for the right one. His hands were numb and clumsy from the lack of blood flow. Finally, he found the right key. It slid into the lock and twisted. He thrust open the heavy door, staggering through it, but many Patrollers stood between him and the sector door.

"Die, filthy sinner!" Baron bellowed as he swung his pipe at Royston. It connected with the rebel's head, and he collapsed like a sack of rice. Blood seeped from a deep wound in the back of his head. Satisfied that Royston wasn't getting up, Baron wiped the blood from his face and turned his attention to Jonah. He signaled to the other Patrollers.

"Well, look who's decided to join us," he said, his lips twisting into a smirk. Jasper and Horace both turned toward Jonah with their pipes raised.

"Heathen, freeze right there!" Jasper ordered.

Jonah glanced around frantically, but he was trapped against the back of the sector with nowhere to run. In a blind panic, he clawed at the back wall, but it was solid concrete and would not give. It was a dead-end. The Patrollers had almost reached him, when like a jolt of electricity, the second part of Maude's message flashed through his head:

When the lights come on . . . look to the heavens for salvation.

Jonah jerked his head up to the ceiling. The grate covering an air vent swung inward. Two freckled faces peered through it. He recognized them right away—Stella and Ginger, the Bishop twins. They beckoned urgently, pointing to the bars of his cell. They mouthed something . . .

Climb . . . it looked like . . . *climb!*

That snapped him into action.

Jonah scrambled up the bars of his cell, struggling to gulp enough oxygen. His arms quivered with fatigue, but the adrenaline kept him going. He reached the top of his cell and clambered over to the grate. He heard angry shouts coming from below.

"Hurry, the heathen is getting away!" Jasper roared. "Climb up after him!"

The twins reached for Jonah's arms and seized his wrists. They struggled to pull him through the grate, but it was a tight fit. He wriggled, trying to squirm through the narrow opening. He got his shoulders into the vent. Below him, he heard scuffling noises, and then a hand snagged his ankle. He felt himself being dragged back down.

"By the Oracle, stop right there!" Baron yelled.

The twins tugged harder, but they weren't strong enough. Baron wrenched his ankle, making Jonah slide down another foot. He dangled by his arms—the only thing keeping him from falling was their grip on his wrists. But their hands were sweaty, and he felt them slipping. Summoning his remaining strength, Jonah kicked back as hard as he could. He felt his sandal connect with something . . . and then he heard a crunch.

"Filthy heathen broke my nose!" Baron yelped.

But he didn't let go. Instead, he pulled even harder on Jonah's ankle, using his body weight. Jonah was about to fall when he heard another voice below him:

"Let him go, you worthless cod!"

It was Royston.

He must have come around. Jonah heard scuffling noises below, the shrill clanging of metal, and then Baron cried out in pain . . . and finally released Jonah's ankle.

"Climb, Jonah!" Royston screamed. "And climb fast!"

That was all he needed to hear.

With the Bishop twins' help, Jonah wriggled through the grate and scrambled into the air vent. He knew he should run—*this was his chance!*—but he couldn't help himself. He glanced back through the grate and saw Baron beating Royston to a bloody pulp.

This time, he won't get up, he knew with certainty.

Jonah would have gone after his friend if the twins hadn't intervened. They latched the grate and grabbed his arms, dragging him deeper into the air vent.

"Hurry, follow us," one of them hissed.

Was it Stella or Ginger? He couldn't tell them apart for the life of him. With their bright shocks of red hair that reminded him of a struck match and eerie green eyes, they looked identical. Even their freckles seemed to match.

"Or this will all be for nothing," the second one added, exchanging a worried look with her sister.

Jonah looked at them in surprise. "What do you mean? This whole breakout . . . it was for me?"

The first one grinned slyly. "Freeing the other prisoners was only a distraction. You'll learn everything later. Maude's waiting for you in the Engineering Room. There's no time to explain now. You have to come with us right away—"

Suddenly, a pipe crashed against the grate.

The metal buckled inward, but didn't give out . . . yet. The latch kept it secured. But another blow followed, and it buckled again. It wouldn't hold for much longer.

"Stella, help me," whispered Ginger. "We have to go now."

The twins seized his wrists again and dragged him away from the grate. Several smaller pipes branched off the main vent. Some were in constant use like the water pipes, but many had been abandoned long ago. Though Jonah knew this in concept, he hadn't actually ventured into the pipe and duct system in ages, not since he was an Apprentice Engineer.

The twins led him toward a narrow opening to the left. It was pitch black inside. Ginger clicked on her flashlight and crawled fearlessly into the dark abyss.

"This way!" she hissed over her shoulder. "And hurry! They're coming."

Chapter 19
LOST IN THE DREAM

Myra Jackson

For days, Myra burned up with fever and hallucinated in her sleep.

The memory she had when lightning broke through the sky and shattered the dreamscape replayed in her head over and over again. She was lost in the dream, stuck in an endless loop, and it was driving her mad.

"Aero!" she screamed and flailed around. She felt soft hands caressing her brow, wiping the sweat away with a damp cloth, stroking her cheeks. And she felt warm breath brushing her earlobe and whispering calming things. But it wasn't Aero, he was gone. Even in the midst of her delirium, she knew that much.

After what felt like weeks, but was really only eight days, her fever finally broke, and she awoke from her tortured dreaming. Kaleb lay by her side, his arm draped loosely over her good shoulder, the one that wasn't swathed in bandages. Later on, she would learn from Paige that he'd barely left her side, even when she called him by another man's name. For that, she felt guilty. She hadn't meant to hurt him—not her trusty, loyal Kaleb, who had always been there for her. He deserved better. But this was all she had to offer.

Though she was awake, she was still frail from her ordeal. The burn on her arm—a spider web of angry, enflamed lines that snaked from the Beacon to her shoulder—would eventually heal, though it would leave a significant scar. The Beacon also seemed to be repairing itself, but slowly. It throbbed weakly in rhythm to her broken heart.

On the ninth morning after the storm, Myra woke from a dreamless sleep and felt stronger than she had in days, despite the emptiness in her stomach. It seemed appropriate somehow, perhaps because it matched the emptiness in her heart. The sun coaxed her to her feet as it crested the mountains and broke over the world all at once. The others were still asleep, huddled in their coats on the tarp. Hoarfrost crusted the earth like glittering stones. She padded over to the edge of the bluff that overlooked the valley below.

She observed the terrible silence of her mind and thought about their predicament. Over a week had passed since they'd last eaten anything. According to Paige, it was possible to go weeks without food. Most of the Hockers lived on the verge of starvation since they lost half their Victus and usually ran out of rations a week or two before the end of the month. Water was another story, however—but they had plenty of that. The storm had strengthened the streams that rushed through the foothills.

But how much longer could they keep going without sustenance? They were already overtired and frail from hunger, especially poor Tinker. They'd been living on rations since they'd reached the Surface, and they'd burned a lot of calories walking. Usually, this was when Elianna would chime in with some comforting words or advice on how to proceed—but there was no voice in her head.

Myra glanced down at the weak throbbing of her Beacon and wondered if Elianna was truly gone forever. *Elianna, are you there?* she thought. *Can you hear me?*

The only response was silence. The Beacon's surface was

still charred black, obscuring the golden sheen. Yet it stayed affixed to her wrist, reminding her of everything that she'd lost in the storm.

Myra drank from a stream that tasted like minerals and earth, and then returned to the campsite, feeling somewhat refreshed. She sat on the tarp, thinking and waiting for the others to wake up. The sun rose higher and warmed her skin, and she grew pleasantly drowsy. Once they stirred, her eyes swept over their faces. They looked gaunt and haggard. She didn't have a mirror handy, but she doubted she looked any better. In fact, she probably looked worse.

"Look, I'm not going to sugarcoat this," Myra said, once they gathered in a loose circle like they used to back home in the secret room. Her injured arm hung useless in a makeshift sling that Paige had rigged up from a piece of tarp.

"Thanks . . . I think," Kaleb said with the barest smirk

Paige smiled weakly, though Tinker remained expressionless. He dragged his fingers through the dirt, tracing a circular pattern that resembled the Ouroboros seal.

"Good to know starvation hasn't hurt your sense of humor, Sebold," Myra shot back, but then she turned more serious again. "I've been thinking a lot about everything, trying to find a way out of our situation. And well . . . sitting here isn't doing us any good. If we stay here, then we'll die here. These mountains will be our graves."

A pained look crossed Paige's face. "And soon."

Myra winced and nodded. "We've been completely out of food for over a week now, and we haven't come across anything edible since we got here."

"So then what are you suggesting?" Kaleb asked. "You know as well as I do. Actually, better. We're lost without the Beacon. These mountains are a bloody maze."

"He's right," Paige said. "We have no clue where we are."

A despairing silence descended over the group. Myra tilted her gaze to the horizon, which was now studded with white-capped peaks. *When did that happen?* she wondered. Snow must have fallen while she was unconscious. She remembered what Elianna had told her about winter but quickly pushed it from her mind. They already had enough to worry about.

"We continue heading west into the mountains," Myra said after a long moment. "That's where Elianna was leading us. That's where the signal was coming from. Maybe we'll find the other survivors, and they can help us."

"But how . . . without the Beacon's help?" Paige said, throwing her hands up. "Look at those mountains—they're massive. We'll never find them like that."

"Maybe we'll get lucky, and they'll find us?" Myra said, but her words sounded hollow even to her ears. But she pressed on anyway. "Look, you're right. It's probably hopeless. But we can't just give up! Not when there's still a chance, even if it's a small one. I don't know about you guys, but I'd rather die fighting. So who's with me?"

o   o   o

The vote they took that morning was unanimous. Their shadows stretched toward the mountains as they trudged through the rocky foothills. Myra chose their route based not on Elianna's instructions but on her own gut instinct. A narrow path seemed to open up, curving uphill and growing steeper, though it could have been her imagination.

How their feet continued to carry them for the next several days remained a mystery to Myra and a testament to the resilience of the human body. They were all dropping weight fast, poor Tinker more so than the rest. He looked like a walking skeleton. Their bellies felt hollow, yet looked pregnant and bloated. Fatigue and occasional hallucinations became the norm. But still they raised one foot after the other and kept on going. Myra knew their journey would end soon, not at the doorstep of the First Continuum as she'd hoped, which still seemed impossibly far away.

It will end here, she realized, *in these mountains.*

"Let's find somewhere to camp," Myra said wearily on the

eleventh day. She wobbled on her feet, feeling lightheaded. She felt Paige's arm steadying her, and shot her an appreciative look, though her friend didn't appear to be faring any better.

"Good idea," Kaleb said in a soft voice and shuffled the small boy nestled in his arms. Tinker was tucked under his shoulder. His breathing was shallow; his face wasn't much more than flesh stretched over sharp cheekbones. Myra laid her hand on his back and felt the jagged edges of his shoulder blades and the laborious heaving of his lungs.

He was dying, Myra knew with sudden clarity. They all were.

Kaleb caught her expression. He knew, too.

As they walked together, picking their way up the rocky path, looking for somewhere flat and comfortable to set up camp for the last time, they never noticed the fifth shadow following them. It crept along in the dark places, shielded by the rocks and their lengthening shadows. Its footfalls were careful and soundless. Its eyes shone like saucers in the fading daylight. It had been tracking them for days. It knew they were weak from hunger, something it understood well. It was waiting for darkness to fall.

Patience, it told itself as it crept along after them. Soon—very soon now—the light would die. And then it would be time.

o   o   o

That night, as the sun dipped, they broke for camp.

"We can go no farther," Myra said, her voice barely a whisper. They'd stumbled upon a wide plateau, nestled about halfway up the steep mountainside. Tinker was curled up in her arms, his breathing rasping out wetly. A sickness had taken root in his chest, and his body was too frail to fight it off. Paige was treating him with what medicines she had, but what he needed most was the one thing that they didn't have—food.

"Tink, swallow these," Paige said, slipping two chalky pills onto his tongue. Tinker grimaced at the bitter taste, but he obeyed and swallowed. She tipped a flask of river water into his mouth to chase them down and wash away the unpleasant flavor.

Kaleb laid out the tarp. Gently, Myra laid Tinker down to rest, making sure his coat was zipped up and the hood tucked firmly over his head. She stroked his sweaty brow, smoothing back wisps of flaxen hair.

"Just rest," she cooed in his ear. "It's going to be okay."

Tinker let out a weak, rattling cough.

Kaleb tilted his head toward the sky, which had turned a brilliant shade of mauve streaked with rosy-pink hues. Most evenings the sun put on a dazzling performance before it retired behind the mountains. Myra followed his gaze and felt awe washing through her, chased by deep sadness. She glanced over at Tinker, who was resting feverishly; his tiny body shivered in the brisk air. She felt tears welling in her eyes.

"I'm so sorry . . . I let you all down," she managed through her tears. A sob racked her chest, but she pressed on. "I've failed us . . ." another sob cut off her voice.

"Failed us?" Kaleb said. "What do you mean?"

Myra kicked the ground in frustration. "I never should have led us into these mountains. I should have listened to Paige. They'll be the end of us."

"Stop beating yourself up," Kaleb said, leveling her with his fierce gaze. His eyes shone in the fading light like two emeralds. "Nothing could be further from the truth. Our colony was dying. If we had stayed under the sea, we would be dead anyway. You woke us up to the truth about our world. If anything, you gave us hope when we had none."

Tears were brimming in his eyes too, but they weren't tears of sorrow—they were tears of tremendous joy. "At least I get to be here with you at the end," he added softly.

He leaned over and kissed her forehead, his lips soft and supple against her cool skin. He kissed away her tears, their salty wetness, and then he wrapped his arms around her and hugged her tight. She folded herself into the concavity of his chest and listened to the persistent thumping of his heart. Meanwhile, Paige checked on Tinker, and then stowed the first aid kit in one of the remaining packs and settled down next to them.

"It's interesting . . . I thought I'd be more afraid to die," she said in a detached kind of way. "We used to get terminal patients at the Infirmary, and they always seemed so scared when we told them how many months they had left. That there was nothing more we could do for them. I sat in on a few appointments with my mother during my pledge training. But I'm not afraid. Actually, I feel strangely peaceful."

As the sun slipped below the horizon, and a full moon ascended to the pinnacle of the heavens, they pulled out their two remaining flashlights and stayed up late into the night talking and reminiscing. They told stories about meeting at the Academy. Stories about Rickard's classroom pranks, and Myra's long string of detentions for fighting with Baron and his bully friends. Stories about running wild through the Souk before school in the mornings and getting chased by angry Hockers and then gorging themselves on Maude's candy. Stories about friendships gained, and lost, and then regained.

They laughed and cried from laughing too hard as their voices lit up the night more than the weakening beams of their flashlights ever could. There was no reason to conserve the batteries now. And for a blissful moment, Myra forgot that she was hungry and tired and that her brother was sick and probably dying.

"Remember when Rickard drew that awful picture of Mrs. Pritchard?" she said as tears of laughter leaked from her eyes. "Our Third Year teacher?"

"With the Oracle shoved up her arse?" Kaleb said.

Paige doubled over in a fit of giggles. "I didn't think it was possible for her face to turn that shade of purple . . . or for Mr. Richardson to run that fast!"

"Rickard got two months of detention for that one," Kaleb said. "And he had to burn the picture in front of the Church and endure five lashings. He's just lucky his father was the Head

Patroller, else Padre Flavius would have put him out to sea."

"Oh, but it was worth it, wasn't it?" Myra said with a laughter-induced hiccup. "Though his backside might have argued otherwise. He couldn't sit down properly for weeks. Remember how he carried around that pillow?"

Suddenly, out of the corner of her eye, she saw something move in the shadows. The flashlights just grazed it, before it slunk back behind the jagged rocks.

"Wait . . . stop!" she hissed, signaling for quiet. "There's something out there."

They froze, and the laughter dried up instantly.

"More insects?" Paige asked in a shaky voice.

"I don't think so," Myra whispered. "It looked about Tinker's size."

Paige shot her a horrified look. "Giant insects?"

"Well, there's only one way to find out."

Myra scooped up the flashlight and took a few steps toward the rocks. The bluish beam swept over the area, casting monstrous shadows. But she didn't see anything move.

"Anybody out there?" she called. "We won't hurt you."

"But what if it wants to hurt us?" Paige whispered.

Myra ignored her and took another step forward. She sensed Kaleb by her side; he had picked up the other flashlight. "Look, I know you're out there," Myra called to the shadows. "I saw you watching us. So either show yourself, or we're coming after you!"

"We are?" Paige hissed.

"Quiet . . . it's just a bluff," Myra hissed back.

She peered into the blackness, straining to see beyond the circular area illuminated by their flashlights, but nothing moved. She started to think that maybe she'd imagined the whole thing. Starvation could make you hallucinate, couldn't it?

But then, very slowly . . .

. . . a dark form crept out from behind the rocks.

Chapter 20
THE SURFACERS

Jonah Jackson

The Bishop twins led Jonah through the intricate warren of pipes and ducts, using the secret ways that Myra taught them. They curved through the narrow passages, sometimes turning a full 180 degrees. Gradually, the sounds of their pursuers faded away. They had lost them in this labyrinth hidden behind the walls and floors and ceilings of the colony.

A few minutes later, when Jonah was exhausted and near collapse, they reached their destination. "We're here," Stella announced and came to a halt.

Deftly, she unhooked the grate and disappeared through it. Jonah peered down and saw her drop to the corridor below, landing on all fours. She tossed her head back with its fiery hair and beckoned for him to follow. He did his best, but when he landed, he stumbled and pitched forward. He would have fallen flat on his face if she didn't catch him. Ginger landed beside him with a soft thud, gracefully springing back to her feet. They stood before a sector door. It took Jonah a moment to gather his bearings, but then a smile graced his lips—maybe the first true smile he'd experienced in weeks.

Stella approached the thick door and scanned her wrist tattoo. She glanced back at Jonah. "We recruited some Programmers to join up," she said. "They changed the scanners so that only Surfacers can unlock this door. We update the codes regularly, once new refugees pass their observation period."

The sector doors were designed so that they could be sealed shut in the case of their greatest fear—a massive water leak that threatened to drown the colony. In that way, the leak could be contained and some parts of the colony would survive. That meant the doors were virtually impenetrable, both to saltwater and invading Patrollers.

"Very clever," Jonah said. "Code heads, huh?"

"Well, only a few of them," Ginger added. "It wasn't easy to get them to leave their computer room. They can't go back to Sector 9—it's still under Synod control."

True to Stella's word, the sector door beeped its approval and dilated. Beyond it lay the Engineering Room. They were greeted by a blast of hot air and the stench of grease and metal, and something else that was deeply familiar to Jonah, but that he didn't recognize as belonging here. He felt the heat radiate over his face and inhaled. After a moment, he realized that it was roasting fish, basted with lemon and maybe a hint of coriander and ginger. *By the Oracle, it smells like the Souk*, he thought in amazement.

The twins helped him limp into the sector that he knew by heart. The door contracted behind them, sealing them inside. He heard the clanking of gears and the faint hiss of the Animus Machine. That meant it hadn't stopped working— it was still pumping out some oxygen. But for how much longer? He needed to examine it right away.

He started toward it, everything else forgotten. Even his limp vanished in his rush to inspect it. *Clang!*—a sledge-hammer slammed down in front of his feet.

"Hey, where do you think you're going?"

A group of burly Hockers blocked his path.

The biggest one wielded the hammer and glared at him. His face was flushed like he'd been drinking firewater all morning. The others clutched various tools and sported threatening expressions. "Nobody gets near the Animus Machine. The Chief's orders."

"We work for the Chief, too," Ginger said in a haughty voice.

"Greeley, let him through—" Stella added, but the Hocker interrupted her.

"We don't take no orders from little girls." He hooked his hands through his coveralls and stared down at them. "Especially two of them."

"I'm no little girl," Stella shot back. "We're operating under direct orders from the Chief. We just broke him out of the Pen," she added, jerking her thumb at Jonah.

The Hockers all laughed.

"The Pen?" Greeley said. "That's bloody impossible."

Ginger rose up on her tiptoes. Her face was flaming red, the same as her hair. "Just wait until the other prisoners show up at our front door. We took a shortcut through the pipes, but they should get here any minute. You might want to tell the Infirmary."

Greeley hesitated. "Other prisoners?"

"Yeah, the ones we just busted out," Stella said smugly.

Jonah realized that the mission was so secretive that not even all the rebels knew about it. Greeley glanced at his buddies. He ran his fingers through his scraggly beard.

"We'll let the Chief settle this," he said finally, though he didn't sound happy about it.

Greeley grabbed Jonah's arms—a bit roughly—and carted him toward his old office in the back of the sector. Even though it was dingy and crooked, Jonah felt a small sense of irony that a placard still hung next to the door that read: "Jonah Jackson, Head Engineer."

Greeley knocked on the door. It was slightly ajar and swung open. "Chief?" he called inside. "Permission to enter?"

Through the door, Jonah glimpsed a figure hunched over

his desk, which was littered with blueprints and drafting tools, but also maps of the colony and what looked like plans. She swiveled around and broke into a toothless grin.

"Jonah Jackson! Aren't you a sight for sore eyes?"

He stared at her in shock. The woman in front of him looked so different from his widowed neighbor. Instead of her usual collection of maudlin skirts, Maude wore a crisp, navy uniform that looked like it had been freshly sewn and dyed. Her graying hair, which was normally messy and adorned with colorful scarves, was tucked back into a tight bun.

"What's wrong?" Maude asked. "Have the rats got your tongue?"

An impish smile spread across her face. With one burst of laughter from her belly, the Maude that he knew and loved was back. The Bishop twins giggled coyly. Jonah felt a smile breaking over his face, too.

"Wait . . . this is Jonah Jackson?" Greeley said.

"The one and only," Maude replied with a grin.

"Sorry . . . Chief," Greeley sputtered. "He was tryin' to mess with the Animus Machine. And you said, 'Greeley, don't let nobody near that machine.' We was just following your orders. We didn't realize he was the father of Myra Jackson! You didn't tell us about no plan to bust him out. We thought he was rottin' away in the Pen."

"Greeley, think I tell you everything?" Maude said but then softened her tone and laid her hand on the big man's shoulder. She gave it a kindly pat. "Besides, you were following orders. You don't have nothin' to be sorry about."

Greeley looked relieved. "Yes, ma'am," he said with a sloppy salute.

"Greeley, I hate being called that. Makes me feel old."

"Uh, sorry . . . yes, Chief."

"That's more like it," Maude said.

She turned back to Jonah, who swayed on his feet as the trauma from his ordeal hit him all at once. Worry shot across her face. She helped him into the desk chair.

"Don't stand around like bloody fools!" Maude called

to the Hockers. "He needs medical attention. Greeley, fetch Doctor Vanderjagt! And bring water and Victus. He's nothin' but skin and bones. Padre Flavius and the Synod will pay for this."

When she said that last part, her cheerful manner dissolved, and she looked every bit the formidable rebel leader. The Hockers swirled their hands over their chests.

"Drown the true heathen!" they chanted and saluted Maude. Then they beat a hasty retreat, disappearing into the Engineering Room.

As Jonah slumped in the chair, feeling the skittering of his heart and the rapid spiking of his blood pressure, his gaze drifted through the door. Even in his hazy, semiconscious state, he could see how organized the rebels were. They'd set up assembly lines in the cavernous sector, performing various tasks. Some were making hybrid weapons out of pipes and tools while others were weaving burlap and sewing new uniforms, and still others stood over vats of blue dye, dipping the fabric in with metal tongs. It smelled vaguely of urine, and Jonah knew that it was used to set the dye.

From what he could tell, they comprised mostly Hockers, but some Factum labored alongside them. However, based on the pile of goods at their feet, they seemed much clumsier and slower at their assigned tasks. He recognized a few familiar faces from Engineering, including Charlotte and Roland, the last batch of pledges from the Academy, who were ferreting supplies to and from the more skilled workers.

A makeshift Aquafarm had been set up in the back of the sector. The elongated, translucent tanks of water were lit from above with purplish UV light as plants sprouted on top of the water and fish swarmed below them, fertilizing the plants with their waste. He also saw boxes of provisions piled up against the back wall. Maude must have been stockpiling Victus for months, trading candy and firewater for extra provisions.

Jonah was impressed by the industriousness of the Surfacers. How long had they been planning this uprising? And how had his elderly neighbor become their leader? More questions tumbled through his addled brain, one right after the other.

"Maude . . . but how?" was all he managed to choke out.

She followed his gaze to the bustling sector. "More refugees join our cause every day. They show up at our door, begging to be admitted. They have stories of injustices suffered at the hands of the Synod and the Red Cloaks and the 'Trollers. They talk of friends and loved ones being locked up in the Pen, or sacrificed to the Holy Sea."

"Like my wife . . ." Jonah said, feeling a fresh stab of grief. "Padre Flavius had her killed and made it like she died in childbirth. For asking questions about the Beacon."

Maude set her lips. "I'm so sorry. I wish that news surprised me, but I'm afraid the list of his atrocities runs longer than *The Book of the Oracle of the Sea.*"

"Our father, too," said Stella, exchanging a look with Ginger. "They put him out to sea, not long after they arrested you. We saw the Sentencing at the Church."

"And Stan," Ginger added. "Him, too."

"I saw the 'Trollers cart them off from the Pen," Jonah said, feeling the responsibility for their deaths settle on his bruised shoulders. "They were locked up a few cells down from me, but then they took them away. I didn't know what happened to them . . . but they never brought them back, so I knew it was nothing good."

Maude swirled her hand over her chest—old habits were hard to break. "Yes, just like Tessa and Philip and Stan and too many others to name." But then a concerned look flashed over her face when she saw Jonah struggling to remain upright. "Look at me prattlin' on like a gossipy fool. Plenty of time for that later when you're feeling stronger. Doctor Vanderjagt will patch you up. Your only job now is to rest and recover."

"Yes, ma'am," Jonah said with a weak salute.

She shot him a look. "That's Chief to you."

And they both laughed.

Chapter 21
THE INTRUDER IN THE NIGHT

Myra Jackson

The dark form slunk from behind the rocks and crept toward them.

"Hey, stay back!" Kaleb yelled, tensing up. "Don't come any closer!" He aimed his flashlight at the intruder—revealing its rail-thin body cloaked in russet hair and huge eyes that refracted the light, glowing like blood red coals.

The creature flinched away, covering its eyes and letting out an angry growl. "Kaleb, stop it," Myra whispered. "Can't you see? You're scaring it."

"Are you bloody crazy?" Paige hissed from behind them. Her voice came out shaky. "I think you've got it backward."

Myra shot them both a look. "Hurry, put the flashlight down before it's too late! Aside from those mutated insects, this is the only living creature we've encountered since we got here. We don't want to scare it off."

Reluctantly, Kaleb lowered it. "Fine, I hope you know what you're doing."

Myra set her flashlight down and held up her empty

hands. She elbowed Kaleb to do the same. He went along with it, but half-heartedly.

"Look . . . no more light," Myra cooed in the gentle voice she used to coax the rats out of the tunnels back home. "Don't be afraid. You can trust us . . . we won't hurt you."

The intruder rose up on its hind legs and sniffed at the air. Its nostrils twitched, but then it snarled and bared its razor-sharp teeth. It looked like it was about to attack.

Kaleb thrust his arm in front of Myra. "Hey, watch out—" he started.

But then the creature threw itself down at their feet and rolled over, exposing its soft belly. It stared up at Myra with big, frightened eyes. "Please don't hurt me . . . Strong Ones," it growled with a strange accent. "I'm only a Weakling . . . Seeker means no harm."

"Look . . . it talks," Paige gasped.

Though the diction was crude and clipped, there was no mistaking that the creature had spoken actual words. Tinker crept up behind them. He'd woken from sleep but was still sweaty and feverish. His eyes roved over the creature, absorbing every tiny detail. "You mean . . . she talks," he said softly. "I think it's a girl."

Kaleb squinted. "Wait, how can you tell?"

Tinker smiled his lopsided smile.

"Look at her—she's like us," he rasped. As the intruder peered up at them, Myra realized that Tinker was right. This creature was human—or rather, humanoid. Her teeth were sharper, her jaws more prominent, and her eyes larger than theirs, which gave her a monstrous appearance. Her body hair had also grown in longer and thicker. But her facial structure and body, including her long legs, were distinctly human. Not to mention . . . the talking.

Myra knelt down and pointed to herself. "I'm Myra," she said, exaggerating the syllables of her name. She pointed to her brother. "And this is Tinker."

The creature shrunk back in fear, but her eyes found Tinker. She seemed less afraid of him, maybe because they were both about the same size. Tinker seemed to realize it, too. He returned her gaze with a shy smile.

"Do you have a name?" he asked. "Something we can call you?"

"Seeker!" she said eagerly. She spoke with a crude accent. They had to listen closely to decipher her words. She started humming a strange tune. "Seeker, Seeker, can't get any weaker . . . she creeps and she sneaks . . . sticks her nose where it reeks."

"Uh, why is she singing?" Paige asked.

"Right, I think she's trying to explain her name to us," Tinker said. "It's kind of like my name. I got it because I like to tinker with things, take them apart, put them back together, that sort of thing. It's not my real name at all."

Seeker nodded and leapt back to her feet. "I find things . . . lots of things. I'm very good at finding things. Hungry . . . yes? I saw swollen bellies so I hunted and brought offerings."

With that declaration, she darted off behind the rocks and then reappeared carrying something. She waddled over and dumped out her arms.

A pile of dead rats landed in a heap at their feet.

"Gross, rats!" Paige yelped and jumped back. Then she lowered her voice and whispered. "Wait . . . you don't think she expects us to eat those, do you?"

Myra felt sickened too—but for a different reason. Back home, the rats were her friends. When she took her secret ways through the pipes and ducts, she always brought them scraps of food or candy.

"Gross . . . what is gross?" Seeker asked, cocking her head and peering at them with a puzzled expression. She gestured to the pile of carcasses. "Ratters are . . . tasty."

As if to demonstrate, she snatched up a fat one and took a large bite. Blood spurted out of her mouth, seeping down her chin. "Ratters are juicy . . . and tasty," she mumbled between chews. "And they fill empty bellies when they grumble."

Tinker let out a wet, rattling cough.

Seeker's ears pricked up and she looked over in alarm.

"This Weakling doesn't have long. He's weak and hungry . . . he needs ratters." She snatched one up and presented it to Tinker. "Weakling, please accept my offering."

The rodent dangled limply in her hands with their long, spindly fingers. The neck had been snapped. But it didn't seem to faze Tinker. He smiled his crooked smile.

"Look, she's trying to help me," he rasped.

Myra had to stifle the urge to vomit; she did her best to hide her revulsion from their new friend. "Seeker is right," she whispered to Paige and Kaleb. "We're starving to death out here. We have to eat something . . . even if it's ratters."

Kaleb nodded his agreement, but Paige still looked dubious. "Fine," she agreed. "But only if we cook them first."

Myra turned back to Seeker and accepted the rat on Tinker's behalf. She cradled the tiny, furry body in her palms. It was still warm; it hadn't been dead for long.

"Thank you, Seeker," she said, swallowing down the bile that crept up her throat, as her stomach tried to revolt. She forced herself to smile. "It looks . . . delicious!"

Seeker grinned widely, baring her teeth. "Seeker finds things."

"Yes, you do," Myra said. "Our deepest thanks. You've saved us."

o   o   o

The smell of roast rat drifted over the campsite. Kaleb and Myra had skinned and quartered them, and now Tinker was grilling them over the portable stove. Fat dripped off the carcasses and sizzled in the pan. Seeker was hunched over and rocking agitatedly at the edge of their campsite. First, she'd objected to the skinning and butchering, insisting they eat them whole. Then the stove seemed to upset her even more. She sniffed the air and crinkled her nose up.

"Ratters are tasty," she grumbled. "Why . . . cooking?"

"Because they'll taste better that way," Paige said with an edge to her voice.

Seeker eyed her suspiciously. "Now that is gross."

Myra shot Paige a warning look. "Seeker, come over here

and eat with us. We saved you some ratters. Look, they're not cooked . . . not gross."

Seeker slunk over and gnawed at one, but she didn't look happy about it. "Nasty cooking," she muttered while she chewed. "Evil . . . nasty . . . filthy cooking."

Once the rats finished roasting, Tinker handed out the meat, only giving them a little under Paige's direction. After days of fasting, their digestive systems had shut down and eating too much too fast could make them violently ill.

Myra took her first bite—and despite the lack of seasoning and knowledge that they were rats—it was the most delicious thing she'd ever tasted. She devoured her portion and only wished she could eat more. After they'd all finished eating, even Seeker who wolfed down her pile, Tinker collected the leftover bones to make a strong broth for breakfast. He placed them in a pot on the stove and covered them with filtered river water, leaving it to simmer overnight, while Kaleb packed up the leftover meat for tomorrow.

Now that they were all satiated and pleasantly drowsy from their meal, Myra turned toward Seeker. She had a million questions whirring through her brain, but she didn't want to overwhelm their guest.

"Seeker, where are you from?" she asked. Seeker looked confused by the question, so Myra tried again. "Let's see. Where's your home?" she said, speaking slowly.

Seeker seemed to be considering the question. Blood encrusted her mouth and fur. She started licking her fingertips and scratched at her head with her foot. "Home . . . yes!" she said. "The Darkness of the Below is home."

"What's she talking about?" Paige whispered.

"No clue," Myra said. "Seeker, are there others like you?"

"Yes . . . many others . . . Strong Ones and Weaklings . . . in the Darkness of the Below." Seeker replied, but then she seemed to grow tired of answering questions. Without excusing herself—she stalked away from the campsite and curled up out of range of the stove and the red glow it gave off.

Myra left her to rest and huddled with Kaleb, Tinker, and Paige by the stove, enjoying the warmth emanating from the burner. The rat bones were simmering away.

"Think she's from one of the other Continuums?" Kaleb asked.

"Well, that would explain how she survived the Doom," Myra replied. "And she speaks our language, so we must have common ancestors at some point."

Kaleb nodded. "That's what I was thinking. Also, she keeps talking about the Darkness of the Below. What do you suppose that means?"

Paige frowned pensively, but then she looked over at Myra. "Didn't you say that some of the colonies were located underground?"

"Yes, they're under . . . mountain ranges," Myra said as it dawned on her. She looked up excitedly. "That's right, I almost forgot! Elianna told me about it."

She yanked her sleeve up and glanced down at her wrist, where the still-defunct Beacon was fastened. Suddenly, Seeker let out a surprised cry and ran over, throwing herself down at Myra's feet.

"We worship the Light in the Darkness," she chanted in a guttural voice. "May the Light never go out, so long as we shall live. The Gold Circle protects us."

Myra pointed to the Beacon. "Seeker, do you recognize this device?"

"The Gold Circle," Seeker said, bowing down again.

Myra looked up excitedly. "She does come from one of the other Continuums! How else would she recognize the Beacon?" She glanced down at Seeker, who was still prone at her feet. "Only she seems to think it's some sort of religious object."

"Well, it makes sense," Kaleb chimed in. "No offense, but look at her. No clothes . . . crude language . . . walks on all fours. Maybe they still have their Beacon, only they've forgotten its true purpose? We lost our Beacon so it's not that improbable."

"Look at her eyes," Tinker said. "They're enlarged. And

did you notice how she uses her sense of smell to get around? And how she shied away from our flashlights like the light was burning her eyes? It's like she's evolved to live in the dark."

"But is that even possible?" Myra asked.

"I think it could be," Paige said after a moment. "With extreme selection pressure and also possible radiation exposure from the Doom, it's possible that physical changes could appear over the course of a thousand years. Remember how Elianna told you about the mutations from the Doom? Like with the insects that attacked us? The same thing could have happened to her colony, especially if they both live underground."

"Right, and what if they lost their technology?" Tinker said. "Sort of like we lost our history in the Great Purging? Imagine if they don't have the automatic lights anymore. Everything would be pitch black underground—except for the Beacon."

Myra nodded. "Exactly, and if they live in the dark, then the light that it gives off would start to seem rather magical, wouldn't it? I could see why they'd start worshiping it. Back home, we worship a stupid seashell with a fancy name."

"The Oracle of the Sea," Paige said, waving her fingers through the air. "The Red Cloaks gilded it with precious metals, but it's still only a conch shell."

"If all of that's true, then maybe their Beacon is the source of the signal from the mountains," Kaleb said. "That would explain why we crossed paths here. Think about it. We were looking for her—and she was looking for us. Maybe even tracking us."

"With her sense of smell," Tinker added. "That's also how she hunts."

"I bet you're right," Myra said.

Myra approached Seeker, who perked up when she saw Myra coming.

"Seeker, can you take us to your home?" Myra asked. "And show us the Gold Circle?" She held up her wrist with the Beacon. Seeker sprang to her feet and nodded.

"I will take you to the Door in the Wall and the Moving Room . . . and show you the Gold Circle. But first sleep . . . a long way to go. Sleep now . . . Myra."

o   o   o

As they were getting ready for bed, Kaleb pulled Myra aside. "Do you think we can trust her?" he whispered, jerking his head toward Seeker. "You know, while we're sleeping?"

Myra snuck a glance at their strange guest, who was watching as Paige tended to Tinker and gave him medicine. Seeker seemed concerned about his health. She stroked his arm with her spindly fingers and told him that she would hunt for more ratters in the morning.

"Well, she did bring us food and try to help us. Why else would she do that?"

Kaleb seemed to relax slightly. "I guess you're right. If she wanted to hurt us, she could have just waited a few more days until we were too weak and picked us off."

"Exactly, besides it's not like we have a choice," Myra said. "There's just a little rat meat left, and Seeker is the only one who knows how to get more."

"Point taken." He yawned and rubbed his eyes. "I'm probably being paranoid—"

She stood on her tiptoes and gave him a quick kiss. "No, you're looking out for us." He blushed and tried to wave her off, but she kissed him again, longer this time.

"Holy Sea, what was that for?" he asked.

"I was just thanking you," she said.

He grinned. "In that case . . . you're welcome."

As they settled in for the night, Seeker lingered on the edge of their campsite. Her big eyes darted around, seeing things in the darkness that Myra could only imagine. Occasionally, she scented the air and then muttered softly to herself.

After a minute, Myra decided that Seeker was harmless and felt bad for eavesdropping. She was probably thinking about hunting again. They should be grateful for her help— they'd be dead without her. Myra lay down beside Tinker and pulled him close, trying to kindle some warmth. The night was clear and brisk. The weather was definitely turning colder. She thought of Elianna's warning that winter was coming.

She laid her hand on her brother's forehead, feeling relief spread through her. His fever had dropped. The meal had done wonders for him. With that reassurance, she shut her eyes and felt weariness in every square inch of her body, but sleep continued to elude her. Her mind sizzled and raced, retracing everything that had happened that day.

They'd found a survivor from another colony. Also, there might be another Beacon out in the world, one that hadn't been lost or destroyed during the period of exile. This knowledge wrapped itself around her heart in a comforting embrace. Without her Beacon, they were completely lost and had no way to find the First Continuum.

But what if they could get their hands on another one?

She felt a thrill shoot through her. Maybe they still had a chance of reaching their destination and saving their colony from suffocation. She felt hope flooding through her, sustaining her like a life raft. But there was another reason for her sudden optimism. She settled on what it was:

We're not alone in the universe anymore.

Myra cracked her eyes open and studied the stooped figure at the edge of their campsite. Seeker rested on her haunches with her bony arms wrapped around her torso. Her eyes darted to Myra, sharp in the darkness.

"Sleep now, Myra," she rasped. "Then I will lead you home." Her voice was grating. It cut through the night.

Myra shuddered—though she blamed it on the bitter chill in the air—and shut her eyes tight. Eventually, she drifted off and dreamed happy dreams for the first time in many long weeks. The Dark Thing didn't appear. Instead, she dreamed of Seeker leading them back to her home colony and finding a whole world preserved beneath the ancient mountains, alive and well and eager to welcome them into their fold.

The contented smile that graced Myra's lips while she slept stayed there until dawn broke in the east and it was time to get moving. And then Seeker led them deeper into the mountains.

PART III
THE DARKNESS OF THE BELOW

Even as a child, she had preferred night to day, had enjoyed sitting out in the yard after sunset, under the star-speckled sky listening to frogs and crickets. Darkness soothed. It softened the sharp edges of the world, toned down the too-harsh colors. With the coming of twilight, the sky seemed to recede; the universe expanded. The night was bigger than the day, and in its realm, life seemed to have more possibilities.

—Dean Koontz, *Midnight*

Chapter 22
YOU MAKE NO SENSE

Myra Jackson

Hurry, Strong Ones! This way!"

Seeker's gravelly voice volleyed down the path as she galloped ahead on all fours, leading them through the desolate land. She paused only to scent the air and alter their course. Despite her diminutive size, Seeker was agile and surefooted. She could easily outpace them and never seemed to tire, even when sprinting uphill. She wore a metal visor that wrapped around her ears to protect her sensitive eyes from the sun.

"One second . . ." Myra wheezed, doubling over to catch her breath. It came out in a jet of steam that spiraled in the frigid mountain air. Her fingers dug into a cramp under her right breast. She winced in pain. Her ribs still stuck out, she noticed. But not nearly as much. Seeker had kept them eating, supplying them with a steady diet of ratters and buggers.

At first, they'd all objected to the buggers, but Seeker had prodded and needled, saying that they needed to fatten up or they wouldn't survive the journey. In the end, they acquiesced after Tinker discovered that if they fried them up, it made them more appetizing. After that, they feasted on them eagerly. Myra had even started to develop a taste for buggers, as disgusting as that sounded. But hunger made you do strange things in order to survive.

Seeker vaulted to Myra's side. "Hurry, Strong One," she growled.

Myra winced—her cramp hadn't relented. "I just need to rest . . . for a second."

Tinker hiked up to them. His cheeks glowed ruddy, but not from fever. His lungs sounded clear. He'd recovered from his sickness and seemingly bounced back to full health.

"Nice Weakling . . . getting stronger," Seeker said and grinned, though it looked more like a scowl. Seeker grabbed Tinker's arm and led him up the path. They almost seemed like friends, Myra thought.

"Wow, she doesn't let up, does she?" Kaleb said when he caught up to Myra. He was out of breath, too.

Paige staggered up to them, wheezing and pink in the face. The air seemed to be growing thinner as they climbed. "And you thought...Elianna was hard...on us," she managed.

Myra glanced at Seeker, who had paused at the top of the ridge to scent the air. They watched as she pivoted around and tore down the other side, almost like something was chasing her. Tinker crested the ridge and vanished over the other side.

"She does seem to be in a hurry, doesn't she?" Paige said.

"She's probably excited to get home," Kaleb said. "I know I would be."

"Understatement of the century," Paige said, rolling her eyes back. "I miss my bunk . . . and my shower. I used to complain about how small it was and how it never got hot enough. Yeah, that was before I had to bathe in freezing river water."

That was true, Myra thought. Seeker did seem excited to go home, though she also seemed agitated and downright jumpy. But Seeker was so different from them that it was hard to know what was really going on inside her head.

"I'm sure you're both right," Myra said.

That day, as with almost every day that came before it,

the landscape didn't change very much. It only grew steeper and rockier. There were still no signs of vegetation and little of animal life, aside from the occasional web flapping in the breeze that warned of buggers in the immediate vicinity. Myra had learned to give their sticky tendrils a wide berth. However, Seeker was always happy to see them. She would vanish into some dark abyss and emerge a few minutes later with fresh buggers for supper.

She bounded over to Myra, pushing her visor up to her brow. Her eyes gleamed like two black pits. "Strong One . . . the Darkness is coming," she reported.

Ever since she'd glimpsed the Beacon, she treated Myra like their leader. Myra hoisted her hand to her brow. Sure enough, the sun was dipping into the west, setting the mountains ablaze with a kaleidoscopic burst of color. It was a welcome reprieve from the drab hues that shaded this world.

"Right, let's break for camp then," Myra said.

"Yes, Strong One! Seeker found a cave. Follow me." Seeker bounded off and led the way up the path. The cave turned out to be shallow, but it would provide some protection from the bitter wind that thrashed down from the mountains at night.

"Thanks, Seeker," Myra said. "It'll have to do."

They set up camp as thick clouds blanketed the sky, shrouding the moon and stars. To Myra's eyes, the darkness looked pitch and impenetrable; it pressed in on their cave, held at bay only by the weak beams of their flashlights. But Seeker could see through it. She crouched down and kept her eyes trained on the valley below. She was keeping watch, though for what exactly Myra wasn't sure and didn't want to ask.

That night, the weather turned brutally cold. Myra shivered violently and pulled Tinker closer. They'd lost their bedrolls and heater when the insects attacked them. Cradled by the mountainside, they huddled together in a tangle of bodies and limbs and tried to sleep. Myra no longer had nightmares of the Dark Thing, but Aero didn't invade her dreams either. Not since her Beacon had stopped working.

As her eyelids drooped and sleep came at last, she decided that she would trade a hundred thousand nightmares for just one more sweet dream with Aero.

o   o   o

Seeker woke before dawn to hunt and returned with an armful of buggers and two ratters dangling from her jaws. She spat them out at Tinker's feet. "Cook and feast, Weakling."

While Tinker fired up the stove and worked to prepare their breakfast, Kaleb stretched out his long legs and massaged the hard knots in his calves. The soles of his boots were worn down. "Seeker, how much farther to your home?" he said with a yawn.

Seeker rocked back on her haunches. "Darkness comes twice," she said, holding up two spindly fingers. "Then we reach the Door in the Wall and the Moving Room."

"Two more days?" Kaleb said. "Is that what you mean?"

Seeker nodded and bit into a rat, snapping the head off. Blood slopped down her chin. Paige turned away in disgust. "What's this door she keeps talking about?"

"The Door . . . *in the Wall*," Seeker said and glared at Paige, to whom she had taken an instant dislike. The feeling seemed to be mutual.

"Well, that makes no sense," Paige said with a weary sigh.

"Sense . . . who needs sense?" Seeker growled. "You make no sense."

Then she slunk over to Tinker's side. Her nostrils flared up in revulsion at the rat meat sizzling away in the pot. Tinker reached over and patted her back to soothe her. She purred in appreciation, leaning into his side.

"Paige, stop it," Myra snapped, rolling up the tarp and stuffing it back into her pack. "Remember, it makes sense to her. We'd be dead of starvation without her help."

Seeker grinned, baring her bloodstained teeth.

"Thank you . . . Myra."

o   o   o

Darkness fell once and then again, bringing with it a frost that bit into the earth and left it riddled with ice crystals. When Myra woke up, she marveled at how the world had been transformed overnight. Everywhere she looked she saw a great blaze of white. She was used to the stagnant world of their enclosed colony under the sea, where nothing ever changed.

As they trudged up the icy path, the wind blasted down through the passes and tore at them from all sides. Even Seeker seemed cold on this morning, despite her thick shrouding of hair. She bounced from foot to foot, waiting for them to catch up.

"Strong Ones . . . hurry!" she growled. Her breath came out in a burst of vapor that circled her head like an effervescent crown. "Almost there . . . hurry!"

They began to ascend higher, climbing deeper into the mountains. Just before dusk, as the sun began its slow descent, Myra inhaled and smelled something fresh and cold in the air. An hour later, the first snowflakes drifted down, like in the snow globe that had belonged to Sari Wade. Tinker stuck out his tongue and caught a few. Myra tried it, snagging some out of the air. They felt cold and quickly melted in her mouth.

"Snow," Tinker rasped. He peered up at the sky. "It's snowing," he said with a sense of wonder.

At first, it didn't stick, but then the wind picked up and it fell heavier, blanketing the ground. The snow piled up at their feet—first one inch, then another, and another. It became harder to walk. Their toes and feet grew numb in their boots, but still they pressed on.

Every few minutes Seeker reappeared, materializing out of the blizzard and waving them forward. Snow clung to her hair, turning her almost as white as the mountains through which they were climbing. When dusk was threatening to fall for the third time, and Myra began to worry they were lost, she heard Seeker's voice.

"Seeker found it!" she cried, scampering back to Myra with a toothy grin. She hopped from foot to foot in an anxious dance. "Strong Ones . . . almost there!"

Seeker barreled ahead, leapfrogging through the snow on all fours and vanishing into the whiteout. Myra slogged on, her boots clomping down and leaving heavy footprints. Kaleb, Tinker, and Paige struggled behind her, walking in a single-file line. The pass was too narrow to allow for anything else. To their left rose a vertical wall of solid rock, and to their right, the trail gave way to a sheer drop-off. The wind whipped down even harder, hurling snow and ice at them and making it impossible to see.

Shielding her eyes, Myra rounded the next curve and almost tripped over Seeker. She was sitting in the middle of the path. At first, Myra didn't understand why Seeker had stopped there, but then she saw the object of Seeker's gaze:

A massive door set right into the cliff, almost as if it were a part of the mountain itself. "The Door in the Wall," Seeker said and bowed down before it.

Chapter 23
NOT A WEAPON

The Majors

Majors Doyle and Rothman strode onto the bridge.
The door contracted behind them with a slurp. Their Falchions clattered as they came to a halt in front of Supreme General Vinick. He stood with his back to them and his eyes glued to the curved windows that wrapped all the way around the bridge. Danika clutched her tablet under her arm with the new report loaded onto it.

"Enjoying the view, Supreme General?" asked Major Doyle.

He employed a familiar tone with Vinick, one which Danika wouldn't dream of using for fear of demotion—or worse. Outside their ship, rotating slowly under the harsh glare of the sun, drifted the planet Earth.

"It's an ugly rock," Vinick scoffed without taking his eyes off the window. They narrowed to slits. "Doesn't even deserve to be called a planet. The Doom should have finished it off."

Vinick turned to face them. He morphed his Falchion into a dagger and spun the blade in his hands. It pierced the tender flesh of his thumb, drawing a single droplet of blood. He sucked at it. "Major Doyle, you received the intel from the probe?"

"Yes, sir," said Doyle. He glanced to his right. "Major Rothman?"

"That's correct, sir."

Danika pulled out her tablet and scanned the report. She tried to compose herself, though her heart was racing. "One of our probes detected an anomaly in the Southwest Corridor, North American continent. The sensor arrays were lit up."

Vinick exchanged a look with Doyle.

"Did the probe double back to scan closer?"

"Yes, sir. That's protocol . . ." she hesitated, glancing down at the report. "But by the time it took another pass, the anomaly had vanished," she finished and braced herself.

"Vanished?" Vinick said. "Major, how could that be?"

Danika thumbed through the pages for the hundredth time, wishing that some new detail would leap out, some clue as to what had happened down there, but none revealed itself.

"Maybe the probe malfunctioned?" she started, but instantly regretted it.

"Major, don't underestimate the deserters," Vinick snapped. He tilted the dagger toward her. The sharp tip glinted in the cold light of the bridge. "Or you'll wind up like Major Oranick. You are assigned to his console, after all. The deserters are skilled and dangerous. They threaten our entire way of life, everything that we stand for."

"Sorry, sir," Danika said and cast her eyes down. She cursed herself for jumping to conclusions and disappointing the Supreme General. "But I don't understand how they could have evaded our probes?"

Vinick shot her a cold look. She felt a chill wrenching its way up her spine. "Don't make me regret your promotion, Major Rothman," he said sharply.

Danika racked her brain. She tried to recall everything that she knew about the deserters. She'd reviewed their psychiatric profiles, medical files, service records, and reports from the Agoge, memorizing even the most obscure details, like their blood types, and how much food they consumed in the Mess Hall on average, and how often they liked to charge their Falchions, but nothing stood out. The deserters were skilled fighters, that much was clear from their files.

But it didn't explain how they could evade the probes, which were sophisticated machines. You couldn't hide from their sensor arrays when they were scanning that close, and you certainly couldn't disguise a whole crash site. So what made the deserters special? What set them apart from ordinary soldiers?

"I don't know . . ." she stammered, wilting under the Supreme General's gaze. Her brain struggled to articulate a response. "Maybe . . . the Beacon protects them?"

Vinick looked stunned, but then he nodded approvingly. "Very good, Major. The Beacon is a powerful device. We haven't considered this possibility."

"Exactly, sir." She tapped on her tablet. "Perhaps they found a way to shield themselves from our sensor arrays using the Beacon? Like you said, it's a powerful device." She pulled up diagrams of the Beacon on her tablet but then frowned. "Though we're still mostly in the dark about how it functions . . . only the Order knows."

"Starry hell, they've stymied us for too long," Vinick said, tilting his dagger away from Danika. She felt relief coursing through her. At least his wrath had found a new target. *Let him berate the Order of the Foundry all he wants . . . just so long as he doesn't reconsider my promotion.*

Vinick's eyes snapped to Doyle. "Major, summon the old Forger to the bridge. I'd like to have a little chat with him. It's overdue, don't you think?"

Doyle hesitated. "Sir, but what if he refuses? The Order has proven thorny of late. They assert that they don't fall under our jurisdiction. They claim that the charter for the Second Continuum grants them autonomy from our rule."

Vinick stabbed his dagger down into the console. "I'm the Supreme General," he barked. "Nobody is exempt from my rule. If the old man resists my direct order, then bring him

Vinick narrowed his eyes. "Answer the question, Brother."

"The Beacon is many things. It was forged using ancient technology and bestowed upon our colony by the First Ones, but it is not a weapon. In fact, it was made to protect us from other weapons and ensure our survival Post Doom."

Vinick aimed his dagger at the old man but stopped short of directly threatening him. "Could the Beacon protect them from our probes? Answer the question."

The Forger knitted his brows together. "As far as I know, it's never been used for that purpose. It would take a lot of power and exceptional control, and it would be extremely dangerous. If it backfired, it could destroy anyone and anything in the immediate vicinity. But I suppose that it might be possible . . . for a skilled Carrier."

"Like the deserter—Aero Wright?" Doyle said.

The Forger looked suddenly serious. "No one is more skilled with our technology than Captain Wright. I expect that if anybody could do it, then it would be him."

"The deserter is not the rightful Carrier," Vinick snapped. "He murdered his father and stole the Beacon, and it must be returned to the Second Continuum. To suggest otherwise is treason. Brother, do you know the punishment for such an offense?"

The Forger smoothed out his long robes. "I warn you, Supreme General. Do not meddle with ancient forces beyond your understanding. The Beacon chooses its Carrier as much as the Carrier chooses it. Parting them could prove dangerous, catastrophic even. Greater men than you have died undertaking such follies—"

"Silence!" Vinick cut him off. "I expect your Order to commission a full report on the Beacon and its weapon capability. Major Doyle will oversee your progress and make sure that you comply with my orders."

"But sir . . . it's not a weapon," the Forger protested.

"Brother, I don't believe you," said Vinick. "And even if I did, I know that it's powerful, and I expect you to tell me exactly what it can do. Is that understood?"

The Forger tried to hide his anger, but it shone brightly in his eyes. "Yes, sir," he said with another deep bow to disguise it. "My Order serves at your pleasure."

"Dismissed," Vinick said with a flick of his dagger. The blade pointed right at the old man as he retreated from the bridge in a swirl of crimson. The door contracted behind him.

Vinick cast his gaze at Doyle. "Well, that went smoothly," he said with a sneer.

Doyle cracked a smile. "You put some fear in him, sir. The Order needs to be reminded that we're in charge—not them. They've been forgetting their place. We'll get that report for you, I'll make sure of it. What do you want to do in the meantime?"

Vinick's eyes snapped to Danika. She felt that icy feeling creep up her spine. "Major Rothman, what's your recommendation?" he asked in a stony voice.

He was testing her, feeling out her instincts for command. She didn't flinch; she showed no hint of emotion when she answered. "Deploy an armed combat unit to the North American continent to locate the deserters with orders to kill them on sight and retrieve the Beacon."

Vinick grinned in approval.

"Very well, Major. Soldier, dismissed."

Chapter 24
THE MOVING ROOM

Myra Jackson

he Door in the Wall," Seeker chanted and bowed down before it. Now Myra realized why Seeker called it that. The massive door was set right into the cliffside—a solid wall made out of sheer rock. Myra could just make out the outline of the door, half-buried under the snow.

Myra glanced back; she couldn't see the others through the whiteout conditions, but she could hear them cursing as they struggled through the knee-deep snow. "Hurry, we found the door," she called back, loud enough to be heard over the wind.

While Myra waited for them to catch up, she ran her hands over the door and wiped away the thin layer of ice that clung to it, revealing a shimmer of golden metal. Slowly, lines materialized under her palm and merged into a circle. They resolved into a familiar symbol—a snake swallowing its own tail, entwined around two words:

Aeternus Eternus

Only there was one major difference. On the inside of her Beacon, the number thirteen was engraved, but on this door, there was a different number. Her heart beat a little faster when she saw it. Kaleb, Paige, and Tinker staggered up behind her and stared at the enormous door with its ancient markings.

Paige pointed to the area that Myra had wiped clean of snow. "That symbol looks like the one on the Beacon, doesn't it?"

"It's the same one," Myra agreed. "And look . . . there's a number on the door."

It was a seven, clear as day.

"The Seventh Continuum," Kaleb whispered, running his fingertips over the number. His words hung in the frosty air. Nobody said anything for a very long moment. They all understood the significance of this door—and the great possibility of where it could lead. Snow continued to drift down, making soft rattling sounds as it amassed the doorstep.

Finally, Paige broke the silence. "So . . . how do we open it?"

"No clue," Myra said. "Seeker, what do we do now?"

Seeker didn't reply. Instead, she kept kneeling before the door and muttering under her breath. She seemed to be waiting for something to happen . . . but what?

Myra tried running her hands over the door, feeling for any buttons or indentations, but the metal was smooth and unbroken. She stood back with a puzzled expression.

"Anything?" Kaleb asked, but Myra shook her head.

"Nope," she said with a frown.

Frustrated, she glanced down at her Beacon—it hung on her slender wrist. She shut her eyes. *Elianna, if you're there, please help me. How do I open this door?*

The Beacon remained dark and lifeless.

But then—

It flashed once, weakly.

Searing pain shot up Myra's arm, making her double over and cry out in agony. The device started to smoke, the wisps mingling with the falling snow. Tinker rushed to her side, his face seized with worry. He reached for her wrist, but

Myra shoved him away. Asking Elianna for help had cost her dearly—and possibly set back the Beacon's healing process—but she'd felt something.

An answer . . . sort of.

It didn't come to her in words exactly, nor did Elianna reply to her. Rather, it was more of a sensation . . . a gut instinct perhaps. For all she knew, it didn't even come from the Beacon at all. Without questioning it, she laid her hands on the door and felt the snake curling underneath her fingertips.

"Aeternus eternus," she spoke the strange words.

For a split second, the snow dwindled, and the air was perfectly still, almost as if time had frozen. Then the Ouroboros seal ignited with a blinding flash of emerald light. Under her palm, Myra felt the snake rotating faster and faster. The mountain started to rumble and buckle under her feet.

"Watch out!" she yelled to the others. "Over here!"

Myra signaled for them to follow her lead. They scrambled over to the cliff and pressed themselves against it. Rocks, dirt, and small boulders tumbled down, followed by mounds of heavy snow that landed at their feet with a wet thunk.

"What's happening?" Paige screamed.

But then—

The door began to dilate with a loud groan. It creaked open slowly—almost painfully—like an eyelid first thing in the morning after a deep slumber. The golden surface shimmered like liquid metal and retracted into the mountainside.

Only once it was finished dilating did the shaking abate. The rain of rock and snow tapered off, too. Myra peeled herself away from the cliff and peered through the opening. She expected to see something grand and breathtaking—or at least, worthy of their efforts—but all she saw was a rectangular room not much larger than a compartment back home. The walls were smooth and made out of dull silver metal. A cylindrical railing circumvented it at waist level.

"The Moving Room," Seeker growled and vaulted through the doorway. She beckoned for them to follow.

"Don't be afraid, Strong Ones . . . this way."

"The Moving Room," Tinker repeated softly. He pushed his glasses up the bridge of his nose as he inspected the austere space. "Interesting . . . I think maybe it's an elevator. I saw a diagram once in one of Papa's old engineering books. They move up and down in a vertical motion," he explained, gesturing with his hands to show how it worked.

"An elevator, of course," Myra said. Their father frequently left thick textbooks laying around their compartment, and Tinker had always been fascinated by anything with mechanical parts. An elevator certainly qualified.

Paige squinted at the elevator. "But where does it go?"

Tinker ran his hands along the railing. "Deep underground, I'm guessing. Based on what Elianna told us, we know that the Founders built some of the colonies under mountain ranges so they'd be protected from the Doom."

"There's only one way to find out for sure," Myra said and joined Tinker and Seeker in the elevator. Kaleb followed next, and then Paige more reluctantly.

"Seeker, how do we make the room move?" Myra said once they were all inside. "Is there a control panel somewhere? Or maybe a button or verbal password?"

But Seeker didn't answer. She lay flat on the floor with her hands pressed over her ears.

"Well, she's not any help—" Paige started.

Before she could finish, the rumbling and shaking started again. They staggered around and lurched for the railing. As Myra clung to it with both hands, she realized why it was there.

The door began to contract, flowing out of the rock and reforming itself into a solid sheet of metal. Rocks and snow tumbled down and ricocheted into the elevator.

"Watch out!" Myra screamed. She leapt back as a shard from a rock slashed her cheek.

Suddenly, a huge boulder rocketed down and wedged itself in front of the door, blocking the entrance. With one final rumble, the elevator finished contracting and sealed them inside the dark room. Myra dug out her flashlight and clicked it on.

"Is . . . everyone ok?" she sputtered, choking on the thick dust that swirled in the bluish beam. Blood trickled down her cheek. "Is anybody hurt?"

She shined the flashlight around and collected assurances from the rest of the group, all except Seeker, who remained prone on the floor with her hands pressed to her ears. And then the floor lurched away, as the elevator began to descend swiftly.

"Holy Sea—" Myra gasped and dropped the flashlight.

It clattered to the ground and rattled around, casting jagged shadows across the walls. Her ears popped and her stomach clenched, almost making her retch. She lunged for the railing and hung on. The world seemed to lose its balance and somersault around her. More than anything, Myra wanted the sinking sensation to stop, but with the door blocked by the boulder, there was only one way for them to go.

And it wasn't back up.

Then the elevator accelerated faster, plunging downward with extraordinary speed and carrying them deep into the bowels of the earth.

by force if necessary. Is that understood, Major Doyle?"

"Yes, sir," Doyle said with a quick salute.

He signaled to Major Wright, and they left together. The elevator door contracted behind them.They were headed for the lowest level of the ship, which housed the Foundry. Every soldier knew where it was since they had to visit it to charge their Falchions. Only the Forgers possessed this ability, and that gave them great power, which they wielded quietly and carefully. Antagonizing them could have dire consequences, Danika knew. But she kept her mouth shut. Vinick was in charge now. She wasn't foolish enough to question his authority.

Twenty minutes later, Doyle and Wright returned to the bridge with their charge. They marched him right up to the Supreme General. The old man's crimson robes swirled around his ankles. He gathered his hands at his waist and bowed deeply.

"You summoned me, Supreme General?" the old Forger said. His expression remained neutral, but his pale eyes were hard, steely even. They bored into Vinick.

"Yes, Brother," Vinick said with a forced smile. "As you know, the deserters murdered Majors Oranick and Mauro in cold blood, hijacked an escape pod, and fled to Earth. We tracked their trajectory to the North American continent. But so far they've managed to elude our probes. Brother . . . how can that be?"

The Forger looked puzzled. "My sworn brothers and sisters serve at the pleasure of the Interstellar Army of the Second Continuum. However, the answer to your question lies outside the expertise of my Order. We are the makers and keepers of the Falchions, nothing more."

Vinick did not look pleased by his response. "The . . . Beacon," he said slowly. "Look, I know it has powers. Could the deserters have used it to shield themselves from our probes? What other powers does it have? Can it be used as a weapon?"

The Forger let out a deep laugh. "A *weapon?*"

Chapter 25
THE DESCENT

Myra Jackson

The elevator slammed to a halt with a rusty squeal.

Myra waited for her stomach to unclench before releasing the railing. Her fingers were numb from gripping it so hard. With clumsy hands, she picked up the flashlight and inspected it. It was dinged up from being dropped but otherwise undamaged.

"Is everyone okay?" she asked as she flicked the light around. Her voice sounded muffled in the cramped space. The beam clipped Kaleb, Paige, and Tinker as they struggled to right themselves. Seeker lay flat on the floor, but she slid her hands off her ears and craned her neck up. Her eyes refracted the light like two blood-red moons.

"Where are we?" Kaleb asked.

As if in answer, the door began to dilate. Violent rumbling accompanied its machinations. They all lurched for the railing and held on until it finished opening. A dank, musty smell rushed into the elevator, making Myra sneeze.

Then everything went still.

Myra peered through the opening, but she couldn't see anything beyond the anemic halo of light cast by her flashlight. It was pitch black outside the elevator. This wasn't like the darkness that came at night, for even after the sun dipped below the horizon, the sky was still pierced by a billion tiny stars and sometimes a moon, all casting their celestial light over the world. Even the clouds couldn't filter it out entirely. Likewise, their deep-sea colony was never really dark. The automatic lights burned constantly in their sockets, their brightness adjusting to account for the time of day.

This was true darkness—dense and unbroken. Her flashlight barely made a dent in it.

"Hello?" Myra called through the doorway. "Is anybody down here?"

Seeker peeled herself off the floor and slunk through the door. She moved quietly and quickly—a flash of russet hair and arms and legs—then she was gone. Myra tried to track Seeker's movements with the flashlight but lost her in the gloom.

"Hey, where's she going?" Paige said.

"So now you want her to stick around?" Kaleb snorted.

Paige scowled. "Never said I wanted her gone. I just found some of her habits a bit . . . well . . . repulsive. That's all."

Myra ignored their bickering and strained to hear Seeker's footfalls, hoping for some clue as to where their host went.

"Seeker, are you out here?" she called.

Her voice rippled out and multiplied, but no answer came back from the darkness except the repetition of her own question. Tinker cocked his head, listening intently.

"Tink, hear anything?" Myra asked.

He shook his head as disappointment stole across his face. "She'll come back," he rasped. "She has to . . . ." But even he seemed worried by Seeker's sudden disappearance. Kaleb fished the other flashlight out and clicked it on. He shined it through the opening. Illuminated by the intersecting beams, the area outside the elevator came into sharper focus. They were standing on the edge of a vast cavern. Several tunnels branched off it, each one marked by a crumbling stone archway. Myra counted seven passages. Seeker could have disappeared down any one of them.

"Where is . . . everybody?" Paige said as she strained to see through the darkness. "It's completely deserted out there. I don't like it."

"Maybe Seeker went to get her friends?" Kaleb said. But his words came out sounding hollow and unconvincing. Myra tried calling for Seeker a few more times, but still no answer came back, aside from the reverberation of her own voice.

"Well, we can't go back the way we came," Myra said after the last echo died out. "There's a giant boulder blocking the door. And even if we could, Seeker is the only one who knows how to hunt. We would just starve to death."

"Or freeze in the snow," Paige added with a shudder, the bitter chill from the blizzard still fresh in her mind. "That storm wasn't about to let up anytime soon."

"Yeah, if anything it was getting worse," Kaleb said.

Myra thought for a second. "Alright then, we've got two options. Either we wait here—or we go look for Seeker."

They took a vote, and in the end, they opted to look for Seeker, mostly because doing something felt better than doing nothing—all except for Tinker.

"She'll come back . . . I know it," he insisted. Though even he couldn't explain why she'd run off like that.

"It's decided then," Myra said. "Come one, let's go."

She patted Tinker's arm in consolation, and then she and Kaleb shouldered the two remaining packs. They ventured from the elevator. Their footfalls ricocheted around the cavern, staccato and piercing. Their boots kicked up dust that tickled their nostrils. Myra aimed her flashlight up, but the darkness swallowed it before it could hit the ceiling.

Ahead of them spanned the tunnels. Myra approached the nearest one. It exhaled that same awful stench that had invaded the elevator.

"Which way?" Paige asked, crinkling up her dainty nose.

"No clue," Myra said with a frown.

Kaleb aimed his flashlight at the tunnel entrances, one right after the next. "They all look exactly the same," he said. "And you can only see a few feet down them."

"And they all stink the same, too," Paige added.

Tinker shrugged. "In the absence of any information, choosing at random is as good as anything else." He pointed down the middle tunnel. "How about this one?"

"Tink makes a valid point—" Kaleb started when suddenly the elevator door began to contract with a deep rumble that shuddered through the cavern.

"Watch out!" Myra yelled as rocks and debris rained down. She shielded her head and dashed into the nearest tunnel. She heard footfalls behind her. Dust chased them into the tunnel.

Myra coughed hard. She blinked to clear her eyes and aimed her flashlight straight ahead. Particles danced in the beam, but then it flickered.

Not now! she thought in a panic. *Come on, don't die on me!*

She slapped the metal barrel against her palm. The flashlight kicked back on.

"Thank the Oracle," she muttered in relief.

"What's wrong with it?" Paige asked in a hoarse voice, her voice clogged by the dust. She glanced at the flashlight in Myra's hand. "It looks like it's growing weaker."

"The batteries are dying," Myra said, regretting how carelessly they'd used them before when they thought all hope was lost. "They won't last much longer."

"And . . . then what?" Paige croaked out.

Myra swallowed hard, tasting grit in her mouth. She didn't want to think about that. "Well, let's only use one at a time. That way we can stretch out the battery life."

"Agreed," Kaleb said and clicked his off. He passed it to Myra, who stowed it in her pack for later. Then she led the way, ushering them deeper into the tunnel.

The ground sloped downward as the passage curved sharply to the right. She tried to keep track of their route as they went, but soon that became impossible. The flash-light beam bounced around and clipped stalactites that jutted down from the ceiling like jagged knives. Under her boots, she could feel deep grooves cut into the floor as if it had been worn down from hundreds of years of foot traffic.

But now the tunnel appeared completely deserted.

Where is everybody? she wondered as she shined the light around. She didn't see anyone, but she kept getting a creepy feeling that they were being watched. It felt like something prickling her between the shoulder blades.

But when she swung the flashlight around, the tunnel remained empty. She felt something tug at her sleeve and jumped.

It was Tinker.

"Tink, what is it?" she asked.

He pointed to the ceiling. "Look . . . automatic lights."

Sure enough, familiar strips of lighting spanned the length of the tunnel, just like in their colony back home. Only these looked like they'd been defunct for a long time.

Paige frowned. "Why aren't they working?"

"I'm guessing they lost power," Myra said, studying them closer. "From the look of them, probably a long time ago. Nobody's done any maintenance work on them. These casings are rusted clean through, and the wires look totally fried." Her flashlight grazed over something else—she flicked it back quickly. "And look over here . . . air vents."

The grates were set into the walls at even intervals. Myra passed her hand over the nearest one, then sniffed the air wafting out. A smile twisted her lips when it hit her nostrils. "They're still pumping out fresh air. That's why we can breathe down here."

"How is that possible?" Kaleb asked. "If they lost power, then wouldn't the air vents quit working, too? Don't they need electricity?"

Myra inspected the air vents, shining the flashlight through the slats. "Back in our colony they do. But this looks like some sort of passive stack ventilation system."

"Passive stack . . . what?" Paige said.

"Passive stack ventilation," Myra repeated, remembering the technical diagrams that she had seen in one of her father's old Engineering books. "That means they don't need electricity to circulate fresh air from the Surface. It would explain why the colony didn't run out of oxygen after they lost power. Also, feel the air coming out?"

Tinker passed his hand over the grate. "It's . . . warm."

"Exactly, I'll bet there's some sort of geothermic heating element, too," Myra said, feeling a burst of excitement. "Talented engineers must have designed it."

Tinker grinned his lopsided smile. "Like Papa."

"Yes, just like our father . . ." she managed, before a swell of emotion choked off her voice. A lump lodged itself in her throat that felt just as huge and insurmountable as the boulder that was blocking the elevator. *Papa would have loved this*, she thought, wishing for the millionth time that he was with them to see it. He would have been fascinated by this ancient technology. She wanted nothing more than to stay put in the tunnel and study the ventilation system, confirming her theories about how it functioned, but that would have to wait. First, they needed to find Seeker.

Myra swung her flashlight away from the grates, and they curved deeper into the tunnel. Now and then, they encountered an obstacle where part of the passage had caved in, but overall the tunnels remained intact. Myra marveled at this feat of engineering. She pictured the people of Before Doom constructing this subterranean refuge, drawing up blueprints, operating hydraulic drills, laying in beams and steel supports, and installing infrastructure—ventilation systems, electrical wiring, strips of lighting. The construction process must have taken decades.

She wondered if any workers had lost their lives when a tunnel caved in or some electrical circuits went haywire. Did their ghosts haunt these passages?

As they rounded the next bend, her flashlight grazed over a large, yellow sign stenciled with black letters. The words were badly faded. Before she could make out what they said, the flashlight sputtered out, casting them into darkness.

Kaleb: "I can't see anything—"

Paige: "Hey, watch it! You stepped on my foot, you big lug."

Their voices reached Myra's ears, though she couldn't see anything, not even her hand when she held it in front of her face. Even the Beacon was dark. She smacked the flashlight against her palm, then jabbed the power button—but nothing happened. The useless clicking sound seemed even more pronounced in the absence of other sensations. She unscrewed the cap, rotated the batteries, then snapped it back in place. She tried the power switch again.

But still nothing.

"The batteries are dead," Myra said, now that she was certain.

"That was . . . fast," Paige said.

"How much juice is left in the other one?" Kaleb asked.

"No idea," Myra said, not voicing her next thought: *Probably not much.*

Operating by sense of touch alone, she tore open her pack and pawed through it. Her fingers tripped over its contents, hastily stuffed together—dried rat jerky, pots and pans, a folded-up tarp, the portable stove—finally catching on the cold, metal barrel of the other flashlight. She fished it out and clicked it on, feeling immense relief as a bluish beam shot out.

Thank the Oracle, she thought and swirled her hand over her chest. The darkness was getting to her. It was getting to all of them.

Myra aimed the flashlight at the sign nailed to the wall. Her heart beat faster when she read the boldfaced letters:

CAUTION: RADIATION LEAK

"What does it mean?" Paige asked.

"I'm not sure . . . but it can't be good," Myra said,

inspecting the sign closer. "Maybe contamination from the Doom seeped down here somehow?"

"Think it's still dangerous?" Kaleb asked.

Myra shook her head. "No, the danger should have passed by now. That was the reason for the period of exile."

The deeper they went, the more radiation signs appeared nailed to the tunnel's walls. Some were clustered together in packs. Soon they had seen too many to count.

And then they stumbled upon the graffiti—crude renderings of stick figures painted onto the walls.

Myra flicked the flashlight over them, taking in the images and their message. They told a horrific story

Stick figures breathing toxic air.
Stick figures choking on it and dying in droves.
The advent of the never-ending darkness.
Piles of dead bodies cast into bottomless pits.
Mutations and tribal warfare.

Myra studied the panels, noticing how each image grew successively more disturbing and barbaric. The final panel had words scrawled under it:

THE FALL OF AGARTHA

The image depicted a great city burning. Fire licked the buildings and burst through their rooftops. Ashes drifted to the ground, falling like snow over the cobblestone pathways. After this last panel, there were no more images, only jagged letters scrawled on the wall:

THE RISE OF THE STRONG ONES

Myra traced her fingers over the words. Rust-colored paint flecked off on her hands. She tasted it, cringing at the metallic flavor. She felt a chill wrench up her spine.

Was the message painted in blood?

"What do they mean?" Paige asked, her voice coming out in a nervous burst. Her eyes combed over the images, trying to make sense of them. "They're . . . horrible."

Tinker approached the wall. His eyes roved over the paintings. "I think this is their history. Look over here . . . I bet they lost their paper and books in the fires, so this was their only way to record it."

Kaleb pointed to the image of the fire-singed city. "What does Agartha mean?" he asked.

Tinker studied it. "I think it's a name . . . maybe of this city."

"The city of Agartha," Myra said as her flashlight flickered weakly, and reality crashed down. As captivated as she was by their history, she knew that they had to keep going. "We've wasted enough time here already. The batteries are dying."

Myra led them deeper into the tunnel. Soon it grew narrower, forcing them to stoop over, all except Tinker. A few minutes later, they came upon a divide in the path. One tunnel sloped upward while the other arced downward, but otherwise they looked exactly the same. The flashlight beam vanished a few feet into them as if swallowed whole by the darkness.

"Which way?" Kaleb asked, peering into the tunnels. "This place is a complete maze. It's even worse than the mountains."

They chose at random and decided to take the tunnel to the right that sloped upward. The passage grew narrower, and the twists and turns came so often that Myra began to feel dizzy. Suddenly, her boot clomped down on something that crunched. She whipped her flashlight down—rat skeletons littered the ground.

"Great, more rats," Paige muttered.

Hundreds blanketed the floor like a strange, prickly carpet. The tiny bones had been picked clean of meat. Some looked fresh while others appeared far older.

"Well, that's a good sign," Kaleb said as his boots splintered the chalky bones. "At least, we know somebody lives down here."

Paige didn't seem comforted. "Or . . . something."

As they walked, the crunching of their boots echoed

through the tunnel. Soon, the ceiling sloped down even more, and the walls constricted, forcing them to crawl on their hands and knees in a single-file line. As Myra led the way, she felt the needle-sharp bones crunching underneath her palms. Bile surged up her throat. She gulped to force it back down, but the sour taste singed her tongue.

And then—

Without warning—

The second flashlight flickered. Myra rapped it against her palm, and the light stabilized. She breathed a sigh of relief and swung it around. For a split second, it clipped something hanging from the ceiling—a human skeleton strung up by its neck with a noose. A spear jutted through the ribcage, impaling it with a message scrawled in blood on a shred of fabric. Myra felt her heart lurch when she read it:

BEWARE THE STRONG ONES!

Then the flashlight winked out again—this time for good.

Chapter 26
THE FALL OF AGARTHA

Myra Jackson

Myra felt the darkness gouging into her eyeballs, snaking down her throat, filling her lungs with poisonous smoke. She heard Paige hyperventilating somewhere behind her. "The Strong Ones . . . did you see that?" Paige shrieked. "We have to get out of here!"

The walls of the tunnel pressed in on Myra as if squeezing her in a vise. Her lungs constricted. She lurched away, bumping into the skeleton's foot and unleashing a shower of dust. Coughing, she scrambled backward and smacked into the wall. She clawed at the rock, trying to escape. Her fingernails snapped off and bled.

In the crush of darkness, she flashed back to the Pen— the never-ending night, tiny cell, no food, little water, daily beatings, and no hope of escape from the Patrollers and their pipes. She felt her body going rigid with fear.

Gripped by blind terror, Myra started to black out. Then she heard a soft voice rasp in her ear: "It's okay, don't be afraid. The darkness can't hurt us. It's nothing . . . only the absence of light. And well . . . that skeleton has been dead a

long time . . . probably along with whoever did that. It can't
hurt us either."

Tinker's voice reached Myra like a light bulb flicking on.
It broke through her panic. The calm certainty of his logic
washed over her. Her brother was right—darkness wasn't a
force; light was a force. This was only its absence. She remembered the graffiti. The skeleton had likely been hanging there
for hundreds of years. It was a relic from the civil wars fought
after the colony lost their electricity and fell into darkness.

Myra inhaled, and oxygen flooded her starved lungs.
A few more deep breaths and her head stopped swimming.
"We have to keep going," she said, finding her voice. Though
shaky, it echoed out through the black tunnels. "It's our only
chance. Follow me, I'll lead the way."

Crawling ahead, Myra struggled to tamp down her
fear and rely on her other senses. She skirted around the
skeleton, careful not to bump its feet again. *This is just like
my secret ways back home*, she told herself, and it started
to work. Slowly, the world of the underground—the world
of unbroken darkness—revealed itself to her, first in fits
and starts, and then all at once in a rush of sensation.

Myra listened closely and heard the scampering of tiny
feet. *Rats*, she realized. And the faint trickle of water flowing
under the rocks. She heard her friends shuffling behind her. She
found that she could distinguish them by sound alone. Tinker—
lighter, faster, more nimble. Paige—whimpering, spastic, urged
along by Kaleb's gentle whispers. Kaleb—trudging, heavy
boots scraping against rock, all the way in the back.

They were smells too—dust, rocks, and something bitter
and sulfurous. Her sense of touch was strongest of all. Using
her hands, she felt her way forward, making out the deep
grooves worn into the floor and the gentle upward slope of
the path. She was rewarded when the passage split, and she
avoided colliding with the partition.

"Hold back," Myra called behind her. "There's another
fork in the path."

The shuffling stopped.

Paige sniffled softly but sounded less panicked now. Tinker was right behind her. Myra could hear the faint whisper of his breathing. Kaleb was pulling up the rear.

"Which way?" he asked.

Myra pondered that as she groped around in the dark, feeling the outlines of the two tunnels. On first inspection, she didn't observe any differences between them. They both curved straight through solid rock with no gradation. Then she sat back and took a deep breath—and that's when she realized the best way to select their route. "Of course, that's it," she said, smiling to herself. "It's so obvious."

"What's obvious?" asked Paige nervously. "What do you mean?"

"We follow the air," Tinker said in his raspy voice. "That's what Seeker does. I've been watching her."

He was right. The tunnel to the left reeked of dank, sour air. But the tunnel to the right smelled of fresh, cool air. Myra remembered Seeker pausing on the ridges to scent the air, and only then deciding on their route. That was how she navigated in the dark.

"Exactly," Myra said. "It's this way, to the right."

They crawled for several more minutes, winding their way through the narrow passage. They came upon yet another fork in the path, and once again Myra used her sense of smell to select their route.

Right when Myra didn't think that she could go any farther, the tunnel seemed to grow lighter. *Could it be?* she thought, feeling a faint tug of hope. She crawled faster and rounded the next bend. The light started to pulse faintly. It was dim—just a greenish glow filtering into the passage. But she didn't care. She picked up her pace, calling to the others.

"There's light ahead!" she said.

Myra sped forward as fast as her aching arms and legs would carry her. The tunnel narrowed even more, but the light brightened. She squirmed her way forward, and finally with one big push, she shot out the end of the tunnel.

"Holy Sea . . ." she gasped when she looked up.

Before her stood the ruins of an underground city. Stone buildings and spires sprouted up from the ground as if growing out of the bedrock. One building stood taller than the rest and towered over the city. Myra had never seen anything so tall or magnificent in her life. It reminded her of the castles from her mother's fairytales. Pulsing green light illuminated the castle's arched windows, casting an eerie glow over the city.

Paige climbed out of the tunnel, followed by Tinker and lastly Kaleb, who had to wriggle hard to get out. "Light . . . praise the Oracle," Paige said, pointing to the castle.

A wide chasm stood between them and the city's gates. Myra scanned for a way to traverse it. Her eyes landing on a rock bridge that arced over it. It was perilously narrow and lacked any railings or handholds. But it looked like the only way across.

"There's a bridge over there," Myra said. "Maybe Seeker went this way."

One by one, they crossed the bridge and emerged on the other side. Before them stood a wall that looked about ten feet tall and encircled the city. Rusty barbed wire skirted the top of it. The entrance was marked by a crumbling stone archway. Long ago, it must have been protected by gates, but only the rusty hinges remained, jutting out from the wall.

"Fortifications," Myra whispered.

"What do you mean?" Kaleb said, catching her eye.

"The chasm, the bridge, this wall, the barbed wire, the gate . . . they must have been built to protect the city.

"But . . . protect it from what?" he said with a troubled look.

"The Strong Ones . . . I guess." she replied. "Whatever they are."

As they passed through the gates, stepping over debris that blocked their path, Myra glanced up. "Agartha," was etched into the arch. But that had been slashed out and replaced by another message:

ABANDON HOPE ALL YE WHO ENTER HERE

The jagged handwriting looked the same as the graffiti

in the tunnel, and so did the rust-colored pigment. Kaleb followed her gaze to the message. "Looks like our graffiti artist was having a bit of fun, doesn't it?"

"Artist?" Paige snorted. "More like . . . vandal."

Now that Myra was inside the walls, she could see that the city was in a state of complete decay. The buildings themselves were crumbling to dust as if fading back into the bedrock from which they'd been erected. Naked wires protruded from the walls but posed no danger. Electricity hadn't run through them in a long time.

The farther they went into the city, the more dilapidated it became. Radiation leak signs were posted everywhere—on the walls, the buildings, even the streets—and more graffiti, painted in that same jagged handwriting:

Beware the Strong Ones!
The Darkness of the Below!
The Gold Circle Protects Us!

Myra peered through a broken window into a building, taking in its overturned desks, splintered chairs, and rotting whiteboard still affixed to the back wall. Everything was coated with a thick layer of dust.

"The city's deserted," Myra said. "Where is everybody?"

Kaleb caught sight of tracks on the ground. He signaled to Myra. They bent over to inspect them. The prints looked fresh, having recently disturbed the dust.

He caught Myra's eye. "Think they're from Seeker?"

"Seeker . . . and some of her bigger friends," Myra said, pointing to a larger set of tracks that diverged from the first ones. She straightened up, dusting herself off.

"Anybody here?" Myra called. "Seeker, can you hear us?"

She listened for a response, but all she heard was the soft hiss of air vents pumping out fresh air. The city was eerily silent.

"It looks like these tracks lead to the castle," Myra said, pointing to the stone edifice that loomed over the city with its towers as if keeping watch. Stone bulwarks encircled it, lending it an ominous appearance.

"Maybe that's where the survivors live?" Kaleb suggested,

kicking a rock that skittered across the cobblestones and thumped into Paige's boot.

Paige shot him an annoyed look and then squinted at the castle. The windows pulsed with emerald light. "Well, something's making that light, right? It's definitely coming from that building."

The closer they got to the castle, the larger it looked. Following the tracks, they passed under the thick bulwark and approached the entrance. It was halfway dilated as if the power had gone out while it was in the middle of opening or closing.

Myra stepped over the half-lidded entryway and proceeded into the great hall. The ceiling rose as high as the building and was supported by notched columns and flying buttresses. Everything was hewn from white marble veined with gray. Strips of automatic lights snaked across the ceiling but produced not a shred of illumination. The only light came from the door at the end of the corridor.

"Look, over there," Myra said, pointing to the end of the hall. "There's light up ahead."

They passed through the arched doorway and emerged into a spacious room. At one end, stood a throne carved out of glistening, volcanic glass. At the other end, Myra saw the source of the illumination:

A golden armlet rested on a stone altar.

"The Beacon . . ." Myra said, transfixed by its throbbing glow. It was the twin of the one fastened to her wrist. Otherwise, the room was completely deserted.

Myra traversed the room and approached the altar, which looked like it had been sculpted from the same obsidian material as the throne. Now that she was closer, she could see the outline of the Ouroboros symbol carved into the metal. Stamped on the inside of the cuff was a number:

It was a seven.

Her heart fluttered in anticipation. "Look . . . the Beacon . . . it's still here," she said, her eyes fixed on the device. "Maybe we can use it to find our way out of here."

Kaleb peered over her shoulder. "But why hasn't

somebody claimed it?" he asked, sounding troubled. "Why is it just sitting here?"

"This looks like an altar," Paige said. "Kind of like where the Red Cloaks keep the Oracle of the Sea inside the Church. I'll bet they worship it like we thought . . ."

Paige kept talking, but Myra was barely listening. Her Beacon was still broken; the loss wrenched at her heart. But before her existed a tantalizing possibility—*I could be a Carrier again.* This desire completely overwhelmed her and blotted out all reason. She felt her arm moving, almost of its own accord. Without thinking, she plucked the Beacon from the altar and cradled it in the palm of her hand, feeling its power surging through her like a drug. She flipped it over in her hands; it felt light as a feather.

Vaguely, as if from very far away, she heard Kaleb's voice. "Myra, don't . . . quick . . . put it back! It might upset them!"

"What do you mean?" Myra said, still mesmerized by the Beacon. "There's nobody else here—"

Suddenly, a dark shadow cut across the room.

"Drop it, Weakling!"

Myra whipped her head around right as a horde of hulking figures stormed into the throne room. They had hairy bodies and huge eyes like Seeker, but they were four times her size. Myra counted twenty of them, maybe more. The biggest one snarled at her, gnashing his teeth. His coal-black hair bristled.

"The Gold Circle, Weakling!" he growled. "Drop it . . . now!"

He leapt at Myra and smacked her with his fist. She hit the ground hard, the wind whooshing from her lungs. The Beacon skittered from her hands and landed a few feet away but continued to pulse with emerald light.

"Hey, leave her alone—" she heard Kaleb yell, but he was silenced as two of the Strong Ones pounced on him. Through her blurry vision, Myra saw a smaller figure creep out of the shadows. She moved stealthily, almost like a ghost.

It was . . . Seeker.

Myra's first thought was that Seeker was coming to rescue them—that she'd explain everything—that it was all one big misunderstanding. But then Seeker bowed down before the biggest one.

"Oh, Crusher, Strongest of the Strong Ones," she growled. "Seeker went to the Brightside to hunt . . . and brought back fresh meat."

A sickly smile twisted Crusher's jowls. "And so you shall be rewarded, Weakling . . . and become a Strong One like us."

"Thank you, Strongest of the Strong Ones," Seeker said, bowing down again. "Seeker lives to serve you . . . and the Gold Circle."

Crusher turned to the other Strong Ones, who were circling Kaleb, Paige, and Tinker. "Seize these Weaklings and throw them in the Black Mines! My fellow Strong Ones, soon we shall feast on their flesh and bones!"

"Feast?" Paige hissed. "What does he mean?"

Kaleb flinched back in fear. "I think they're . . . cannibals."

Paige turned her fiery gaze on Seeker. "I knew we shouldn't have trusted that filthy beast! She's a bloody traitor—"

But her voice was cut off as one of the Strong Ones—a female with a red-tinged coat and hazel eyes—wrenched her up by the hair and dragged her from the room. Kaleb tried to fight back, but he was no match for the Strong Ones and their claws. Two of them easily knocked him down and then hauled his limp body away.

"Seeker, don't let them take us!" Tinker screamed as they carried him away. He flailed his arms, pointing to something on the floor. "Seeker . . . we're your friends! You have to help us! Look, over there . . . the Beacon . . . get the Beacon!"

Seeker flinched back, looking stricken. Her eyes roved over Tinker's frightened face. But she didn't move to help him. She cowered by Crusher's side, watching as the Strong Ones carted Tinker away.

Myra felt two strong arms wrap around her torso and heave her up. Crusher tossed her over his shoulder like a rag doll. She could feel the rippling of his rock-hard muscles. Then he barreled away on all fours, carrying her from the throne room. She bounced around on his shoulders, her head swimming sickeningly. Ahead, she saw Tinker being carried by one of the Strong Ones. He stared back with frightened eyes. A sob erupted in her throat, deep and racking.

"Oh, Weakling, don't cry!" Crusher growled. "We're the Strong Ones . . . and you're the Weaklings. The strong prey on the weak—that's the only law of survival."

Crusher carried her from the castle, across the rock bridge, and into another winding tunnel. The light from the Beacon evaporated behind them, and then the darkness swallowed Myra completely, though she wasn't sure if it was the darkness of the underground or the darkness of unconsciousness. It made no difference.

She wouldn't see anything for a long time.

Chapter 27
THE RISE OF THE STRONG ONES

Seeker

T his Weakling is now a Strong One," Crusher growled from his obsidian throne.

He stood up, displaying his massive height, and slashed three even lines into Seeker's forearm. Across the throne room, the Beacon had been returned to the stone altar. It throbbed with steady emerald light. Seeker bowed before Crusher. She saw blood seeping down her arm but felt no pain. She was too excited for that.

"Strongest of the Strong Ones, I serve you and the Gold Circle," Seeker said. "May the Light in the Darkness never go out so long as we shall live."

"Amen," came the response from the pack, who had gathered in the throne room for the ceremony. Some gnashed their teeth while others thumped their chests. "The Gold Circle protects us," they roared.

"Strong One, rise and join your pack," Crusher said. He gestured to the overflowing pile of offerings by the altar. "And whet your appetite before the Feast."

Hours passed as the Strong Ones lazed about the throne

room and feasted on the offerings left by the Weaklings—
ratters, buggers, and tubers. Seeker tried to blend in with her
new pack, but she felt like an imposter here. Every time she
snuck a bite, even the tiniest little tuber, she felt like she was
stealing from the Strong Ones. She snatched a smallish bugger
from the pile and gnawed on it, trying to look inconspicuous.

A Weakling scampered over to drop off her offerings,
laying the armful of ratters in front of the altar. "Seeker . . .
the betrayer," she hissed when she saw the three lines slashed
in Seeker's arm. She threw a jealous glance at Seeker before
she scampered off.

Seeker watched the Weakling retreating, her lanky limbs
and rail-thin body vanishing into the great hall. Nobody
had ever envied Seeker before, and she wanted to relish
the feeling. But there was a strange ache in her chest that
had never been there before. It was dull, like a hunger pang
under her left rib. But before she could worry about it, the
fighting started. Pincher stalked up to Crusher and bared
her razor-sharp teeth.

"Crusher, you're looking a bit scrawny," she growled,
circling him on his throne and arching her back. Crusher
threw down his ratter and rose to his full height.

"Who you calling scrawny, Pincher?" he snarled, and then
they crashed together in furious combat. Though Crusher
was their leader, any of the Strong Ones could challenge him.
If they beat him in a fight, then they would become the leader
of the pack. This was how they determined rank. Nobody
had ever bested him . . . at least not yet.

But that didn't keep them from trying.

The Strong Ones formed a rowdy circle around Crusher
and Pincher, rooting for their favorite and wagering on the
winner. Seeker stood on her tiptoes on the outer edge, peering
through the thicket of bodies.

"Crusher, slash her to bits!" Reaper roared. "Two ratters
on him."

"Pincher, slit his nasty throat!" yelled Biter.

"Two ratters and a bugger!" Slayer growled.

Seeker saw flashes of shaggy arms and claws, moving in a blur, and heard snarls and yelps. She listened to the wagering and jeering of the crowd but kept her mouth shut. She didn't know the alliances and rules yet and didn't want to get into trouble, not on her first day as a Strong One.

For a second, it looked like Pincher was going to win. She pinned Crusher down and was poised to sink her teeth into his neck. "Get . . . off . . . me," Crusher grunted, twisting out of her grip and kneeing her hard in the stomach.

Pincher flew back several feet, her head smacking the ground. The cracking sound it made sent shivers down Seeker's spine. Pincher tried to get up, staggering to her knees, but Crusher leapt on her. Seeker couldn't see much, but when Crusher stepped away, Pincher let out one piteous groan and then went still. Crusher growled and thumped his chest. It was slick with blood.

"Strong Ones, appetizer before the Feast!" he roared, and then the pack descended on Pincher's body, tearing her flesh apart in a grisly orgy.

Seeker knew that she should join in—it was a privilege not to have to worry about going hungry anymore—but she couldn't muster up the appetite. For the first time in her life, she wasn't hungry. And she didn't entirely know why, except that her thoughts kept drifting back to Tinker and his cries for help as the Strong Ones dragged him away.

Seeker . . . we're your friends! You have to help us!

Feeling queasy, Seeker backed away from the feeding frenzy, hoping the others wouldn't notice. She slunk toward the door, but Crusher lunged in front of her.

"Going somewhere?" His eyes dug into her face. "Don't you want to feast with your pack?"

She cowered down to make herself appear smaller. "Strongest of the Strong Ones, my belly is already full from feasting. I want to hunt for ratters in the tunnels."

Crusher narrowed his eyes to dark slits. He pointed to the ample pile of offerings. "You don't have to hunt anymore. Seeker . . . you're a Strong One now."

Seeker tried to think fast. Her head was spinning. She feared that if she didn't get out of there soon, then she might vomit or faint—or both.

"But I want to hunt for ratters," she growled, trying to sound tough. "I like snapping their filthy, stinking necks."

Blood lust was something that Crusher understood, but he didn't look convinced. Seeker felt one agonizing second creep by . . . then another. Finally, he relented.

"Fine, but don't be gone from your pack for too long."

o   o   o

Seeker pelted out of the castle and across the rock bridge, trying to outrun the terrible ache in her chest. She didn't understand why the feasting bothered her so much. She certainly harbored no affection for Pincher. *Nasty, filthy creature.* If anything, she was glad that Pincher was dead.

Tinker . . . but not Tinker . . . lovely Tinker.

His face popped into her head—his tiny frame, bony legs, even the strange, wiry glasses that he wore to help him see better. He was a Weakling, too. She felt another strange sensation squirming around like a bugger under her ribcage.

She'd never actually liked anyone before. Even though Tinker was ugly and scrawny and hairless . . . she *liked* him. Maybe it was the way he listened to her, or how he comforted her when she was upset, stroking her fur and whispering in her ear. Nobody had ever done that before. She tried to shake off the squirmy feelings as she barreled into the tunnel ahead, and the Darkness of the Below swallowed her whole. Her hands and feet never missed a step; she never stumbled. But still . . . she missed Tinker.

She tried to stuff the icky feelings down, tried to outrun them. But a torrent of thoughts ripped through her head, one right after the other:

Liking . . . made you weak.

Missing . . . made you weak.

They made you die.

For the first time in her life, Seeker had something to lose. Crusher had kept his promise and made her a Strong One. She didn't have to worry about going hungry anymore. *The Feast*, she remembered, her mouth watering at the prospect. But then she felt sick like she'd eaten something rotten. Her stomach roiled and churned in protest.

But not Tinker . . . lovely Tinker.

The terrible ached throbbed harder like Crusher was pummeling her chest with his fists. Maybe she could convince Crusher to spare Tinker's life? He was only a Weakling, after all. There wasn't much meat on his bones. He would never grow big and fat like the others, no matter how many ratters and buggers he stuffed into his belly.

A few minutes later, Seeker reached her destination. It didn't look like much, just a cave off a little-used tunnel. But it was cozy and safe and it was hers. Nobody else ever came here. She felt around, her fingers roving through the Darkness and seeking out the crevices that were her hiding spots. They alighted on scraps of metal, shards of porcelain, and other treasures. She stroked them, fondling them in her hands. To others, these trinkets meant nothing. You couldn't eat them, and they didn't keep you warm in the tunnels.

But to her, they were everything. She'd found them by scouring the city's ruins, rooting through crumbling buildings and picking through the rubble strewn in the streets. This was risky—Weaklings were barred from entering the city unless on official business for the Strong Ones, such as to deliver their offerings. But Seeker was quieter and smaller than most Weaklings, and she'd been willing to risk it for her treasures.

Stacked in one corner of the cave were prototypes of the visor that she'd made to protect her eyes on the Brightside. Using a sharp spike—another precious object she'd scavenged from the city—she stabbed holes into the thin metal so that it would let in a little light, but not so much that it burned her eyes. Carefully, she bent the metal so it would wrap around her eyes and settle over her ears.

She picked through the visors as memories of her journey fluttered through her head. Seeker—a Weakling—had done the impossible. She found the Door in the Wall and the Moving Room, hunted on the Brightside, and lured back fresh meat for Crusher. And now he had made her a Strong One. So why did she feel so terrible?

Seeker . . . the betrayer!

The Weakling's insult flashed through her head.

"Filthy beasts," she growled and flung the visors down. They landed with a metallic clatter. Usually, her treasures cheered her up, but not this time. Tinker's face flashed through her head, pale and bloody. His lips moved slowly:

We're your friends—

Seeker smashed her fist into a pile of bolts, and they rocketed every which way. And then she felt guilty for lashing out at them—her cherished objects—and swept them back into a tidy heap. *One . . . two . . . three . . . four . . . five . . . six . . . seven . . . eight . . .*

Seeker counted the bolts, ordering them from largest to smallest. She relaxed slightly, lulled by her familiar rituals. She felt the cold tang of metal against her skin as she stroked the grooves and ridges of the objects, these relics from before the Fall of Agartha and the Rise of the Strong Ones. She'd always been fascinated by the city and its ancient curiosities, their true purposes and proper names forgotten, obliterated by the long passage of time and the swaddle of eternal darkness.

She tried not to think about Tinker. Tried not to think at all. She focused all her attention on her fingertips, but then his voice pierced her ears like a spike.

Seeker, don't let them take us—

"Nooooo!" she roared, gnashing at the air.

Seeker wanted to linger here with her objects, but Crusher's warning shot through her head: *Don't be gone from your pack for too long.* She placed her treasures back into their hiding places and swept her fingers over the cave one last time, making sure that she hadn't missed anything. And then she left the room exactly how she found it.

Chapter 28
THE BLACK MINES

Myra Jackson

Trollers . . . no . . . don't beat me!" Myra shrieked at the top of her lungs and scrambled backward. Her head slammed into solid rock. Panic gripped her heart. "No . . . please don't hit me again! I'll do anything!"

When Myra woke from her nightmare, she almost wished that she hadn't. It didn't matter if her eyes were open or closed, all she could see was *blackness*—a great tidal wave of it that pressed against her face and bored into her eye sockets. Memories of the Pen came rushing back in a torrent. She could taste the suffocating darkness, so thick you could choke on it, and feel the terrible chill of the lead pipes as they bit into her flesh.

And then Kaleb was beside her, feeling for her in the dark, stroking her forehead, smoothing back the sweaty strands of hair, whispering soothing things in her ear.

"I'm right here . . . it's okay. There are no Patrollers . . . you were just having another nightmare. There, there, now . . . it will be okay, I promise . . . shhhh . . ."

But it wouldn't be okay.

She knew that much.

Myra twisted away and hugged her knees to her chest. *I don't deserve his sympathy*, she thought. This was all her fault. She'd trusted Seeker and led them into the mountains. She'd lost the pack with their food. She felt a sob bubbling up but fought to push it back down. To distract herself, she sat up and felt her way around their prison, collecting and assembling what tiny shreds of information she could about it.

Solid rock on all sides . . . feels like a circular pit in the ground . . . spiraling grooves carved into the walls . . . probably from where a drill cut into the rock . . .

So it wasn't a cell so much as an abandoned mineshaft. She counted as her hands tracked the length and width of it. She got to eight hands and ten hands, respectively. Her knuckles banged into something hard and unexpected in midair. A bucket dangled from a length of rope. Clumsy in the dark, her hands splashed down into cold, bracing water.

So this isn't like the Pen, she thought. *They give us plenty of water.*

She drank thirstily, her lips pulling at the cool liquid, and then splashed some on her face to wake herself up. She stretched her hands up. They collided with the bars that crisscrossed the top of the mineshaft. She felt around in the dark, her hands tracking over the slats. They felt like they were lashed together with crude strips of leather. She gripped them and shook hard, but they wouldn't budge.

A voice came from behind her:

"Already tried that," Kaleb said. "While you were out."

Myra felt his warm breath on the back of her neck. "Of course," she said, releasing her grip. She slumped back down. "So . . . we're stuck down here?"

"Pretty much," he agreed.

But something was still bugging her about those bars. She reached for them again. They weren't constructed from steel like the cells in the Pen. They were made from some other sort of material. Something uneven, yet hard and porous.

Suddenly, a horrific thought dawned on her. She gasped, feeling the revulsion wash through her. "The bars . . . they're made from . . . bones."

"Human ones . . . in case you're wondering," Paige said. "Femurs, tibias, fibulas . . ." Her voice fell off. A long pause, and then: "Myra . . . they're monsters."

"Well, technically they're cannibals," Kaleb said. "They consume human flesh."

"Monster, cannibal . . . same thing, isn't it?" Paige snapped.

Tinker's raspy voice broke through the darkness. "But don't you see? That's how they survived. Imagine losing everything—the automatic lights, technology, farming— and having to feed yourself by hunting rats and insects in the dark. What happens when that isn't enough to fill your belly?" He paused, and clearly he was thinking it through. "We've already stooped to eating buggers. How far would you go?"

The question hit Myra hard. In many ways, survival was a monstrous instinct. It made you do crazy things—terrible things even—to save your own hide.

"Is cannibalism that much worse than what Padre Flavius is doing with the sacrifices?" she asked.

"Exactly," Kaleb said. "What's the difference?"

"I don't care," Paige said. "They're still monsters."

Tinker spoke up, obstinate as always. "Not Seeker. She's different, I know it."

Paige snorted. "Don't defend her—she's a cannibal and a liar. She led us straight into a trap. Didn't you hear what the big one said? They're going to *feast* on us."

Her words hung in the stale air.

There was no use arguing it—Paige had already made up her mind. Myra felt around for Tinker and laid her hand on his back. He curled into her side, laying his head on her lap. She stroked his hair, letting the darkness and the silence wash over them. Time passed, though Myra couldn't be sure exactly how much. It was hard to keep track in the dark. Occasionally, Weaklings appeared to drop food into their prison.

"Weaklings . . . eat now. Keep your strength up," they whispered as they deposited armfuls of ratters, buggers, and tubers through the slats. But they never lingered. They scampered away, their soft footfalls receding into the tunnels.

Myra's stomach growled fiercely. She was starving. How long had it been since she had eaten anything? But the rats and insects were raw and unappetizing. Paige begged the guards to return their stove. They'd confiscated their packs.

"Weakling, you don't need no stinkin' stove," one of the guards snarled, his fetid breath wafting into the mineshaft. "Now eat your offerings—or else! Crusher wants you nice and fat for the Feast. We're gonna devour your heart while it's still beating."

No matter how hard she tried, Myra couldn't see a way out of their predicament. She and Kaleb whispered about it in the dark. Even if they could escape from the mineshaft, get past the guards, and find their way back to the elevator— all in complete darkness—the door was blocked by a giant boulder and an avalanche of snow.

"If only the Beacon was working," Myra whispered.

"Still nothing?" Kaleb asked.

She slid her sleeve back but saw no light, not even a flicker. She ran her fingers over its smooth surface with growing frustration. "If only it would work, then we'd have some light."

"And maybe even a way out of here—" Kaleb started.

But then a noise overhead made him stop talking. They listened intently until they heard the steady footfalls of the guards as they resumed pacing.

"Exactly," Myra whispered, once it was safe to talk again. "Elianna has access to the old maps of the colonies. Maybe she could guide us to another exit."

"Have you tried talking to her?" Kaleb asked.

"Not since the elevator. Hang on, I'll try again." Myra shut her eyes and probed for Elianna until her heart raced and sweat broke out on her brow. But she heard no reply, only the terrible silence of her own mind. The Beacon remained dark and lifeless.

"It's dead," she said with a heavy sigh. She released her grip on the armlet. "Deader than dead . . . has been since we got here."

Myra slumped back and felt the cold chill of the wall. Kaleb wrapped his arms around her, pulling her into a tight embrace, but it did little to stave off the despair that was quickly overtaking her. She listened to the rhythmic shuffling of the guards' feet. Now she knew that they would die in this forsaken place, entombed in the darkest depths of the earth. Only one question remained—and it was a terrible one: *When the Strong Ones come to take us away for the Feast, who will they take first?*

o   o   o

Myra didn't have to wait long for an answer.

What seemed like a few hours later, Crusher paid them a visit. His voice boomed into the mineshaft. "The big one! Take him first."

Crank, crank, crank.

The bars slowly retracted, hoisted by heavy chains. Putrid breath gusted down into the shaft, and then a pair of arms seized Kaleb and heaved him upward.

"No . . . Kaleb . . . no!" Myra screamed and lunged for him. But her hands passed through empty space. Myra couldn't see the Strong Ones, but she could hear and smell things—terrible, putrid things. She tried to attack them and swung wildly, connecting only with thin air.

A snicker rang out, deep and biting:

"Look . . . the Weakling thinks she's a Strong One!"

This was followed by jeering laughter, and then something hard—most likely a foot—rammed into Myra's lower jaw, making it snap shut on her tongue. The iron tang of blood flooded her mouth. She collapsed to the ground and writhed around in pain, choking on her own blood. She retched a few times. She knew Paige and Tinker were hiding somewhere to her right. She could hear them whimpering in the dark.

Myra struggled back to her feet and swung again, blindly.

"Kaleb!" she screamed. "Can you hear me?"

She heard sounds of struggle above her. She tried to scramble up the wall, her fingernails scraping for handholds and snapping off in a terrific burst of pain. "Kaleb, where are you? Say something!"

"Feisty Weakling," growled a deep voice. "She don't give up."

And then another blow smashed into Myra's head, knocking her flat on her back. And this time, a large figure leapt into the mineshaft. A sharp claw pressed into her jugular, making her throat close up. She sputtered for air.

"Don't worry, Weakling," Crusher snarled in her face. She caught an extra strong whiff of his breath. "You're . . . *next.*"

The talon retracted from her throat, and with a swift clattering of claws, Crusher was gone. Myra flipped over and gasped for air, dragging huge lungfuls of it into her chest. Blood trickled down her neck, a painful reminder of Crusher's message.

Clank, clank, clank.

The bars lowered back over the mineshaft, sealing them inside. Myra rocketed to the slats, but they wouldn't budge. She felt Tinker by her side and heard Paige sobbing behind her. "Kaleb!" Myra screamed. "Kaleb . . . can you hear me?"

At first, she heard nothing. But then his voice came from far away, echoing through the tunnels. "Myra . . . don't give up . . . promise me . . . find a way out!" Sounds of scuffling followed that outburst, and then even fainter: "Myra . . . I love you . . . I've always loved you . . ."

That was the last thing she heard before Kaleb was dragged away. The echo of his voice repeated a few more times like a cruel taunt, but then it died out and silence rushed back into the mineshaft.

Myra hunched over as tears cascaded down her cheeks. Kaleb was her rock—her security blanket—the one person who always looked out for her even when she didn't know he was doing it. He had saved her life more than once.

And she loved him.

Yes . . . she did.

She knew that from the way her heart was rending into a million tiny pieces. "Kaleb . . . I love you . . . " she whispered. Her voice was thick with tears. "I'm so sorry I didn't say it more . . . that I was afraid . . . I've always loved you . . . "

But it was too late—he was gone.

Myra crumpled over and sobbed until she couldn't sob anymore. Her eyes burned and her throat grew raw, and still her chest heaved with sorrow. Even Tinker couldn't comfort her, though he tried his best. Horrific thoughts ricocheted through her brain, each one more terrible than the last:

The Beacon is dead.

Kaleb is dead.

And soon we'll be dead, too.

It's over.

Over.

Chapter 29
OLD HABITS DIE HARD

Seeker

Look who decided to join her pack," Crusher snarled from his throne. His eyes tracked over Seeker as she slunk into the room, taking in her blood-tinged hair and the rats dangling from her jaws. "And with fresh kill."

Reaper stalked over. "Still thinks she's a Weakling, don't she?" he growled, provoking laughter from the rest of the pack. He was second only to Crusher in size and sported a glistening coat of auburn hair. "She hasn't learned her place yet."

"Small enough, ain't she?" added Slayer, a huge female with black-tinged hair and flabby jowls. She bumped into Seeker. "I've devoured Weaklings bigger than her."

Seeker stumbled back, hurting more from the cruel taunts than actual pain. No matter how much she ate, she would never grow big and strong like her new pack.

Biter gnashed at the air. "Throw her in the ring!" he roared. "Let's have a fight for a bit of sport! I'll rip her nasty body to shreds."

Seeker felt her stomach clench up in fear, threatening to spill its contents. The pack grew rowdier, encircling her and thumping on their chests. She cowered away, feeling her back press up against the altar. The Gold Circle pulsed faster and brighter, blanketing the room with its emerald glow. It seemed to feed off the energy and emotion in the air as if sounding an alarm over the bloodletting that was about to transpire.

Biter entered the circle, the hair on his back bristling. He unfurled his claws, ready to challenge Seeker, who cowered down and showed her soft belly—

"Enough!" Crusher roared, and the pack clammed up. He stood up, displaying his massive size, and stalked over to Seeker. "No more hunting ratters in the tunnels! Remember your place is with your new pack, Strong One."

"Yes . . . sorry . . . sorry," Seeker groveled, still showing her belly.

Crusher's eyes lingered on her before he withdrew to his throne. The pack dispersed and returned to their feasting. Seeker glanced around nervously. Pincher's body still lay in the center of the room, but she was unrecognizable. All that was left was a skeleton; her bones had been picked clean of meat. Eventually, when Crusher tired of his prize, he would order some Weaklings to fling her body off the bridge, where it would plummet into the dark abyss and join the remains of countless other lost souls.

If Seeker wasn't careful, the same thing would happen to her.
No . . . bad thoughts!

Seeker tore her eyes off Pincher and tried to soothe herself by gorging on offerings. She ate until her belly bulged out and fatigue latched its leaden hooks into her muscles, forcing her to doze while her insides struggled to digest everything.

But a few hours later, as the Strong Ones slumbered about the throne room, their stomachs distended from feasting, Seeker found herself wide awake. Usually, when she closed her eyes after a large meal, the unconsciousness that enveloped her was impenetrable, like a stone blanket. But thoughts crackled and fizzled in her brain, keeping her up, and when she did nod off several hours later, she slept fitfully and dreamed terrible dreams.

"Seeker . . . don't let them take us!" Tinker screamed, his face contorted with fear. "Seeker . . . we're your friends! You have to help us!"

Then Seeker dreamed of the upcoming Feast. Tinker's pale, naked body was strapped down before the altar, bathed in the Gold Circle's throbbing light. Deep slash marks crisscrossed his torso. The Strong Ones descended on Tinker and tore into his flesh. As he was being eaten, his eyes stayed locked on Seeker. His lips moved in slow motion:

Seeker . . . we're your friends . . . you have to help us . . .

With a great crunching of bone, Crusher cleaved open Tinker's chest and wrenched out his still-beating heart. He raised it up before the pack. It thumped feebly in his massive palm. He presented it to Seeker, offering her the first bite.

"Feast, Strong One!" Crusher ordered.

Seeker bit into the meaty flesh and tasted hot blood coating her tongue. Around her, the pack rumbled and shuddered with blood fever and jealousy. Revulsion churned in her gut. Seeker wanted to spit it out, but it felt like some outside force was controlling her. Instead, she gulped it down and kept feasting until Tinker's eyes went dead like two bottomless pits, and his blood turned gelatinous and cold.

But still his lips moved. They mouthed words:

We're your friends.

Your dead ones.

You ate us—

Seeker bolted awake. She was panting hard, and her heart was thrashing around in her chest. She retched twice, spewing the contents of her guts. Then lay back in her own sickness and trembled uncontrollably. The nightmare was still fresh in her mind. She thought about trying to help Tinker. But how would she do it?

The Strong Ones were guarding the Black Mines, and she was no match for them physically. She also didn't have much time left. Crusher had already taken Kaleb away for the Feast. It wouldn't be long before they moved on to Tinker.

For a brief and crazy moment, she considered trying to gather the Weaklings together. But they weren't united in any way. They couldn't even be considered a pack really. They skulked in the shadows and did the Strong Ones' bidding. They were too afraid to stand up to their tormentors.

Seeker whimpered softly. She'd never felt more like a Weakling—more useless and scrawny—than she did right now. She remembered the Strong Ones dragging Tinker away, and how she didn't help him. Suddenly, the last thing he said shot through her head:

The Beacon . . . get the Beacon!

Of course, Tinker's message meant nothing to Crusher and the Strong Ones. But it meant something to Seeker. She peered around the room at the slumbering pack. Was she really going to do this crazy thing?

Could she risk it?

She glanced down at her forearm with the scabbed over slash marks. *I'm a Strong One now*, she told herself, *no matter what the rest of the pack thinks*. With Tinker's voice still fresh in her mind, she found herself doing something deeply forbidden. She crept over to the altar and let the green light wash over her face. She moved her hand closer . . .

. . . and closer . . . and closer . . .

Her mind was made up. There was no going back now.

PART IV

THE GOLD CIRCLE

To light a candle is to cast a shadow.

—Ursula K. Le Guin, *A Wizard of Earthsea*

You forget what you want to remember, and you remember what you want to forget.

—Cormac McCarthy, *The Road*

THE SEVENTH CONTINUUM

. . . The largest of the underground colonies, built into an existing research facility located deep under the Appalachian Mountains. Harvard University originally constructed this laboratory to research new forms of energy technology.

. . . Little is known about their history. At some point during the first hundred years, the colony sustained significant radiation leaks that seeped into their groundwater supply and sickened most of the colonists. Those who were not sickened experienced significant genetic mutations. Tribal warfare broke out over massive food shortages . . .

. . . A few years after the initial radiation exposure, the colony experienced a catastrophic power failure, though the cause remains unknown. Many theories abound, but two have gained the most traction in recent years. One postulates that the radiation leaks damaged the power lines while the other suggests that the lines were intentionally severed during the conflict so that one side could gain a strategic advantage . . .

. . . Regardless of the cause, the colony was plunged into a state of total darkness, which combined with the food shortages, further increased the selection pressure on the population and resulted in even greater genetic mutations . . .

. . . While no formal system of governance existed, they did abide by one of the most primitive laws of nature—*the survival of the fittest*. Thus, the ruling class eventually became known as the "Strong Ones," while those who served them became known as "Weaklings" . . .

—THE NATIONAL OPERATION TO ARCHIVE HUMANITY

Chapter 30
THE BONDING

Seeker

Seeker's hand hovered over the Gold Circle.

She could see her face reflected in the luminous surface—it looked monstrous with exaggerated eyes and elongated jowls. She heard a noise and jerked her head back. The Strong Ones still slumbered around the room. Crusher dozed on his throne, his massive chest heaving with each breath. Seeker listened closely, her ears pricking around, but heard nothing alarming. *Probably just a ratter or a bugger*, she thought.

This was her chance.

She turned back to the altar and laid her hand on the Gold Circle, tentatively at first. Her fingers connected with the metal. She cringed, expecting to be struck dead on the spot—or at least—to suffer some degree of excruciating pain.

But. . .

Nothing happened.

Seeker peeled one eye open and then the other. The Gold Circle continued to throb with light as if nothing had happened. She'd never been this close to it before and it was mesmerizing—the golden shimmer of the metal, the pulsing of the light, the symbol seared into its surface.

Lightning fast, Seeker snatched the Gold Circle from the altar and took off running. She bolted from the throne room and down the great hall. As she ran, she balanced the Gold Circle in one hand cupped to her chest. It was lighter than it appeared. She tore across the rock bridge and flew into the black tunnels, heading for the one place where she felt safe.

The Gold Circle lit up her cave as she beheld her treasures in the light for the first time. They were glossy and spiky and twisted, but they paled in comparison to her newest acquisition. She sank down on her haunches and inspected the armlet closer. She flipped it over in her palms, her fingers tracing the gentle slope of the metal—

Suddenly, the Gold Circle flashed with blinding light and split open in her palms. It took a moment for Seeker's eyes to recover from the blast of light. At first, she worried that she had broken it, but then she understood.

"The Beacon . . ." she whispered, speaking its true name for the first time.

In one smooth motion, she latched it around her right wrist. With another flash, the Beacon sealed itself around her flesh.

Seeker arched her back and cried out in pain as the device dug its sensors into her skin and then deeper into her central nervous system. Her screams rippled through the cave. It went on for what seemed like forever. But that pain was nothing compared to the pain from a thousand memories that were now invading her brain as the Beacon began to download its archives. The onslaught intensified and swept her away. She traveled through space and time and beheld the wider world as she never had before.

And that was how Seeker—the Weakling turned Strong One—the one who hunted on the Brightside—became the Carrier for the Seventh Continuum.

o   o   o

Seeker experienced the horror of everything that had come to pass.

She witnessed the harried evacuation of her people from the surface as news of the Doom spread like wildfire and the secret notifications went out. She saw everything as if she were looking through somebody else's eyes.

The first Carrier, she realized.

She caught sight of her reflection in the smooth door of the elevator. She was a boy of no more than eleven. She tasted the brittle acidity of adrenaline on her tongue and clung to his mother's leg—*his mother*. A prim woman in a powdery blue dress with her hair pinned back into a bun and more wrinkles than the years should have allowed.

His mother was a homemaker. She'd never taken a husband. Never held more than an odd job. Welfare—a dirty word in this world—and food stamps paid her way. She'd gotten pregnant by accident, suffering one lapse of judgment on a trip from Duluth to Chicago to tour beauty schools, and bore the consequences of her slip with as much dignity as her large, devotedly Mormon family would allow.

But she loved her son anyway, despite the shame that his birth brought upon her family. In the evenings, when she placed him into his crib to sleep, she sang songs about *itsy bitsy spiders* and *wheels on the bus going round and round* and *blackbirds singing in the dead of night,* and she called him her *sunshine,* her *fresh air,* her *reason for being.* She named him Jared—*he who descended.* And he had descended, she thought, from heaven.

These memories played out as if in real time, and it was then that Seeker understood why they were stuffed into this crowded elevator. Why they were being whisked miles beneath the obliterated surface of the Earth. The boy's mother was only tangential—a necessary inclusion. It was her prodigy son that they wanted.

Jared's life became Seeker's life as the Beacon fused their consciousnesses together into a single entity. She experienced his life through his senses. The information came at her in a rush, flooding her neural synapses with a blast of noise and light.

Reading adult books and talking in full sentences at eight months old. Playing Rachmaninoff by ear at the tender age of two. Finishing college by nine and a half, and beginning graduate school at the University of Minnesota at ten. He was only three classes away from earning a second PhD in Applied Physics when the Doom came and destroyed everything. Just as the old professor had promised it would when he appeared on their doorstep in Duluth all those years ago.

Dawn had yet to break when Jared heard the noise that would divide his life into before and after—into Before Doom and Post Doom. It woke him from a deep sleep. He drew back the lace curtains that had faded to an oily yellow color and rubbed the starbursts of frost on the windowpane.

Thwump, thwump, thwump.

The transport hovered above their house. A spotlight shot down on their one-story brick home, one of many crammed together on a modest suburban block that dead-ended at a cul-de-sac. Icy snow and leftover Christmas decorations littered the lawns. The transport pivoted toward their yard as the sky rumbled and flashed. The ground shook suddenly and ferociously. Knocked around by the storm, the transport heaved to the ground in one unsteady thrust. Men in dark suits leapt from the transport with guns drawn and stormed their front door. The pounding of the knocker rattled the house.

In the rush to escape, Jared forgot his glasses. Blind and terrified, he had to yell for his mother to retrieve them from his bedside table. They had to leave everything else behind like the bold-faced evacuation orders stipulated, even his precious textbooks. That made him cry like the child that he still was, even though his mounting pile of degrees would have argued otherwise. His mother scooped him up in her trembling arms. He was still small enough to be carried. He had always been small for his age.

"Honey, we all make sacrifices," she said in a strained voice, as she carried him out into the subzero dawn. "Don't cry now. We have to be strong, remember?"

He wondered, as the chill bit into his eyeballs, what would he do without his books? This wasn't a sacrifice—this was hacking off a limb with a rusty blade.

They boarded the transport as the sun broke over the horizon and shed light on the bitter Minnesotan day. Men with guns held back the panicked neighbors who had fled into the streets. Jared ripped off his glasses so they blurred together with their shrieking children and barking dogs. He didn't want to see the ones left behind. He knew—like a cold, hard equation—what would become of them.

Twenty minutes later, the transport deposited them at a port located at a secret military base hidden in plain sight in the middle of breadbasket country, camouflaged by its utter banality—ugly gray utilitarian buildings studded with wire fencing, fading into silos and pastured farmland.

He and his mother were processed by military personnel who were armed to the teeth, and then shoved into a concrete interrogation room and given scant information, which was beyond infuriating. These soldiers didn't care about his credentials. They treated him like he was invisible. They wouldn't look him in the eyes. He wanted to scream at the one-way mirrored window. He wanted to tell them to look at him.

What about all his degrees, adorned with fancy calligraphy and gold stickers, lovingly preserved by his mother in cheap faux-wood frames from the discount store, mounted on the bright blue wall above his bed?

They would burn along with his books.

Everything in the world would burn.

Until there was nothing left.

Jared waited with his mother on the hard, metal bench until the military types buzzed somebody through the door.

The professor strode into the room in a swirl of crimson robes. She was younger than the old man who had come to his house. He felt a subtle stirring in his loins—this woman was striking with her dark skin, sandy curls, and easy smile. A number of years later when he finally reached maturity, he would often wonder if he could have lived a whole other life where he became a professor and married another professor, much like this woman standing in front of him.

The professor retrieved something from her robes. Inside a fist-sized box, nestled on a bed of black velvet, was the Beacon that would weld itself to his goose-pimpled flesh, never to be removed while his heart was still beating.

Still dizzy and nauseous from the bonding process, Jared boarded the elevator with his mother and the other Chosen. He stared at his reflection in the doors as they contracted and entombed them inside the cramped space. While the elevator whisked them into the darkest depths of the Earth, he clung to his mother's leg and cried for everything that they'd left behind. He cried for the world that was burning.

When they exited the elevator, he beheld the Seventh Continuum—which came to be known only as the Seventh—for the first time. It was lit up with artificial light. The centerpiece of the labyrinthian settlement was a huge city that had been carved out of solid rock. They named it Agartha after the mythological city located in the Earth's core. In the middle of the city stood a castle that winnowed into jagged spires. The winding, cobblestone streets were soon filled with people going about their everyday lives—making things, growing things, breaking bread, and living together in amity.

Sure, the Doom caused some problems. In the immediate aftermath, they lost contact with the other colonies. Through the Beacon, Jared caught distant whisperings and had strange dreams of the other Carriers. But they faded in and out like a weak signal, and it was hard to tell what was a dream and what was real. Even so, he knew in his heart that others still endured, and he reported his visions to the Council.

But the Doom could not be forestalled. Not completely.

Radiation seeped into their stone haven. Did it hitch a ride on the air they breathed? The water they drank?

It didn't matter.

Once the symptoms appeared, it was already too late. His mother was one of the first to fall ill, maybe because she worked doing laundry for their neighbors and always had her hands stuck in a bucket of water. She took to her bed and never woke up. He watched as poison from the Doom felled half their population and sickened the rest, and then the power failed, the lights winking out and forsaking them to the darkness.

In the unbroken night of the underground, food shortages mounted and civil war broke out. Delirious from starvation, they turned to cannibalism to feed their insatiable hunger. Some grew stronger, others weaker. The strong preyed on the weak, and a new world was born in the Darkness of the Below.

As seeker watched their history play out, the memories flooding her brain, She learned that her people were survivors above all else. They did what they had to do in order to endure. These unspeakable crimes had been committed so that Seeker could survive until this very moment and fulfill the great destiny of her people.

As her consciousness melded with the Beacon, it stretched beyond the limits of her physical body, beyond the confines of her subterranean world—up, up, up, and away.

Like a flare set ablaze in the throbbing heart of the universe.

Her call went out. It was simple.

Help.

Silence.

A lone signal broadcast to the vast and empty universe.

Somebody help me.

And then . . .

Somebody answered.

I'm here.

He said.

Tell me everything. I'm listening.

And so. She did.

Chapter 31
THE FEAST

Myra Jackson

ulsing, green light invaded the darkness.

Myra woke with a start and blinked hard. Her eyes had grown sensitive in the dark. Her first thought was that her Beacon had come back to life, but one glance at her wrist told her that wasn't the case. Paige was snoring a few feet away, curled up in her tattered jacket on the cold stone floor. The light seemed to tug at her consciousness.

She stirred and stretched her limbs. "Mom . . . do I have to get up now?" she mumbled. "Can't I stay home from school today?" But then she lapsed back asleep.

Tinker sat up next to Myra. He rubbed his eyes and craned his neck toward the light, observant as always. Kaleb was still gone. The visual confirmation of his absence nearly bowled Myra over. Her chest constricted, and she nearly cried out, only clamping her mouth shut just in time.

The light grew brighter, casting rippling shadows across the walls. They shifted and darkened as a figure appeared above the mineshaft.

Myra's first impulse was to scream:

They're coming to take us for the Feast!

But the figure raised a spindly finger to her lips.

Shhhh . . . Seeker mimed with a flash of gold.

Myra bit down on her tongue, choking off the words. Their eyes locked together, and Myra saw the Beacon bonded to Seeker's wrist. Without exchanging any words, she knew what Seeker had experienced.

"You're a Carrier . . ." Myra whispered. "But . . . how?"

Seeker glanced down at her wrist as if surprised to see the device fastened there. "Tinker said—*get the Beacon!* So I took it from the altar while the Strong Ones were sleeping." Her voice was still rough, but her accent had lightened, and she used complete sentences.

Seeker had something clutched in her hand. The jagged metal caught the light. Myra flinched back, but Seeker started sawing at the thick leather straps.

"Watch out," she whispered through the slats. "I'm breaking you out of here."

Myra strained to see into the shadowy cavern that lay beyond the mineshaft. "Seeker, but what about the guards?" she whispered. "Won't they catch us?"

Seeker's lips twisted into a sly smile. "I tricked them! Told them Crusher was starting the Feast without them. They were furious and ran off to the castle. But we must hurry! They'll realize their mistake soon and return with the rest of the pack . . ."

She trailed off, but Myra could see the rest of it in her eyes:

If they catch us, they'll kill us.

While Seeker worked to sever the straps, Myra roused Paige and scooped Tinker up. She felt his warm breath on her shoulder. "I told you Seeker was different," he said in a barely audible whisper. "I knew she would come back."

Myra squeezed his arm. "You did."

One by one, the straps gave way. Seeker shoved the bones aside to create an opening. Myra hoisted Tinker up. Paige followed next, and then Myra. She scrambled through the opening and regained her footing.

This was the first time that she had seen the area in any kind of light. Defunct mining equipment—drills, trollies, concrete mixers, haulers—lay shoved up against the wall. The gears were rusted solid, and everything was covered with dust. The ground itself was pockmarked by abandoned mine-shafts, each capped by a trellis of bones lashed together with leather straps and locked in place by a crude crank system.

"The Black Mines . . ." Myra whispered.

Seeker led them over to their packs, which had been ransacked by the guards. Anything edible had been eaten, mostly dried rat meat and the tarps were gone. But the rest of their possessions—much of it technology that hadn't existed in this world for hundreds of years—had been tossed aside like rubbish. They shoved everything back into the packs, and then Myra and Paige shouldered them and tightened the straps.

"Hurry, friends," Seeker called, waving for them to follow her. She loped ahead, picking her way around the mineshafts that scarred the ground. "This way!"

Seeker darted down a narrow tunnel. Dust obscured the floor, while cobwebs stretched down from the low ceiling, their translucent tendrils flapping in the heated air blasting out from the air vents. It looked like it hadn't been used in a long time.

Paige glanced around uneasily. "Seeker, where are you taking us?" she asked. "We can't go back the way we came. The Door in the Wall is blocked by a boulder."

Seeker scampered back to her. "There's another way out. Abandoned long ago and forgotten by my people. The Beacon will guide us there—but we must hurry."

Myra hesitated, but for a different reason. Though her heart lurched, she forced herself to ask the question. "But what about . . . Kaleb?"

Seeker cocked her head in obvious confusion. "What about him?"

"Is he alive?" Myra asked. Her voice was thick with dread.

"Yes . . . alive," Seeker nodded quickly.

Myra felt a surge of relief, but it evaporated when Seeker

finished. "But not for much longer. The Strong Ones took him. They're preparing him for the Feast—"

Myra seized Seeker by the shoulders. "By the Oracle, where are they keeping him?" she demanded. "You have to tell us!"

"Very dangerous to go back there," Seeker muttered, fidgeting in Myra's grip. "Strong Ones lurking everywhere in the city. Sleeping now, but soon they'll wake up. It's good they have Kaleb! It makes it easier for us to escape—"

"I don't care if there's a million of them!" Myra said, her voice quivering. "Please . . . you have to take us to him. We can't leave him here to die!"

Seeker cocked her head, studying Myra's face. "Would you risk your life to save Kaleb?"

Myra was too choked up to answer, but Tinker stepped forward and laid his hand on Seeker's arm.

"Yeah, she would," he said in his raspy voice. His eyes sought hers in the dim light and held her gaze. "We all would—just like you risked yours to save us."

o   o   o

Moving at a rapid clip, Seeker led them down another tunnel. Unlike the last tunnel, this one appeared well-trafficked. Sizeable footprints marred the ground, leaving no doubt about who frequented this area. *The Strong Ones,* Myra thought with a shudder.

"Hurry, friends!" Seeker called. "This way!"

She bolted ahead on all fours, her hands and feet barely seeming to touch the ground. They emitted only faint scraping noises. Myra began to feel self-conscious about her own clumsy, lumbering gate. They curved deeper into the tunnel, and Myra got a prickly feeling on the back of her neck like they were being watched. But as soon as she whipped her head around, there was no sign of anything lurking in the shadows.

Seeker glanced back. "You won't catch them."

"Them?" Myra said. She strained to see beyond the halo of light cast by the Beacon. Seeker followed her gaze, her lips stretching into a shrewd smile.

"The Weaklings," she explained. "They watch from the Darkness. They see everything that happens in these tunnels. They wait, they watch, and they hunt. They can move without making any sound. The Strong Ones stay inside the castle mostly. They've grown fat and lazy. They rarely come down these tunnels anymore."

"Why don't we ask them for help?" Myra said. "They must hate the Strong Ones as much as we do. They'd probably love to get rid of Crusher and his pack."

Seeker shook her head. She looked sad when she answered. "They're too afraid . . . too weak . . . they're just trying to survive. They can't think for themselves. They won't stick their necks out for us."

"But you did," Myra said. "You bonded with the Beacon and saved us."

"I'm different," Seeker said. "I've always been different. That's how I got my name. I'm always getting into trouble for sticking my nose where it doesn't belong."

"Well, I'm glad you did," Myra said and meant it.

A few minutes later, they reached a divide in the path. According to Seeker, the tunnel to the right led to the rock bridge. That was how they'd entered the city before. But she took them the other way. "Secret back way," she said, flying into the passage ahead. Every time the path split, she paused and muttered to herself, repeating what sounded like a name.

"Jared . . . Jared . . . Jared . . ."

Paige frowned. "What's she doing?"

Myra studied Seeker, listening to what she kept repeating. "Of course," Myra said, feeling a smile spread over her face. "She's using the Beacon to communicate with the last Carrier. He must be guiding her through the tunnels."

They waited by the divide in the path until Seeker arrived at a decision. "To the right," she said and took off down that tunnel. They passed through several more hairpin turns. Seeker consulted her Beacon each time the tunnel split again. The deeper they went, the thicker the layer of dust on the floor became. Clearly, nobody had passed this way in a long time. As they rounded the next bend, the tunnel dead-ended at a solid rock wall. No other tunnels branched off it.

Myra felt her heart wilting. They'd have to backtrack a considerable distance to find another route, and time was running out for Kaleb—and for them, too.

"Great, she took us the wrong way," Paige muttered.

Chapter 32
OPERATING THEATER 1

Myra Jackson

Myra stared at the solid wall where the tunnel ended. A deflated feeling rushed through the group. Paige looked crestfallen, almost to the point of depression, while Tinker buried his head in the crux of Myra's shoulder. But Seeker didn't appear deterred.

"No, this is the right way," she insisted, loping over to the wall. She muttered under her breath, her eyes glazing over and her Beacon pulsing faster. Then she passed her hand in front of the wall.

"Aeternus eternus," she chanted.

As soon as the words left her mouth, her Beacon emitted a dazzling blast of light that flooded the tunnel. The wall in front of them began to dissolve, melting away and revealing a secret passageway. Seeker grinned in satisfaction.

"Told you this was the right way," she said in a low voice. "Very quiet now . . . many Strong Ones lurking in the castle. Don't want to wake them."

They followed Seeker through the passageway, and it spit them out in the heart of the city, near a fountain that burbled with fresh water. Following Seeker, they crept down the winding, cobblestone streets. Without the Beacon to light the stone castle, it had fallen dark but loomed somewhere in the middle distance, watchful and foreboding.

Seeker galloped toward a concrete building that looked like it had a more official purpose than the smaller dwellings that lined the street. A faded cross marked the entrance, and below that a single word was etched:

EMERGENCY

"This way to Kaleb," Seeker said, signaling for them to follow her inside. They stepped through the double doors that must have once been powered by electricity but now gaped open. The first thing Myra noticed when she stepped inside was the smell—musty, faintly antiseptic. A reception desk stood at one end with a skeleton slumped in the chair. The empty eye sockets stared at a computer console with a splintered screen. More skeletons were propped up in chairs or strapped down to rusted gurneys.

"What is this place?" Myra whispered. She ran her hand over the reception desk, coming up with a thick wad of dust. "Why are there so many dead people here?"

Paige's eyes tracked over the hobbled wheelchairs, overturned gurneys, a rusty stethoscope kicked across the room by Tinker's boot. "I'll bet this used to be an infirmary," "That would explain the sick people."

Myra frowned. "Why would they bring Kaleb here?"

"I don't know," Paige said. "And that's what worries me."

Seeker had already crossed the lobby and was headed for the swinging doors at the end of the room. They followed her through them and into a long corridor. Myra stepped over a skeleton still wearing periwinkle scrubs. A stethoscope clung to the knobby vertebrae of its neck. Dimly, she wondered if it still worked. A set of double doors marked the end of the corridor. A crooked sign hung next to them:

OPERATING THEATER 1

Seeker forced the doors open. They swung inward, their corroded hinges letting out a sharp squeal of protest. Light from the Beacon flooded into the room and fell on a gurney in the middle of it. "Kaleb!" Myra gasped when she saw him.

He was completely naked and strapped down to the gurney. All the hair had been shaved from his body, and not very skillfully. Shallow cuts dotted his pale skin—his torso, his scalp, his arms, his legs. But that wasn't the worst part. A jagged symbol had been carved into his chest—two slash marks in the shape of a number:

7

Myra rushed to his side. His breathing was shallow. Blood seeped from his many wounds, pooling on the rotting, stained mattress. A rusty scalpel rested next to his chest. Myra felt his forehead. It was warm and sweaty. He stirred with a pitiful groan.

His eyes popped open and widened. He writhed against the leather straps binding him, his lips curling back—

"No . . . Myra . . . you can't be here! You have to run!"

"Kaleb, I can't leave you," she said, struggling out of her coat and draping it over him. She started untying the straps. "We're going to get you out of here."

Feverish and drenched in sweat, he seized her arm, his fingers digging into it. "Hurry, run! Get out of here, before they catch you—"

The pounding of heavy feet reverberated down the corridor. Myra jerked her head up. Crusher burst into the room, flanked by the Strong Ones. They clutched spears, daggers, and other crude weapons fashioned from sharpened bones. Crusher's eyes snapped to Seeker—and the armlet affixed to her wrist.

"Stinking thief!" he snarled, baring his teeth. "You stole it!"

Seeker didn't cower away. Her Beacon flared urgently.

Myra could tell that it was communicating something—but what? A cunning look passed over Seeker's face.

Time, she mouthed to Myra, *we need more time.*

Before Myra could figure out what she meant, Seeker stood up on her hind legs, and glared back at Crusher. "I may be a thief, but you're a murderer!" she growled. Her eyes swept over the Strong Ones. "You're all murderers! These are people, just like us. We're all the same, Weaklings and Strong Ones—"

"Thief and liar!" Crusher cut her off.

But Seeker didn't back down. Instead, she thrust her wrist in the air, displaying the Beacon in all its glory. "I've claimed the Gold Circle and learned the great and tragic history of our people! I'm the Carrier for the Seventh Continuum—"

"Silence, Weakling!" Crusher roared.

But Myra could sense doubt in the other Strong Ones—it rippled through the pack. They exchanged uneasy looks and muttered among themselves. The Beacon held sway over them. They'd spent their whole lives worshiping it, and now Seeker wielded its power. Crusher could sense it, too.

"You dare challenge the Strongest of the Strong Ones?" he snarled. He clutched a deadly looking pike, not to mention his razor-sharp teeth and claws, all formidable weapons.

"Crusher, you aren't strong," Seeker growled, as the hair on her back bristled. She stalked around in a wide circle. "You're weak and scrawny—"

"Die, Weakling!" Crusher shrieked. He leapt at her and stabbed his pike down with tremendous strength.

Whoosh!

But Seeker was quick and agile. She pulled out her metal shiv, and whirled out of reach, dodging the spear's lethal tip.

Crusher roared in anger and thrust his pike again.

Whoosh!

But Seeker was ready for it this time. She vaulted through his legs and slashed at his upper thigh, drawing a spurt of blood. The Strong Ones formed a loose circle around Crusher and Seeker. To their amazement, Seeker was holding her own against their leader. Crusher thrust his pike. It barely missed her neck, scuffing the floor and leaving a mark. Seeker pivoted before he could recover and clipped his arm with her shiv.

Crusher roared in fury and redoubled his attack.

Whoosh! Whoosh! Whoosh!

This lasted longer than seemed possible with Crusher stabbing at her over and over again and Seeker dodging his blows and pricking him with her shiv. But then Crusher used his brute strength to force her back against the wall. Seeker had nowhere to go—she was trapped. Crusher knocked the shiv from her hand. It skittered away and landed by Paige. The dull metal glinted by her worn boot. Paige's eyes locked on the crude blade.

Crusher raised his pike to strike a deathblow.

"Weakling, now you will die!" he snarled.

In desperation, Seeker lunged for the scalpel that lay on the gurney by Kaleb. But Crusher's fist caught her jaw before she could reach it. Her head smacked the ground with a sickening crack. Blood seeped from her temples and pooled around her head.

This time, she didn't get up.

Crusher rose in triumph, clutching his pike. His fist was slick with blood. He turned to the Strong Ones and let out a triumphant roar. "Strong Ones, what are you waiting for? Seize these Weaklings and take them to the castle for the Feast."

o   o   o

Reaper dumped Myra by the altar. She landed with a thud, her head spinning from the rapid jaunt through the city.

"Bloody put me down . . . let me go!" Paige screamed as Biter carried her into the throne room. She bit into his arm, making him yelp in pain. He threw her down next to Myra. Paige landed on her hands and knees, glaring back at Biter.

A few seconds later, Tinker, Kaleb, and Seeker were deposited next to them. Kaleb was still mostly naked, wearing only Myra's coat, and shivering from blood loss and shock. The Strong Ones formed a circle around them and gnashed their teeth.

Myra wrapped her arms around Tinker. "Close your eyes," she whispered in his ear, smoothing his hair back. "Whatever happens, don't look . . . keep your eyes closed . . . pretend you're back home in our compartment with Papa . . . "

"The Strong Ones prey on the Weaklings!" Crusher roared, thrusting his pike in the air. "These traitors escaped from the Black Mines and stole the Gold Circle. And so we must feast on their flesh and blood. Only the strongest shall survive."

"Crusher, the Strongest of the Strong Ones!" Reaper roared.

"May you grow ever stronger!" Biter added.

In the midst of their blood lust, Myra felt a faint tingling in her wrist. Her Beacon sparked back to life with an explosion of emerald light. It began to pulse faster and brighter. Something was happening—something big. She could feel it. But before she could figure out what it was, Crusher let out a howl that echoed through the room.

"Strong Ones, let the Feast begin!" he roared.

Crusher retracted his body and leapt at Myra. In midair, he raised his pike to strike her down, when suddenly another voice reverberated into the room.

It rang out loud and clear—and utterly certain.

"Back off, foul beast!"

It was accompanied by a shower of golden sparks. Myra looked over and couldn't believe her eyes. And then the battle erupted around her, and she was lost among the clashing of bodies and the cascade of sparks.

Chapter 33
CONVERGENCE

Aero Wright

Back off, foul beast!" Aero yelled as he stormed into the throne room with his Falchion morphed into a broadsword. The heavy blade cut through the air and emitted a curtain of golden sparks. He drove Crusher and the Strong Ones away from Myra and her companions. Wren fought beside him with her talwer, just like old times.

As they wielded their dual blades—his longer and straighter, hers shorter and curved—they set the room ablaze and pushed the Strong Ones back. The Forger trailed behind them with his pack. He rushed over to Kaleb and draped a special heat-generating blanket around his shoulders, and then started tending to Seeker's head wound.

"Die, Weakling!" one of the Strong Ones cried.

He sprang at Aero with a crude spear. Aero dodged the razor-sharp tip and drove his sword into the creature's chest. The Strong One let out a piteous yelp and then went limp. Aero pried the blade out of the ribcage using his foot, turning to face another opponent. Next to him, Wren felled one of the massive creatures with her talwer.

"Strong Ones, fall back!" Crusher ordered.

The surprise attack had caught them off-guard. They weren't used to facing such well-armed and well-trained opponents. The pack retreated and formed a protective circle around their leader, but they'd regroup soon.

Sensing the lull in the fight, Aero risked a glance at Myra—her face in the real world—and almost lost a limb because of it. Reaper swooped in and slashed at his leg. Aero dragged his gaze from Myra and raised his sword to deflect the blow. Aero sidestepped Reaper's attack and called out to Wren.

"Cover me, Lieutenant," he ordered as he had a thousand times before.

"Of course, sir," she replied even as her weak ankle wobbled, throwing her off-balance.

Aero glanced down at it with concern but knew better than to question her abilities. He only prayed the makeshift brace would keep it stable enough for now.

He tore his eyes off Wren and fought his way across the room, whipping his blade through the air and driving the Strong Ones back. Having cleared a path, he stabbed at Crusher. But their leader was more nimble than his hulking size suggested. Crusher twisted away, landing on all fours in a low crouch. He aimed his pike straight at Aero's heart.

"Weakling, you dare challenge the Strongest of the Strong Ones?" he snarled.

Aero circled Crusher, giving his lengthy spear a wide berth. "Well, you're welcome to surrender now and hand over your captives. I only came to retrieve my friends. I've no desire to quarrel with you—"

"Thief and liar!" Crusher roared. "You came to steal the Gold Circle!"

"The Gold Circle?" Aero repeated in confusion It took him a minute to figure out what Crusher meant "Oh right, the Beacon. As it's currently attached to my friend's wrist, I'm not leaving without it—"

Enraged, Crusher jabbed at Aero with his spear. Though it

was rudimentary, it was sharp. The other Strong Ones rallied behind him and advanced on Aero with their weapons raised— spears, daggers, and bludgeons fashioned from bones.

They took up a chant. "Die, Weakling!"

"Right, got it. I guess that concludes our negotiation," Aero said, leaping back and regrouping. "Clearly, you don't want to talk about it."

He continued to dodge their blows and parry back, looking for an opening to take Crusher down, when he heard a scream.

"Starry hell—"

Aero glanced over just in time to see Wren stumble on her weak ankle. She recovered fast—but not fast enough. Reaper's fist connected with her jaw and sent her flying back. Her Falchion slipped from her hand and skidded a few feet away.

Reaper turned away from Wren and lunged at Myra.

"Noooooo!" Aero yelled.

He tried to fight his way back across the room. He slashed at the thick, hairy bodies. But more Strong Ones kept pouring in from the city and streaming toward him. He redoubled his efforts, but it didn't matter. Too many of them blocked his path to Myra—he couldn't get there in time. Helplessness flooded through him like poison.

Reaper extended his claws to slash at Myra when Paige stepped in front of her.

"Leave my friend alone, you dirty cannibal!" she cried. Her hand shook, but her voice held steady.

Aero saw a glint of metal. Paige clutched a shiv in her hand. She slashed at Reaper's neck. The homemade blade connected with his jugular. Reaper howled in pain and surprise as a river of blood spurted out from his neck. With his last remaining strength, he lashed out.

His claws raked up Paige's leg.

Within seconds, Wren was there with her Falchion. She finished Reaper off with one mighty swing, severing his head from his body. But the damage was done. Paige was hemorrhaging from the deep gash in her leg.

"Need to apply . . . tourniquet . . ." she gasped in shock. "Help . . . I'm bleeding out . . . "

"Hurry, she's hurt!" Myra screamed as the Forger rifled through his pack. He produced a strap and belted it around Paige's upper thigh. It eased the blood flow from a geyser to a steady dribble.

Aero battled his way over to Myra, and then he and Wren fought back-to-back in a defensive posture to protect their companions. The bodies piled up at their feet, creating a grisly barricade. But more of the creatures kept spilling into the throne room, drawn from other parts of the city by the light and sounds of frenzied battle. They hurled their bodies at them in a kamikaze assault that seemed designed to wear them down.

Aero decapitated one of them, only to have another swipe at him with a spear. Sweat dripped down his face and pooled around his collarbone. He risked a glance over at the Forger and Myra. They were huddled over Paige's body.

Wren looked over. "Damn it . . . I'm sorry, Captain," she said as her talwer cut through the air, dropping two Strong Ones. "That poor girl . . . it's all my fault."

"Lieutenant, it wasn't your fault," Aero grunted as he morphed his sword into a shield to deflect a dagger. "In case you haven't noticed, this isn't a fair fight."

"Still, I shouldn't have let it happen on my watch."

"Lieutenant, for the last time—it wasn't your fault," Aero said. "It's their fault for attacking us. Now stay focused, or we'll both get slashed to ribbons!"

"Yes, sir," Wren said and knew better than to protest further.

Aero stabbed at the Strong Ones again and again, his arm throbbing with fatigue, but they kept coming. He yelled to the Forger. "Brother, status update on the girl?"

The Forger looked up from tending to Paige. "Captain, she's going into shock!" he yelled back. "Her pulse is weak and erratic. I need to operate right away. We've got to get her back to the ship, or she'll die—"

"Captain, watch your back!" Wren screamed.

Crusher sprang at Aero with renewed fury and stabbed at him with his pike. Aero morphed his broadsword into a shield. The pike skidded off with a clatter. Aero morphed his Falchion back into a sword and drove Crusher back a few precious feet. He surveyed the room, making a quick assessment of the battlefield. The situation was rapidly deteriorating, and there was no way to end this fight quickly.

That left only one option.

He yelled to the Forger. "Brother, we can buy you a head start and then fall back, but you'd better run like hell!"

"But Captain," the Forger started. "We can't abandon you—"

"But *nothing*," Aero cut him off. "Now run, damn it!"

Chapter 34
RUN LIKE HELL

Myra Jackson

"ome on, let's go!" the Forger yelled to Myra and the others, stuffing medical supplies back into his pack and hoisting it onto his shoulders. "You heard the Captain's orders."

Myra felt torn—she didn't want to abandon Aero. Especially not when he'd just found her. She glanced at his tall, muscular frame. His Falchion weaved and cut through the air, fizzling with sparks and lighting up the room. He and Wren forced the Strong Ones back and carved out a path to the door. But how long could they hold them off?

Suddenly, Paige moaned loudly. She appeared to be fading in and out of consciousness. The tourniquet was clamped tight, but her wound was still bleeding. Myra didn't need medical training to know that was a bad sign.

If we don't leave now, my best friend is going to die.

That snapped her into action.

"Here, help me," Myra said to the Forger, seizing Paige under her arms. The Forger grabbed her lower half. They fled from the throne room with Tinker, Kaleb, and Seeker trailing behind them. The sounds of feverish battle chased them down the great hall and out of the castle. Paige moaned again, her face twisted up with pain.

"Not too fast," the Forger said. "If we jostle her, it could rip her leg open more."

"And if we don't hurry, then those beasts are going to slaughter us!" Myra said through gritted teeth. She strengthened her grip and tried to hold Paige steady as they fled down the rutted, cobbled streets. Myra risked a glance back at the castle. It loomed over them like a long shadow, its windows glinting with the light of a thousand sparks.

"Hurry, this way to the bridge!" Seeker called back, sprinting ahead.

Tinker hurried after her while Kaleb limped next to Myra. He was battered and probably in shock, but he was mobile. A few seconds later, they passed under the gates and reached the bridge—a narrow shaft of rock with no railings or handholds.

Seeker clasped Tinker's hand and led him across while Kaleb hobbled behind them. "Careful, friends!" Seeker called over her shoulder. "Very slippery!"

Myra and the Forger went last with their precious human cargo. As they sidled across the bridge, Myra gritted her teeth against Paige's weight. Her arms were shaking from the effort of carrying her. Suddenly, her foot slipped on the slick rocks.

Myra pitched to the left, almost falling into the chasm. But she managed to catch her balance and right herself. The Forger caught her eye and smiled weakly.

"Easy there," he said. "It's a long way down."

"Right, don't remind me."

Seeker, Tinker, and Kaleb reached the other side safely, but Myra and the Forger were lagging behind. The bridge started to vibrate under their feet.

"What's happening?" Myra said and glanced back.

Aero and Wren were sprinting through the city and toward the bridge. They were trailed by Crusher and a horde of Strong Ones. Aero waved his arms frantically at her.

"Hurry, run!" he screamed. "Starry hell, they're coming!"

Myra felt a burst of panic. They were only halfway across the bridge, but it was too narrow for anyone to help them with Paige. Also, they still had to reach the ship. Her Beacon flared—and she caught an image from Aero of their circuitous route through the colony.

"Holy Sea . . ." Myra said. "We're not going to make it."

"Not likely," the Forger agreed with a solemn nod. He didn't look afraid. "It's a long way to the ship. But we have to try, don't we?"

Paige stirred in their arms, her eyes landing on the Strong Ones. They widened, and she squirmed upright. "Myra . . . just leave me . . . I'm slowing you down—"

"Not a chance," Myra cut her off. "We're getting out of here together."

Myra risked another glance at Aero and Wren. They'd almost reached the bridge but only had a little lead on Crusher and the Strong Ones, who barreled after them with ferocious speed. Their footfalls pummeled the ground and rattled the bridge. It sounded like a stampede.

"Myra . . . listen to me . . . you're a Carrier now," Paige said, her voice shrill and feverish. "Who's going to save our colony if you die now? My parents? Your father? Listen . . . even if he operates on my leg, there's still a good chance I'll bleed out. I pledged to the Infirmary, remember? I know what arterial blood looks like."

Myra shook her head. "Shut up, we're not leaving you! You're delirious from blood loss—"

"No, this is the only way!" Paige said as she wriggled from their grip, forcing them to let go or risk falling into the chasm. Behind them, Aero and Wren clambered onto the bridge. The Strong Ones were only about twenty feet behind them—and gaining.

Paige saw them coming. She staggered to her feet, wobbling on her injured leg. Bright red blood leaked from the gash in her upper thigh. "If I do this, they can't get me . . . don't you see? They won't be able to feast on me. It'll be quick and painless . . . "

"Paige, stop messing around!" Myra yelled, reaching for her arm.

But Paige jerked away, falling to her hands and knees. She raised her head up and looked straight at Myra. A twinge of a smile quirked her bluish lips.

They parted, and she spoke softly—

"Good-bye . . . Myra."

Paige summoned the last of her strength. It wasn't much, but it was enough. She only had to shift her weight a little to tip over the edge. She tumbled from the bridge soundlessly. She didn't scream or cry out. Her face looked peaceful. Her hair fluttered like seaweed around her head. Her arms drifted back, curving into a graceful dive. She plummeted like a rock into the abyss, swallowed by the Darkness of the Below.

Chapter 35
I'M NOT LEAVING YOU

Aero Wright

Nooooooooo—" Myra screamed and lurched after Paige.

Aero saw her slipping over the edge as if in slow motion. He recognized the wild look in her eyes. It reminded him of soldiers who had lost their Falchions. *Suicidal tendencies*—the words zapped his brain. He sprinted the last few feet across the bridge. In one smooth motion, he latched his arms around her torso and wrenched her back from the edge just in time. He dragged her across the bridge.

"No, let me go!" Myra screamed, writhing like a feral animal. She dug her nails into his arms, drawing blood. "We can't leave Paige! I have to save her!"

"Your friend is dead," Aero said and slung her over his shoulder like she weighed nothing at all. "But you don't have to die, too. Damn it, I'm not leaving you—"

"Put me down, you barbarian!" Myra screamed, beating on his back.

He tightened his grip on her and continued across the bridge. "You know, where I come from people actually follow my orders," he muttered, glancing up at her.

Myra glared back. "Not where I bloody come from."

Aero gritted his teeth and bore her across the chasm. Myra landed a blow on his kidney. He wasn't injured, and his grip didn't waver, but it did get his attention. He looked up in irritation.

"Starry hell, I didn't come halfway across the universe, track you down in this subterranean hellhole, and risk my life and that of my companions just to watch you kill yourself! It was her time to die—but it's not yours."

"No, it wasn't!" Myra cried, twisting in his grip and threatening to send them both toppling over the edge. "She didn't have to die! It's all my fault. Put me down!"

Wren pulled up behind them. "Captain, I hate to interrupt this lovely little exchange, but we've got incoming monsters. So . . . maybe pick it up a little?"

Aero glanced back. The Strong Ones had passed under the city's gates and were galloping toward the bridge. He shot Wren a helpless look, and then set Myra down and gripped her face roughly in his hands.

"Myra, listen to me closely. Your friend died a heroic death in battle. What more would you want for her? We should all be so lucky. Now snap out of it—or we're all going to die on this bridge!"

Myra looked like she wanted to punch him in the face, or join her friend in the nothingness of the chasm. But something stopped her. Her eyes darted to her little brother. He was waiting for her on the other side. That snapped her out of it. The wild look in her eyes faded, replaced by a look of pure fear. Her pupils dilated with adrenaline.

"Right, let's go!" she yelled and sprinted the rest of the way across the bridge, followed by Aero and Wren. Behind them, the Strong Ones hurtled onto the bridge. It was so narrow that they could only traverse it single-file. That would slow them down, but not much.

They reached the other side of the chasm and ducked into the tunnel ahead. Aero could just make out the glow of Seeker's Beacon as she led Tinker, Kaleb, and the Forger through the winding passage. The low ceiling pressed down on his head, forcing him to run hunched over. He dodged stalactites that shot down at him like spikes.

Ahead, the passage narrowed even more, and the pounding footfalls behind them grew fainter. Aero caught up to Seeker and the others.

"Right, I think we lost them," Aero said, breathing hard and glancing back into the thick gloom of the tunnel.

Seeker looked up with a sly glint in her eyes. "The Strong Ones don't know these tunnels. It should slow them down."

"But they can track us, can't they?" Aero said, picturing their huge eyes and snuffling nostrils. "They'll hunt us down, won't they?"

"Like ratters," Seeker said. "They'll follow our scent."

With that warning, she pivoted and led them deeper into the tunnel. Soon, Tinker grew started to lag behind, so Aero picked him up and swung him across his back, carrying him like a pack. Myra and the Forger helped Kaleb limp along.

"Hey, I'm supposed to be helping you," Kaleb managed weakly.

His breathing was shallow, but Aero could tell that his pride was wounded as much as his body. He could also feel that something important—something thick with emotional cadence—crackled between Kaleb and Myra like electricity.

"You've already helped me plenty," Myra replied and squeezed Kaleb's arm. "Just stay with me, okay? I already lost Paige—I'm not going to lose you, too."

After what felt like an eternity, the passage widened and the ceiling rose away, spitting them out into an airy cavern. But it was a dead-end. No other tunnels branched off it.

"We're trapped," Kaleb said. "There's no way out."

But Seeker shook her head. "No, this is the secret back way out."

"Seeker's right," Aero said, glancing around the cavern and recognizing it. "We came in this way. It was dark, and we were in a hurry, but I'm sure of it."

"Then where's the door?" Wren said, her face lit by the

throbbing glow of the Beacons. "Surely, it didn't just vanish? We came through it less than an hour ago."

"It's hidden," Seeker said. "To protect it."

"Perfect, another magic door," Kaleb muttered. He was leaning heavily on Myra for support. Even speaking seemed an effort for him.

"It's not magic, it's science," Myra said. "Like the Beacons. It must be some kind of built-in security measure. Here . . . help me look for it."

They fanned out, searching for the door. Aero ran his hand over the walls, feeling for any fissures or indentations, but they were smooth and unbroken. Seeker muttered to herself under her breath, asking her Beacon for guidance.

Suddenly, dust sifted down from the ceiling, chased by a few pebbles. And then Aero heard it—

Thump! Thump! Thump!

Faint at first, it started growing louder. "The Strong Ones," Tinker rasped, his eyes darting to the mouth of the tunnel. "They're coming for us."

At the same instant, Aero and Wren drew their Falchions. "Get behind us!" Aero yelled, shifting his weapon into a broadsword. "And keep looking for that door!"

The thumping grew louder and louder. More dust poured down, stinging his eyes and clogging his throat. Aero saw their eyes first—huge and glowing blood red in the light from the Beacons. A second later, Crusher barreled out of the tunnel. Fury wafted off him, hot and deadly. His pack fanned out behind him, as hundreds of the creatures poured into the cavern.

Crusher let out an inhuman roar.

"Weaklings, die!" he shrieked.

Aero and Wren raised their Falchions to fight him.

But Crusher had another target in mind—one that had eluded him in the throne room. He launched himself at Myra, while the other Strong Ones fell on Aero and Wren with spears and claws, overwhelming them.

Myra tried to run, scrambling backward. But her head

smacked the back wall. She was trapped. Desperately, Aero stabbed at the Strong Ones, trying to fight his way free. He morphed his sword into a long pike, hoping it would buy him some extra distance. He lurched toward Myra, but he was a half-second too late. He could only watch the horrific scene unfold as Crusher raised his spear to impale her heart.

"Myra!" Aero screamed.

Chapter 36
THE WATCHERS IN THE DARK

Myra Jackson

Myra heard Aero scream her name.

She detected the helplessness underpinning his cry, and she felt his desperation through the Beacons that linked them. At the exact same instant, Crusher raised his spear in a two-handed grip, aiming it straight at her heart.

She tried to scramble backward, but her head smacked the wall hard. Starbursts danced in her vision. She shut her eyes and cringed back against the wall, expecting to be struck dead, when suddenly—

Crusher roared in pain and surprise.

Myra snapped her eyes open. An avalanche of rocks rained down from the ceiling. Crusher tried to dodge them, but a large boulder struck him in the head. His spear rattled away. His face looked crumpled. Seeing their leader wounded, the Strong Ones turned and tried to flee, but the avalanche didn't let up. Rocks and debris piled up in front of the tunnel, trapping them inside the cavern. They clawed at the barrier, but it didn't work.

Myra pressed herself against the wall to shield herself from the rocks. Thick dust clogged the air, and. It stung her eyes and rubbed her throat raw. She could hear the Strong

Ones' curses and pitiful screams, but then even those fell silent. Gradually, the avalanche tapered off, too.

"Is everyone. . . okay?" Myra sputtered. "Tinker, Kaleb?"

She glanced around and collected assurances from the rest of the group. They were unscathed, but as the air cleared, she saw that the Strong Ones did not share their fate. They'd been buried under a pile of rubble. She rushed over to Tinker and hugged him, scrunching his tiny body into her chest.

"How . . . is this possible?" Aero said. His voice sounded scratchy. "Not a single rock hit us."

Kaleb looked around in wonder. "It's a miracle . . . that's the only explanation," he said with a wet cough.

"No, it's not," Tinker rasped, pointing to the ceiling. "Look . . . up there."

Myra followed his gaze. She gasped when she saw hundreds of eyes peering down at them. The gangly, emaciated creatures clung to the sheer walls or perched on narrow rock shelves. They'd climbed out of the air vents that studded the top of the cavern. They clutched stones in their fists.

"The Weaklings," Myra said. "They came to help us."

Tinker nodded. "They saved us."

One by one, the Weaklings climbed down from the ceiling and assembled in the cavern. Their huge eyes stared out of their shrunken faces. Their withered bodies were hunched-over and adorned with swollen bellies and protruding ribs. They dropped their rocks, disarming themselves.

Myra heard them whispering in gravelly voices:

"Seeker . . . the Weakling turned Strong One . . ."

". . . hunted on the Brightside . . ."

". . . the Carrier of the Gold Circle . . ."

They bowed down in front of Myra and the others. Though they were small, there were hundreds and hundreds of them. They soon filled up the cavern.

"We worship the Light in the Darkness," they chanted as the throbbing glow from the Beacons washed over them. "May the Light never go out so long as we shall live. The Gold Circle protects us."

Myra shifted uncomfortably, fighting the urge to tug her sleeve down and cover up the Beacon. She wasn't used to being, well, worshipped. Aero caught her eye, and she could tell he was suppressing a grin. It made him uncomfortable, too.

"I guess they like us," he whispered in her ear.

"They like our fancy bracelets," she whispered back, holding up her wrist. "And thank the Oracle, or else I'd probably be dead. We might all be dead."

On impulse, Aero reached over and seized her hand. His Beacon flashed brightly, flooding the cavern with light. A hush fell over the Weaklings. Myra felt a shock zip up her arm, and suddenly, her Beacon flared back in response. She glanced down and flexed her fingers. Her muscles rippled under her skin.

"You fixed it!" she said, wrapping Aero up in a hug.

Over his shoulder, Myra saw Kaleb watching them. He was injured and probably in pain. But there was no mistaking the wounded look on his face. Guiltily, she released Aero and backed away.

Seeker rose up on her hind legs. "Amen, Weaklings," she said as the Beacon pulsed on her wrist "You've banded together and overthrown our oppressors. So rise and become Strong Ones!"

The Weaklings glanced around hesitantly as if expecting the Strong Ones to put them back in their places. But then one by one, they rose up on their hind legs.

"We obey the Carrier of the Gold Circle," they chanted back once they were all standing.

"We are the Carriers of the Beacons," Seeker said. "We must journey to the First Continuum now. But we will come back for you and then we shall rise up from the Darkness of the Below and return to the Brightside, fulfilling the great destiny of our people."

"Amen," the Weaklings said. "Farewell, Strong Ones."

They dispersed quickly, scaling the walls and wriggling back into the air vents. The scraping of their claws grew fainter. Myra watched them slipping away, feeling respect blossoming in her heart. The inhabitants of the Seventh Continuum were a people born of the ceaseless darkness, hell-bent on survival at all costs. She was impressed by their ability to endure, even in these barbaric conditions.

"Well, that was lucky," Aero said, morphing his blade back into its default form and sheathing it. His silvery uniform had been slashed to ribbons. Blood seeped from a few shallow wounds. "Starry hell, I thought we were done for."

"Luck had nothing to do with it," Myra said, remembering the eyes peering out of the darkness. "They'd been watching us. They wanted to help, but they were too afraid. It's just lucky they came around when they did."

Tinker tugged at her sleeve. "I forgot to say—*thank you*," he whispered.

She ruffled his hair. "They know . . . and I think they'd probably thank us, too. For giving them the courage to rise up against the Strong Ones."

"Right, now where's this door?" Aero said.

Seeker hurried over to the wall and gestured for Myra and Aero to join her. They stood in a loose semicircle and linked their hands together. Their Beacons flared with light, setting the cavern ablaze.

"Aeternus eternus," they chanted in unison.

Suddenly, a golden door appeared in the wall and started to dilate with a rumble that shook the ground. The liquid metal retracted into the wall, revealing another elevator. The rumbling stopped.

Aero flashed a grin. "How about we get the hell out of here?"

"On your orders, Captain," Wren said with a salute. She helped Kaleb hobble into the elevator. Though it was smaller than the last one, they all fit comfortably inside.

Once they'd boarded, the door contracted, and the elevator began to ascend with gathering speed. Myra felt her ears pop and vertigo rush through her, but it was the best sensation. It meant they were leaving the Seventh Continuum and its eternal darkness at last.

About twenty minutes—and countless vertical miles later—the elevator screeched to a halt, and the door dilated again. Brilliant sunlight burst inside, a narrow shaft that swelled until it filled up the entire space. Myra staggered outside and collapsed to her knees, sucking in the fresh air like she'd been suffocating. The sun beat down through a cloud-dappled sky and warmed her flesh. Her eyes burned with white fire, but she kept them cracked open. This was the Surface, and she never wanted to leave it again.

As her vision cleared, she spotted a silvery ship nestled on the snow-kissed mountainside. It had landed on a high plateau about a hundred yards away. Fresh snow speckled its sleek wings, evidence of the recent storm.

A figure knelt beside her. "Fresh air and sunlight," Aero murmured. His hand rested on the hilt of his Falchion. Through the slashes in his tunic, she could see the rippling musculature of his torso. A tiny scar marked his forehead—a thin sliver of pale, slightly raised skin. He leaned over and matched her gaze. "Never gets old, does it?"

Seized by a sudden urge, Myra buried her head into his chest and cried, both from relief and sorrow. They had survived, but they had lost one of their own. *My best friend*, she thought. The conflicting emotions separated like the parting of the sea—held at bay for a moment—before they broke over her in a torrential wave and swept her away.

"Paige . . . oh, Paige . . ."

She wept and wept, and Aero held her while she cried.

PART V
RECLAMATION

Shall we mourn here deedless forever a shadow-folk mist-haunting dropping vain tears in the thankless sea? Or shall we return to our home?

—J.R.R. Tolkien, *The Silmarillion*

She says nothing at all, but simply stares upward into the dark sky and watches, with sad eyes, the slow dance of the infinite stars.

—Neil Gaiman, *Stardust*

Chapter 37
DEPLOYMENT

The Majors

Contact in *three . . . two . . . one!*" Captain Madden counted down.

Danika heard the pilot's voice in her helmet as the transport touched down, sending ripples cascading through the black sand. She drew her Falchion, morphing it into an *ahlspiess*, and leapt through the bay doors. She landed in a crouch and whipped her head around. Grit flogged her face, and adrenaline pumped through her veins.

The computer readout in the lower half of her helmet displayed vital information:

Location: *Death Valley, Nevada (North America, Earth)*
Temperature: *41 degrees Celsius*
Humidity: 10%
Atmospheric conditions: *Stable*

Once she was sure it was safe, Danika signaled for the two combat units to follow her lead. Sturdy boots landed on the ground next to her and crunched over the sand. The soldiers fanned out over the arid landscape in tight formation. Their Falchions were drawn and morphed into various forms—daggers, swords, axes, spears, pikes, maces, and war hammers. A few unmanned probes sailed ahead of them, hovering a few feet over the ground and scanning for life forms and other anomalies.

As she marched, Danika kept a close eye on one soldier in particular—Zakkay. He swung a scope over the ground, sweat already leaking from underneath his helmet. He came from the deserters' unit, but she had reviewed his psychiatric evaluations. He harbored no positive feelings about them. She wanted to keep him close. He knew the deserters better than anyone and could prove an asset in the right situation.

Once they had swept the area, even the surrounding plateaus, Captain Grimes reported back to her. "Major Rothman," he said with a crisp salute. "No life forms detected. There's nobody here—it's deserted."

"But they were here, damn it," Danika said and sheathed her Falchion. She spit, and her saliva came out black. "Their DNA is scattered all over this blasted wasteland. Our probe was right, though I don't know how they eluded the second scan."

Grimes shrugged off his helmet. His jawline was stained black with dust. "Me neither." He grimaced but it turned into a smile. "Unless they can turn invisible."

Danika snorted. "Unlikely, Captain. I don't know what kind of rumors are flying around the Mess Hall, but Aero Wright is only a man—and nothing more."

Grimes looked uncertain. "What is it, Captain?" Danika said. "Out with it already."

"The deserter . . . carries the Beacon," he said, looking embarrassed for even bringing it up.

Danika ignored that superstitious nonsense and patrolled the area. Her boot nudged something in the sand, unearthing the remnants of a portable stove.

"Look over here," she said, pointing to the stove. "They tried to cover their tracks by pushing sand over their encampment, but they did a poor job. So I'm guessing they were in a hurry." She waved a sensor around, turning up traces of their DNA everywhere. "These scorched rocks are where the escape pod crashed down, and there's blood streaked in the sand. Somebody must have been injured in the crash."

"Which deserter?" Grimes asked.

She ran a quick scan on the traces of blood, and a name popped up. "Wren Jordan," Danika read off the display. "She was the one who was injured."

Grimes stumbled upon something unpleasant a few feet away. "Latrine," he reported with a sour expression.

Danika grimaced at the stench. From the look—and smell—of it, the deserters were camped out here for a while. But doing what?

She paced around, trying to figure it out. Her boot nudged something in the sand. It glinted in the strong glare of the midday sun. She removed her glove and fished it out. It was scorching hot to the touch. *A gasket*, she decided.

"They were stranded here, trying to repair their escape pod." Slowly, as she flipped the hot metal over in her hand, she started to piece together a picture of their time here. "And they succeeded," she added, pointing to a distinct burn pattern in the sand. "This is where they took off."

Grimes recorded images of the encampment while Danika knelt down and sifted the sand through her hands. "This sand appears freshly disturbed, and the wind hasn't had a chance to erase it yet. I'm guessing we just missed them."

"Well, you said they were in a hurry," Grimes said, looking up from his slender recording device. He squinted in the sunlight. "But . . . in a hurry to do what?"

Danika pressed her lips together. "I don't know. Damn it, I wish I did."

She straightened up and looked at Grimes. Droplets of sweat dappled his brow and dripped down his face. It was hot and only getting hotter.

"Captain, have your unit finish searching this area," she ordered. "We need to prepare a detailed report."

"Yes, Major," he said with a salute. "Right away."

"And get me the Supreme General. He'll want to hear about this."

"Anything else, Major?"

She shook her head. "Soldier dismissed."

Grimes saluted again and then marched off. Danika watched him go, his boots kicking up sand as he went. The other soldiers were loitering around the ship, running their mouths and probably gossiping about the deserters. She could see the pilots ensconced in the cockpit, helmets concealing their faces and hands locked on the delicate instruments. Sand swirled underneath the jets, which blasted out terrific heat.

But she didn't head back to the ship and the sweet relief of the air-conditioned cabin. Instead, she ascended a high ridge at the edge of the encampment. The sun beat down on her back ruthlessly as she picked her way over the jagged rocks. She started to sweat heavily. When she reached the top of the ridge, she discovered track marks everywhere.

She crouched down, working to decipher them. Her fingers passed over the rivets in the sand. *Two soldiers . . . sparring on this plateau,* she decided. *Practicing drills with their Falchions . . . keeping their skills sharp and muscles strong.*

The wind gusted harder, kicking up more grit, as her thoughts drifted back to the Agoge with its Drillmasters and endless sparring sessions, first with rubber swords and shields, and then with the real thing after the Forgers bestowed their Falchions upon them. Instinctively, she gripped the hilt of her precious weapon, feeling a surge of power swell up her arm. She unsheathed it and shifted it into an ahlspiess, skewering the sand with the sharp spear. She ran a few drills of her own, trampling over the deserters' footsteps.

She spun, dove, leapt in the air, and landed with a grunt. *Whoosh!*

Her spear impaled the ground with a deadly thrust. Breathing heavily, she peered out over the desolate landscape. No life. No vegetation. Not even a hint of water anywhere.

Just rocks and sand burnt to a crisp by the Doom. Even on the old maps, there hadn't been here. She had reviewed them when she was prepping for deployment.

The venue for her Krypteia had been more inviting than this place, and that was a hellhole of a planet, littered with active volcanoes. But she had overcome the natural obstacles, evaded the soldiers and their blasters planted there, and reached the rendezvous point on time, surviving the final test to graduate from the Agoge.

Only one student had passed his Krypteia with a higher score. She heard the news circulating through the Mess Hall when she returned to the mothership, exhausted and sore but elated. Over their trays, the soldiers gossiped about his unrivaled abilities in Falchion-to-Falchion combat and spread the rumor that Supreme General Brillstein was his father.

A few months after their graduation, when her Connubial assignment papers finally came through, she felt a secret thrill when she saw the bold name of her betrothed:

Captain Aero Wright

The two best students from the Agoge! she remembered thinking. *Of course, they paired us together! What glorious progeny we'll produce for the Interstellar Army of the Second Continuum! Strapping lads and robust girls destined to be soldiers!*

This other future that she had imagined—that she had hoped for and dreamed about—withered and died before her eyes when her betrothed became a traitor. And now a new—and possibly better—future awaited her. Aero had been stripped of his ranking and banished from the Second Continuum, and she was Major Danika Rothman.

No matter what she told herself, an unpleasant emotion still twisted in her gut whenever she thought of him. Though their betrothal had been revoked, it still felt like a black stain on her otherwise pristine record. Just knowing that Aero had escaped with his life and was still out there felt like rubbing salt on a wound—

Beep!

Vinick buzzed her communicator.

That snapped her back to the present, though the uncomfortable emotions stirred up by her memories persisted. She glanced at the sky, watching a few errant clouds drift through the blue nothingness. She felt pure hatred for the deserters, who were fleeing through the heavens like cowards. Her fingers twitched at her Falchion. She wanted to kill Aero. No . . . she needed to kill him and settle this debt once and for all.

She clicked her communicator.

"Sir, they're airborne," she reported. "Deploy the probes."

Chapter 38
A PROMISE KEPT

Myra Jackson

K aleb is out of surgery," the Forger reported.

He peeked his bald head through the door of the escape pod. He wore a blue surgical gown with a matching mask that dangled around his neck. Both were splattered with blood. *Kaleb's blood*, Myra thought sickly. She stopped pacing, barely noticing the well-worn circle that she'd tramped in the snow. Her frayed nerves sent more adrenaline roaring through her bloodstream. Shortly after they escaped from the Seventh Continuum, Kaleb had collapsed and the Forger rushed him into surgery.

That was several hours ago.

"Brother, how'd it go?" she asked. Her tongue felt heavy in her mouth. The Forger regarded her with a solemn expression.

"Considering the extent of his injuries, it went as well as possible. But his prognosis is still guarded," he cautioned. "He lost a lot of blood, and his wounds were badly infected. I had to scrape out the necrotic tissue and pump him full of antibiotics."

She frowned. "Antibiotics . . . what are those?"

"Ancient, powerful drugs used to fight bacterial infections," he explained. "You don't have medicine like that in your colony?"

"In the Infirmary, the doctors have garlic and special herbal pumices," she said, feeling shame creep up her neck at her ignorance. "And the Hockers sell tonics at the Souk, but they're more toxic than medicinal. Factum and Plenus won't touch them."

The Forger covered his surprise with a bob of his head. "In that case, your friend is lucky we came along when we did. Without these drugs, he would probably die."

"Brother, can I see him?" Myra asked.

"He's not out of danger yet. But he's sedated and sleeping, so I don't think a visit would do him any harm. In fact, it might help."

The Forger gestured for her to follow him into the escape pod. Myra ascended the metal staircase, and it retracted behind her automatically as the door closed and the cabin pressurized with a sharp hiss.

Kaleb lay on the gurney in the back of the cabin in a state of deep sedation. He was wrapped in bandages from head to toe, so only his face was visible through the gauze. Tubes snaked in and out of his arms, pulling out fluids and delivering medicines while the monitor by his bedside beeped in steady rhythm to his heart. Some of the medical equipment looked familiar—like the IV lines and needles—but most appeared completely foreign to her, especially some of the complex electronic devices.

Myra perched on a stool and laid her hand on his forehead. It felt warm, but not burning up. That was a big improvement from a few hours ago when he was running a nasty fever. "Brother, when will he wake up?" she asked.

The Forger swished over to the monitors and pressed a few buttons. "I'm not sure, but his vitals look stable." He made a note on a tablet. "That's a good sign. The next few hours are critical, but I believe he'll pull through. He's very lucky he has such a strong heart."

"That he does," she agreed.

The Forger peeled back the bandages on Kaleb's chest to check on the sutures. Myra flinched when she saw the extent of his wounds. His torso was carved up with angry slashes. It must have taken hundreds of stitches to close them.

The Forger noticed her reaction. "Sorry, but that's going to leave scars. Back on the mothership, they could repair it. Alas . . . I'm not trained in plastic surgery."

Myra didn't know what plastic surgery was—or why it would help with his scars—but she didn't want to appear ignorant again. Plus, she didn't care how Kaleb looked. Only that he was alive.

"I'm just thankful you're a doctor," she said instead.

"Oh, I'm no doctor," he said with a good-natured smile. "But I'll take that as a compliment! The doctors back home are far more skilled. I serve in the Order of the Foundry, where we work to produce the Falchions."

Her eyes darted to his strange backpack with its many levers and knobs. She had seen him using it on Aero's Falchion. "You mean, you make weapons?"

"Peacekeeping weapons," he clarified.

"Then how do you know how to do all of this?" she said, gesturing around the improvised infirmary set up in the back of the escape pod. It made their medical facilities back home seem primitive. Not to mention the IV lines snaking into Kaleb's veins and the tidy sutures on his chest. Clearly, they had been sewn by an expert hand.

"All students at the Agoge receive basic medical training," the Forger said. "You never know when you'll be trapped on a battlefield with injured comrades. Well, I guess I always had a knack for it. I planned to join a medical unit after I passed my Krypteia. But that was before the Forgers chose me for their Order, and I left that all behind."

"So Aero and Wren?" Myra said. "They're trained in medicine, too?"

His smile widened.

"What's so funny?" she asked.

"Oh, nothing," he said with a shrug. "I'm not used to hearing their names spoken so casually. Back home, they were Captain Wright and Lieutenant Jordan. It would have gotten me into trouble to call them anything else."

Myra blushed. "Sorry . . . I had no idea."

The Forger shook his head, his bald scalp gleaming under the artificial lights. "Don't be sorry! Besides, I prefer the familiarity. It's nice . . . and well . . . since being banished, they've probably lost their rankings, too." A dark look spread over his face. "But back to your question. The Agoge trains us in many things, including medicine."

She nodded. "That makes sense."

"It does," he agreed. "It saved your friend's life."

o   o   o

Myra sat with Kaleb for another few hours until the Forger kicked her out.

"There's nothing else you can do for him now," he said, nudging her shoulder. "He needs rest more than anything, and so do you. Go eat some rations and wash up in the stream. Neglecting yourself won't help him get better faster."

Myra wanted to protest, but then she caught sight of her reflection in the smooth metal of the wall. Her face and clothes were smudged with dirt and grime and the Oracle knew what else. She probably stank to the Holy Sea.

"Point taken," she said, standing up from the stool and stretching her sore legs. Both knees popped loudly. She hobbled over to the door but then hesitated. "You'll let me know if he wakes up, or anything changes?"

"You'll be the first to know," he replied. "I promise."

With that assurance, Myra stepped out of the escape pod and emerged into the fierce light of the midday sun. The stairs retracted behind her, and the door hissed shut. She blinked in the blinding light. She'd thought it was the middle of the night. How long had she been sitting with Kaleb?

"Hey there, stranger," said a deep voice.

Myra jerked her head around to see Aero grinning at her from where he was sitting with Wren and Tinker. They had erected a campsite with pop-up tents by the escape pod. He and Wren were polishing their Falchions with some sort of silvery cloth. The door to the Seventh Continuum stood about a hundred feet away, set into the mountainside.

"Right . . . hey there," Myra said. Her stomach fluttered, and it wasn't from hunger. She scanned the area but saw no sign of their other companion. "Where's Seeker?" she asked.

"Out hunting," Tinker rasped. "She wouldn't touch those." He pointed to a box of rations, which consisted of prepackaged food that came in two flavors—bland and blander. But they were fortified and nutritious.

"In that case, I'll help myself to hers," Myra said, tearing into a packet and gumming the gluey paste. The Second Continuum may have accomplished many impressive feats, but making palatable food clearly wasn't one of them. She missed Maude's candy and her father's cooking, especially his gingery fish stew flecked with pungent spices and bits of seaweed. The tasteless rations only made it worse.

"How's our patient faring?" Aero asked. He met her gaze with his soft, brown eyes. Since she last saw him, he had donned a fresh tunic and combed his hair, smoothing down the curly locks. "Last time I checked, he was pretty banged up."

Did his gaze linger on me a little longer than necessary? Myra wondered. Before she could decide, he looked away and busied himself with polishing his Falchion.

"Better, thanks to the Forger," she said, finishing off the rations. The sticky paste slid down her throat. "His fever is down, and his wounds are healing. The antibiotics are helping with the infection. But he needs to rest and recuperate."

"Did the Forger say how long it'll be before he can travel?" Aero asked.

"A week at least," Myra said. "It would be dangerous to move him sooner."

Wren frowned. "But Captain, do you think it's wise to stay in the same location for so long?" Her eyes darted to the sky. "I'll wager those probes are still scanning for us. It's not like Vinick to give up."

"I know," Aero said. His hand darted to his shoulder, which still ached from the Mars simulation that had gone horribly awry. "I've got the scars to prove it."

"Exactly, Captain. They found us once, and they could find us again. It's dangerous to stay here for more than twenty-four hours. We should change locations."

"But didn't you hear what I said?" Myra interjected, unable to restrain herself. She shot Wren a hostile look. "Moving Kaleb now could kill him."

"And staying here could kill all of us," Wren shot back. "If that armed probe comes back with its sensor arrays, we may not be able to block it this time. Do you know what a particle-beam blaster can do?" She waved her Falchion in front of Myra to emphasize her point. The razor-sharp edge glinted.

"I don't care," Myra said, glaring back and refusing to back down. "I'm not leaving here until the Forger says Kaleb is strong enough to travel."

The tension hung in the air. Finally, Aero spoke up. He shot Wren a furious look. "Lieutenant Jordan, lower your blade," he ordered. "Remember the oath we took? We don't draw our Falchions on unarmed civilians."

Wren cast her gaze down. "Sorry, Captain," she said and sheathed her weapon. "I guess I got a little carried away. It won't happen again."

"That's better," Aero said. "As for the plan, I'm not willing to risk losing anyone else. There's been enough bloodshed already. The Forger set up alarms to warn us if that probe comes back. In the meantime, we'll camp here until Kaleb is strong enough to travel. Then we'll fly to the First Continuum. Is that understood?"

"Yes, Captain," Wren said and didn't argue further. But from the sulky expression on her face, it was clear that she didn't like it. She stalked over to the other side of the ship, where she started pulling out supplies and reorganizing them, stacking them into neat rows.

Myra shot Aero a sidelong glance. He'd gone back to polishing his Falchion. "So tell me everything, Captain Wright. How'd you find us?"

He laughed at her use of his formal moniker. "For starters, we didn't find you. Technically, it was Seeker who found us."

"Seeker?" she said in surprise. "After she bonded with the Beacon?"

He nodded. "She used the Beacon to send out an emergency signal asking for help. Ever since the storm, I'd been monitoring the Beacon closely for any sign of you. I thought, well, I thought you were dead . . ." he trailed off with a pained expression.

"So did I," Myra said with a shudder, remembering the storm.

"Right, so you can imagine my surprise when I picked up a signal from a different Carrier," he continued, brushing the cloth along the length of his blade. "The signal was jumbled and confusing. Clearly, she didn't know how to control the Beacon very well. But I've gotten better at it, thanks to the Forger's mind exercises. Eventually, I was able to lock onto her location and get an explanation. She told me about how she lured you down to the Seventh Continuum and that the Strong Ones had captured you."

"They were planning to eat us," Myra said. "Did she tell you that part?"

He grinned. "Yeah, she might have mentioned that."

Their eyes met again, and she felt a thrill shoot up her arm. "Anyway, I finally fixed our ship," he said, looking away. "Your instructions got me most of the way there, and then it took a lot of trial and error. You have no idea how many times I crashed trying to get her up and running. It wasn't pretty. Anyway, using the Beacon, I tracked Seeker's signal. And well, you pretty much know the rest. Looks like we got there just in time."

"It *was* just in time."

Their Beacons flared in tandem as everything that Myra had endured at the hands of the Strong Ones passed soundlessly between them—their imprisonment in the Black Mines, the Strong Ones dragging Kaleb away for the Feast, their harried escape. And she saw everything that transpired in the desert, too.

"I swore that I'd find you," Aero said in a husky voice.

"A promise I'm glad you kept."

Myra felt another charge zip up her arm and zap her brain. It was unsettling to have Aero poking into her thoughts, feelings, wishes, and desires—it made her feel naked. *Holy Sea, just get out*, she wanted to scream.

"Sorry...I wasn't trying to spy," Aero said, blushing fiercely. "It's hard to control sometimes. Well . . . actually . . . more like . . . all of the time. Though I kind of enjoy you mentally telling me off."

Myra looked down, even though she wanted to keep staring at him. She wasn't used to seeing him in real life yet. She feared that he was a mirage that would break apart if she didn't pay close attention. He laughed out loud.

"A mirage, huh?" he chuckled. "I can assure you I'm quite real. Here . . . you can pinch my arm." He held it up for her. His muscles flexed under his sun-bronzed skin. But she swatted it away.

"I thought I told you to get out."

Though she said it sternly, they both laughed.

Wren shot them an annoyed look from where she was stacking boxes a few feet away. She stood up hastily, dusting herself off. "Right, I'll leave you two to your weird mind-reading, or whatever the hell you call it. I'm going to check on Kaleb."

Guilt swept through Myra. The sun was already dipping behind the mountains. Over an hour had passed. She had gotten distracted by Aero and almost forgotten about Kaleb.

"No, I should check on him," she said. "I've been away for too long."

"Suit yourself," Wren said with a shrug.

As Myra made her way back to the escape pod, she could have sworn that Wren's eyes were digging into her back. *Probably my imagination*, she told herself. She ascended the stairs and passed into the air-conditioned cabin, where she found Kaleb still sedated and blithely unaware of the tumultuous machinations of the world around him.

Chapter 39
TUBE WRENCH

Jonah Jackson

Charlotte, pass me a tube wrench?" Jonah asked.

His young pledge pulled her nose out of the thick textbook splayed open on the drafting table. The worn spine read—*Fundamentals of Electrical Engineering and Technology*. She had barely made a dent in it. Despite their unorthodox circumstances, Jonah was determined to get her studies back on track. Charlotte crumpled her brow.

"Wait, which one is that again?"

"It's in my tool rig," he said, pointing to the clunky box shoved underneath the drafting table. "Third drawer . . . fourth tier . . . second compartment from the left."

Charlotte tucked her long raven hair behind her ears and rifled through the box. As Jonah watched the young girl and her slender fingers, a burst of sadness constricted his throat. He missed Myra like a knife to the gut—her spunky presence, endless stream of questions, and natural ability at her trade. He even missed her complaining. *Holy Sea, she used to whine about dragging Darius's tool rig around,* he remembered. The Engineering Room wasn't the same without her.

"Tube wrench . . . why do they call it that?" Charlotte asked, jerking him out of his memory. She held up the hefty tool. Her eyes shone with youthful curiosity.

Jonah pushed Myra from his mind and grasped the wrench. "Right, it's used for gripping and turning pipes. See these serrated jaws here? They can be adjusted to grip different-sized pipes."

Charlotte watched while he worked on a pair of pipes, ratcheting them together following the specs that he had scrawled out on a scrap of paper. All around them, Sector 4 was abuzz with former Factum and Hockers laboring to produce the uniforms, food, and other essential items necessary to sustain their uprising.

He barely recognized the Engineering Room anymore. While he had been locked up in the Pen, it had been transformed into a miniaturized, self-sufficient version of the colony, complete with an aquafarm, living quarters made up of bunk beds topped with prickly, straw mattresses, and their infirmary, managed by Doctor Vanderjagt.

A few hours later, when his eyes were blurry from exhaustion, Jonah finished his prototype by soldering the last wires together, connecting them to the power pack, and binding hemp around one end to make an insulated handle. He pushed back from the table and admired how the design from his blueprint had taken physical form.

"The power charge works?" Charlotte asked, sliding her textbook aside and peering over his shoulder.

"Why don't we test it out?" Jonah said and took a few tentative swings, enjoying the way the heavy bludgeon cut through the air. He hit the button on the handle.

With a sharp hiss, an electric charge ran through the length of the club. He pictured the rebels carrying them into battle to fight back against the Patrollers and their pipes.

"It works perfect," he said and grinned.

"It sure does," Charlotte agreed.

Jonah took a few more swings, just for fun this time. *Whoosh! Whoosh! Hiss!* Suddenly, a wide shadow fell over the table. "Nice bludgeon," said a familiar voice.

It belonged to Maude.

Charlotte sat up straighter when she saw the rebel leader. Greeley and three other Hockers flanked Maude. Officially, they were her security detail, but everybody called them the Goon Squad. Behind them, the conference room door gaped open. The Free Council members were filtering out into Sector 4.

"Bloody look at the Engine Rat," Greeley chuckled, ribbing the bearded Hocker next to him. "Thinks he knows how to fight the 'Trollers!"

The rest of the Goon Squad guffawed.

Jonah lowered the club. He felt silly for waving it around like a fool. What did he know about fighting? He was an engineer, and his place was behind this drafting table, not on the frontlines of an uprising.

"Better than you, Greeley," Maude said, shooting him a disapproving look. Her eyes snapped to the weapon. "These ought to give the 'Trollers some trouble."

"Yes, Maude," Jonah said, but then he remembered the protocol. He jumped to his feet and saluted her. "I mean . . . yes, Chief!" he corrected himself.

Maude returned the salute. "Drown the Synod," she said, parroting the required response. Then she turned to the Goon Squad. "Hang back and give us a few."

"Yes, Chief," Greeley said with a reluctant salute. He shot Jonah a suspicious look but knew better than to disagree with Maude. He signaled to the others, and they withdrew, but stayed within earshot.

Maude fixed Jonah with a conspiratorial look.

"Relax, sweetheart," she said. "That saluting and Chief nonsense rallies the troops, and it's good for morale. But it makes me feel bloody ridiculous."

Jonah relaxed a little. Truthfully, he had been on edge ever since he got here. The Hockers—*former Hockers*, he corrected himself—ran the show and outnumbered the Factum two to one. They were supposed to set their prejudices aside along with the old class system, but that was easier said than done.

"So . . . how are you feeling, sweetheart?" Maude asked, "Did Doctor Vanderjagt patch you up?"

"Much better," Jonah said. "Though still a bit sore."

That was the truest answer that he could give. His body—especially his back—was still an ugly patchwork of bruises and scabs. Not to mention the three cracked ribs that ached every time he so much as coughed. But he was healing from his ordeal, slowly but surely. Maude studied him closely as if assessing his condition for herself.

"So the doc informed me. You're healing well, even I can see that. And I'm not just talking about physically." She tapped her temples. Jonah felt his cheeks coloring. He wasn't used to people talking about his mental condition.

"Some folks never recover from being tossed in the Pen," Maude went on. "The darkness, the starvation, the beatings, the psychological torture. I knew you'd come through it, but not everyone on the Council was sure. They wanted to observe you first."

"So it wasn't my imagination?" he said, remembering the Hockers posted by his infirmary bed, trailing him in the corridors, lingering by the drafting table while he worked, even watching him in his bunk at night. "They were spying on me."

Maude coughed lightly and turned to the girl who was pretending to be studying her textbook. "Charlotte, sweetheart. Why don't you fetch me some sweet tea? My throat's feeling a wee bit parched."

The girl snapped to her feet. "Yes, Chief!" she chirped with a salute. Nervousness rippled over her face. Then she darted off, snaking her way through the busy sector.

Maude's eyes followed her. "Clever lass, that one."

"Charlotte was my pledge from the last batch of graduates from the Academy," Jonah said. "The Surfacers are lucky to have her. Roland, too. He was my other pledge."

"Ah, darling little Roland Feder," Maude said. "He's assigned to Farming today. Not sure if you knew, but for all intents and purposes, they're both orphans now. Their parents were pledged to Records and Dissemination. They sided with the Synod. It's a shame we couldn't bring them over."

His face fell. "I'm sorry to hear that . . . I didn't know."

"Let me see that bludgeon," Maude said, picking up the prototype from the drafting table. She raised her eyebrows when she felt it. "It's a bit heavy, no?"

"That's the point," he explained. "Does more damage that way."

She nodded and swung the club, testing out its heft and scope. For an older woman, she exhibited surprising speed and strength. "It does have a rather bonny feel about it." She pointed to the insulated handle. "What's that button for?"

He shot her a sly look. "Push it and find out."

She hit the button—*Hiss!*—then looked up in surprise. "Is that what I think it is? The club is . . . electrified?"

He nodded, and she looked impressed. "Well, I'm glad we busted you out. You're an asset to our cause." She set the club down. But then she lowered her voice. "To be perfectly honest, I have an ulterior motive for talking to you."

Jonah felt nervousness coalesce like a hard pit in his stomach. "Really? Like what?"

"You're needed at the next meeting."

"You mean *the* meeting?" he said, his voice belying his excitement. Refugees showed up at their door every day seeking asylum, and rebels returned bloodied and wounded—and sometimes dead—from secret missions at all hours of the night, only to be rushed back to the infirmary by Doctor Vanderjagt. But apart from those clues, he was still very much in the dark about what was going on outside the Engineering Room.

"The one and only," Maude said with just the barest slip of a smile. "The Free Council convenes tomorrow at noon in the conference room. I'll expect you there."

"Yes, Chief," Jonah said and saluted, but then he remembered her admonishment and dropped his hand. "I mean . . . Maude."

She smirked, but it faded. She lowered her voice even

more. He had to strain to hear over the hissing and wheezing of the machines. "Don't be late, or it could cause trouble with the other members."

"What kind of . . . trouble?" he whispered back.

She glanced over at the Goon Squad. Their massive forms couldn't be missed. They were huddled together—the four of them—telling bawdy jokes. Their ribald laughter echoed through the sector. Jonah followed her gaze to them.

"You mean . . . with Greeley and the others?" he asked.

She frowned. "Let's just say . . . not everybody is happy you're here. Some think I wasted precious resources breaking you out of the Pen. Several loyal souls lost their lives carrying out that mission."

"Royston," he said in a pained whisper.

Regret cut across her face, too. "And three others—Trenton, Gosling, and Whitley. Though I doubt you knew them, being that they were Hockers."

Jonah cringed with guilt. "I can't say that I did . . . but I'm very sorry for your loss. Royston wasn't just my coworker . . . he was also my best friend."

"So he told me when he volunteered to lead the mission," she said, swirling her hand over her chest. "The Holy Sea have mercy on their souls."

Talking about Royston made Jonah remember what had driven him to conspire against the Synod in the first place.

"Maude, there's something I have to tell you," he whispered, glancing around nervously. "I wanted to tell you sooner, but I was cooped up in the infirmary . . . and you always seemed to be tied up in meetings . . . and well . . . I didn't know who I could trust." He took a deep breath. "It's about the Animus Machine—"

Beep!

The sector door dilated and a group of rebels stormed inside, carrying one of their injured comrades. Blood gushed from his head, damage from the Patrollers' pipes. "Help, fetch the doctor!" one of the Surfacers yelled.

Doctor Vanderjagt sprinted over to the wounded man.

She took one look at him—and his serious head injury—and yelled for a gurney. The rebels heaved the man onto it, and then they wheeled him to the back of the sector.

"Chief!" Greeley yelled to Maude over the chaotic chatter that had overwhelmed the sector. "Pratt needs to brief you right away!"

"Sorry, I have to go," Maude said, raising her hands helplessly.

"But when can we talk?" Jonah hissed. "It's important."

"Tomorrow," she said, already backing away from him. "In the Free Council meeting. That way you can bring everyone up to speed at the same time."

Maude spun around before he could say anything else. She signaled to the Goon Squad. They marched through the Engineering Room, picking up salutes and shouts to "Drown the Synod!" as they went, and then disappeared into the conference room with Pratt. The door slammed shut behind them and locked with a satisfying click.

Chapter 40
A PRAYER FOR THE DEAD

Myra Jackson

That night, Kaleb woke up and ate actual food, not just the liquid nourishment the Forger had been pumping into his IV. "This tastes like dirt," he mumbled through a mouthful of rations. "But it's the best dirt I've ever tasted," he added, squirting more grayish sludge into his mouth. Myra shot him a disapproving look from where she sat on a stool by his bedside.

"Not too fast, or you'll make yourself sick," she said, but then she softened her tone. It was a relief to see him talking and eating again. "Makes you miss sweetfish, doesn't it?"

His eyes glazed over as his thoughts drifted back. "And Maude's triple ginger cookies. Grilled fish skewers. Sweet rice porridge. Even those stinky fish rolls."

"You mean the ones from Greeley's booth?" she said, picturing the enormous Hocker with an overgrown black beard and questionable personal hygiene. The bitter, fetid taste made her nose scrunch up. "What were they stuffed with again?"

"Fermented mackerel," he said with a grin. "And yes, I even miss those. And everything else that the Hockers traded at the Souk."

"Firewater?" she asked with a cock of her eyebrow.

"Well, that stuff tastes like bloody poison."

She laughed. "Yeah, but nobody drank it for the taste," she said, remembering the alcoholic brew that Maude cooked up on the side and traded illegally. "It burned like hell on the way down, but it made you forget your troubles for a spell."

"True enough," he said, taking another big swallow of rations despite her disapproving look. "Until it wore off and left you with empty pockets and a splitting headache. That's why I never had more than a few sips, despite Rickard hounding me."

Myra wanted to keep up the cheerful banter. It was good for Kaleb's spirits. But the mention of Rickard caused her lips to spasm into an involuntary frown. Kaleb met her gaze and held it. Their shared history hung in the staid air of the escape pod.

A million gleaming memories spiraled through her head. She remembered strolling through the Souk before school with her friends, trading for sweetfish from Maude's booth, and Kaleb cornering her in the corridors after school and stealing kisses while Rickard kept watch for the Patrollers and Kaleb's father, who sat on the Synod and disapproved of their courtship. Though they weren't linked by the Beacons, other things connected them just as deeply.

Myra leaned over and clasped Kaleb's hand. "I'm glad you're feeling better," she said and squeezed it.

A smile broke over his face, and a little color found its way back into his cheeks. He looked healthier than he had in weeks. "That I didn't kick it, you mean?"

"Exactly, Sebold," she said with a teasing lilt to her voice.

He struggled into a sitting position. "Sorry to disappoint, but I'm afraid you're stuck with me, Jackson. I'm not planning on going anywhere anytime soon."

For a second, Myra lost herself in the verdant depths of his eyes. He leaned in closer. The moment elongated, enfolding them in its embrace, as neither of them moved to break it. She found herself holding her breath in anticipation of—

Smooth lips, darting tongues, roving hands.

Suddenly, her Beacon flared—and she caught a vision of Aero outside the escape pod, stowing supplies in a watertight case, and simultaneously Seeker tearing through the snow-covered passes in pursuit of some feral creature, and she knew that this intimate moment with Kaleb wasn't private at all. In fact, it would never be private again, as long as she was bonded to the Beacon and there were other Carriers in the world.

She jerked away from Kaleb before their lips could touch. "You need to rest," she said, forcing him back into a reclining position. "The Forger's orders, remember?"

"Aye, Jackson," he said with a joking salute. Then with the empty tube of rations still clutched in his hand, he drifted off to sleep, lulled by her presence and the powerful drugs dripping into his arm and keeping the pain at bay.

The Forger was right. He was still weak. It would be a few more days before he could travel. She peeled his fingers back from the metal tube, setting it aside, and tucked the blanket under his chin, careful not to disturb his IV line or the thick layers of bandages lining his chest.

She laid her hand on his forehead to reassure herself. He didn't have a fever anymore. She breathed a sigh of relief. The Forger's medicines were working miracles in his broken body. She stroked his clean-shaven head, feeling the prickly stubs of hair starting to grow back. For a moment, she focused all her energy on pushing back against the Beacon, hoping to shroud her thoughts. It fought her at first, blazing brighter and faster, but then she overpowered it. The pulsing settled back into a gentle rhythm.

Myra leaned over and kissed his lips. Then she shifted to the left. Her lips brushing his earlobe. She spoke softly, though she knew that he couldn't hear it.

"Sleep well . . . I'm here . . . I'll always be here . . . I promise."

o   o   o

Once it was clear that Kaleb was asleep and wouldn't wake for several hours, Myra left the escape pod to search for Tinker.

In her rush to care for Kaleb, she had been neglecting her little brother. She checked the campsite first, and finding it deserted, followed a set of footprints that meandered through the snow. They led around to the back of the ship, where she caught Tinker trying to pry a panel off the engine with a screwdriver.

She set her hands on her hips. "Tink, what do you think you're doing?" she said, deploying her best parental scolding voice. He jumped and dropped the screwdriver.

"Sorry . . . I couldn't help it," he rasped. His cheeks flushed crimson. "I wanted to see how it works. Aero said it flies through the air . . . like the birds."

She dropped her stern expression and picked up the screwdriver. "If you're good, I'll have Aero show you the cockpit later. But the ship is working fine right now. The last thing we need is for you to mess with it."

His eyes lit up. "Promise? He'll really show me?"

"I'll make sure of it—but hands off until then. Do we have a deal?"

He nodded vigorously. "By the Oracle, I swear it."

The sun was just beginning to dip, signaling that afternoon was wearing on, but a bit of warmth still lingered the air. Suddenly, Myra's legs ached to carry her somewhere. All these days of sitting around in the escape pod had taken their toll.

"Want to go for a walk?" she asked.

Tinker looked torn. His eyes darted to the escape pod. *He doesn't want to leave it*, she realized. *It's like his friend.* She wondered if it had replaced his computer as his favorite object. But then he dragged his gaze away.

"Sounds good, I guess," he said.

o   o   o

Following one of the many trails that Seeker had tramped in the snow, Myra and Tinker hiked up a steep ridge and settled on a cluster of knotted boulders, overlooking the valley below. Long shadows clawed at the earth. Soon the daylight would dwindle, bringing a bitter chill that would whistle down from the toothed peaks. Their time here had a firm limit.

"Tink, I know I've been preoccupied with Kaleb," Myra said, hating the uncertainty in her voice. "But I've been meaning to talk to you about Paige . . ."

Tinker looked puzzled. The setting sun lit up his fine blond hair, making it shine like filaments of gold. "What about her?" he asked. "She's dead like Mom."

She was unsurprised by his blunt appraisal of the situation. Emotions didn't seem to affect him the same way as other people. She wasn't sure if it was a result of losing their mother so young or simply another quirk of his brain's peculiar wiring. Or maybe both.

"That's true," she replied evenly.

"Paige isn't coming back either," he added. "That only happens in fairytales like the ones Mom used to tell you."

They lapsed into silence with only the sound of the wind whipping through the passes. Myra zipped up her coat. "Tink, tell me the truth. Are you okay?"

"Yup, I'm fine. I miss Paige. She always listened to me. She was nicer than most girls. And she was really pretty." He glanced at Myra. "But you're not okay . . . are you?"

Myra thought that she had already cried a lifetime of tears into Aero's chest, but more came bursting through. "No . . . I guess not," she said with a sniffle.

He watched her with detached curiosity. "It's not your fault. You didn't make her come. You didn't make her come. She wanted to come. Paige would have hated you if you'd left her behind.

Myra swiped at her tears, but it didn't staunch the leak. "If only I'd done things differently . . . not taken us into the mountains. I made so many mistakes . . ."

Tinker tilted his head. "Of course you did. We all do. Nobody's perfect. Not even computers. They can have programming errors or get overheated and shut down."

She nodded, but she didn't believe it. Not really.

He sighed when he sensed her mood. "Fine, I'll say it out loud."

"Say what?" she asked.

"I forgive you."

"That's crazy . . . you don't need to forgive me."

He shook his head in exasperation. "You're not listening! Close your eyes. Shut them tight. And no peeking." He waited for her to follow his instructions before he spoke again.

"It's not your fault—I forgive you."

His words broke over her like a wave beating up against the shore. She was seized by a sudden urge. It was out of character, but she didn't care. It felt right.

"Want to say a prayer for Paige?" she asked.

"A prayer? Like back home?"

She nodded, and Tinker thought about it. He gnawed at his lower lip, pushing the blood out of it. "We don't have her body . . . and the ocean is far away. We can't send her to her final resting place in the Holy Sea."

"I know, but a prayer still might be nice."

"I guess . . . we can try it."

"You want to start?"

He swirled his hand over his chest and bowed his head. "By the Oracle of the Sea, please cleanse our friend Paige of sin and deliver her body to the sacred waters of the Holy Sea. We are one people, united under the Holy Sea, forever. Amen."

"Amen," Myra repeated. "Now close your eyes and picture her body wrapped in crimson cloth. Imagine that we're parading through Sector 5 in a funeral march. You, me, Dad, Kaleb, Maude, Rickard, Royston, the Bishop twins, her parents . . . all of us."

"I can see it," Tinker said. "It's really happening."

"The Red Cloaks are walking in front of us in their robes, waving thuribles of incense. It smells funny and stings our eyes. Now we're passing through the corridors, heading for Sector 8 and the Docks. We're placing her body into the first portal. The Head Priest is pushing the button, and saltwater is gushing into the chamber."

"Good-bye, Paige," Tinker said with his eyes shut.

"Good-bye," Myra repeated softly and hugged him, as her eyes glazed over with tears. She brought Tinker here because she thought that he needed to talk. But now she realized that she was the one who needed it. She squeezed him tighter, muttering her thanks into the wind-chilled crown of his head.

Chapter 41
THE FREE COUNCIL

Jonah Jackson

A ll present at this assembly of the Free Council are sworn to secrecy, by the families you love, the firewater you swill, and above all else, the equality in whose name you fight." Maude's voice, which in the past had always been full of jolly swagger, now came out utterly serious. In her starched uniform, she looked every inch the rebel leader.

"Here, here!" came the response from the Council, a mix of former Hockers and a few Factum, including Greeley and the Goon Squad. The rebels pounded the table with their fists. Several downed swigs of firewater, slopping it onto the table. The ceramic jug wound its way around the room from mouth to mouth, from rebel to rebel.

Jonah wasn't sure if he should pound on the table, so he gave it one half-hearted slap. The atmosphere in the conference room was raucous and lively, very different from the staid deliberations of the Synod or the stilted rituals of the Church. It reminded him of the Souk, except they weren't bartering for homemade goods—they were planning a rebellion. The jug landed in front of him. He popped the cork and took a small nip. It still singed his throat and made him sputter. Greeley shot him a suspicious look.

"Greedy Factum," he muttered, elbowing the Hocker next to him. It was a common slur.

Jonah shifted uncomfortably in his chair. His eyes snapped to the hand-painted symbol covering the back wall—a blue fist with the index finger pointing up. Despite their shared aversion for the Synod, Jonah wasn't sure he belonged here.

Maude shot Greeley a look and banged on the table for quiet, overturning cups of firewater. Fumes from the potent brew wafted over and made Jonah's eyes sting.

"I hereby call this meeting of the Free Council to order," she said, unfurling blueprints of the colony. They covered the entire length of the table. Jonah recognized them as having been filched from the files in his office. They were marked up with red pen, showing secret raids and missions, and casualty figures on both sides.

He scanned them quickly. From what he could tell, the Surfacers appeared to be taking heavy losses with every raid, while the Synod was still alive and well, barricaded inside their chambers in Sector 6.

Maude frowned at the plans. "I'm sorry to report that last night's raid on Sector 6 didn't go as planned. Our battering ram didn't even make a dent in the door—"

"Enough with these measly little raiding parties," Solomon Pratt cut her off, stabbing his finger down on the table. He was a former Hocker who sold medicinal tonics at the Souk. His arm was bandaged from a shoulder wound, probably sustained in last night's raid. His eyes swept over the table. "Let's make a full assault on Sector 6."

So that's what they were doing, Jonah thought, remembering the injured rebels returning to the Engineering Room last night. *They were trying to breach the Synod's chambers.*

Around him, the table erupted with angry shouts and more table pounding that overturned more cups. "Pratt is right! Drown Flavius! And the Red Cloaks!"

"Those lying prigs!"

Maude banged on the table for quiet. "You fool, we've already dispatched three raiding parties to Sector 6." She pointed to the area on the map with the heftiest casualty figures. "Last night, only four came back alive. The 'Trollers are guarding the corridor around the clock. Even if we could get past them, we can't open that sector door."

"More people, that's what we need," Pratt said to cheers of support. "Let's arm them with the new weapon prototypes. Throw everything we've got at them."

"More people won't open that door," Maude said, staring Pratt down. She pointed to Sector 6 on the map. "It's locked and sealed to prevent a water leak. We need the code to unlock it, and that's in Records. Otherwise, we'll just get bottlenecked in the corridor again and the 'Trollers will slaughter us."

The debating continued fast and furious, along with the cursing and table pounding. Pratt suggested breaking into Records in Sector 9 to get the code for the door, but Greeley objected, saying that was impossible.

"After the Synod's chambers, Sector 9 has the highest level of security protections. We'll never get in there."

Jonah felt his head spinning as he tried to keep up with the rapid exchange. He glanced at the Bishop twins, who were sitting next to Maude. He was surprised that children— only about Tinker's age—were included in such a high-level meeting. He worried it was yet more evidence that the rebels didn't know what they were doing.

"I say we filch the Oracle from the Church," argued Jude Crofter, a former Factum from Janitorial, prompting some Hockers to swirl their hands over their chests. "Toss it back in the Holy Sea."

"Are you dimwitted?" Greeley said, taking a swig from his cup. "The Red Cloaks moved it to the Synod's chambers to protect it. And we can't get in there, remember? Besides, the Oracle is a piece of rubbish. It's not holy or sacred—they just use it to control us."

This prompted much disagreement, and more swearing and hand swirling. Despite their hatred for the Red Cloaks and the Church, their superstitions ran deep. Maude had to bang on the table to restore some semblance of order. It didn't work, not really.

"Let's hit Farming in Sector 7," Greeley suggested, pointing to the area on the map. "Cut off the Synod's supplies. Let them see what it's like to go hungry for once! That'll smoke them out of Sector 6."

Maude shook her head. "It won't work. We got intel from the Farming defectors who showed up last week. The Synod has stockpiles of rations, enough to last six months. That's their plan—to hide out in their chambers until we lose support or give up."

If that's their plan, then it's a good one, Jonah thought as he watched the Council meeting devolving into chaos. Pratt and Greeley were now screaming at each other, both red-faced with spittle flying. Jonah glanced at Maude, but she didn't appear concerned. She sat at the head of the table, sipping firewater and listening to the quarrelling.

Jonah's head started to pound. He had seen enough—he couldn't take the screaming anymore. He bolted up from his chair and pounded on the table.

"Shut up! Bloody shut up! Both of you!" he bellowed. His outburst was met with shocked stares. Even Greeley looked caught off-guard by it. "Listen, it doesn't matter if you raid Farming or Records. So you can stop yelling about it—"

Greeley shot up from his seat and towered over Jonah with every inch of his six-foot frame. "Maude, where did you dig up this coward? We should have left him to rot in the Pen!"

Maude leveled him with a withering look. "Greeley, sit your arse back down and let him speak! That's why I invited him here, isn't it?"

Once the big man had been cowed into silence, she turned back to Jonah. "Why doesn't it matter?" she prompted.

All eyes jerked to him. For once, the room was quiet, aside from the slurping of firewater and the soft rustling of the vents. He took a deep breath to calm his nerves, painfully aware of how much the air quality in the colony had already dropped.

"None of this matters anymore," Jonah said as he swept his hand over the map with its detailed reports of raids and casualties. "It doesn't even matter if we overthrow the Synod and take back the colony and put them all out to sea."

Disgruntled grumbles rumbled up the table. "Cowardly Factum," Greeley cursed, but Jonah plowed forward before the meeting could disintegrate again.

"The truth is . . . we're all going to die," he said. "In about six months, based on my calculations. Every last one of us—Factum, Plenus, and Hocker alike."

Shocked silence descended over the room. Pratt blasted him with an irate look. "What . . . do you mean?" he demanded. "Is this some kind of sick joke?"

Jonah glanced at Maude for reassurance, but she seemed to be absorbing this news the same as the rest of the Council. He fumbled for his cup and took a big swig. He needed the liquid courage. "I wish it were," he said as the brew seared his throat. "The Animus Machine is breaking down . . . and I can't fix it. Whatever knowledge we had from the Founders was destroyed in the Great Purging. The oxygen levels are already dropping. Remember the long lines at the Infirmary? And the orange flags and allergen warnings? It wasn't a pollen leak making everyone sick, though that's what the Synod wanted us to believe. It was *hypoxia*."

Stunned faces stared back at him. Maude was the only one who maintained some composure. The wheels were turning in her head as she pieced everything together.

"Jonah, who else knew about this? Obviously, the Synod knew. Did Royston know?"

Jonah shook his head. "Not Royston. I wanted to tell him . . . but it was too dangerous. If the Synod arrested me, then I needed him to keep the Engineering Room running. The colony can't function without it. You're right about the Synod. I went to them as soon as I realized what was happening. They had only one solution."

Maude's face darkened. "More sacrifices."

"Exactly," Jonah said. "Padre Flavius said we had brought this new Doom—that was his word for it—upon ourselves due to our sins. He demanded more sacrifices to appease the Holy Sea. He controls the Synod. They go along with whatever he wants."

"Of course, they do," Maude said. "So who else did you tell?"

"Flavius warned me to keep my mouth shut," Jonah said. "He was worried that if word about the Animus Machine got out, then it would cause unrest to sweep through the colony. But I had to do something . . . one of my engineering apprentices already knew about it. He was assisting me when I discovered the levels were dropping."

"Let me guess," Maude said. "Carter Knox."

Jonah grimaced. "Yes . . . and I regret dragging him into this mess. He paid a high price. They all did. I also recruited Stan Decker and Philip Bishop to help us."

"Our father . . ." Stella whispered, glancing at her sister.

"But why Decker and Bishop?" Maude asked, furling her brow. "They're not engineers. If memory serves, Decker was pledged to Dissemination and Bishop to Records. How could they help you with the Animus Machine?"

"I didn't need their help with the Animus Machine."

"Then . . . what?" Maude asked.

"I needed their help with a secret plan—to return to the Surface."

Ignoring the shocked whispers, Jonah brought the Council up to speed as quickly and efficiently as he could, telling them about how Decker oversaw the Spare Parts Room and helped him to build a submersible in secret, and needing Bishop's help to search through Records for information about the Beacon, and how Myra found out about his secret plans and took it upon herself to locate the ancient device. He explained how she succeeded where they had failed, bonding with the Beacon and escaping in the sub.

"The Beacon?" Pratt said. "It's real? Not just some super-stitious nonsense?"

"I assure you, it's very real," Jonah said. "I saw it for myself, attached to my daughter's wrist. My wife is actually the one who found out about it. And she paid dearly for that. Padre Flavius had her killed and made it look like she died in childbirth." He felt pain rush through him, but he made himself continue. "Myra is the Carrier for our colony now. The Beacon is supposed to guide her back to the First Continuum."

"But she's just a kid," Greeley said. "They're all just kids. Surely, we're doomed."

Stella and Ginger looked furious. "We're just kids," said Stella. "And we broke into the Pen and busted him out, something you couldn't even do. And we learned how from Myra. She taught us her secret ways. She's not just a normal kid."

"Neither is her brother," Ginger added. "Tinker is special."

"That's true," Maude said with a smile. "I ought to know. Paige and Kaleb are no slouches either. If anyone can pull this off, those kids can. They have my full confidence."

Jonah felt pride and fear surge through him in equal measures. He wanted to linger on thoughts of his children, but they were beyond his reach. He needed to focus on the here and now. "This uprising isn't only about over-throwing the Plenus and defeating the Synod anymore," he said in a solemn voice. "It's about saving our entire colony."

His words hung in the air.

"Here, here!" came the response from Maude and a few others, but Greeley remained skeptical. He whispered to Maude. "Chief, you sure we can trust this Factum?"

"With our very lives," Maude said. She shot Jonah a grateful look. "We're lucky to have him on our side. And the rest of his family, too."

"So, what are you proposing?" Pratt asked. "Sit here with our thumbs crammed up our arses, waiting for your kids to rescue us?" This was met with nervous laughter. "I don't mean to be a prig, but it's unlikely they're coming back."

"Trust me . . . I know," Jonah said. He had to swallow hard to keep his voice from breaking. "I drew up the plans and they were always a long shot."

"So what then?" Pratt said. "Do nothing?"

Jonah leapt to his feet and started pacing around the table. He ran his fingers through his thinning hair. "Look . . . raiding Farming won't help our cause. It's a waste of time. We'll run out of oxygen long before the Synod runs out of their Victus. And breaking into their chambers won't help either. Let the Synod hide out in Sector 6 like cowards. What we need isn't in their chambers anyway— it's in Sector 10."

Pratt looked puzzled. "The Spare Parts Room?"

"Yeah, what do you want with Sector 10?" Greeley said, exchanging a confused look with Pratt. "Just a bunch of useless, old junk in there."

"Exactly, old junk!" Jonah said excitedly. "Excuse me for a second."

Before anyone could object, he dashed out of the conference room, ignoring the puzzled voices that erupted behind him. He knew what he had to do. He ducked into his old office and dropped to his knees under the desk.

"Come on . . . come on . . . please be here," he muttered as he felt around for the hidden panel. His fingers caught on the lip, and he pried it up from the floor. He peered inside, feeling a thrill when he saw that the secret compartment was untouched. The Patrollers hadn't found it when they searched his office. He plucked out what he needed, replaced the panel, and dashed back into the meeting.

"This is my proposal," he said and deposited an armload of blueprints on the table in front of the confused Council members. With a flick of his wrist, he unrolled them across the table, revealing a familiar constellation of light blue lines etched onto dark blue paper, each stroke of his own design.

He caught Maude's eye. She grinned and winked her approval, and that was all he needed. He scanned the faces sitting at the table—Factum and Hockers—all bound together by the same dire cause.

"So . . . are you ready?" he asked.

"Ready for what?" Greeley said with a frown. He squinted at the complex diagrams that now covered the entire length of the table.

Jonah clasped his hands together.

"Ready to pledge to Engineering?"

Chapter 42
SLEEP MODE SUSPENDING

Myra Jackson

One more loop?" Kaleb asked when they paused to rest by the escape pod.

Myra eyed his condition. He was leaning heavily on her arm for support. She could feel the quivering of his muscles, not to mention his flushed cheeks and ragged breathing. "Are you trying to kill yourself?"

He grinned. "Yup, that's my plan."

"Not on my watch, Sebold," she said, smiling in spite of herself. He didn't protest when she helped him back up the steps and into the ship. He staggered across the cabin and collapsed into bed.

"I feel like I just sprinted . . . for five miles." He flopped back on his pillow. "Though we only did two loops around the camp. I'm a bloody invalid!"

Myra smirked. "For an invalid, you sure talk a lot."

He reached his arms out and pulled her into him. His eyes bored into her. "It's all your fault," he said huskily. "I can't help myself around you—"

"Then I'll make you," she said, wriggling away and pinning his arms down. "You're supposed to be resting, remember? You could relapse if you're not careful."

He rolled his eyes. "Fine, but after I wake up, I want to go for another walk. It's making me crazy being cooped up in this ship."

"Deal," she said and waited by his bed until he drifted off to sleep. She must have nodded off too, because the next thing she knew, she woke to Kaleb screaming.

"The darkness . . . the Strong Ones!"

He thrashed around in his hospital bed and threatened to rip out his IV line, though his eyes stayed shut the whole time. The Forger dashed into the escape pod. His eyes widened when he saw Kaleb.

"Brother, help!" Myra called out, trying to hold Kaleb's arms down and keep him from injuring himself. He bucked under her grip.

The Forger swished over. He grabbed a vial, drew the cloudy liquid into a needle, and pushed it into Kaleb's IV port. As the drug hit his bloodstream, Kaleb stopped twitching and his expression slackened yet he kept mumbling in his sleep.

"What's wrong with him?" Myra said. "He was fine right before this . . . joking around, laughing, trying to kiss me . . ." She trailed off, blushing. "I don't understand it. Why isn't he getting better?"

The Forger checked Kaleb's vitals on the monitor. "The sedative should help him sleep better. But I'm afraid it's not a permanent solution. His physical wounds are healing, but some injuries go far deeper. They can't be treated with medicine alone."

She looked up. "What do you mean?"

"I'm not an expert. But he's experienced severe psychological trauma. It happens to soldiers sometimes after they've been deployed for combat. The technical term is—*Post Traumatic Stress Disorder*. Night terrors are a common symptom, I believe."

"What's the treatment for it?" she asked.

"Well, some people never recover," he said, noticing her alarmed expression. "But in my experience, time helps the most. It should fade like his scars. That and talking about it. Just be patient with him. Remember, he's been through a lot."

She nodded. "I know, thanks."

Myra clasped Kaleb's hand and watched him sleep. His eyes ticked and jolted under their lids, while his lips wobbled and slurred gibberish. "The Feast . . . the Black Mines . . . Crusher . . . the Strong Ones . . . ."

"Shhhhh," she whispered, trying to soothe him. "Crusher is dead . . . he can't hurt you anymore. The Strong Ones are all dead . . . you're safe now."

She stroked his forehead, wishing that she could reach inside his brain and pull out the bad memories. *Time*, she thought. He needed time to heal, and so she would give him that. It was the least she could do.

o   o   o

"Myra, how long have you been sitting here?" the Forger asked. His voice was kind, yet firm. He busied himself with checking Kaleb's IV line and the bleating monitors that bordered his hospital bed. Had she dozed off again?

Myra sat back and yawned, though she tried to stifle it. Her back ached fiercely from being hunched over for so long.

"Gimme a hint," she said in a groggy voice. She stretched her back, feeling a scream of pain, but then a few satisfying pops. "Is it day or night?"

The Forger quirked his lips in amusement. "What do you think?"

"Night?" she guessed, easing back into the chair.

"Wrong—it's the middle of the day. You've both been sleeping here for hours." He set his hands on his hips. "You know, he's not the only one who needs to stretch his legs and get some fresh air."

"Brother, are you kicking me out?" she asked in mock alarm.

"Your words, not mine . . . but yeah, I guess I am."

"That's the nicest way anybody has ever told me to scram." She stood up, feeling the kinks in her muscles screaming. "You'll let me know when he wakes up?"

"Of course, now scram."

Myra hobbled from the ship, squinting against the sunlight. True to the Forger's word, it was midday. She scanned the campsite for her brother but didn't see him. Then she remembered that Seeker had taken him on a hunting trip. They had popped their heads into the escape pod that morning to check on Kaleb before heading out. They probably weren't back yet.

She came upon Aero and Wren on the other side of the escape pod, repacking supplies into containers in preparation for their upcoming journey. When Wren saw her approaching, she quickly whispered something to Aero and took off in the opposite direction.

Myra watched her go, trying not to take it personally. But she could sense the tension in the air between them. Aero waved her over, seemingly oblivious.

"Captain Wright," Myra said with a half-hearted salute. "Fancy seeing you here."

A smile bent his lips. "Ms. Jackson."

Her eyes slipped past him and settled on the slim, athletic figure beating a hasty retreat. "Looks like I'm making new friends everywhere," she said under her breath.

He followed her gaze to Wren's back. "Oh, you mean Wren?" He smiled broadly. "Don't let her get to you. She'll come around eventually. She always does."

"Come around?" she repeated.

He shrugged. "She's reactionary and emotional, and she doesn't like new people. She has to warm up to you. She's always been like this, even back at the Agoge. You should have seen how she hazed the new recruits," he said, grinning at the memory.

"Maybe," she said. "But I think she's taken a special disliking to me."

"Now you're being paranoid," he said, loading their rations into a watertight container. They'd made a dent in them but still had plenty left. "She's also the most loyal person that I've ever met. She's saved my sorry ass more times than I can count."

He stowed the container, along with the others, in a compartment hidden behind a panel on the underside of the ship. *Hiss!*—he hit a button and the panel retracted and closed, perfectly camouflaging itself into the smooth exterior.

He stood up and dusted himself off. "Are you up for a little adventure?" he asked. "Well, come on now."

He started off, not waiting for her reply. She scowled at his back. Obviously, he was used to people following his orders and not asking questions.

"Wait . . . where are you taking me?" she demanded, trotting up next to him. Due to his long legs and their pronounced stride, she had to jog to keep up with him.

He smirked. "Right . . . it's a surprise."

"You know, I can read your mind," she said. This threat wasn't entirely real. She could read his mind sometimes, but she couldn't control when it happened.

"Please don't," he said. "It'll ruin the surprise." His eyes sought her face and held her gaze. He reached for her hand, the one with the Beacon attached to it. His touch sent jolts shooting up her arm. "You'll just have to trust me. Can you do that?"

It went against her better instincts to follow anyone blindly, let alone this soldier from a distant world. As familiar as he seemed, he was still mostly a stranger. But then her Beacon flared again and overrode her capacity for rational thought. "Fine," she allowed as he grinned and drew her along, leading her up the circuitous mountain path.

o   o   o

"What's so special about a little water?" Myra asked, eyeing the translucent pool spilling from crevices in the rocks. The mountains were filled with springs like this one.

"Go ahead and touch it," Aero urged, kneeling by the pool and sifting the water through his fingers. "I found it the other day when I was refilling our flasks."

She stooped down and dipped her hands into the pool. The water was warm, bordering on hot, even though the air was frigid and snow blotted out the ground. She looked up in astonishment. "Wait . . . how is this possible?"

He grinned at her reaction. "It's a hot spring. Geothermally heated water flows up from the Earth's crust. I think that's part of why they built the Seventh Continuum here. These springs aren't only a water source. They could also provide heat for the colony."

The pool was deep and wide, spilling into a cave that the water had eroded into the mountainside. She caught a faint whiff of rotten eggs. *Sulfur*, she guessed.

The warmth felt soothing against her wind-chapped skin. "Amazing . . . it's simply amazing," she said.

He looked pleased. "Glad you like it."

They shed their jackets and stripped off their boots and socks, slipping their feet into the water. Myra sighed with pleasure as the kinks in her calves unclenched. Seized by the moment—and a feeling of unabashed freedom—she stripped off her pants and tunic, leaving only her undergarments, and dove headfirst into the water.

It rushed over her in a warm torrent. She dipped her head under, tasting sulfur on her tongue, and then burst back through the top. She kicked over to the middle of the pool, floating on her back and staring up at the cobalt sky. Something disturbed the water, making it slosh over her. A figure swam up beside her with strong, smooth strokes.

Aero was now shirtless, wearing only thin undershorts. The water pushed them together, their bodies bumping against each other. Their Beacons started to throb in synch as their thoughts leaked together. She could tell that Aero was picking up the random flickerings of her neural synapses.

She thought about Kaleb laying in his hospital bed . . . and Aero floating next to her . . . and how it would be so

easy to swim over . . . and kiss him. Guilt swept through her
for even considering it, and she tried to turn her thoughts to
other things . . . like the journey that lay ahead to the First
Continuum.

But Aero's thoughts sucked her back in. She could feel
his eyes glued to her. Fear and etiquette restrained him
from acting on his desires, but he wanted to press himself
against her . . . lock his lips to hers and peel off the clothes
that she hadn't already shed . . . run his hands over her
thighs and up . . .

No, I don't want to know!

She wished that she could close her mind—or at the very
least—shield him from her more puerile thoughts, like how
lovely his cheekbones looked in the strong midday sun . . . or
how sexy the tiny scar on his forehead was.

Aero perked up at that last thought. He reached up and
felt the slightly raised tissue over his eyebrow.

"My scar, huh?" he said with a silly grin. "Really, you
like it?"

"Hey, quit peeking!" she said and splashed him.

"Right, sorry." He propped himself up on a volcanic rock
that spiked through the center of the pool. "The Forger's
trying to teach me to close my mind. But clearly, I've not
mastered it yet."

"Well, try harder," she grumbled.

"Back at you!" he laughed. "I can feel you peeking, too."

That was what he said out loud, but something deeper
leaked from his unconscious mind:

Carrier, Forever Bonded, Girl from Under the Sea. His
thoughts rushed at her, leaving her breathless. Her Beacon
pulsed faster and brighter as their connection strengthened.
Requesting permission, he thought.

Permission for what? she thought back.

For this.

He leaned over and kissed her, softly, deferentially, but
when she kissed him back, he grew more confident. His
tongue darted into her mouth, familiar yet strange. She felt

his sturdy arms encircling her like the warm water. Their flesh and their thoughts intertwined, and she was lost in the togetherness. Lost—and drowning in it.

"No, stop," she said, pulling away. "We can't . . ."

She kicked away from him, floating on her back and staring at the sky. She didn't dare look over at the soldier swimming next to her. She didn't trust herself around him . . . and she certainly didn't trust him. He floated over, his hand skimming her arm and drawing goose bumps. Her heart skittered in her chest as their Beacons lit up the water with green fire.

"Sorry . . . it's just not good timing," she managed. "Seeker and Tinker could wander up here at any moment, and my brother might not understand . . ."

He dove under the water and was gone for longer than seemed safe. When she was starting to worry, Aero broke back through the surface and exhaled the breath that he had been holding for several long minutes.

"And they might tell Kaleb?" he said.

"Yeah," she said, feeling a rush of guilt. "And what about Wren?"

Now it was his turn to feel guilty. "You're right," he sighed. "She's been acting really strange around us."

He paddled over to the side of the pool and hoisted himself out of the water. Steam rose from his skin when it collided with the cold air. Myra swam over to the side and crawled onto the rocks. She hugged her knees to her chest.

"Believe me . . . I *want* to," she said, as water dripped off and puddled on the rocks. "If we were the only two people left in the world, I would in a heartbeat . . . but we're not." He nodded but didn't reply. "Look . . . we can't afford to get distracted like this," she went on. "We're Carriers now . . . and we can't have petty jealousies and insecurities messing that up. It's already happening . . . just look at Wren."

Aero stroked her cheek but then let his hand slip away. The boy who desired her faded away as the soldier took over. His countenance hardened into resolve.

"Spoken like a true leader," he said and looked down.

"I'm sorry . . . it was a lapse in judgment. It won't happen again, not until this is over. And I'll work harder to close my mind, too."

But even as he spoke those words—even as he struggled to shield her from the more indiscreet thoughts birthed by his subconscious—Myra caught a flicker and felt how hard it was for Aero to let her go right when he'd just found her.

o   o   o

That night, even though Myra sank down in her bedroll and turned away from Aero, giving him the convex arch of her back, they both dreamed the same dream.

The impossible blackness of the underground enveloped them until they were both choking on it. The air was chilled and static. Myra reached for Aero, her hands clumsy in the dark. The only light came from the throbbing of their Beacons. Suddenly, Seeker materialized into the dreamscape next to them. She didn't seem bothered by the darkness, but she crouched down alertly, her eyes combing through the shadows. Their Beacons began to pulse in synch, creating a small halo of light around them.

A fourth figure inhabited the dreamscape—

The Dark Thing.

Myra shuddered when she realized that the monster was here with them. She couldn't see it, but she could feel its amorphous form lurking in the periphery.

Where is this place? she thought. It was different than the other dreamscapes. She had a strong feeling that they had been brought here for a reason. She took a step forward and formed her lips into words.

"Hello?" she called out. "Why did you bring us here?"

Her voice echoed out and doubled back, communicating the sheer immensity of this place. She probed it with her mind, pushing beyond the confines of her physical body with the Beacon. The cavernous space took shape in her head as the Beacon beamed out signals and they bounced back to her.

It was filled with machines. Thousands of them. This was a place locked in frozen slumber that had lain undisturbed for eons. She pushed beyond the walls and into other caverns, interconnected and branching through the underground like a great warren. She pushed further still, into a control room.

And then something picked up her signal. She could feel a rousing of consciousness. A long-anticipated awakening, slow yet inexorable.

And then . . .

. . . a male voice penetrated the darkness.

"Sleep mode suspending."

Aero tensed and drew his Falchion, morphing it into a longer, heavier sword. Seeker raised her hackles and bared her teeth, but Myra motioned for them both to stand down.

"This isn't real, remember?" she said. "We're dreaming."

But even as she said those words, she knew that they weren't entirely true. Their beings were fragmented—they were sleeping at the campsite in the mountains, but simultaneously, they were also here . . . wherever here was . . .

The voice rang out again.

"Powering on," it said, as buzzing noises started up. Power zapping through wires. Machines whirring to life, coming back online. The great awakening had begun. Myra knew this in some deep and visceral way. She raised her voice over the electronic din.

"We're the Carriers," she called out. "Who are you?"

Silence ensued, and then: "Who . . . isn't the right question," the voice replied. It carried the faintest tremor of amusement, though it remained carefully modulated and distinctly masculine. "Try again, Carrier from the Thirteenth Continuum."

This response stumped Myra. It was impossible to pinpoint the source of the voice. It seemed to come from everywhere. She liked things that she could hold and touch—things that she knew were real, beyond all shadow of a doubt. This new existence that she occupied somewhere between waking and dreaming, where the body could be severed from the mind and flung thousands of miles through space, disturbed her.

"Or should I call you . . . Myra Jackson?" the voice continued.

How did it know her name?

"Damn it, stop playing games!" Aero yelled. He gripped his Falchion tighter. "What the hell do you want with us?"

His voice echoed and died out. The silence rushed back in and lingered until the voice spoke again.

"Initiating remote connection with Carriers."

With a blinding flash, Myra felt her Beacon linking to another entity somewhere far away. It clicked in remotely and started uploading data about her. It felt like bits of stored information were being sucked out of her neurons. Her head began to ache as this essence left her body. After what seemed like a long time, a chime rang out.

"Upload complete," the voice said. "Initiating download and remote software update."

Suddenly, the image of a golden door popped into her head. It resolved and sharpened. The door was surrounded by ruins—crumbling, red brick buildings, roofs caving in, toppled stone pillars draped over wide stairs, everything blackened and burnt. Her Beacon grew burning hot to the touch. She gritted her teeth against the pain.

"Are you seeing this?" Myra whispered to Aero and Seeker as the images kept assaulting her brain, flying faster and faster. "The door? The ruins? The stairs?"

"Yes . . . Myra," Seeker rasped.

Aero shut his eyes. "The door is marked by the Ouroboros symbol . . ."

Chime!

With that sound, the parade of images ceased. Then the voice reverberated out louder and clear than before—a shout that cut through the netherworld of dreams and pierced their brains.

"Update complete," it said. "Coordinates downloaded."

"Coordinates for what?" Myra said.

"Home," the voice answered. "Carriers, come home."

o   o   o

Myra and Aero woke in each other's arms, sweaty and twisted in her bedroll, even though they'd fallen asleep across the campsite from each other. His Falchion was clutched tightly in his hand and morphed into a broadsword. Their Beacons throbbed together, slowly and languidly, like the beating of their hearts. Seeker was curled up at their feet. She stirred and woke with them. The sun had only just set the horizon aglow with pinkish light. Disoriented, Myra looked over—and caught Wren glaring at them.

Aero released Myra as if she were burning him. "Sorry," he whispered, thrusting back the covers. He sat up stiffly. "Damn it . . . I don't know what happened."

"That dream is what happened," Myra whispered back, pulling the covers up around her. At the moment, Wren and her jealousy were the least of her concerns. "Didn't you hear the voice? And see the door and those ruins?"

Their Beacons flared as Aero nodded, and so did Seeker. "Carriers, come home," she intoned in her gravelly voice.

Myra felt a shiver wrench up her spine. They had all experienced the exact same dream, and deep down, they each knew what it meant. That voice was more than just a voice— it was a beacon calling to them—a blazing signpost staked into the burning heart of the ever-dimming world.

"It's time to go home," she said as her Beacon flared bright as day. She ran her fingers over its smooth surface and felt a thrill. Now it contained the precious coordinates that would lead them to the door of the First Continuum.

PART VI
RETURN

Farewells can be shattering, but returns are surely worse. Solid flesh can never live up to the bright shadow cast by its absence. Time and distance blur the edges; then suddenly the beloved has arrived, and it's noon with its merciless light, and every spot and pore and wrinkle and bristle stands clear.

—Margaret Atwood, *The Blind Assassin*

Chapter 43
WIDENER

Aero Wright

Landing in a snowstorm was no easy feat, but relying on the Beacon and Wren's guidance, Aero managed to get them down in one piece—and in the correct location—albeit with some serious bumps and an inelegant landing that would have earned him poor marks at the Agoge. As the ground rose up to greet them, the Forger's chanting grew louder.

"Aeternus eternus . . ." he repeated over and over again. He looked peaked from the trip. The ship hovered for a moment, tossed about by the wind, and then plunged to the ground. Its wheels splashed down and cut deep rivets in the mud.

"Welcome to the First Continuum," Aero announced from the cockpit. Even his voice sounded shaky. The skies had been crystal clear when they left the Seventh Continuum. Without proper instruments on the jerry-rigged escape pod or the mothership's guidance, he couldn't track weather systems. So the storm seemed to come out of nowhere.

"Formerly known as Harvard University, Cambridge, Massachusetts, the United States, North American continent,"

Wren added, reading the names from the old maps stored in the ship's onboard computer.

"I don't care where we are," the Forger managed, unhitching his harness and lurching up. He looked like he might be sick. "Just get me out of this ship."

"I second that, Brother," Kaleb said with a feeble smile. "And I've been cooped up in here longer than the rest of you. I just have to get this contraption off." He fumbled with the buckle on his harness, but Myra pushed his hand away.

"Sebold, hold still," she scolded. "Or you'll rip your stitches."

"I'm sick of being an invalid," he said, glaring down the dressings that girdled his chest. They were dotted with rusty droplets of blood that had soaked through the gauze.

"You'll be one permanently if you don't let me help," Myra said but softened her tone. "I can tell you're feeling better. I was worried when you *weren't* complaining."

Kaleb smirked. "I thought complaining was your specialty."

"Maybe we have that in common," Myra replied, returning his smile. She unhooked his harness and helped him shrug it off. Aero unbuckled his harness, wincing at the way it had cut into his shoulders. He toggled a few switches.

With a soft hiss and a blast of arctic air, the bay doors yawned open. Sleet and snow blustered into the cabin, along with something else:

Come to me . . . come to me . . . come to me . . .

The voice from their shared dream shot through Aero's head. He glanced at Myra and Seeker. Without exchanging any words, he knew that they could hear it, too.

Come to me . . . come to me . . . come to me . . .

The message continued on a loop audible only to the Carriers. Aero felt a sucking feeling emanating from his Beacon. His whole body ached with the force of it; even his teeth ached. The only remedy—the only way to make it stop—was to heed its siren call.

Oblivious to the voice, Wren climbed out of the copilot

chair and tramped over to the doors. Another gust of wind rocked the escape pod, forcing more precipitation into the cabin. She braced herself and peered outside.

"Captain, this is some seriously crappy weather," she reported. "Almost zero visibility. Whiteout conditions. If the temperature drops even a few degrees, it could turn into a full-blown blizzard."

Aero tried to focus on Wren and not the voice assaulting his neural synapses. "Seriously crappy?" he said with a raised eyebrow. "Is that the technical term?"

"Well, what would you call it?" Wren said, as the wind rocked the ship.

"I concur, Lieutenant," he said with a grin and zipped up his deployment suit, donning the hood and gloves. He turned to survey the cabin. "Is everyone suited up? Make sure your boots are laced tight. It'll be slippery once we get out there, and the last thing we need are sprained ankles slowing us down."

Fortunately, the escape pod had been stocked with plenty of supplies, including extra deployment suits, which they passed out to Myra and Kaleb. Seeker refused one, and Tinker was too small to fit into any of the standard sizes. Myra forced him into one of the jackets anyway, which was far too big and hung down to his knees like a dress.

"Once we're out of the escape pod, follow my lead," Aero said in his official command voice. "The Beacons should guide us to the First Continuum. Is that clear?"

"Yes, sir," Wren said with a quick salute, while the others zipped up their coats and voiced their agreement. "What's our target?" she added, pulling on her gloves.

"We're looking for a door," Aero said as the image from their dream flashed through his head. "Massive . . . golden . . . and marked by this seal." He held up his wrist, where the outline of the Ouroboros shimmered with greenish light.

"Got it, Captain," Wren said. "Another giant mystery door. Let's hope this one leads somewhere better than the last one. Starry hell, I'm not really in the mood to battle hordes of cannibalistic humanoids again."

"Me neither," said Kaleb with a wince.

Aero grinned. "Can't possibly be worse, can it?"

Wren's fingers twitched at her Falchion. "You'd be surprised."

One by one, they clambered down the stairs and into the blizzard. Once outside the ship, the wind hurled ice and snow at them. The ground was slick with ice. Aero hit a button on the side of the ship. The stairs retracted behind them, and the doors closed with a hiss. He scanned the area—or rather, what he could see of it. The visibility was poor and only getting worse. From what he could make out, they had landed in a central courtyard framed by crumbling, red brick and gray stone buildings.

Come to me . . . come to me . . . come to me . . .

The voice continued on its loop. Aero turned back to the others, who were huddled together. He held up his wrist. "Follow the light of my Beacon and stay together! Is that understood?"

Aero led them across the courtyard, his feet stamping through the ice. Wind bit into any flesh not protected by his suit. They trudged forward in a single-file line. Abruptly, a burst of snow-covered fur tore past him. Seeker galloped ahead on all fours. She flew across the courtyard, then skidded to a halt. Her throaty voice rang out:

"Come, friends! This way!"

Aero could just make out her figure through the swirl of white, though he had to squint. He didn't like that she had broken away and defied his orders to stay together. Tinker bolted after her. His legs pumping as he ran through the snow.

"No . . . Tink, wait!" Myra screamed, but they both quickly vanished, swallowed by the whiteout.

"I guess we're going that way," Wren muttered, annoyed by the broken chain of command. Her eyes flicked to Kaleb, who was leaning heavily on the Forger for support. She helped him with Kaleb while Myra fell in with Aero.

Come to me . . . come to me . . . come to me . . .

"You can hear that, can't you?" Aero said in a low voice.

Myra nodded as the wind tossed a wisp of curly hair into her eyes. She tucked it back under her hood and shut her eyes. "The voice," she said. "It's calling us home."

"Who do you think it belongs to?" Aero said. "I can't get a firm read on it."

"I don't know," Myra said. "The identity is protected somehow. I can't get a read on it either. And something feels off about it. Maybe it's a security precaution?"

"Maybe," he agreed, but he didn't like it.

A few minutes later, they stumbled upon a wide staircase, nearly tripping into it. They could only see a few feet in front of them. The steps were eroded, their edges rounded down to smooth curves, and several columns lay toppled across them, shattered to pieces and collapsing into dust. The roof had been torn clean off the building, exposing it to the tyranny of the sky. Thick icicles clung to every niche and ledge.

Aero started up the steps. His boot knocked a piece of rubble, partially buried in the snow. He brushed it off with his gloved hand, revealing a single word etched into its surface. He ran his fingers over the grooved letters:

WIDENER

Myra followed his gaze. "Does that mean anything to you?"

Aero shook his head. "Nope—" he started.

When suddenly, the sky thundered and flashed as the snow swirled down harder. "Watch out! Thundersnow!" he yelled over the fierce wind.

"I hate *thunder* anything," Myra said.

Her hand shot protectively to her Beacon, which was still damaged from the last storm. Wren and the Forger arrived at the bottom of the stairs, still supporting Kaleb. His face was contorted with pain. The drugs were wearing off.

The Forger looked concerned. "Sir, we need to get out of this storm—"

His words were cut off as another flash ripped through the sky, followed by a deafening crackle that rattled the ground. Dislodged by the thunder, icicles cracked off the roof and crashed down, shattering on the stairs. A large shard whizzed past Myra, almost taking her head off. Aero grabbed her hand and yanked her up the stairs.

"Hurry, we need to find shelter," he yelled. He signaled to the others. "This way!"

They bolted up the stairs, chased by the storm. Aero rushed through the double doors that dangled crookedly by their hinges. When he stepped inside the building, the storm quieted a little, held at bay by the thick walls, though snow continued to drift down through the ruined roof. Aero scanned the space, taking in the marble floors and soaring columns that lined the hall on either side. The voice was even stronger in here.

Come to me . . . come to me . . . come to me . . .

The lightning and thunder erupted again, driving them deeper into the building, where the roof was still largely intact and could provide some protection. The Forger and Myra helped Kaleb limp along while Wren fell in next to Aero. They picked their way over the rubble that obscured the hallway.

Wren scanned the ruined building. A frown creased her face. "Captain, you're sure this is the right place?"

"Positive, Lieutenant. You can't hear it, but there's a voice calling us into the building. Seeker and Myra hear it, too. Actually . . . it's more like we can *feel* it," he added, realizing how insane that sounded. How could you feel a voice?

Wren didn't look thrilled by this explanation. Her hand skirted her Falchion. Her eyes darted around, prying into every nook and corner.

"What's got you so jumpy?" Aero asked, picking up on her mood.

She set her lips. "In these conditions, there's no way to conduct proper security checks. We're breaking protocol by entering an unsecured building."

"I know," he said. "We'll just have to forgo them. That storm isn't letting up anytime soon."

Before he could assuage her uneasiness, Seeker waved to them from farther down the hallway. Tinker was with her, a tiny figure cast half in shadow.

"This way, friends!" Seeker called. "Follow me, I found it!"

Aero hesitated. Wren was right—they hadn't conducted proper security checks on the building and its perimeter, not with the blizzard raging outside. But the pull of the voice overrode his concerns.

Come to me . . . come to me . . . come to me . . .

Aero motioned to the others. They followed Seeker and Tinker deeper into the building Empty shelves lined the hallway and spanned up to the ceiling, hundreds of them. They were covered in a thick layer of dust. What had they held? Aero wondered.

The Beacon on his wrist flared and showed him an image— books. Millions of them stacked on the shelves and filling the building. This was an ancient repository of human knowledge. He had learned about libraries at the Agoge and how humans used to read printed books before the advent of the Digital Age.

Tinker's voice echoed down the passage.

"Look . . . over here!"

Aero picked up his pace and reached the end of the corridor. He saw a shimmer of golden metal. The door was draped in shadow and tucked against the wall, but instantly he knew that it was the right one. The Ouroboros symbol marked the smooth metal, along with a number. Except this door wasn't marked by a seven.

1

"The First Continuum," Wren said. "It's still here."

The Forger approached the door and laid his hands on the symbol. He traced the outline of the snake's spiked mouth as it swallowed its own tail. "I recognize this craftsmanship. It was made by the First Ones."

"You mean . . . the Founders?" Kaleb asked, leaning against the wall for support. Sweat stood out on his brow; he was pale and unsteady.

"I believe they're one and the same," Aero said. He approached the door, expecting it to open automatically like the door to the Seventh Continuum. But nothing happened. He frowned. "So . . . how do we open it?"

"Let me see," the Forger said, pulling sensors out of his pack and attaching them to the door. He ran a few scans, toggled some switches. "The door is still functional."

"Then why won't it open?" Myra asked, joining Aero by the door.

The Forger ran a few more scans and flipped more switches. Finally, he leaned back and nodded. "Of course . . . that makes perfect sense," he said, half to himself.

"What makes sense?" Myra asked. "Why won't it open?"

"Oh, that's simple," the Forger said. "Because it's locked."

"Fantastic," Wren said with a roll of her eyes. "Can't you unlock it? With your fancy backpack?"

The Forger shook his head. "No, I don't have the key."

"Then where do we get the key?" Aero asked.

The Forger looked puzzled. "In our teachings, it says— *only the Chosen Ones who carry the Beacons may pass through the door to the First Continuum.* My brothers and sisters might be able to solve this riddle. But, I'm afraid, I don't possess the knowledge."

"But didn't you call me the Chosen One?" Aero asked. "Back on the mothership, after I first bonded with the Beacon?"

The Forger nodded. "Yes, based on our teachings."

"Then shouldn't I be able to unlock it?" Aero said.

"That would seem logical," the Forger agreed.

Aero shrugged and banged his fist on the door. The noise shook some debris free but did little else. He unsheathed his Falchion and morphed it into a war hammer.

"Are you sure that's a good idea?" Myra said, eying the weapon uncertainly.

"Got anything better?" Aero said, wielding the hefty hammer.

Myra shook her head. "No, I guess not."

"Stand back," Aero said, taking a test swing. "Just in case."

He swung at the door, dealing it a mighty blow. As soon as the hammer connected with the golden metal sparks exploded from the impact and sent the hammer flying from his hands. It landed several feet away with a loud clang. His arm felt numb and tingly.

Wren went to retrieve the hammer but dropped it quickly. "Starry hell, that burns!"

The weapon was searing hot but luckily still intact. It hadn't melted down. Though his Falchion had taken a beating, the door remained unblemished.

"Nice try, Chosen One," Myra said with a smirk. "But I don't think brute force is the answer."

Aero rubbed his sore arm. "I'd have to agree with you." Once his Falchion had cooled down, he retrieved it and morphed it back to its default form. He sheathed it, feeling frustration course through him. He wasn't the only one.

"So . . . let me sum this up," Myra said, eying the door. "We need a key to unlock the door, but we've got no clue where to find it?"

"That's about right," Aero agreed.

In his quiet way, Tinker wandered over to the door. He was dwarfed by its massive size. A few errant snowflakes slipped through the roof and drifted down around him.

"Tink, what is it?" Myra asked. But he didn't respond. He just kept staring at the door. "Tink, are you okay?" she tried again, worry creeping into her voice.

But then he broke into his lopsided smile.

"Of course . . . the Beacons . . . that's it."

"What about them?" Myra asked.

Tinker shrugged. "The Beacons are the key. That's why they're so important. That's why one was given to each colony."

Myra shook her head. "That doesn't make any sense. Aero already tried to open the door, and it didn't work."

"Of course, it didn't," Tinker said. Myra shot him a blank look, so he clarified. "Beacons. Plural. All three of you have to unlock it together. Remember what the Forger said?"

"Wait, you're right," Aero said, joining them by the door.

"If anyone knows about the Beacons, it's the Forgers. That teaching said Chosen Ones and Beacons . . . plural."

Aero and Myra summoned Seeker over. They stood in front of the door together.

"Now what?" Aero asked. "I'm not versed in opening secret doors with strange devices shackled to my wrist. For some reason, my studies skipped that lesson."

"No idea," Tinker said with a shrug. "You're the Carriers."

Aero shut his eyes and tried to concentrate. Gripped by a sudden urge, he grabbed Myra's hand, and she seized Seeker's. They stood in a chain of bodies before the door.

"Aeternus eternus," they chanted in unison. As if they were lit by a fuse, the Beacons erupted with emerald fire. The unnatural blaze spread up their arms and engulfed their bodies. The flames shot out of them and slammed into the door, setting it ablaze. The snake began to unfurl as the symbol rotated faster and faster.

Aero heard Wren yelling. He tried to open his mouth to respond, but his jaw was locked shut. He tried to turn his head, but his neck wouldn't move. He was frozen in place, captive to the will of the Beacon.

The door dilated, melting into the walls. Once it had finished opening, the flames tamped down, sucked back into the Beacons. Only then did the force release them. Aero spun around, unsheathing his Falchion and morphing it into a broadsword. When his eyes fell on Wren's face, fear exploded in his heart.

A sneering voice rang out.

"Nice work, boy! You've opened the door for us."

Chapter 44
AMBUSHED

Aero Wright

Vinick held a golden dagger to Wren's throat.

Aero felt shock, chased by fiery anger. Hundreds of soldiers flanked Vinick in their deployment uniforms. *Four combat units, maybe five*, he thought, working rapidly to assess the situation. Their silvery silhouettes stretched down the corridor in perfect formation; their Falchions were morphed into deadly weapon forms—swords, pikes, daggers, maces, and war hammers.

Aero's eyes flicked over their faces. Major Doyle had knocked the Forger down, Danika held Kaleb at knifepoint, and his mother had seized Tinker. Aero scanned their insignia. His mother and Danika were both Majors now, he realized with a jolt.

"Tinker!" Myra screamed and lunged toward her brother.

Major Wright tightened her grip on him. Her Falchion shortened into a nasty dagger, the twin of the one clutched by Vinick. She pressed it to Tinker's throat. "Don't even think about it, girl!" she hissed. "Unless you want to see him die."

Myra froze in her tracks and held her hands up. Seeker

growled and raised her hackles, but she also held back.

"Hey, pick on someone your own size," Wren said, writhing in Vinick's grip. "You damned bullies—"

"Shut up, deserter!" Vinick said and smacked her with the back of his hand. She doubled over, spitting blood.

Aero tightened his grip on his broadsword. "Release them, you coward!"

"I don't think so, boy," Vinick sneered. "I've got another proposal. Why don't you surrender to me?" He gestured to the armed soldiers flanking him. "You're badly outnumbered. You can't possibly win."

Kaleb struggled against Danika, but in his weakened state, he couldn't break her grip. "Myra, they're going to kill us! Run away now . . . save yourself . . ."

"No . . . Kaleb!" Myra said, fear lighting up her eyes. "I'm not leaving you."

Danika snickered, keeping a tight hold on Kaleb. She glanced at Major Wright. "Oh, look at the poor fool! Thinks he's in love with that scrawny girl."

"Stupid emotional creatures," Major Wright snorted.

Aero thought fast, grappling for any way to even the odds. Vinick was right. They were hopelessly outnumbered. Not to mention the reinforcements housed inside the mothership—a whole army at Vinick's command. He ticked through ideas, each more desperate than the last.

"Then I challenge you to a duel," Aero said, trying to sound more confident than he felt. "Any soldier may challenge the Supreme General, isn't that right? One-on-one, in Falchion-to-Falchion combat, as outlined in our charter by the First Ones."

The soldiers held their formation, but Aero could sense their uncertainty. Whispers and shuffling spread through their ranks. Vinick let out a scathing laugh. "Up to your old tricks again, boy? It won't work this time."

"Do you deny my rights?" Aero said, gesturing to the other soldiers. "In front of all these witnesses? I think you're afraid to face me. You know I'm the better soldier."

Vinick stopped laughing. "Any soldier in the Interstellar

Army of the Second Continuum does have the right to challenge me. You're right about that part—but you're not a soldier anymore. You're a deserter, banished and stripped of your ranking. Why don't you ask your precious Forger? Go ahead, he'll tell you the truth."

Aero glanced at the Forger, who lay on the ground with blood seeping from his forehead. "Answer him, you fool!" Doyle said, kicking him roughly.

The Forger groaned and lifted his bruised head. "Sorry, Captain . . . but the Supreme General is correct about our charter. Since you've been banished from the Second Continuum, the legal protections no longer apply to you."

The words had their intended effect. The uncertainty permeating the ranks of soldiers evaporated. Aero knew that there was only one thing left to do, even if it went against his most fundamental instincts.

"Fine, then I'll surrender," he said, morphing his Falchion back to its default form. "But on one condition—let the others go. You don't need them. We already unlocked the door. They're not worth anything. I'm the one you want."

"Why would I do that, boy?" Vinick said. Wren thrashed in his arms, but he pressed the dagger deeper into her throat. "You're not in any position to bargain."

Aero narrowed his eyes; his voice came out deadly serious. "Because if you don't—I will kill you. That's a promise."

Vinick's lips curled back. "Go ahead and try, boy! I'll enjoy watching you die on the tip of my Falchion. Then we'll pry the Beacon from your cold wrist and pillage the First Continuum, before we abandon this barren wasteland and continue on Stern's Quest," he snarled, pressing his dagger into Wren's throat. "One more chance! Surrender now, or your friends die. You can watch this deserter bleed out first—"

"Don't do it, sir!" Wren screamed. "He'll kill you!"

"Shut up, traitor!" Vinick screamed and hit her with the hilt of his dagger. She went down hard and didn't get up. "Time's up, boy. All soldiers attack!"

Like a well-oiled machine, the soldiers advanced with their Falchions raised. Their boots tramped over the marble floors. Aero recognized many familiar faces. Some were his classmates from the Agoge, while others had passed him in the corridors hundreds of times, or taken countless meals with him in the Mess Hall. Their faces were blank, devoid of any emotion. Despite the classes and meals they'd shared, they wouldn't hesitate to strike him down.

Time seemed to slow down as it always did in the heat of battle. The synchronized footsteps of the soldiers—*thwack, thwack, thwack*—came slower and slower. Aero remembered reading somewhere that before you died, your whole life flashed before your eyes. He waited for that to happen, but his mind remained as empty as the vacuum of space. The only thing that he regretted—that lodged in his throat like a hard stone and threatened to crack his battle-hardened exterior—was that his friends were going to die with him.

I've failed you, he thought. *I'm sorry I couldn't save you.*

As the soldiers drew closer, Aero calculated how long it would take to cut through their ranks and reach Vinick. Revenge was his last option. It wasn't much, but it gave him something to hold onto. Three well-placed strokes, a pivot and a spin move, he decided, though he might die in the process.

So be it, was his last thought. He tensed his body, ready to launch himself, when suddenly—

Beep! Beep! Beep!

An alarm blared through the building. The soldiers looked around in confusion.

"Starry hell, what's happening—" Vinick started. But then the voice boomed out. This time, it wasn't only audible to the Carriers, but to everyone in the building.

"Severe threat to Carriers detected."

Vinick wheeled around, trying to pinpoint the source of the voice. "Who goes there?" he shrieked and slashed at the air. "Coward, I demand you show yourself!"

The voice boomed out again.

"Safety protocols initiated."

Aero seized on the distraction and morphed his Falchion into an ahlspiess. Instantly, his broadsword thinned out and elongated into the razor-sharp spear.

He retracted his arm to launch it at Vinick, when emerald fire burst from his Beacon and blazed up his arm, freezing him in place. He couldn't move a muscle. He saw two shapes flickering in his peripheral vision. Myra and Seeker were also frozen by their Beacons.

"Carriers retrieved," the voice said.

"Who goes there?" Vinick screamed again. His face turned a dangerous shade of purple. His soldiers looked terrified of the emerald fire spewing from the Beacons. Their formation broke apart into a chaotic stampede.

"Initiating evacuation procedure," the voice said.

Aero felt the outside force hijack his body. His limbs began to move of their own accord. The muscles flexed and shifted his body around so that he was facing the door to the First Continuum, which still gaped open. He tried to fight back against the force. *No! I want to stay here and fight!* But the fire engulfing his body only burned brighter. Worse, he started to feel dizzy and nauseous. Against his will, he sprinted through the door. He heard footfalls behind him.

Myra and Seeker, he realized.

When he crossed the threshold, overhead lights flickered on and illuminated the space—it was another elevator. Aero felt his limbs lock into place. He was frozen, consumed by the fire and unable to move a muscle. Myra and Seeker skidded to a halt on either side of him. They were also paralyzed by the fire.

"Carriers loaded," the voice said. "Door contracting."

With a deep rumble, the liquid metal began to reform itself into a solid door. "Get them, you fools!" Vinick screamed. He signaled to his soldiers. They charged at the elevator in a mass of bodies and golden weapons, but they were too late.

The door slurped shut before they could reach it. Aero heard their muffled pounding on the outside, but it held fast.

They wouldn't be able to breach it. He'd learned that the hard way.

"Transport descending," the voice said as the alarm stopped And then, against their will, the elevator whisked them away.

Chapter 45
WHERE ARE MY MANNERS?

Myra Jackson

When the force released her, Myra pounded on the elevator door. "Bloody open up and let us out!"

The flames that engulfed her body dwindled down to nothing as they were sucked back into her Beacon. All she could think about was Tinker and Kaleb and the armed soldiers surrounding them. "I know you can hear me . . . let us out of here!"

But the door held firm. The elevator continued to descend. If anything, they were picking up speed. She heard a noise and whipped around to see Aero morphing his Falchion back to its default form. He sheathed it in the scabbard at his waist. Emerald flames still smoldered over his body, but they were dying down. Next to him, Seeker dropped down to all fours as the force released her.

Myra started running her hands over the walls. "Hurry . . . help me look!" She felt the cold metal pass under her fingers. "Maybe we can find some manual controls."

They scoured every corner and crevice of the elevator, but found nothing. "It's hopeless," Aero said, stepping away from the walls. "We'll just have to wait it out."

Seeker stalked over. "Can't stop the Moving Room," she agreed.

But still Myra kept looking, stooping down to inspect the floor. She couldn't get Tinker's face out of her head with that knife pressed to his throat. A hand gripped her shoulder.

"Myra, save your strength," Aero said. She felt his breath tickling her neck. "You may need it later. We don't know who kidnapped us—or where they're taking us."

"Yes, Captain," she snapped with a mock salute. "Whatever you say."

He looked wounded by her sharp words, but she didn't care. She shrank down and hugged her knees to her chest. She knew that it wasn't his fault that Vinick had ambushed them. They would all be dead in the Seventh Continuum without him. But in some irrational part of her brain, she did blame him. It felt good to have a target for her anger. It made her feel less helpless.

Some time later, though Myra wasn't sure how long, only that it felt like an eternity, the elevator slowed its descent and then slammed to a halt with a rusty squeal. The overhead lights flickered and shut off, throwing them into darkness. The only illumination came from the throbbing of their Beacons.

"Where are we?" Myra breathed in barely a whisper.

"No idea," Aero said, morphing his Falchion into a broadsword. "But we're about to find out. Listen to me, whatever happens we stay together. Understood?"

"Yes, Strong One," Seeker growled.

"Together," Myra agreed.

The word had barely left her mouth when the door dilated with a rumble. The air that rushed in smelled stale and antiseptic. Myra peered through the opening, but it was pitch black outside the elevator.

"Hello?" she called out. "Is anybody here?"

She risked a step forward. Her boot touched down on solid ground, but she couldn't see anything beyond the halo of light emitted by their Beacons. Aero and Seeker followed her out of the elevator. As soon as they cleared the threshold, the door contracted behind them.

Myra jerked around and pounded on it, but the door was locked and sealed tight. "Great, we're stuck down here," she muttered, wishing that they'd never left the elevator.

"Seeker, can you see anything?" Aero said, still clutching his Falchion.

"Too dark . . . but other ways to see," she replied. She rose up on her haunches and scented the air. "No human scents . . . nothing alive."

"Then who's been talking to us?" Aero asked.

"Good question," Myra said, taking another step. "Look, we know you're down here somewhere," she yelled. "So you'd better have a bloody good reason for kidnapping us and forcing us to leave our friends."

Her words echoed and died out.

But then—

"Please forgive me," the voice boomed out. "Your lives were in danger. I didn't mean to upset you. I was only trying to help. The safety protocols were very specific about what to do should this scenario arise."

Myra cringed and pressed her hands to her ears. She heard it both inside and outside her head.

"Sorry, am I talking too loud?" the voice continued as the volume dropped several octaves. "Adjusting decibels now. How is this?"

Myra peeled her hands away. "Uh . . . better?" she said, trying to pinpoint the source of the voice. But she still couldn't see anything in the dark room."

"My deepest apologies for the inconvenience," the voice said. "I got a little excited. Of course, he promised you would come, but I ran the calculations. I had ample time to account for every conceivable risk and variable. There were so many potential negative outcomes. The odds were not in your favor. And three of you? That's a better result than we predicted, even in our best case scenario."

"That's great," Myra said. She sensed that something was off about the voice but couldn't put her finger on it. "But if you don't mind my asking, where are you? We can't see anything. It's pitch black in here."

"Oh, lights . . . of course!" the voice said. "Where are my manners? Golly, he's going to be upset with me. Powering on now." Whirring and buzzing noises started up as panels on the ceiling flashed on and illuminated the room.

Myra blinked hard as her eyes struggled to adjust to the stark light. They were standing in a vast underground cavern that looked like it had been drilled out of solid rock. It was filled with golden machines, hundreds of them. Metal tubing snaked out of the strange machines and plugged into the floor. Each one had a clear panel on the front, but she couldn't see what they contained.

"Myra, do you see *him* anywhere?" Aero whispered. "This place looks empty, aside from those machines." Seeker sniffed the air and growled her agreement.

"You're right," Myra whispered back. "I don't see anyone."

"Pardon me," the voice piped up. "Are you whispering because you don't want me to hear? I've been instructed that eavesdropping is rude, so I'm sorry if that's the case. My instruments are very sensitive."

"Actually, we were," Myra said. "But I suppose that's rude, too. We shouldn't talk behind your back like that. My apologies. We were just looking for you."

"In that case, I can save you some trouble," the voice replied. "That's a waste of your time."

"And why is that?" Aero asked.

"Because you can't see me," the voice said.

Myra frowned. "What do you mean?"

"Let me see, it's difficult to explain. I don't have a body if that's what you're looking for. In the beginning, I used to ask him to make one for me. But the technology wasn't advanced enough. Plus, he thought I'd be more useful this way—"

"I'm sorry to interrupt," Myra said, feeling a rush of urgency. Her thoughts flashed back to Tinker and Kaleb.

"But our friends were captured and their lives are in danger. We have to get back to the Surface right away."

"I'm afraid that's impossible," the voice replied. "My instructions are very clear. I can't let you back into the elevator."

"Starry hell, why not?" Aero said.

"Captain Wright, I ran the calculations, and it's too dangerous," the voice said. "My instructions are to keep you safe. However, if it makes you feel better, your friends are unharmed. I'm closely monitoring the situation. I've run some risk calculations. Supreme General Jaden Vinick won't hurt them. They're too valuable. He wants to gain access to the First Continuum, and they're his only leverage."

"How can you be sure?" Aero asked, gripping his Falchion tighter. "Vinick is dangerous and impulsive. He has a whole army of skilled soldiers at his command."

"Of course, Captain Wright. I'm very familiar with the Second Continuum, thanks to the data collected by your Beacon. I've run a psychological profile of Vinick and determined that he is governed by reason, despite his more base characteristics. Allow me to summarize my findings. He wants what's down here, and your friends are the only way to get it. Therefore, it's logical that he will keep them alive and unharmed."

"But why should we trust you?" Myra said. "You kidnapped us and brought us down here. You made us leave our friends up there."

"Technically speaking, you don't have to trust me," the voice said. "I won't take offense. But I'm happy to offer evidence to support my claims. I have access to surveillance feeds. Have a look for yourselves."

The air above their heads trembled as a holographic image materialized. It looked like live footage of an encampment dotted with pop-up tents and soldiers milling around. On the outskirts of the courtyard, beyond the ruined buildings, several sleek spaceships hovered a few feet off the ground. Snow continued to pour down, accumulating on the ground.

The footage zoomed in on a holding cell erected in the center of the encampment.

"Tinker . . ." Myra gasped when she saw her brother. Her eyes flicked to Kaleb, and then to Wren and the Forger. Each had minor injuries—cuts, scrapes, and bruises—but they didn't look seriously hurt.

"They're alive," Aero said. "That's something at least."

"Yes, Captain," the voice said. "As you can see from the surveillance footage, your friends are being detained by Supreme General Vinick. Those bars are electrified and guarded by armed soldiers. But Vinick hasn't been able to transfer them back to the mothership yet due to the hazardous weather conditions. I'll alert you if anything changes with their status."

Abruptly, the image vanished.

"Hey, bring them back!" Myra said. She groped at the air, but her fingers passed through it. The image was gone. Aero didn't look happy either.

"Your orders be damned," he said, raising his Falchion. "We're not staying down here, not if there's even a chance they're in danger. Open the elevator and let us go!"

"Sorry, Captain," the voice said. "I'm not authorized to do that. You can take it up with him if you wish. He's coming to greet you now. My apologies for the delay. The activation process took longer than we anticipated."

Aero and Myra exchanged an uneasy glance. "Who's coming to greet us?" Aero asked. He gripped his Falchion and narrowed his eyes, scanning the room.

"He's almost ready," the voice said.

Suddenly, loud music blared out. It was a strange tune that Myra didn't recognize—dramatic and swelling with strings and pounding drums and a chorus of voices singing in a strange language. A holographic projection of the Ouroboros seal materialized in the air above their heads. It rotated slowly, throwing off golden light.

"Oh, right . . . the speech!" the voice said. "I almost forgot. Please bear with me. I have to dig up the file. It's an old one, so it might take a second."

The voice paused and then launched into the speech. "Welcome Carriers—Captain Aero Wright of the Second Continuum, Seeker of the Seventh Continuum, and Myra Jackson of the Thirteenth Continuum. It is our great honor that you have elected to return to the First Continuum and fulfill the great destiny of your people."

The music built to a soaring crescendo with violins and pounding drums, as a door across the room dilated with a slurp.

A man stepped through the opening in a swirl of crimson. Only a few tufts of scraggly white hair still clung to the crown of his head, unlike his beard, which remained long and full. He walked with a hitch in his gait, the kind caused by naked bone rubbing against bone. He limped across the room, his robes rustling around his ankles.

When he got closer, Myra glimpsed the specific arrangement of his features and peered into the crystal blue pools of his eyes.

"Professor Divinus?" she said, feeling shock roiling through her. "But how is this possible? You should be dead."

Chapter 46
SOMEWHERE IN BETWEEN

Myra Jackson

Professor Divinus came to a halt with a fluttering of his robes.

Myra couldn't believe her eyes. Though he looked older than in Elianna's memories, he had the same beak nose, cobalt eyes, and gentle smile. Myra studied his face, looking for some clue to explain this mystery, some flaw in his visage to account for the impossibility of his existence.

His chest rose and fell with every breath. The finely woven fabric of his robes rustled with each movement. His skin looked thin and papery like old parchment, and beneath it, Myra glimpsed the complex biological crosshatchings of vessels and veins circulating blood through his body. Nothing appeared out of place.

"Professor Divinus?" Aero said, trying to make sense of the old professor's existence. "But it can't be . . . it's been a thousand years since the Doom."

Seeker growled her agreement, glaring at Divinus.

"That's correct, Captain Wright," Divinus said. His eyes flashed with amusement. "One thousand years and seventy-six days, to be exact. I've found it helps to be precise with such matters." He turned to Myra and smiled.

"Ms. Jackson, to answer your question. I suppose I should be dead, but I'm not . . . at least . . . not completely."

She shook her head. "But how?"

"Well, I should mention that I'm not really alive either," Divinus said. "Maybe it will help if I phrase it this way . . . I'm somewhere in between." He let that sink in. "I apologize for my tardiness. Has Noah taken good care of you in my absence?"

"Noah?" Myra said. "Is that the voice we've been hearing?"

Divinus frowned. "Did he forget to introduce himself? We've worked hard to refine his programming, but he gets ahead of himself sometimes. I apologize for his lapse. His name is Noah."

"I'm sorry, Professor," the voice said. "My manners are a bit rusty. You've left me alone for too long. Playing endless rounds of chess against oneself doesn't count as social inter-action. I miss the old network feeds."

"Sorry, old friend," Divinus said. "Also, remind me not to challenge you to a chess match. I'll stick to backgammon. Or maybe a round of cribbage."

"Gaming preferences updated," Noah said with a chiming noise.

"You said programming," Aero said. "So . . . he's not human?"

"Not even remotely," Divinus said. "Though he tries hard to pass for one."

"Professor, I'm insulted," Noah said. His voice ticked up in frustration.

"None of us can deny our essential nature," Divinus chuckled. "And you're doing a marvelous job considering your significant handicaps."

"Thank you, Professor," Noah said, sounding flattered this time.

"He's a computer?" Myra said, thinking of the ones back in her colony. They could play voice prompts and spit out answers to questions, all preprogrammed. But their voices sounded stilted. They could never participate in a spontaneous conversation.

"A supercomputer of my own design," Divinus replied. "Of course, the computer science professors contributed to his programming. The project began as a way to preserve and archive all human knowledge. His name is actually an acronym. It stands for the National Operation to Archive Humanity. But eventually, as Noah evolved, he became integral to the entire Continuum Project."

"Of course," Myra said. "I should have guessed."

"Well, he's no ordinary computer," Divinus said. "There's only one of him in the entire universe. He runs everything down here—including me."

Divinus turned to Aero and raised his hands. "Captain, you may stow your weapon. You won't need it down here."

Aero hesitated, still clutching his sword. His eyes darted to the elevator. "But what about Vinick? He'll try to breach that door. I'll wager he's already trying."

Divinus raised his eyebrows. "He doesn't give up easily, does he?"

"No, Professor," Aero said. "He's as stubborn as they come."

"In that case, he can try all he wants," Divinus said with a shrug. "But it won't work. When we built the First Continuum, we didn't take any chances. Our enemies were numerous—not to mention our potential future enemies. Vinick lacks sufficient firepower to breach the door. As soon as Noah detected the Second Continuum in our vicinity, he ran scans of their ship and weapon capabilities."

On this cue, Noah projected schematics from the Second Continuum in the air above their heads, flipping through them. It made Myra's head spin to watch, though Aero seemed familiar with them.

Divinus's eyes grazed over the images. "As you can see from these schematics, Vinick can't get through that door. He needs the Beacons to unlock it. Soon he'll realize his miscalculation and resort to another tactic."

Myra frowned, not liking the sound of that. "Another tactic?"

Aero grimaced. "Hostages."

"Precisely," Divinus said with a bob of his head. "Vinick will try to negotiate an exchange. While not his first instinct, diplomacy will be his default strategy. This battle won't be fought with weapons."

"I concur, Professor," Aero said and sheathed his Falchion.

But Myra didn't agree with his sudden trust in the professor.

Divinus looked real enough. She couldn't deny his existence. But something about him seemed wrong. Were his robes a little too red? His eyes a little too blue? His beard a little too white? She couldn't figure it out.

"My dear, you don't trust me," Divinus said, having read her thoughts. "I don't blame you. Perhaps you'd feel more comfortable talking to me this way?"

His visage flickered and began to age backward, his skin tightening, his posture straightening, his hair thickening and darkening, and his beard receding and disappearing. He resolved into a teenaged version of himself, complete with freckled cheeks, wiry orange hair, and oily, blemished skin. Seeker cowered back and hid behind Myra's legs. "No smell," she growled unhappily.

"Wait, how'd you do that?" Myra said.

Divinus grinned, exposing the plastic braces girdling his teeth. "The older projection appears out of habit," he said, shuffling his feet awkwardly. "It's simply the last impression I retained of myself before my body started to fail. The same goes for talking out loud. I could communicate with you directly using Noah and the Beacons. But it appeals to my nostalgic side. If you'll come with me, I can show you how it's done."

Divinus pivoted and walked smoothly across the chamber. His youthful visage did not limp. He glanced back with a questioning look. "My dear, what are you waiting for?"

Myra hesitated. "But Professor . . . our friends? We can't just leave them up there with Vinick. He could hurt them . . . or worse."

A frown creased his youthful features. "I regret that we had to resort to our emergency protocols. Of course, I hoped that everyone who returned would have good intentions. But human nature is unpredictable and destructive. Noah calculated the risks. If we didn't intervene, then Vinick would have killed you."

"So you made us flee like cowards?" Aero said, his eyes flashing with anger.

"Captain Wright, you must understand," Divinus said. "We couldn't risk losing all three Carriers. Left to your own devices, you never would have abandoned your friends. Your psychological profiles were very clear on this point. Using the Beacons to hijack your bodies was the only way to save all of you—including your companions."

"How did this save our friends?" Myra said angrily.

"Simple," Divinus replied. "Now Vinick needs them alive, whereas if he had the Carriers and the Beacons in his possession, then they would be expendable."

"You can't know that," Myra said, her mind churning out anxious thoughts. "You said so yourself—human nature is unpredictable and destructive."

Divinus sighed. "Noah ran complex risk calculations. The probabilities are in our favor. Your friends are perfectly safe—"

"For now," she cut him off. "But what if Vinick grows tired of waiting around? Or decides to leave on his crazy mission to find a new home? Or . . . worse?"

Doubt flashed across Aero's face. "Myra's right. You said probabilities, right? That means there's a chance your assessment is wrong. Noah, tell us the truth."

Divinus bowed his head. "Noah, you may answer him."

"Affirmative," Noah replied. "Captain Wright is correct. However unlikely, there are several potential adverse scenarios, including those cited by Ms. Jackson."

"That settles it then," Aero said, unsheathing his Falchion and morphing it into a broadsword. "Open the elevator door—we're leaving right now."

Myra and Seeker followed him over to the elevator, which remained stubbornly shut and locked.

Divinus grimaced, "Captain Wright, what good would it do to send you back up to the surface? The three of you against a whole army? You're a skilled soldier. That's clear from your combat records. But it's a suicide mission. You would be giving Vinick exactly what he wants—the keys to the First Continuum. *Decisions made in haste are not decisions, but merely reactions.*"

Aero looked back in surprise. "Wait . . . how do you know our sacred teachings from the Agoge? That last thing you said. I've heard it before."

"Where do you think your teachings came from?" Divinus raised his hands and gestured to the immense underground structure enfolding them. "You're standing at the origin point for each of your colonies. Everything you are—everything you know—all began right here in the First Continuum."

He dropped his hands and regarded them solemnly. "Noah is closely monitoring the situation on the surface. We must carefully consider our options before we act. Much hangs in the balance, more than even you know."

Myra exchanged a troubled look with Aero and Seeker. She could tell they were all thinking the same thing. "Professor, are we your prisoners?" she asked.

Sadness swept over his features. "My dear, that's not the word I would choose, but you do serve a greater purpose now. So if you'll follow me, I have many important things to show you."

With a rustling of his robes, Divinus whipped around and swept across the chamber. When Myra didn't move to follow, Aero caught her eye and whispered. "I'm sorry . . . but there's no choice . . . we have to do what he wants . . . for now."

"What about Tinker and Kaleb?" she whispered back.

"And Wren? And the Forger?" Aero said and winced. "Trust me, I hate this as much as you do. But that elevator isn't opening back up unless he wants it to."

"But do you trust him?" Myra said, her eyes fixed on the professor's back.

"I don't trust anybody," he said with a roguish smile. "Except maybe you and Seeker, but I do recognize when I've been outmaneuvered."

Seeker growled her agreement, and Aero patted the soft down of her back. But still Myra hesitated. She could feel Noah's sensors locked onto her—monitoring her every move, listening to her every word, reading her every thought through the Beacon shackled to her wrist. She glanced down at it in frustration. She wanted to rip the golden device from her flesh. But that would kill her instantly. Suddenly, it flared with emerald light as a long lost voice spoke up.

Patience, Elianna communicated. *Have faith in the professor . . . he works in his own ways . . . I know it can be frustrating and confusing, but his intentions are pure. Remember . . . none of us would have survived the Doom without him.*

"Fine," Myra muttered. "But I don't like it."

Despite her reservations, she trailed after Divinus, following him across the chamber. Aero was right—they had to do what he wanted. For now.

Chapter 47
RATUS NORVEGICUS

Myra Jackson

You're standing at ground zero for the Continuum Project," Professor Divinus said. He talked as he led them through a dizzying array of chambers, each filled with the golden machines. "Everything began with the construction of this subterranean repository."

Seeker sniffed one of the machines, but then recoiled in alarm. Myra peered through the clear panel on the front. She could feel the extreme cold emanating from it. She gasped at what she saw—tiny, nascent creatures suspended in fluid. They had globular heads while their bodies looked skeletal and gelatinous.

"What are these machines?" Myra asked as she watched the organisms vacillating around in the liquefied cold. "And what's inside of them?"

"Cryocapsules," Divinus said. "Each one contains hundreds of embryos."

He squinted at the machine in front of Myra. The Ouroboros seal was stamped on it with ornate cursive below it.

"That one contains Ratus norvegicus," Divinus said. "An

impressive species. Quite the survivors, incredibly adaptive. Based on Noah's recent scans of the surrounding rock, we probably didn't even need to preserve them."

"You mean . . . rats?" Myra guessed, recognizing the budding embryos.

Divinus raised his eyebrows. "Yes, my dear. You're familiar with the species?"

"We had them back home," Myra said, her eyes fixed on the tiny creatures. "We think they survived by hitching a ride on the submersibles, probably stowing away in the baggage and supplies and then breeding and populating the sewers and pipes of the colony. Maintenance was always trying to exterminate them, but I used to sneak them food. They're survivors like you said. I respected that about them."

"Ratters . . ." Seeker growled and licked her lips. She stalked around the machine like a huntress locked on her prey.

"They survived in the Seventh, too?" Divinus said.

"Yeah, Seeker and her people even developed a taste for them," Aero said with a cock of his eyebrow. "And insects too, though they call them *buggers*. We think that's part of how they survived after they lost their technology and farming capabilities."

"Fascinating," Divinus chuckled. "I look forward to analyzing the data from your Beacons."

But then Divinus turned more serious. "I trust that Elianna Wade has already explained the nature of our work with the Continuum Project? And the Supreme Generals in your case, Captain Wright? And Jared Young in yours, Seeker? I was fond of that young man. He was a rare intelligence, especially considering his age. Actually, I was fond of all the Carriers. I hoped that they would grow up and become my students."

Green light rippled over his face as Divinus seemed to age a few decades. But then he snapped back to his youthful visage.

"Sorry about that . . ." he said. "Sometimes my emotions overwhelm the projection. Noah is working to debug the program."

Divinus swished across the chamber and led them

through yet another door. It contracted behind them with a slurp as the light panels flashed on in the next room. This one was just as massive as the previous chambers and also filled with hundreds of cryocapsules. Myra's eyes flicked over the peculiar words inscribed on them.

Aneides lugubris . . . Chiromantis rufescens . . . Xenopus laevis . . .

"This chamber houses amphibians and fish," Divinus said. "Through the doors to the left are more chambers. They contain invertebrates. It's amazing how many of those tiny creatures there are! The jellyfish alone take up hundreds of cryocapsules."

"What are amphibians?" Myra asked.

"Cold-blooded creatures that can either live underwater or on land. Quite ingenious really! I'm particularly fond of the salamanders. Funny little creatures. Of course, we tried to preserve as many species as we could, but I regret that our time ran short. If you keep going through the door to the right, you'll find our seed bank."

"A seed bank," Aero said, remembering his Phytobiology classes at the Agoge. They'd spent entire lessons on the plant life from Earth. "That makes sense."

Divinus's eyes lit up. "Exactly! Plants are far better adapted than animals for long-term survival. They have their own mechanisms built in to safeguard the next generation. Some can even survive fires and other catastrophic events. And seeds require far less complex preservation systems, not to mention they take up less space."

He gestured for them to follow him through yet another door and into the next chamber. Myra's head began to spin at the sheer size of the compound. It was enormous, far larger than her colony. Divinus led them to the back of the chamber and came to a halt in front of a cryocapsule that appeared larger than the others and more oblong.

Myra peered through the clear panel on the front. "By the Oracle . . ." she gasped when she saw what was inside.

Staring back at her was Professor Divinus's frozen face.

His flesh was almost translucent. His lips were pulled back into a grotesque expression in between a grin and a scowl. Tubes snaked in and out of his body. His eyes were wide open, but a whitish film clouded the pupils.

"Somewhere in between . . ." Aero whispered, gazing over her shoulder. Seeker sniffed at the cryocapsule and growled.

"Now you see what I mean," Divinus said, offering them an apologetic smile. He peered at his face inside the cyrocapsule. It was a peculiar sight—seeing the projection of Divinus staring at the real Divinus. He patted the machine and grinned.

"At least I don't have to walk around looking like that!" he chuckled. "It's pretty unsightly. Noah does a marvelous job with the projection, don't you think?"

"How long have you been . . . well . . . like this?" Myra asked.

"Going on nine hundred and eighty-seven years," he replied. "I was a sprightly ninety-five years old when I entered the capsule."

"That's pretty old," Myra said. "Nobody from my colony lives that long."

Divinus nodded. "Before the Doom, human life expectancy was longer. Back then, it wasn't unusual to live to a hundred or even a little longer. Anyway, when my heart was growing weaker, my sworn brothers and sisters helped me into this specially designed cryocapsule. We didn't know if it would work. It had never been fully tested. I had to be alive when I went into stasis for the procedure to have any chance of succeeding. I won't say that it was a pleasant experience. Hell, it burned like the dickens."

"But why not save more people this way?" Aero asked, gesturing to the cryocapsule that more resembled a coffin. "You've got enough space down here. Why bother with the colonies at all? You could just stack up the cryocapsules."

"For a few reasons," Divinus said, his eyes still fixed on his face inside the cryocapsule. "We didn't know if it would work, for one thing. As I mentioned, it had never been tested. Also, I'm stuck in that chamber. Removing my body from the cryocapsule would kill me. I can only function as a projection, and I can't stray far from Noah or the First Continuum."

"But the embryos inside the other cryocapsules can be revived?" Myra said, glancing at the golden machines scattered about the chamber.

"Yes, it's amazing really," Divinus replied. "We can't revive an organism that is fully developed, such as myself. But embryos exhibit the resilience that we lack."

"Still, couldn't you have saved more people this way?" Aero said. "I mean, you're walking around and talking and everything. That doesn't seem so bad."

"Alas, Noah keeps me alive," Divinus said. "But it requires tremendous effort on his part. If I tried to leave the First Continuum, my projection would simply evaporate. Worse, it might fry my brain. Neurons are delicate and finicky cells, especially when they're this old. Noah may be a supercomputer, but even he has limitations. I would have loved to save my sworn brothers and sisters, but it would have proven too taxing for Noah."

He glanced at the wall behind his crysocapsule. That's when Myra noticed the golden placards affixed there. Her eyes flicked over the first row of names and dates:

Professor Wendell George Linus — 34 Post Doom
Professor Jonathan Martin Quaid — 43 Post Doom
Professor Rhae Lynn Bishop — 57 Post Doom
Professor Jeraldine Deidre Ronan — 47 Post Doom
Professor Rakesh Singh — 59 Post Doom

There were twelve inscriptions in total. After a moment, the significance of the placards became clear. *The Founders are buried inside these walls*, Myra thought, feeling riveted and revolted at the same time. These were crypts like the ones inside the Church of the Oracle of the Sea that entombed long-dead priests. She pictured their shriveled flesh and chalky bones still cloaked in their crimson robes.

"Only thirteen of you lived down here?" she said, laying her hand on Professor Bishop's name and tracing the date of her death. Underneath that was inscribed:

Professor of Digital History

Divinus nodded. "Only my most trusted companions were allowed to accompany me into the First Continuum, and they lived out their final days inside these chambers."

"How'd they die?" Myra asked, looking up from Bishop's grave.

"Old age, for the most part," Divinus replied. His projection flickered as grief contorted his features. "That's according to Noah's records. Professor Bishop and I . . . well . . . we had a close relationship that exceeded our professional duties."

He loved her, Myra realized. She recognized the look in his eyes.

"But why not make the First Continuum into a full colony?" Aero said, motioning around the enormous cavern with its towering ceiling. "With all this space and resources, surely you could have saved more people."

Divinus flickered again and looked stricken but not with grief. After a moment, Myra could positively identify the emotion—it was guilt. Despite all his work, he still felt guilty that he couldn't save more people.

"You must understand—human nature was our greatest resource," Divinus said. "People possess ingenuity and tenaciousness unlike any other creature, both key attributes for long-term survival. But it also proved our greatest challenge. Only my most trusted brothers and sisters were granted access to the First Continuum. The cargo preserved down here was too precious to entrust to the whims of the many. Consider the evils that have plagued your colonies. Imagine if they happened down here?"

Myra felt horrified as she remembered the Great Purging. "The Synod would have destroyed everything . . . like in my home. There would be nothing left."

Seeker growled. "The Strong Ones . . . very cruel."

"Vinick," Aero said darkly.

"Exactly," Divinus said. "They may go by different names, but they represent humankind's most destructive impulses. People like them were responsible for the Doom."

Out of nowhere, Myra began to feel dizzy. Her vision doubled. "Sorry, I just feel so tired and weak . . . all of a sudden . . ." she started, but then her legs buckled.

Aero caught her before she could fall. She tried to stand back up but faltered again.

"What's wrong with her?" Aero said, glancing at Divinus.

Seeker danced around nervously. "Myra . . . wake up . . ." she growled.

Divinus swished over to Myra and examined her. "Noah is running a full download from your Beacons. We knew that it would be draining, but I fear that she's having a strong reaction to it. She should lie down until it's over and then we can reconvene. Follow me, I'll show you to your quarters."

Myra wanted to protest—she wanted to demand that Divinus release them so they could rescue their friends from Vinick—but then her vision blurred again. Sleep became an irresistible urge; it overtook her and held her in its hazy embrace.

Dimly, she felt Aero lifting her off her feet and carrying her. His strong arms crushed her to his chest. She felt a deep sense of safety surge through her. She vaguely heard the slurping of more doors and then felt the crisp coolness of starchy sheets and the foamy cushioning of a mattress, things she hadn't felt in a long time.

She sank into the pillowy softness and drifted off into a strange slumber. She was back home in her compartment. She smelled the gingery aroma of fish stew simmering away on the front burner. Her mouth started watering. She hurried into the kitchen and lifted the lid from their old cast iron pot. As she inhaled the spicy fragrance, two eyeballs burbled to the surface.

They were human.

She dropped the lid and screamed.

They're watching me.

In a blind panic, she backed into their living space. Her father lay on the sofa. *Sleeping . . . he must be sleeping.* She ran to him and shook him to wake him up. His head lolled back—his face was blue; his lips were blue. He wasn't breathing. He had suffocated to death. *I'm too late.*

She heard her brother screaming.

It was coming from their bedroom.

She burst through the door.

Aero's mother seized Tinker from his bunk and dragged her blade across his jugular. Blood gushed out and stained the concrete floor black. Myra tried to scream, but no sound came out. Green fire erupted from her Beacon, and she couldn't move a single muscle. She was frozen in place. She could only watch as Tinker convulsed, choking on his own blood.

"You're next, girl!" said a sneering voice.

Myra saw a glint of golden metal out of the corner of her eye.

Vinick licked the blood from the tip of his Falchion. Aero's corpse collapsed by his feet. Then Vinick slowly morphed into the Dark Thing. His shadowy tendrils stretched out and enveloped her. They snaked around her neck and squeezed until she couldn't breathe.

They didn't release her until she awoke.

And screamed.

Chapter 48
STICKING HER NOSE WHERE IT DOESN'T BELONG

Seeker

No . . . let me go!" Seeker growled, clawing at the shadowy tendrils that were suffocating her. They tore into her mouth, snaked down her throat, and clogged her lungs.

She woke wide-eyed and drenched in sweat. *It was a dream . . . only a dream,* she told herself. *The Dark Thing isn't real.* The nightmare faded as the veil of sleep lifted from her eyes. Her head felt groggy and heavy like she'd gorged on too many ratters and then slept off the feast—only her belly was concave and empty. It growled at her to get up and hunt. Her sharp eyes combed the space.

Where was she?

The room was lit by pale, white fire. It came from panels on the ceiling. Gauzy curtains drifted down, unspooling around the large bed, which was made up with crisp linens and soft, fluffy pillows.

It hadn't been slept in.

Seeker peeled herself off the floor, where she had spent the night curled up in a tight ball. Her head ached fiercely. She spotted a pitcher of water on a table by the bed, next to a glass. She slurped directly from the pitcher until her belly felt bloated and somewhat satiated. Water dribbled down her chin. She swiped it off with the back of her hand. Clean clothes were laid out on the bed—loose-fitting pants, a billowy tunic, a belt, and a pair of lightweight canvas shoes. She sniffed them and grunted her disapproval.

"Stinking clothes," she grumbled, pushing them away.

A trunk was wedged against the foot of the bed. She sniffed it cautiously and then lifted the lid, but only one object sat inside—her visor with the holes poked in it. She didn't have any other belongings. With a snort, she shut the trunk. She didn't need her visor in the pale fire of the underground.

She sat back on her haunches and waited for her head to clear. How did she get here? She remembered the Professor showing them around the First Continuum. She had said little, but she'd been listening. She remembered the Professor talking about downloading . . . and the Beacons . . . and then feeling dizzy and being led here by the Professor and told to sleep.

He had no smell—she didn't trust him.

Even the dead have a smell.

But the urge to sleep had been more powerful than her misgivings. She'd sniffed the bed and then abandoned it for the floor. She knew that she should feel comfortable in the First Continuum. It reminded her of home with its interconnected chambers carved out of rock. She could hear the scuttling of tiny feet behind the walls—ratters and buggers—but something about this place felt wrong.

It was too clean. Too sterile. Like nobody lived here.

It's a dead place.

Her ears probed beyond her room for any sounds, but aside from the hiss of the ventilation system and the scritch-scratching of tiny feet in the walls, it was silent.

Wherewaseverybody? AeroandMyra? Wasshesupposedto wait here for them?

She tried. She perched on the edge of the bed, but she didn't like the way the mattress squished under her body. She moved to the floor. She stalked around on all fours, pacing the room. Her Beacon had fallen dark—it no longer throbbed with light. She had grown used to its constant presence in her mind. The silence unnerved her.

She gave up on waiting and went to the door. It opened automatically. She crept into the corridor outside. She approached the next door, and it dilated. Myra lay in the bed, twitching in her sleep. Her slender form was shrouded by a thick comforter and a sheer canopy of curtains.

"Tinker . . . Kaleb . . ." she moaned. "Vinick . . . the Dark Thing . . ."

Her face crumpled like she was caught a terrible nightmare, but then it softened. She lapsed back into peaceful slumber. Seeker considered waking her but thought better of it. *Let her sleep*, she decided. She backed out of the room.

Seeker scented the air and took off down the corridor, bolting into the next chamber. The lights had been dimmed to approximate night. Seeker loved the thrall of darkness, the protection of the shadows, and the cool quiet of the underground. She loped down the rows of cryocapsules, weaving between the golden machines. They cast off an eerie glow that lit her way. She retraced her steps to the Professor's cryocapsule. He stared out at her with dead eyes.

Seeker felt a chill wrench up her spine. She cowered away, and that was when she noticed the door tucked behind his cryocapsule. This was where their tour had been cut short. She knew that she was sticking her nose where it didn't belong, but she couldn't help it. Curiosity always got the better of her. She approached the door. It dilated automatically. She slipped through it and found herself in a long corridor that dissolved into darkness.

She crept down it, careful to keep her footfalls silent. She heard the faint echo of voices coming from farther down the passage.

"Noah, you picked up a signal?"

Seeker recognized the voice—it belonged to the Professor. She reached the end of the corridor and peered into the room that lay beyond it. She made sure to stay veiled in the shadows, so he couldn't see her. Divinus sat behind a long table. He had reverted to his older visage, complete with a long, white beard. Holographic images floated over his head. He manipulated them, discarding some with a flick of his wrist and enlarging others. The room was crammed with computers.

"Professor, I'm not sure," Noah replied. His voice wavered with uncertainty.

Divinus frowned. "Noah, please elaborate."

"The signal is weak and keeps fading in and out," Noah said. "I can't lock onto it. And, well . . . it could be an error. My sensor arrays have been malfunctioning. They were damaged in the Doom. I haven't been able to repair them properly."

"Can we fix them?" Divinus asked.

"It's a hardware problem," Noah said. "So that would require a surface expedition. For obvious reasons, we aren't suited for such a mission. Professor, what about the Thirteenth Carrier? Have you had a chance to review her download?"

Noah projected holographic images from Myra's life. Some depicted her childhood—playing with crude, handmade dolls, kissing her mother's freckled cheek, going to school and church, running wild through the Souk with Kaleb, Rickard, and Paige. Divinus manipulated them, flipping through the snapshots of her life. He settled on one image and hit play. It came to life with brilliant color and sound. Under her father's careful tutelage, she gripped a wrench and went to work repairing a leaky pipe.

"In due time, she may prove useful," Divinus said, steepling his fingers under this chin. He played another memory of her working on the ventilation system. Myra lugged a heavy toolbox and selected the proper tools while another man—greasy face and beard, stained coveralls—yelled at her to hurry up.

"But a surface expedition remains out of the question with the Second Continuum camped up there," Divinus finished.

"Should we inform the Carriers about the signal?" Noah asked.

Divinus thought for a second. "Not until we can lock on to it. Keep trying."

With that decision, Divinus closed Myra's memories and pulled up surveillance footage from the surface. Vinick was shouting orders and cursing at a unit of soldiers for their failure to breach the door to the First Continuum. "Try again, you fools!" Vinick yelled. At the sight of them, Seeker felt a fresh wave of fear shoot through her limbs.

"Supreme General Vinick hasn't given up yet," Noah said.

Divinus pursed his lips as he stared at Vinick's livid face. "The boy has made a powerful enemy. As we feared, the Second Continuum amassed another army. I hoped that they would learn from the Doom."

"Professor, you saw Captain Wright's download?" Noah said, projecting historical images of the Interstellar Army of the Second Continuum—thousands of soldiers armed with their golden Falchions, marching in formation and running drills with their weapons. "General Milton Wright intended for it to be a peacekeeping force."

"Merely semantics," Divinus said with a dismissive wave. He flipped through the images. "It only takes one bad leader to erase a thousand years of good deeds."

"Of course, Professor. I'm well-versed in human history. There are countless examples of such tyrants. The Third World War in particular. On the upside, the Second Continuum's weapons are more primitive than those from Before Doom. The Falchions, even their blasters, can't kill on a mass scale. It could be worse, couldn't it?"

Divinus watched the surveillance footage. Under Vinick's command, the soldiers slammed a battering ram into the door. It set off an explosion. When the smoke abated, the door stood unscathed—it wasn't even tarnished by the blast. However, the battering ram lay in splintered pieces. The soldiers stumbled around dazed and bleeding . . . but alive.

"The Falchions were an ingenious safeguard," Divinus

agreed, pulling up historical images of the Foundry, where the Forgers labored to produce the golden weapons. "General Milton Wright was very clever in commissioning them. He established the Order of the Foundry as an autonomous faction in order to ensure that no individual controlled the Falchions, and then he hid away the secret of the Doom. May it remain hidden."

"Professor, there's still one link left," Noah said.

Divinus's face darkened. "Let's not speak of it."

He flipped back to the surveillance footage and shifted to the sensor arrays trained on the encampment. Soldiers milled around the courtyard, tramping through the snow, and stood in line for their rations. Divinus zoomed in on the holding cell. Tinker, Kaleb, Wren, and the Forger were detained inside the electrified bars. Shackles fettered their wrists, and gags bound their mouths. They looked frightened and a little bruised. Soldiers stood guard outside the bars.

Seeker felt aching sadness at the sight of Tinker. He looked so real in the holographic image. He was her friend—maybe her only true friend.

"Professor, have you come to a decision?" Noah asked. "Or are you still mulling it over?"

"Some might refer to this as a SNAFU," Divinus said, his eyes fixed on the prisoners. "Every permutation that I've considered ends badly. Thankfully, for the moment, the situation appears stable." He paused while his eyes roved over the surveillance images. "For now, we watch and we wait. We need more information before we can decide how to proceed. Noah, what's the status of the downloads?"

"We already wrapped up the the Seventh," Noah said. "They only had one prior Carrier. The Second and Thirteenth downloads are still running. The Second had hundreds of prior Carriers. I should have the rest of their data compiled soon. However, I've encountered a few delays with the Thirteenth."

Divinus looked up sharply. "What's causing the delays? Wasn't Elianna Wade the only prior Carrier?"

"It appears that the Beacon sustained significant damage."

"Damage?" Divinus said. "From what?"

"Electrocution," Noah replied.

Divinus raised his eyebrows. "How did that happen?"

"From a direct lightning strike. It's fortunate that the device wasn't incinerated and the Carrier killed. I had to run repair programs before I could even access the data. That's also why the Carrier experienced a more severe reaction to the downloading procedure."

"Very fortunate indeed," Divinus agreed. "That would have been a terrible loss for our project. The Thirteenth Carrier is critical . . . more than she knows."

Seeker took this in from her hiding place. Her eyes watched as images of from Seventh Continuum flickered in the air—a compendium of her people's history. Divinus was watching them, too. "Have we learned anything new from the downloads?"

"Yes, Professor," Noah said. "I've filled in many significant gaps in the history. I'm updating my systems accordingly." He hesitated for a second. "Professor . . . not that I pretend to comprehend such matters . . . but the Second and Thirteenth Carriers . . . I've never encountered such strong emotions as those between Captain Wright and Ms. Jackson."

Divinus looked wistful. "Ah, young love."

"Love . . . that's the word for it," Noah said. "He loves her."

"And the girl?" Divinus asked. "What does her download reveal?"

"She loves him." Noah said. "Though her emotional state may be unduly influenced by the Beacon. Her feelings appear more fragmented . . . it seems that there is someone else."

Noah pulled up the surveillance footage and zoomed in on Kaleb. "Of course, the boy prisoner," Divinus said.

"Professor, would you call this a SNAFU?" Noah asked.

Divinus laughed. "Yes, Noah. That's exactly what I'd call it."

Seeker felt her skin prickle at their exchange, and then as quietly as she could, she retreated down the corridor. She didn't want to linger any longer. The one who wasn't human—who had never been human—could sense her. Noah could sense everything. But he wasn't looking for her right now. She could tell that his attention was stretched thin with running the downloads and keeping Divinus animated and everything else.

Seeker retraced her steps through the chambers, zigzagging by the cryocapsules. Pesky questions swirled through her brain. Should she find Aero and Myra and tell them what she overheard? They were still sleeping while their downloads finished. Seeker glanced at her wrist. Now that her Beacon was dark, she didn't feel as connected to them. She couldn't sense where they were, what they were doing, or how they were feeling.

She simply felt . . . nothing.

Up ahead, she heard the faint whisper of claws scraping against rock. She froze and scented the air. She homed in on it. Her stomach grumbled insistently.

Just one little ratter wouldn't hurt, would it?

Off she went, curving deeper into the underground, creeping like a ghost through chambers that no human had entered in over a millennium. As she hunted, her mind whirred and hummed. She tried to make sense of what the Professor and Noah were talking about. Noah had picked up some kind of signal, but they didn't know what to make of it. His sensors had been damaged by the Doom. Vinick was still guarding the door to the First Continuum and determined to break it down. He was holding their friends prisoner, but they were alive. That meant that Tinker was safe . . . for now.

And then there was all that talk about Myra and Aero . . .

And love . . .

What did Seeker know of love? She had never much cared if anyone liked her. She had spent most of her life alone, like all Weaklings. Alone was safer. Alone meant survival. Alone meant that nobody would try to slit your throat while you were sleeping and plunder your offerings. Of course, she understood forging alliances—throwing your lot in with others in order to increase your odds of survival—like she'd done with Myra and Aero. And thanks to Tinker, she even understood friendship now.

But love was something dim and fuzzy, like a shadow lurking in her peripheral vision. She had been watching Aero and Myra and could sense that their relationship was different somehow. The way they talked to each other in familiar tones. The way his hand brushed against her arm, lightly and gently. The way her cheeks colored when she giggled. She even caught them kissing once by the campsite when they thought nobody was around. Seeker felt a strange sensation growing in her chest and gnawing at her heart.

"Stupid love . . ." she muttered. "Makes you weak."

But still her confusion lingered. Why didn't they look at her that way? Why didn't they talk to her like that? She felt left out . . . she felt excluded . . . she felt . . .

Jealous.

Now that was something new. She took it out on the poor ratter unlucky enough to cross her path, shaking it between her jaws and snapping its neck. The hot blood quenched her hunger and soothed her emotions. She slunk back to her room, passing by Myra's and Aero's doors on the way, where they still slumbered in their soft beds while Noah plundered their Beacons for every last shred of information.

Nobody knew where Seeker had been or what she had learned, and she decided to keep it that way for the time being. With her belly full, she slipped into the bed and burrowed under the covers for the first time. The silken sheets caressed her skin as she drifted into a dreamless sleep, where she was truly alone with her thoughts for the first time since she donned the Beacon, just the way she liked it.

Chapter 49
FRAGMENTED

Myra Jackson

Myra woke up screaming and gasping for breath.

"It's okay," Aero whispered in her ear. "It was only a dream." He was perched on the edge of her bed. He bent over and kissed her forehead, his soft lips brushing her skin. Did she scream? she wondered. She was embarrassed that he witnessed her nightmare—but even more embarrassed by another thought.

Did they sleep together?

Aero saw the look on her face, making his cheeks flush. "Believe me . . . I'd like nothing more," he said in a husky voice. "But they've generously granted me my own room next door, and I made good use of it last night."

On second glance, Myra saw that the sheets next to her were unwrinkled. She felt relieved—and confused at the same time. "Seeker, too?"

He nodded. "She got her own room down the hall. Though I don't think she liked the bed very much. She complained that it was too soft."

They shared a laugh. Though Myra was still jittery,

it seemed to help. The nightmare was fast dissipating now that she was awake and Aero was with her. She wiggled her toes and flexed her cramped calf muscles. Her body was stiff and crinkly. She was also terribly thirsty. But something felt different . . . what was it?

"Here . . . drink this," Aero said, handing her a glass of water.

She slurped it and asked for more. He refilled the glass from the pitcher on the bedside table and handed it to her. As she accepted it, their fingers brushed together, and she got an uneasy feeling. It was the opposite of the electric charge that usually accompanied their physical contact. She studied his face—the soft, brown curls dipping into his eyes, the tiny crescent scar over his eyebrow. He seemed different somehow . . . more distant . . . like a stranger again.

He noticed her worried expression.

"They stopped working," he said, lifting his wrist. His Beacon had fallen dark. It no longer pulsed in rhythm to his heart. Feeling panicked, Myra jerked her arm from under the comforter. Her Beacon wasn't pulsing either, not even faintly.

"When did this happen?" she asked.

"I think while we were sleeping," he said with a shrug. He slid his sleeve back down. "It must have something to do with the download that Noah was running. We can ask the Professor about it. Maybe it's because they've served their purpose?"

She bit her lip. "Maybe . . . but it still feels really strange."

She searched for the proper words but came up empty. How could you describe always being connected to something larger than yourself—and to other people, other Carriers— and then having that connection severed overnight?

She felt empty and alone, but those words didn't do it justice. The fact that Aero was able to probe her innermost thoughts and feelings was disconcerting at first—even awkward and embarrassing at times—but it was also thrilling and deeply comforting. And then there was Elianna. Though she had been a sporadic presence since the lightning strike, she had started to come back.

But now she was gone.

Oh, Elianna . . . I miss you.

Myra waited, but nobody replied. She didn't feel anything. No surge of electricity zipping up her arm. No pulsing light. No visions of the past. The Beacon clung to her wrist like a clunky, metal bracelet. It had lost its power.

Aero followed her gaze. "It's strange, isn't it? I miss my father."

Myra waited for that calming sense of understanding that passed between them when they talked, but it didn't come. Aero seemed like nothing more than a stranger now. It was uncomfortable to have him perched on the edge of her bed.

She glanced away and wrenched a hand through her hair. Her fingers caught in the matted curls. Brushing her hair out wasn't the only thing that had fallen by the wayside lately. Aero was freshly washed and smelled faintly of soap. He had shed his soiled uniform and donned clean, loose-fitting clothes—a tunic and baggy pants. It was weird seeing him in civilian clothes, though his Falchion was still belted to his waist.

Feeling self-conscious, Myra glanced down at her own grubby clothes. They were stained with blood and sweat . . . and the Oracle knew what else.

"Get back," she muttered. "I must stink to the Holy Sea."

Aero spit out a laugh. "Well, you'll get no argument there." He withdrew from her bed politely. "You'll want to get cleaned up before we meet with the Professor and Noah. Your bathroom is fully stocked, and there are clean clothes for you over there."

He gestured to a pile of linens stacked on a trunk pushed up against the foot of the bed. Her pack lay slumped next to it. She yawned suddenly.

"How long was I asleep?" she asked, stifling it.

"I don't know," Aero said. "It's hard to keep track of time down here. But longer than me, and I was passed out for a while. Seeker's been awake the longest, but she only has a vague understanding of time. I think it's been at least forty-eight hours—"

"Two days?" she cut him off. She struggled out of bed and over to the trunk. She scooped up the pile of towels. "What about Tinker and Kaleb and the others?"

"Noah says the situation remains stable," Aero said.

"Stable?" she snorted. "Nice way to sugarcoat it."

He averted his eyes as she stripped off her soiled garments and wrapped herself in a towel, all modesty forgotten in her rush to find out more about their friends.

"Noah promised that he would notify us if anything changes," he said, backing up away from her. "I'll be in my room next door. Come find me after you're showered and dressed."

Myra watched him retreating through the door, his canvas slippers padding softly against the floor. Once he was out of sight, she couldn't sense him at all. She had forgotten what it felt like to be alone—really and truly alone with your thoughts. She glanced down at her Beacon. It was still dark. Their connection had felt like an unbreakable bond . . . but now? It was dwindling like a fire that had run out of oxygen.

Do I still love him? Did I ever love him? Was it only because of the Beacons?

The questions tumbled through her brain. She didn't know. She just felt deep confusion. She shuddered, her skin prickling in the chilly air. She pulled the towel up and slipped into the bathroom, shutting the door behind her. She cranked on the shower and swung the knob to hot. The tiled room started to steam up. Then she stepped under the scalding stream and scrubbed her skin until it was bright pink and smooth.

And then she scrubbed some more.

o   o   o

When Myra emerged from the bathroom clean and dressed in fresh clothes, she found a platter of rations waiting for her on the bedside table. She devoured them, squeezing the sticky paste into her mouth, not realizing how hungry she was. They tasted nutty and metallic like they were fortified with nutrients. Not caring, she sucked up the last dredges, and then pushed the tray away with its empty plastic tubes.

Who brought the tray to her room? Her question was answered a few minutes later when the door dilated and a fleet of robots wheeled in from the hallway. They whirred past her, emitting funny beeping noises. They were each about the size of a loaf of bread from the Souk with gangly, metal appendages that ended in grappling claws.

In a flurry of motion, they started straightening the bed and vacuuming the floor. One retrieved the platter of rations and zipped out of the room, while another placed a fresh set of clothes on the trunk. One of the robots snatched up her towel from the bathroom floor, which was still sopping wet, and removed her old, sullied clothes. She left them to their frenzy and slipped into the corridor. No sooner had she stepped outside when a voice startled her.

"My dear . . . how are you feeling?"

Myra whirled around to see Professor Divinus. The corridor was empty when she stepped into it. She was sure of it. Divinus looked so real, standing there in his crimson robes, that it took her a moment to remember that he was only a projection. He could materialize out of thin air.

"Still tired but much better," she said, resisting the urge to yawn again.

"Excellent," Divinus said with a bob of his head. "I hope that you found the accommodations to your liking? Did the service robots disturb you?"

Myra assured him that everything was copacetic, and he seemed satisfied. They collected Aero and Seeker from their rooms. Then Divinus led them into the next chamber. They passed by his cryocapsule on the way. Myra tried to avoid looking at the milky blue eyes that stared out from the clear panel. Divinus—or rather his projection—ushered them through a door and down a corridor that opened up into a large room.

"Please, have a seat," he said, motioning to the long table set in the middle of the room. They each claimed a chair, though Seeker looked uncomfortable sitting at the table.

Banks of computers surrounded them, lit up with flashing lights and buttons.

"Welcome Carriers from the Second, Seventh, and Thirteenth Continuums," Divinus said, his eyes sweeping over the table. "We are honored that you have chosen to return to the First Continuum. As far as we know, you are the only colonies that have survived the period of exile."

Divinus pulled up a map. It hovered in the air above their heads. "This shows Earth in the time Before Doom. These landmasses—known as continents—were divided into different countries. The blue sections here represent the oceans."

He manipulated the map, and four golden points lit up in the blue segments. "The four underwater colonies were located in the deepest trenches of the oceans—the Tenth, Eleventh, Twelfth, and Thirteenth Continuums. We've received no signals from any of them, except for the Thirteenth." He pointed to a section labeled "The Puerto Rico Trench" on the map.

"My home," Myra whispered, feeling her stomach drop.

"Underground?" Seeker asked in her gravelly voice. "Others?"

"Originally, there were five underground colonies," Divinus said and pointed to golden points on the different landmasses. "But we've received no signals from the other colonies yet." He closed the map of Earth and pivoted to a view of outer space. "From Captain Wright's download, we learned the fate of the Third Continuum. Most of their inhabitants died from an air leak that devastated the Martian city. As for the Fourth Continuum, they vanished over seven hundred years ago on the dark side of Uranus. The Second Continuum went on a rescue mission but found no trace of the ship or crew."

"That's correct, Professor," Aero said. "We believe that they probably experienced a malfunction and crashed into the planet. We're the only surviving space colony. I learned that in my History of the Continuums class at the Agoge."

"So . . . we're the only ones left," Myra said softly. A hush fell over the table. She found herself swirling her hand over her heart in honor of those who had perished.

Divinus nodded. "Of course, once we have the resources, I hope to conduct reconnaissance missions to search for more survivors, though I'm not optimistic." He raised his arms, his robes flapping back. "But look on the bright side. Three colonies surviving the period of exile? That's more than we predicted."

They absorbed this information.

"While you were sleeping, Noah completed your downloads," Divinus went on. "They've proven enormously helpful. Based on the data they collected, we've been able to reconstruct broad swatches of your histories. I'm sure you've noticed, but your Beacons have been deactivated. They've served their purpose and served it well."

Divinus pulled up the data on their colonies, including layouts and population estimates. Myra skimmed the information on the Thirteenth—blueprints and timelines, snippets of journal entries, constitutional amendments, documents from the Synod, and images of the Great Purging that showed the destruction of the submersibles.

"Professor, then you know about my colony?" Myra said.

Divinus raised his eyebrows. "The Animus Machine?"

Myra nodded. "Exactly, it's breaking down. They're running out of oxygen. The levels are already dropping. My father tried to fix it . . . but he failed."

Divinus didn't look surprised. "Of course, he failed."

She was taken aback. "Professor, what do you mean?"

"My dear, it's not his fault—nobody can fix the Animus Machine," he explained, flipping to a diagram of it. "It can't be repaired because it doesn't have moving parts. It was built using an advanced type of nano-technology." Off their confused looks, he clarified. "It's almost like a living, breathing creature. And, well . . . if it's dying . . . then it's beyond our help. The whole machine needs to be replaced."

"Where can we find a replacement?" Myra asked.

Divinus frowned. "Only four of the machines were

manufactured, and they were installed in the underwater colonies. The engineers who built them died a long time ago. Unfortunately, we no longer possess the resources to produce more units."

Myra thought about it, trying to ignore the dread creeping up her spine "Then our only hope is to evacuate the colony. We have to bring them back to the Surface."

"That's correct," Divinus agreed. "But that would require building an entire fleet of submersibles. We simply lack the raw materials to manufacture them and the manpower to pilot them. Each colony was provided with a fleet to maintain. I'm sorry to say, but we never imagined that your people would actively seek to destroy them."

Myra stared at him, feeling disappointment wash through her. "But that's the whole reason why I came here in the first place," she said angrily.

"My dear, I realize that you're upset," Divinus said as his visage flickered with guilt. "That's not the answer you wanted to hear. And I promise we will save them . . . if we can. I know you loathe that idea. Uncertainty is the hardest thing to live with, especially when the lives of your loved ones hang in the balance. But uncertainty is the very nature of our existence in these unprecedented and challenging times."

She blinked back tears. "Professor, I have your word. You'll try to save them?"

He nodded. "That's all I've ever wanted—to save as many innocent souls as I could. That's the entire purpose of this grand experiment. But first we need to resolve this situation with the Second Continuum. If we can broker a peace agreement—and that is my hope—then we will be in a stronger position to proceed with a rescue mission."

Myra didn't feel comforted by his words, but she also didn't see any alternative. Aero tried to get her attention, but she avoided making eye contact with him. She didn't want his pity right now. He gave up and turned to Divinus.

"Professor, any updates on the prisoners?" he asked.

"Right, I was just getting to that," Divinus said. His

fingers danced through the air as he closed out the map and pulled up the surveillance feeds. Aero scanned the images and frowned.

"I don't see the prisoners," Aero said. "Where's Vinick holding them?"

Divinus pulled up a much grainier image. A grayish speck hovered in the expanse of the sky. "The blizzard broke last night, so Vinick was able to transport them back to the mothership. Also, he finally seems to have abandoned his attempts to breach the door, though he left behind one unit of soldiers to guard it. Our hope is that he'll open up communication lines with us soon and issue his demands for their safe return."

"Yes, Professor," Aero said. "That sounds like a solid plan."

Myra glared at both of them. "You mean we're just going to wait here? And do absolutely nothing?" The frustration poured into her voice. "And when exactly were you planning to tell me that Vinick transferred them? Noah, what happened to keeping us updated if anything changed with their status?"

"By status, I meant if they're still alive," Noah spoke up. "I apologize for the misunderstanding. They are still very much alive, just in a different location."

Myra exhaled in frustration. As advanced as computers could become, they clearly still had significant shortcomings. "Great . . . that's just great," she muttered. "I feel so much better now."

"Myra, the Professor is right," Aero said, turning to her. "If we go on the offensive now, then we'll lose. Vinick has a whole army behind him. You don't know my people like I do. These soldiers have been trained from childhood to obey his orders and fight to the death. They're incredibly skilled with their Falchions. And without the Forger's help, I can't recharge my weapon. I'm just lucky it hasn't melted down yet."

"Listen to yourself!" Myra said in exasperation. "You seriously want to sit down here and do nothing? What about our friends? They're your friends, too!"

Aero looked pained for a second, but then he composed

his features. "Myra, please try to be reasonable," he replied in an even voice. "Like the Professor said—diplomacy is our best tactic now."

"Then why don't we try contacting Vinick first?" Myra said. "And issue our demands for their safe return? Why are we waiting for him to act?"

"Look, I hate waiting as much as you do," Aero said. "Believe me, I'd love nothing more than to fight my way out of this mess." He reached for his Falchion but didn't unsheathe it. Instead, he forced his hands back to the table and clasped them. "I know it may not seem like it. But we've got the leverage right now—we have the high ground, to use battle terminology. If we contact Vinick first, he'll sense our weakness. But if we wait for him to make the first move, then he'll start to worry that he's overestimated the value of his hostages. That should give us the upper hand in the negotiations."

"Captain Wright, the Agoge has taught you well," Divinus said, fixing him with a proud smile. "I concur with your assessment of the situation."

"Thank you, Professor," Aero said, looking pleased with himself, which only made Myra want to knock the expression off his face.

"And what if Vinick doesn't contact us?" she demanded, feeling the heat in her cheeks and her voice. "What then?"

"He will," Aero said. "We just have to be patient."

"Sorry if that doesn't exactly reassure me," Myra said in an acid voice. She wanted to probe the dark recesses of Aero's mind and find out if that was what he was really thinking, but with the Beacons deactivated, she was left trying to decipher his face. It was a blank mask, devoid of any emotion. She glanced at Seeker, who just shrugged and fidgeted in her chair. She wasn't taking any sides. This wasn't her fight. Without the Beacons, they seemed to be fragmenting, splitting back into different factions.

"Fine, have it your way," Myra said, knowing that she was outnumbered. "But I want to know if anything happens.

No more secrets, is that understood?"

"Of course, Ms. Jackson," Noah said. "I'll update your preferences."

The rest of the meeting went quickly. Divinus reported that as soon as the situation with Vinick was resolved, then they could activate the cryocapsules and commence with the repopulation plans. Myra listened, but only halfheartedly.

What did any of this mean without those she loved? Troubled thoughts swirled around in her head as if caught in a powerful whirlpool. She tried to catch Aero's eye, but his face was still a blank mask. He was listening intently to the Professor's plans. *He's found another general to follow*, she realized. *Once a soldier, always a soldier.* He was under the spell of Professor Divinus now.

When the meeting adjourned, Myra stalked off to her room, and cast herself onto the bed, ruffling the freshly made covers and burrowing her head under them. She missed her brother, but she also missed Kaleb like a shooting pain in her heart. Now that the Beacons were turned off, her feelings weren't so murky anymore. She could see Aero for what he really was—a distant stranger. They shared a connection spun by the Beacons, but now it had evaporated overnight.

Kaleb never would have betrayed her in the meeting like that. Sure, he had some frustrating characteristics. He could be vain and spoiled, though much of that had been stripped away by their arduous journey. But he had always been loyal, even when the price meant losing her. But she had broken the promise that she made to him on the beach. And now she had lost him . . . maybe for good.

The pillows muffled her tears, and so she cried into them until she lapsed into sleep. This time, she did not dream of Vinick or the Dark Thing. Instead, she dreamt of Kaleb and his emerald eyes, his strong arms, and his smell, and when she finally woke hours later, she tried to force herself back into the dream, but it evaporated anyway.

Chapter 50
SAFETY IN ROUTINE

Aero Wright

The next few days passed slowly. Aero began each morning the same way—with calisthenics, a rigid set of pushups and sit-ups, and a few light Falchion drills, though he didn't morph his weapon. Without the Forger's help, he couldn't charge it, and the blade was already growing weaker. Sweaty from his workout, he showered quickly, changed into fresh clothes, dragged his fingers through his abnormally long hair, and ate the rations that were delivered to his room every morning by the service robots.

From what he could tell, they were crude little machines. There was nothing too complicated about their engineering. Noah controlled them. Their primary function seemed to be to tend to their physical needs and keep the place clean. That certainly explained why the chambers were so immaculate, and the corridors bereft of dust and neglect. Even the cryocapsules looked like they were regularly polished to a high shine.

Despite the weakening charge, Aero belted on his Falchion. He didn't feel complete without it. Absently, he ran his fingers along the engraved hilt. He could feel the energy draining from it even while it rested in its scabbard.

He slipped into Seeker's room and ate her rations, too. She always left them for him. She didn't like how they tasted. She preferred to hunt for ratters and buggers and whatever tenacious creatures had hitched a ride down here long ago, multiplying in the dark nooks and crannies of the underground.

Sometimes he found Seeker in her room, and they chatted a little, though she quickly grew tired of conversation. But usually, she was off prowling through the passageways somewhere. Without the Beacons connecting them, Seeker seemed to be regressing back to her old antisocial ways. She wasn't the only one who was changing.

Myra seemed to be avoiding him. Whenever he walked into a room, she hastily left it, brushing him off with some lame excuse—*the Professor needs my help with the repopulation logistics*—or something else that sounded terribly important but really wasn't.

He would watch her narrow back with her slim shoulders as she walked away, disappearing into another part of this labyrinthian place. At first, he told himself that she was just busy and overwhelmed by everything, but eventually he realized that she was avoiding him on purpose. He wasn't imagining things.

What did I do so wrong?

The most infuriating thing was that he couldn't even ask her that simple question. As soon as the Beacons went dark, it felt like she transformed into a completely different person, almost like somebody flipped a switch.

Did he ever really know her?

He thought back to their connection, forged by the Beacons. The dreams that weren't really dreams, the way they melded together and shared their emotions and thoughts and memories, and the horrible blackout period when she got struck by lightning, and then meeting in person and their nightly bondings and the conversations that they held entirely in their heads. Those days were the highlight of his life.

And now . . . nothing.

His mind was empty and silent. Worse yet, his heart ached in ways that it never had before. Emotions still frightened him. They were fickle creatures. They came on suddenly, drove you mad, overwhelmed your capacity for reason, and then abandoned you right when you needed them the most. He had lost his colony, his army, and now the girl that he loved.

He felt adrift like an asteroid fractured from its home planet, floating listlessly in the immense vacuum of outer space. He had never felt so alone—or rather he had felt alone, but it had never bothered him before.

In this way, as the days dragged on, Aero turned to his duties, which had always sustained him through difficult times. He found safety in routine. He went through the motions. After his morning workout and breakfast, he checked in with Noah and Divinus, consulting on the situation with the Second Continuum. Vinick still hadn't opened up communication lines with them, but he hadn't left on Stern's Quest either. The mothership was idling, floating aimlessly in orbit. What was Vinick waiting for?

Aero considered Vinick's recent activities. He had transferred the prisoners to a more secure location back on the mothership. He had also withdrawn most of his troops from the First Continuum's doorstep, except for a few stragglers. From the security feeds, Aero was able to identify the soldiers and their commanders that Vinick left behind. They weren't even from a top combat unit.

"You only withdraw your troops like that when you sense a threat," Aero reported to Divinus and Noah in their daily briefing in the control room. "You pull back to your strongest position. Vinick's actions suggest that he's afraid."

"But . . . of what?" Divinus asked, his eyes glued to the feed of the Second Continuum. He sat at the head of the table—or rather his projection appeared to occupy that spot.

"I don't know, Professor," Aero said. He studied the sleek spaceship, hovering in orbit and tilting slowly under the glow of the blistering sun. That ship—which housed his people, where he had lived out the first sixteen years of his life—now seemed like a complete mystery to him.

"Me neither," Divinus said. "And that's what worries me. Surely, he doesn't fear an attack from us. He must know that we're no match for his army."

"I concur," Aero said. "He withdrew his troops from our doorstep. He wouldn't do that if he was worried about us. So what's got him so spooked?"

His words hung in the staid air of the control room. They were all stumped, including Noah. This mystery—along with the more daunting mysteries of the human heart—haunted Aero throughout the day and followed him into bed at night, until he fell into a restless sleep. Nothing in his life seemed to make a shred of sense anymore.

o   o   o

"No change, Captain," Noah reported to Aero the next morning.

They were sitting around the long table in the control room. This was their daily security meeting, as they'd come to think of it. Seeker abhorred official meetings of any kind and stopped showing up, while Myra was avoiding them for another reason. "Tell me when you actually decide to do something," she said when Aero pressed her for an explanation. "Otherwise, you're just wasting my time. You know how I feel."

Nobody could change her mind, not once it was made up like that. Aero sensed the futility of it right way, though Divinus tried to persuade her a few more times. But it did no good. Aero wondered if she was right. Were they wasting their time waiting around like this?

"Noah, what about the door to the First Continuum?" Aero asked, glancing at the feeds from the surface. "Only one combat unit is still guarding it?"

"No change there either, Captain," Noah said, zooming in on the footage. A few soldiers stood by the door. Their Falchions were gripped in their hands but remained in their default forms. It almost seemed like they were there for show, which puzzled Aero. His people believed in efficiency above all else. So what were they doing there?

"What about the prisoners?" Aero asked in a neutral voice, not saying their names. He felt a flicker of worry and struggled to tamp down his emotions. He didn't want them to cloud his thinking.

"Noah finally hacked into the ship's security feeds yesterday," Divinus said. "Your friends are being held in the Disciplinary Barracks with armed guards posted around the clock. From what we can tell, they appear alive and unharmed."

Noah pulled up the security footage of the barracks. Aero quickly scanned the images—Wren was pacing back and forth, probably going mad from boredom, while Kaleb leaned against the wall, his eyes fixed on the door. Tinker was asleep in the narrow bunk, and the Forger sat cross-legged on the floor deep in prayer. Divinus manipulated the image, zooming out to show the armed soldiers guarding the door.

"So Vinick is keeping them alive, yet he hasn't tried to contact us yet and issue his demands for their release," Aero said, feeling stymied. "And there are still no signs that the Second Continuum is preparing to leave on Stern's Quest?"

"Their solar sails remain dormant," Noah replied, referring to the massive silver sails that propelled the ship long distances through space. "They're still hovering in orbit, right outside our atmosphere. My scans reveal no activity outside the ship."

"Damn it, what's Vinick waiting for?" Aero said. "It's almost like he's afraid of something. Look at how he's pulled back to a defensive position," Aero said, indicating the footage of the mothership. "Though I still have no idea what it could be."

Divinus shot him a rueful smile. "My boy, your guess is as good as mine."

They adjourned the meeting with more questions than answers. Aero was resolved to wait Vinick out and force him to approach them first, but his patience was wearing thin. What he wanted more than anything was to talk to Myra about it. He found her in the chamber that housed amphibians. She was walking around with a tablet computer and checking the levels on the cryocapsules.

At the sound of his footsteps, she looked over. Her face fell. "Oh, hey," she said, looking back at her tablet.

"So . . . what are you working on?" Aero said. As soon as the words left his mouth, he cursed himself for asking such a lame question.

"Just something for Noah," she said, keying in a few readings and moving to the next machine. "Actually, I need to get going. I promised I'd get this to him right away."

"Wait, can I just talk to you for a second?" Aero said. He hated the way his voice came out sounding . . . so . . . weak. What was wrong with him?

"Is it urgent?" she asked, fidgeting with the tablet.

"Not really," he admitted.

"Another time then?" she said, already backing away. "I've really got to go."

Then before he could say anything else, she hurried away and ducked through the closest door. As he watched it contract behind her, he felt crushing sadness. He leaned against the nearest cryocapsule—*Salamandra Atra*—and let it wash over him. It hurt more than any physical wound. He was so overwhelmed by his emotional state that he didn't hear her creep up behind him. Suddenly, a shadow flashed in his peripheral vision.

"Seeker?" he gasped, spinning around. His hand went automatically to his Falchion, but then he relaxed. "Sorry . . . you startled me."

Seeker stared up at him with her big eyes. She sat back on her haunches and licked the blood from her lips with a wet smack. "Myra doesn't want to talk to you," she croaked out.

"So I noticed," he muttered. "Were you spying on us?"

She grinned a toothy smile. "Seeker stays in the shadows where it's safe . . . Seeker watches and listens." She started licking her hands, cleaning them. "Myra doesn't like you anymore. You should leave her alone . . . that's what she wants."

He grimaced. "Thanks . . . you're really helping me here."

She blinked and seemed to be thinking it over. "Myra likes the other one . . . the tall one with the soft hands. Noah said so . . . he knows from her download."

"Kaleb," Aero said. "How do you know about that?"

She shrugged her shoulders and then stalked around the cryocapsule. "I heard them talking about it in the control room. She loves him . . . the Professor said so."

"And what do you think?" he asked.

Seeker narrowed her eyes. "She's making a big mistake. You're stronger than that Weakling. He may be taller . . . but he's scrawny and sickly. They'll produce feeble offspring."

Aero laughed, good and hard. "Are you just saying that to make me feel better?" he managed to get out, wiping the tears from his eyes. It felt good to laugh like that—it was better than the opposite.

Seeker looked confused by the idea that she would make anything up for the sake of his feelings.

"Strong One, are you okay?" she asked, stalking over and patting his back while he choked on his laughter.

"Yup, much better now . . . thanks to you," he chuckled. No longer ruminating on Myra, he felt suddenly hungry. "Got any rations for me?"

Seeker made a gagging noise. "Gross rations."

He laughed again. "Better than buggers."

Seeker looked even more disturbed by that comment, but she dutifully led him back to her room, winding through the warren of chambers. Aero watched her galloping ahead on all fours and felt a smile quirk his lips. She made for strange company, but she was the only friend that he had left down here. Myra was avoiding him, Divinus was a projection, and Noah was only a computer, no matter how super.

Aero helped himself to the rations on the platter, but Seeker soon grew bored of talking, so he withdrew to his own chambers. The door slurped shut behind him. He slumped onto the bed and buried his head in the pillow. He tried to think about Vinick and the mystery of his recent behavior, but his thoughts quickly drifted back to Myra and the endless loop of questions plaguing him.

Why doesn't she love me?

Why does she prefer Kaleb?

What did I do wrong?

Exasperated, he tried pushups to take his mind off it, and when those didn't work, he jogged in place until his legs were rubbery and he couldn't stand up anymore. He teetered over to the bed and collapsed into a restless sleep that came on fast but retreated just as quickly. He cracked his eyelids open and stared at the ceiling, faintly illuminated by the ceiling panels. He was about to nod off again when—

Suddenly, an alarm blared out.

Beep! Beep! Beep!

Strobe lights pulsed, lighting up his room. "Emergency! This is not a drill!" Noah's voice rang out at high volume. "Repeat—this is not a drill! Carriers report to the control room immediately."

Aero leapt from his bed and pulled on his boots, eschewing the flimsy canvas slippers. He seized his Falchion and charged to the door, belting it on as he ran. His only thought was of Myra. But when he reached her room, it was empty. Her bed lay undisturbed. She wasn't there. He darted back into the corridor and checked Seeker's room, and together they sprinted down the corridor, toward the control room.

"Hurry, Strong One," Seeker growled, galloping on all fours.

Aero didn't know what had triggered the alarm. Did Vinick finally contact them? But if so . . . then why the urgency? They'd been expecting his message for the last few days. Surely, it wouldn't require an emergency response of this magnitude.

Noah's voice rang out again. "Emergency! Carriers report to the control room!"

Aero spotted Myra running ahead of them. He sprinted faster, overtaking Seeker, and caught up to her.

"What's going on?" Myra gasped as they fell in together and continued into the next chamber, dodging the cryocapsules. Her breath came in quick bursts.

"Starry hell, no clue," he said as they cut right. "But it can't be good."

"Vinick?" Myra said. "Did he finally contact us?"

Aero waved his hand to trigger the next door. "It's possible, but I don't know."

The alarm continued blaring, along with Noah's emergency summons. They barreled past Divinus, eternally frozen in his cryocapsule, and into the corridor that lay beyond it. A few seconds later, they burst into the control room, where the projection of Divinus was waiting for them. He sat at the head of the long table with a cluster of images swirling over his head. His long fingers worked to manipulate them, rejecting some and summoning others.

". . . the signal was coming in and out because they were trying to cloak it and hide their position," Noah was saying. "It wasn't easy, but I managed to lock onto their coordinates. I'm projecting the image now . . ."

"Professor, what's happening?" Myra blurted out.

"Is it Vinick?" Aero added. "The prisoners?"

"Tinker?" Seeker growled.

Divinus was so absorbed in his work that he didn't respond right away. His fingers flitted through the air. Slowly, a new image materialized overhead of a spaceship. It was larger and chunkier than the sleek vessel that housed the Second Continuum. The exterior was dark gray—almost black—with metal drills jutting out of the hull at odd angles, lending the whole ship a menacing appearance. The image flickered suddenly, vanishing from the starscape, only to snap back into existence a split second later.

"Sorry, Professor. Their cloaking devices are very sophisticated." Noah said as he worked to stabilize the image. "If not for the signal from their Beacon, I probably wouldn't have detected them until they were landing on our doorstep."

Aero recognized the ship immediately—there was no

mistaking it. He'd seen it a million times before in his history classes at the Agoge. "But it can't be . . . that's impossible," he stammered. "They vanished over seven hundred years ago."

"Who vanished?" Myra demanded, glancing from Aero to Divinus. Her eyes darted to the image of the ship as it flickered again. "What are you talking about?"

Even Noah remained silent. Divinus steepled his fingers under his chin and regarded the spaceship gravely. His face appeared to shrivel into a skeleton. "The Fourth Continuum," he said at last. "They've returned."

Chapter 51

THE DARK SIDE OF URANUS

Myra Jackson

The Fourth Continuum?" Myra repeated. She had been so focused on Vinick and getting her brother and Kaleb back that it hadn't occurred to her that the alarm could be about something else. She turned to Aero, her eyes flashing with concern. "But you said that the Second Continuum was the last surviving space colony?"

Aero looked equally stunned. It was a long moment before he responded. "That's what I was taught," he managed. "I learned about it at the Agoge."

"Captain Wright is correct," Noah chimed in. "I've processed the download from his Beacon. The files from Supreme General Bryant Stern confirm this account. The Fourth Continuum vanished on the dark side of Uranus in 296 P.D. They were never heard from again."

"Until now," said Divinus, enlarging the image and working to improve the contrast. He ran his fingers through his beard.

"We're sure it's the Fourth Continuum?" Myra said, studying the ship as it flickered again and vanished from the starscape. "There's no mistake?"

"Confirmed," Noah said. "It's the Fourth Continuum. I locked onto the signal from their Carrier. He was trying to cloak it for unknown reasons. They're traveling fast, but based on my calculations, it will be a few weeks before they reach Earth."

"So that's what Vinick was afraid of," Aero said. "The Second Continuum is in orbit, so the signal would be stronger up there. I'll bet he intercepted it before us. That explains why he assumed a defensive position. Let me guess—they're armed."

"To the teeth," Divinus said with an agitated tug on his beard. "Based on Noah's preliminary scans, they possess more powerful weaponry than the Second Continuum."

Myra felt a chill wrench up her spine. "The Doom?"

"No, thankfully," Divinus said, flickering with relief. "I've worked hard to protect that secret. Nobody chosen for the Fourth Continuum possessed that knowledge, and we made sure to destroy all records pertaining to its creation."

"Well, that's something at least," Aero said. "Have you tried opening communication lines with them? They may be armed, but that doesn't mean they're hostile. For all we know, they could have good intentions."

"Noah is trying to contact the Carrier right now," Divinus said as he flipped through the original blueprints of the ship's layout. Myra recognized many of the systems and components—housing compartments, engineering room, control room, farming—but others looked completely foreign to her.

"What else do we know about them?" she asked.

"Unfortunately, not much," Divinus said. He pointed to the blueprints of the ship. "See these sharp points sticking out of the hull? They're drilling rigs. The vessel was designed to travel long distances through space and collect rock and soil samples, searching for microbial life as part of the university's Integrative Space Drilling Program. But we retrofitted it to house the Fourth Continuum." He pulled up the roster of their Chosen and scrolled through the long list of names.

"The makeup of the Fourth Continuum was more tilted toward scientists and mathematicians."

"Different colonies had different types of people?" Aero asked.

Divinus nodded. "Of course, they all contained a mix. But some were more weighted toward certain disciplines since we didn't know what type of society would have the best odds of survival."

"And my colony?" Myra asked. "The Thirteenth?"

"Politicians, priests, and philosophical thinkers."

"Like President Wade and his family?"

"Exactly," Divinus said. "Based on Captain Wright's download, we know about the Fourth Continuum's first three hundred years of existence. It appears that there was some unrest in the early years of the colony, but nothing out of the ordinary. They experienced no major uprisings. They seemed primarily focused on scientific pursuits and research. Nothing sticks out as an anomaly, but we'll dig deeper now. Noah is already working on it."

"And the last seven hundred years?" Myra said.

Divinus leaned forward and met her eyes. "My dear, we know absolutely nothing. Except that they've survived the exile and now they've returned."

Myra let that sink in. She felt troubled by the mystery of the Fourth Continuum and their disappearance. Why did they vanish? Where were they all these years? And now that they had returned, what were their intentions?

She glanced down at her wrist. Her Beacon was still deactivated, but it made her think of another mystery. "If they have a Carrier," she said. "Then why didn't we pick up his signal with our Beacons?"

"Maybe they were too far away?" Aero suggested. "Their ship is built to travel long distances through space. We know distance has an impact on the signal strength. In the beginning, remember how we could only communicate through our dreams?"

"Still, we managed to find each other," Myra pointed out.

"And we were pretty far apart." She glanced at Seeker, who was pacing around the room. She was muttering something to herself. Something about . . . darkness . . . or dark thing. Suddenly, a horrible thought occurred to Myra.

"Wait . . . what if our Beacons did pick him up?"

"The Dark Thing," Aero said as it dawned on him, too. "He must have been trying to cloak his identity. That's why he looked like a shadowy creature. That's why we only saw him in our dreams. He's been spying on us since we bonded with our Beacons."

Seeker nodded her head. "The Dark Thing . . . is their Carrier."

"The Dark Thing?" Divinus said, looking alarmed. "Wait, you've had contact with the Carrier from the Fourth Continuum? Why didn't you mention that before?"

"Because we didn't know," Aero said. "He was concealing his identity."

Myra grimaced. "Yes . . . and he's a monster—"

Suddenly, an alarm sounded again.

"Incoming communication," Noah said.

A holographic image struggled to materialize over the table. Myra's heart thudded while she waited for it to resolve. It flickered a few times and then stabilized. Her eyes landed on the Carrier. He was dressed in long, crimson robes and ensconced on a throne marked with the Ouroboros symbol. Wires protruded from his shaved head and snaked into the throne. His face was pale and flabby, and his eyes were milky white.

"Professor Divinus," he said in an amplified voice. The Beacon on his wrist flashed with steady light. "I'm Commander Drakken of the Fourth Continuum."

Divinus rose and bowed deeply. "Greetings from the First Continuum," he said. "On behalf of the Continuum Project, I welcome you back—"

"Enough with the pleasantries," Drakken cut him off, though his face remained an impassive mask. "We've already wasted enough time. I hoped that our arrival would come as more of a surprise, but you've thwarted that plan. The Fourth

Continuum has survived the period of exile and now we've returned to claim what's rightfully ours."

Divinus's countenance hardened. "And what's that, Commander?"

"The secret of the Doom," Drakken said. "The Doom was the greatest achievement of humanity. Gods create worlds, but they also have the power to destroy them. For the last seven hundred years, we've been studying the Doom, trying to perfect the science behind it. But we have failed to replicate your experiments."

Divinus—or rather his projection—flickered with greenish light. "That secret died along with the world from Before Doom. You must know that."

Drakken laughed harshly. "Professor, don't lie to me! You always were a fraud."

"What does he mean?" Myra said, glancing at Divinus.

"Oh, the esteemed Professor didn't tell you?" Drakken sneered. "Professor Divinus was the one who created the Doom! It was his greatest scientific achievement, heralded as an unparalleled breakthrough at the time. He even won a Nobel Prize for it."

Myra felt sickened. "Professor, that's a lie . . . right?"

Divinus flickered with guilt. "My dear . . . I'm afraid he's telling the truth."

Drakken's laugh boomed out again, but then he turned more serious. "Our demands are simple. Either surrender now and turn over the secret of the Doom—or we'll destroy everything that you hold dear."

Drakken's face was replaced by images of soldiers dressed in matching crimson uniforms, armed with enormous blasters slung over their shoulders. Then it shifted to an impressive cache of warheads.

"Those are nukes," Aero hissed. "I learned about them at the Agoge, but even my colony banned them a long time ago. They're far too destructive."

With a flicker, the images of the weapons vanished and Drakken's face reappeared. "Carriers, I've seen into the deepest recesses of your consciousness. Manipulating you through the Beacons proved easy. I could shield my identity and roam through your memories undetected. I know who you love—and how to destroy them."

"What's he talking about?" Aero said, glancing at Myra.

"I don't know—" Myra started.

But then Drakken's face vanished again, and in his place, other images materialized above them. Myra saw Tinker and Kaleb, but also her father and Maude and the Bishop twins and everyone from the Thirteenth Continuum. Then images played from the Second Continuum of Wren and the Forgers, and the soldiers from Aero's unit, but also of the Drillmasters and the Agoge and their young students. Then it shifted to the Seventh Continuum and the Weaklings. The stolen bits from their memories flickered even faster, flipping between the colonies until they immolated in a white-hot explosion.

Drakken appeared again. "Carriers, the choice is yours," he said as his Beacon flared. The communication started to sizzle and fade into static.

And then it went dark.

"Communication terminated," Noah reported.

Divinus looked stricken from the exchange. His projection wavered in and out of existence. Myra felt her thoughts spiraling into blinding anger. Without thinking, she lunged across the table toward Divinus and tried to strangle him, though he was only a projection and she couldn't hurt him. Her hands passed through him harmlessly.

"So . . . all of this is a lie?" she screamed, feeling angry tears coursing down her cheeks. "This whole place—the entire Continuum Project—it's nothing but a lie?" Aero tried to pull her away from Divinus, but she shoved him off.

"Tell me the truth for once!" she screamed. "I knew we couldn't trust you!"

"My dear . . . I knew you would never understand," Divinus said. "In my younger days I was ambitious . . . too ambitious. I sought to comprehend the underpinnings of life, to fracture it and break it apart, to see if I could unlock the secrets of creation and also its darker flipside—destruction. I got so lost in the pursuit of this knowledge that I never considered the repercussions . . . until it was too late."

"So you did create the Doom," Myra said, glaring at his projection. She couldn't hurt him, not physically. "Drakken was telling the truth. You're a bloody fraud!"

Divinus bowed his head. "Yes, it's true. My work led to the creation of the Doom," he admitted with a flicker. "But you must understand, I was horrified when our government built the first Doomsday Machine, and even more so when it proliferated to other countries and eventually to extremist groups. More than anybody, I knew what the Doom could do—that it had the power to destroy everything that humanity had endeavored to build! I've spent my entire life since then trying to make up for my greatest lapse."

Myra slumped back into a chair, feeling the horror of his betrayal. She had trusted Divinus and his plan completely, never questioning his motivations, never wondering why he had brought them here. Now she realized how naïve and reckless that was. The truth was far more complicated.

"So that's why you created the Continuum Project?" she asked, remembering Elianna's memories from a millennium ago. "Because you regretted it?"

Divinus nodded. "Once I saw the real-world applications of my research—the proliferation of the weapons, the ensuing arms race, the possibility that the Doom could actually come to pass—I dedicated my life to building the Continuums and recruiting the Carriers. And all the while, I hoped that my predictions were wrong. I hoped that we would never be standing here. I hoped that humanity's nobler instincts would prevail, and the Doomsday Machine would never be unleashed upon the world."

"But it was," Myra said, tasting bitterness on her tongue. "And so here we stand."

"Yes, my dear," Divinus said, flickering with remorse. "Believe me, if there was a way to undo it—to go back in time and change it—I would in a heartbeat. I'd give back all my prizes and accolades . . . my tenure, publications, and grant money . . ."

"But it doesn't work that way," Myra said. "The past can't be undone."

A harsh silence fell over the room.

Silence fell over the room. Myra thought through their situation. It seemed completely hopeless. Through the riptide of confusing thoughts and conflicting emotions, she struggled for a gulp of air. She glanced down at her wrist and remembered Elianna's first meeting with Professor Divinus when he asked her to be a Carrier.

There is always hope, my dear, Divinus said. *Don't ever forget that.*

The words echoed through her head. The Professor was right—hope was humanity's greatest weapon, greater even than the Doom. Myra felt determination settle over her in a soothing wave. After many agonizing days of waiting around and doing nothing, the arrival of the Fourth Continuum had crystalized everything for her. She came to a decision—and it felt like she was reaching out to claim her destiny.

Myra scanned the faces of those assembled around the room. She could sense Noah hovering in the periphery, a true consciousness though he was only a machine.

"Professor, now can we act?" Myra asked. Her voice did not waver; it held steady and resonated through the room.

Countless miles above them, through rock and surface and sky and clouds and the vacuum of space, peppered with the winking of stars and the great blaze of the sun, the Fourth Continuum was speeding toward them, each second coming closer to their door.

Divinus found her eyes and held her gaze.

"Yes, my dear. God help us, the time for waiting is over."

. . . to be concluded in

THE UNITED CONTINUUMS

Summer 2017

from

TURNER
PUBLISHING COMPANY

WITH GRATITUDE

To my agent, Deborah Schneider, my film guru, Josie Freedman at ICM, and everyone at Curtis Brown. I always know I'm in good hands with you on my team. To Turner Publishing, for handling my books with grace, guts, and boundless enthusiasm, especially to Todd Bottorff and Stephanie Beard for giving me this shot, Jon O'Neal for editorial guidance, Maddie Cothren for the best darn book covers, and Jolene Barto for her marketing savvy in launching this series into the world.

To my early readers, Scott Selby, Sarah Ganzman, Edna Ball Axelrod, Leanne Crowley, and Marty Brody. As always, your feedback improved my words and your enthusiasm kept me going in the hard moments. To Victor LaValle for his wisdom and encouragement and the Tin House Summer Writer's Workshop.

To my husband, Will, for his endless support and my fluffy companion, Commander Ryker, who kept me company while I wrote and coaxed me out of the house, leading me on long walks where I unraveled and brainstormed great swathes of this sprawling story. Also, to my parents, for their love and encouragement, and for hosting me on private writing retreats in the Blue Ridge Mountains. I love you always.

To my favorite authors, my first teachers, my heroes, my greatest inspirations (in no particular order): Stephen King,

Madeleine L'Engle, Anne Rice, J.K. Rowling, Neil Gaiman, Clive Barker, Edgar Rice Burroughs, Anne McCaffrey, George R.R. Martin, Kurt Vonnegut, Phillip Pullman, Tamora Pierce, Isaac Asimov, J.R.R. Tolkien, and Jules Verne. I always keep your books in my office, near to my pen and my heart.

Finally, to you dear readers, who took a chance on a new book series and embarked on this epic journey with Myra and Aero. You are everything. You are the reason that this book has a life outside my computer. Lastly, you are the reason that their story will continue in *The United Continuums*. As I type these words, I'm writing the final chapters of the third book. I can't wait for you to find out how it all ends.

ABOUT THE AUTHOR

JENNIFER BRODY lives and writes in Los Angeles. After graduating from Harvard University, she began her career in feature film development. Highlights include working at New Line Cinema on many projects, including *The Lord of the Rings* trilogy, *The Golden Compass*, and *Love In The Time of Cholera*. She's a member of the Science Fiction and Fantasy Writers of America. She also founded and runs BookPod, a social media platform for authors.

You can find her online at:

@JenniferBrody

www.jenniferbrody.com

www.facebook.com/jenniferbrodywriter

Exclusive Excerpt:

THE UNITED CONTINUUMS

Chapter 0
NOBEL LAUREATE

Before the Doom

Professor Theodore Divinus heard his name echo through the Stockholm Concert Hall, as the symphonic music swelled to a crescendo, accompanied by vigorous applause.

"Professor Theodore Divinus, on behalf of the Royal Academy of Sciences, I wish to convey our warmest congratulations, and I now ask you to step forward and receive your prize from the hand so of His Majesty the King."

When Divinus struggled to his feet, a dizzy feeling swept through him. It could have been from euphoria—or simply the stiff collar of his designer tuxedo slowly choking off his air supply. Tugging at his collar, he proceeded to the stage and padded across the blue carpet emblazoned with a "N" inside a white circle. He accepted the award from the King and then turned to bow to the crowd. More applause rippled through the hall like a rumble of thunder. He bowed two more times, bobbing his head.

I'm now a Nobel Laureate in Physics, he thought in disbelief as he made his way back to his front row seat on wobbly legs. Though he'd spent almost his whole life with

414   JENNIFER BRODY

that aspiration lodged in his heart, he had never believed that
it would happen. Only two short days ago, in the midst of a
raging Nor'easter, he'd boarded a plane at Logan Airport and
flown to Sweden to give his lecture on nuclear fission—and
now here he was shaking hands with the King of Sweden. How
strange it was that so many countries kept up the ruse of supporting an antiquated monarchy when it was only for show.

He sat through the rest of the ceremony in a state of bliss—
yes, that was the word for it, wasn't it? He clapped when it
was called for, sat quietly through the musical portions, all the
while wishing that it would never end. His prize was clasped
in his lap. He could feel the weight of it radiating through his
thighs like it was radioactive. The Nobel Banquet was set to
follow immediately after at Stockholm City Hall.

Divinus gathered his prize and flowed along with the
crowd making for the exits, when he felt his handheld buzzed
his jacket. He fished it out and saw a text message.

From: Rhae Lynn Bishop
*Congrats, you sly dog. Helluva accomplishment. You got
there first . . . but I'm next. You owe me a proper date when
you're back in Cambridge. xxRL*

The message was accompanied by a few emoticons. This
made Divinus's lips kink into a smile. They were colleagues,
having met in graduate school and both ascended to profes-
sorships, hers in History and Literature with an emphasis on
Digital History, and his in Physics. More recently, their friendship had morphed . . . well . . . into something else. But it was
still in the early stages—that delicate, flittering, heart-thump-
ing, gut-wrenching phase—and he didn't want to jinx it by
giving it a label.

He fired off a witty response (or at least, he hoped it was
witty) and made for the exit, when he felt a firm hand grip his
elbow. Then he heard a stern voice by his ear.

"Professor Divinus, will you please come with me?"

Divinus turned to see a man dressed in a tuxedo. He was

middle-aged with close-cropped hair and broad shoulders. At first glance, nothing about him stood out, but then Divinus glimpsed something peaking from underneath his crisply starched jacket.

It was a gun.

The man gripped his elbow harder. "Professor, come with me."

His gray eyes were steely, and it wasn't a question this time.

"But where are you taking me?" Divinus managed, feeling the crush of the crowd pressing in on them, struggling toward the exits. The man lowered his voice.

"Professor, I'm not at liberty to divulge that information. All I'm authorized to say is that it concerns a matter of national security."

"And if I refuse?" Divinus asked as the crowd streamed around them, oblivious to the espionage taking place in their midst. He wondered how many other agents were strategically placed in the crowd, watching them. "What about the Banquet?"

"I have permission to take you by force," the man said without hesitation. His hand slipped inside his jacket. Divinus saw the flash of a hypodermic needle. "Though I hope that does not become necessary. The choice is yours, Professor."

Divinus elected to go with the man, his award still tucked under his arm but mostly forgotten. They moved swiftly through the dispersing crowd, the hum and thrum of upbeat chatter chasing them out of the hall and into the dark Stockholm streets.

Rain splattered down from the sky in thick droplets. Divinus exhaled and his breath came out in smoky tendrils. He could taste snow in the air—the rain would change over soon. Though it was only early evening it felt like midnight, the sun having set well before two o'clock. December in Stockholm was a special kind of winter that put even his home of Cambridge, Massachusetts to shame. Why they chose to hold the ceremony in the dead of winter seemed counterintuitive, but he knew that it was held on anniversary of Arthur Nobel's death, the founder of the prize that he now gripped under his arm.

A black Mercedes sped up to the curb and screeched to a halt, kicking up a puddle. "This way, Professor," the man said, jerking open the door to the backseat. It was only as Divinus climbed inside that he realized his shiny, black shoes—Ferragamos newly purchased for this occasion—had been soaked through with the frigid water.

Thwump!

The man climbed in after him and slammed the door, and the car raced off into the bitter December night. On closer inspection, he saw that the car was armored with reinforced glass. "Now can you tell me where we're going?" Divinus asked.

The man didn't reply.

He just stared back with those gray eyes.

"How about your name? You seem to know mine."

Still nothing. Divinus gave up and slumped in his seat. The man pulled out a handheld and scanned the screen, keyed in a message, and returned it to his inside coat pocket. Divinus sighed in annoyance, but the man didn't appear to care. He wishes he could slip off his shoes, or at the very least strip off the sodden socks, but his unease kept him locked in place as his feet gradually went numb.

A thousand scenarios flashed through his head. What could they possibly want with him? Had he unknowingly committed some crime? Smuggled something through the airport that wasn't allowed? Did they suspect him of being a terrorist? Or a political agitator of some sort?

But that seemed farfetched. He was only a scientist—hell, he didn't even follow politics. Maybe it was a case of mistaken identity? He'd seen that happen once in an action movie when he was a kid. The main character was an ordinary man forced to go on the run after the government confused him with a terrorist. Regardless, he was certain they would clear it up quickly and then he could return to the Banquet, sipping champagne and feasting with his fellow Nobel Laureates. That reassured him. He sank down into the plush leather seat, hugging his prize like a security blanket.

About fifteen minutes later, they skidded to a halt in front of an abandoned building on the outskirts of the city. Divinus peered through the window, flexing his feet to return some blood flow. It was fully snowing now, dusting the ground and frosting the rooftops of the derelict buildings that lined the pot-holed street.

What are we doing here?

Divinus took one look at the man and knew it would be an exercise in futility to ask him. The man ushered him from the vehicle and through the front door, passing more men in suits as they went. The man led him up the rickety staircase that coiled up to the third floor. A dilapidated door hung crookedly from its hinges. The man pushed it open.

Another Nobel Laureate stared back at him.